SERENDIPITY

By

Chris Colby

ser·en·dip·i·ty

/serən'dipədē/   noun

serendipity; plural noun: serendipities

The occurrence and development of events by chance in

a happy or beneficial way.

"It was a fortunate stroke of serendipity!"

Chapter One

NOW

Oliver

Oliver Diamond sat on his balcony, looking out into the bay. Like his wife, Monte Carlo was still sleeping. The pavement below was enjoying a hosing down, ready for the heat of the day, and the marina was crammed with vessels jostling for position like horses at the Derby. A small fishing boat chugged with a 'phut... phut... phut...' looking anachronistic against the backdrop of his super-yacht, *Serendipity*. He smiled at the name, *Serendipity* – a 'happy accident', how very apt.

At six foot four, with raven hair, and a well-toned body, Oliver had eyes that looked deep into your soul. With homes in London, Monte Carlo, and Los Angeles, the tabloids claimed he had it all. Yes, his life was a far cry from his early days as Oliver 'Wilkins', but he'd worked damn hard. Today, Oliver faced losing everything, including Charlie. He could feel his happiness disappearing from his fingertips, like sand in an hourglass. The first blackmail letter arrived a few weeks ago, followed by three more. It was now time to face his past.

As the gentle breeze rolled off the sea billowing the silk curtains into the bedroom, Oliver caught sight of Charlie's face. He could forsake everything else, but not Charlie. She was his destiny, and he couldn't survive without her. Oliver sat back in his chair and reflected over the past... yes, *Serendipity*.

Charlie

The gentle breeze swept over Charlie as she lay sleeping. Born in New York, New York, on 9th February 1977, it was a fateful day on her seventh birthday that changed her world forever. She was haunted by the ghosts of her past. Yet that day had begun so happily on Coney Island...

1984

Charlie buried her head in her father's chest as their carriage pushed through a set of heavy doors with a thud into sudden daylight. She could hear the music of Coney Island and opened one eye to find her mother jumping and waving frantically. Dante's Inferno resembled a castle with a devil-like creature peering over the parapet and wrapped around a large turret a werewolf howled to the moon.

Charlie insisted her father take her on the ride, after all, it was her seventh birthday, and he couldn't deny her anything. James and Elizabeth Black were the happiest married couple you could meet, and they both doted on Charlie. She was christened Charlotte Black, but her father always called her Charlie, as it suited her tomboy demeanor. She was mischievous and inquisitive, spending her days climbing trees and saving wounded birds. Always a daddy's girl, she could have anything she wanted if she put her mind to it.

'Charlie! It looked terrifying, are you alright?'

Charlie pulled away from her father. 'Oh, it was fine for me, but I think Daddy was scared, I had to comfort him.'

James winked at Elizabeth as they climbed out of the car.

'Ok, who's for some cotton candy?'

Charlie shot her arm into the air, 'Me! But first let's have a photo, pleeeaassse.'

Charlie ran behind a cut-out of a werewolf family against a moonlit sky and poked her head through the hole in the face of a young werewolf. Elizabeth laughed and pulled James behind the cut-out where they all made a face at the camera. The photographer gave Elizabeth a numbered slip and when they collected the print from the photo kiosk Charlie giggled hysterically.

James hoisted her onto his shoulders, making her squeal.

'No more horror rides, Charlie!' They walked down the boardwalk, James holding Elizabeth's hand tightly. It was the perfect day, a day that Charlie would never forget. The real horror of her seventh birthday didn't manifest itself until later that evening after they arrived home.

* * * * * * * * *

Two ear-piercing shots and then silence. The body lay before her, twisted, contorted, looking up in agony, imprinting itself on her memory. Charlie stared in disbelief as her world stopped turning for a few seconds. Her mouth moved but no sound came out. She tried to scream as her heart pounded in her chest.

Then came the blood, so much of it seeping out of his shirt, slowly gliding over the polished, parquet floor. She watched as the body convulsed one last time and then... stillness. Footsteps. Someone was running down the hallway. The living room door flung open, and Charlie's mother threw herself into the room. Charlie turned in terror as Elizabeth screamed, 'Nooooooo!!!!!!!!' She stared at Charlie's hand.

'Charlie! What have you done?'

Charlie looked down, and there, in the clutches of her tiny hand, was a revolver. She looked at her mother in disbelief.

'No, no, no...' she started to mutter, shaking her head from side to side. Elizabeth ran back to the hallway and picked up the telephone, her fingers dialing frantically.

'Ambulance... I need an ambulance... quickly! And... and... the police. Get me the police... my husband's been shot...'

Charlie placed the revolver on the coffee table and sat, staring at the body. 'No, no, no...' she repeated the words over and over, again and again. Everything had happened so quickly, but one question repeated itself in her head. Why was daddy dead? Why? In the distance, she could hear the whine of a police siren...

* * * * * * * * *

Charlie opened her eyes, gasping for breath. She reached out, but the bed seemed unusually large, he wasn't there. The silk curtains billowed open from the balcony, and looking out into the bay, she could see the love of her life, Oliver Diamond. A warm sensation spread over her, wiping away thoughts of revolvers, red floors, and police. The full events of that evening remained a macabre puzzle. She locked the terrifying memories away, promising herself that one day she'd lose the key forever.

Today Charlie had an important task to carry out and needed all the energy she could muster. Revenge was revenge, but was she capable of staging such a heist? If all went to plan, Charlie and Oliver could live the rest of their lives with no more secrets. After all, he was her destiny.

Unbeknownst to Oliver, she was meeting Henry later that morning. Henrietta Maria Angelina Diakos was her closest friend. She drifted back to sleep, remembering her first day at school in Switzerland. A day that sealed their friendship, forever.

Chapter Two

THEN

I Should Be So Lucky

Oliver Wilkins lay on his bed looking up at the skylight above. The rain fell hard, leaving trails vying for first position down the pane. He glanced at his alarm clock where Mickey Mouse gaily pointed out that it was ten-forty. The air felt freezing outside the confines of his bed, so why bother getting up? Today's itinerary was blank. Having weighed up the pros and cons of leaving his snug, warm duvet, he decided another hour of sleep was definitely in order.

His Headmaster at Sheffield Secondary Modern School told him he was 'wasting his mother's money' going to Drama School. After graduation, Oliver had played a thief in a tv police drama, handed out a new health bar dressed as 'Peter the Porcupine', and his acting pinnacle was spear-carrying in *Titus Andronicus* at The National Theatre alongside Antony Sher.

Oliver caught sight of his Kylie Minogue calendar on the wall. Through blurred vision, he could make out that today was Friday the 13th, another reason for staying in bed. October 1995, and Kylie was wearing a skimpy black bikini with chains wrapped around her body. *I should be so lucky*, thought Oliver, turning over, encouraging warm thoughts.

As he drifted off in the arms of Kylie, he heard a strange sound. She softly whispered in his ear, 'It's the telephone.' 'Leave it,' he replied as he kissed her neck, 'they'll ring back if...' suddenly Oliver opened his eyes to the shrill noise of the telephone ringing in the kitchen. He looked at the enticing poster, 'I'll get back to you later.' He raced towards the sound, pulling on a sweater on the way.

'Hello?'

'Oliver?'

'Yeah... who else?'

'Oliver, it's me. What are you doing today?'

Dan Goldberg! Exactly what I need right now, thought Oliver. *What exciting job do you have lined up for me?*

'Who's me?' Oliver said abruptly. This always annoyed his agent.

'Dan Goldberg? Your agent?'

'Oh, hi Dan. Well today I have a very busy schedule. At twelve I've got an appointment with a lady at the unemployment office and then this afternoo—'

'Cut the crap Oliver and get yourself down to Shepperton Studios for two o'clock.'

'Shepperton studios?' Suddenly Oliver was interested.

'Go to studio six and ask for Jennifer Castle, she'll fill you in.'

'Dan, what's the job?' Oliver said impatiently.

'Look, do you want a couple of days' work or not?'

Oliver knew it had to be extra work on some third-rate film.

'Well, it would be nice...'

'Just get there for two!'

'Ok... but if I find it's something I don't like, you'll be sorry.' Oliver knew he could push his agent a bit further than his other clients.

'You'll love it! Oh, and by the way Oliver...'

'Yeah?'

'Make sure you have a good wash before you go.'

'What are you talki—?' The phone went dead. 'Dan? Dan!'

Oliver dialed his agents' number back, hopping from foot to foot in the cold kitchen.

'Good morning, DG Artists International, how may I help you?'

'Cassandra? Get me Dan, it's Oliver here.'

'One moment Oliver whilst I put you on hold...' music... beat... 'hello, Oliver? I'm afraid Mr. Goldberg's in a meeting at present.'

'Oh, I bet he is!'

'Can I take a message?'

'You could, but I don't think you could spell it.'

'Very well, thank you for calling.' She replied sweetly.

'No, wait Cassandra, you can give him a message. Tell Dan this is the last job. I've had enough of DG Artists International. He can stuff any future contracts up his big, fat...'

'You're on speakerphone Oliver!' Dan's voice boomed out of the earpiece. 'Now you listen to me Oliver Wilkins, you'll never make it big. After today, our contract is null and void. You'll get your last cheque in the post; see how you survive without me!' A click was followed by Cassandra's sing-song voice.

'Is there anything else we can help you with at DG Artists International today?'

Oliver slammed the receiver down. 'Make sure you have a good wash before you go.' What was Dan talking about?

First things first, Oliver needed a coffee kickstart. His kitchen was reminiscent of a scene from some depressing Mike Leigh drama with its Formica tops and an empty milk carton on the table. He opened the fridge to a chicken carcass staring at him through skull-like bones. 'Alas, poor Yorick,' he muttered. Well, the fridge could offer him no milk, black coffee it was then.

Looking into the mirror, his jet-black hair fell over his face awkwardly. 'Not great,' he muttered. Even unshaven and with tousled hair, Oliver could never look that bad. Shave or no shave? He decided on a five o'clock shadow which looked more like eight o'clock. Testing the water, he grimaced. If anything, it was colder. Removing his sweater and jogging pants, he braced himself. Who needs caffeine in the morning when you have a hot water system like 67b Elgin Crescent, Notting Hill, eh?

Oliver ran into the bedroom. 'Well Kylie, what's it to be, the chinos or the denim?' Plumping for dark and swarthy, he pulled on a black polo neck, black chinos, and Chelsea boots. 'Ta-da!' he announced to himself as he caught sight of Mickey Mouse, who seemed to be pointing more sternly at the time – twelve-thirty.

He winked at his calendar, 'Wish me luck Kylie!' grabbed his jacket, and slammed the front door. His mind was racing, what would today hold for him? After today – no agent, no job, no money, and no more National Theatre. Who wanted to be the third spear-carrier from the right anyway?

* * * * * * * * *

Oliver arrived at Shepperton Studios with minutes to spare. At the main gate, the guard was engrossed in a newspaper.

'Hi, I'm to report to studio six'.

Without looking up the guard grunted, 'Name?'

'Ehm, Oliver, my name's Oliver Wilkins. I'm supposed to report to Jennifer Castle in studio six at two o'clock... can you...?'

'Running late, are we?'

Oliver threw him a withering look.

'Follow the road to the right and use the entrance at the end.'

'Thank you so much.' Oliver glanced down at the newspaper. That explained it. *The Sport* bearing the headline 'Woman Gives Birth To 6lb Trout'. The guard resumed his reading with a sigh and a flick of his newspaper.

After a myriad of corridors, Oliver finally found studio six through a set of large doors where he was suddenly faced with people running in all directions. A young girl clutching the obligatory clipboard approached him.

'Can I help you?' At last, a friendly face.

'Yes, can you tell me where I can find Jennifer Castle?'

'Certainly, follow round the back of this set and you'll see her office in the corner.' She pointed the route out with a feather duster she'd produced from her back pocket, like a practicing magician.

'Are you the new grip?' she asked.

'No, an actor. Are you the cleaner?' Oliver retorted with a twinkle in his eye. She stared at him, then blushed as she glimpsed the duster in her hand.

'Er, no, sorry, I'm Cheryl, Cheryl Stevens. I'm a runner, slash (she made a karate motion in the air) PA. Well, more a general dogsbody really,' she enthused, 'Today, props and odd jobs!'

'Well nice to meet you... Cheryl. I'm a bit late, so... er... I'd better dash.'

'Are you Oliver Wilkins by any chance?'

'Yes, yes I am, how do you know my name?'

'Oh, er, I... ehm... never mind. I'll catch you later.'

With that, Cheryl made a swift exit, nearly colliding with a man carrying what looked like the biggest aspidistra in the world.

Oliver felt unnerved. The sound stage was enormous, and crew were busy scurrying back and forth with cables, lamps, and all manner of what looked like the entire stock of furniture from Harrods second, third, and fourth floors. He approached a glass-fronted office against one wall of the studio where Jennifer

Castle was in the midst of a phone call, looking agitated. Nervously he tapped on the glass, and she waved him in dismissively.

'Michael, I am telling you no! That's not what we agreed!' *Some poor bugger was getting a roasting,* thought Oliver.

'No, I'm busy right now, we'll talk this evening. Michael...' she composed herself, 'we said every other weekend and you damn well know it!' She caught sight of Oliver awkwardly standing by the door. 'Look I have to go, I've someone with me. No, it isn't... not that it's any of your bloody business!' She slammed the phone down. Oliver grimaced; this day wasn't turning out the way he'd planned. Oh, why hadn't he stayed in bed with Kylie?

'Yes, can I help you?' Jennifer stared at Oliver tersely.

'I hope so.' Oliver started... Suddenly, the door flung open and a man barged in, completely ignoring Oliver. He was in his thirties, denim from head to toe, tight curly blonde hair, round glasses, and a splash too much Kouros for Oliver's sensitive nose.

'Jennifer, it's getting worse! He should've been on set an hour ago and now the bloody crew is wanting a lunch break. This movie is never going to get off the ground!' He spat the words out like a fire-breathing dragon.

'Alright Philip, calm down, I'll go see him now.'

'Yeah well, he'd better get his arse in gear or we're going to go way over budget!' With that he turned and slammed the door, shaking the glass windows, making a terrific noise.

Jennifer glared after him. 'Fucking actors and fucking directors!' she snapped.

She turned to Oliver, 'And what's your specialist subject?'

Oliver screwed his face up. 'I'm sorry?' He didn't want to be here. 'Oh er... I think I fall into the category of... "fucking actor"?' He offered hopefully.

Chapter Three

THEN

Smoking Spaniels and Spoon Trees

Freedom at last! Charlie Black screeched down the driveway away from St. Mary's School for girls. The last four years in Switzerland had dragged on, but the day had finally arrived when she could forget exams, rules & regulations, dress codes, timetables, and everything that made St. Mary's tick. A rich school, for rich girls, with rich mummies and daddies. She pulled over, grabbed her camera, and opened the window. A few last shots of St. Mary's as the sun rose over the rooftops. She'd arranged to join up with her accomplice and confidante, Henry, later that week in the South of France.

Henry, or Henrietta, and Charlie had become inseparable over the last four years. They shared the deepest secrets and were nearly expelled on many occasions. 'Bringing shame to the name of St. Mary's!' the governess, Ms. Kleinhaus, bellowed at them, her thin lips stretching over crooked teeth. They stared ahead, noses in the air, knowing that the school's exorbitant fees would prevent Ms. Kleinhaus from doing anything to cease their education.

After Charlie's father died, she had lived in a daze. She couldn't remember much further back than that horrific seventh birthday. Soon after, her mother, Elizabeth, became an alcoholic, and suffering from acute depression, ended her life with an overdose of sleeping pills a year later, on Charlie's eighth birthday. She never celebrated her birthdays after those tragic events.

Charlie was ushered off to boarding school, and in the holidays lived in Boston with her Aunt Sophia. Her aunt had never married and herself led a somewhat troubled life. She'd struggled with dementia since her early forties but managed to live alone, with the occasional health care visit. Her doctor agreed it was good to have Charlie stay, from time to time.

When she was sixteen, Charlie was informed by the family lawyer, a Mr. Thurgood Brown, that she had a trust fund of over ten million dollars which would be hers when she reached the age of twenty. Charlie's father had been a hugely successful entrepreneur and owned three development companies, all under the banner of Black Trading Incorporated. His workaholic lifestyle meant that Charlie would be a very rich young lady. Meticulous to the last detail, James Black had Charlie's education mapped out from when she was five years old.

Charlie was shocked to hear news of her inheritance, but not elated. She would have given anything to have her parents back in her life and from the little knowledge she could glean from her aunt, her father had adored her.

Aunt Sophia relayed happy stories of times gone by when they visited her in Boston. 'My house was full of laughter when you all visited. Oh, Charlotte, how he loved you.'

Charlie wished she could remember those precious times, but the only memory she had was the day at Coney Island. Auntie Sophia shook Charlie from her thoughts.

'I had another brother besides your father, you know...' Aunt Sophia stared ahead, reaching for a distant memory.

'Aunt Sophia? I have an uncle?' This was news to Charlie.

'Yes my dear, but he disappeared a long time ago. William...' Charlie noticed her aunt's face clouding over.

'William... Black. The black sheep of the family.' Her Aunt Sophia snarled as she glanced at a silver-framed photograph on the mantle.

'They were triplets.' Her Aunt said with a worried expression.

'Triplets, Aunt Sophia?' Charlie stood and passed the photograph to her aunt, who looked wistfully into the frame.

'Yes, mother had a time of it. Your father, James, was born first, followed by William. The third triplet died in childbirth. He looked as white as snow. Charlie, that was his name, Little Charlie.' She closed her eyes as a tear ran down her wrinkled cheek.

'Three babies, and now only one remains,' she wiped away another tear.

Charlie hadn't noticed the photograph before, or hadn't paid any attention to it. It showed a young Aunt Sophia standing on a step, in front of an ornate door. There was an identical boy on either side of her, both wearing a cardboard spaceman's helmet with the face cut out, looking like peas in a pod. Aunt Sophia was in her late thirties and the boys were very young, maybe ten or eleven.

They were dressed in long shorts and green jumpers with huge yellow initials on the front. 'J' for James and 'W' for William. William was holding a white rabbit. Her Aunt was pulling a face at the camera with a hand on each of the boys' shoulders. It was the strangest photograph Charlie had ever seen.

Another tear ran down Aunt Sophia's cheek as her face darkened.

'I always thought William had killed little Charlie. Murdered him in mama's womb.'

'Aunt Sophia, don't get yourself upset. A baby can't kill.'

Her aunt followed her with troubled eyes as Charlie replaced the frame on the mantle.

'It's nearly time for the emerald necklace,' her aunt said with a contented smile.

'Emerald necklace?' Charlie frowned.

'Yes, I can go to the necklace and rest with mama and papa.'

Aunt Sophia was getting more and more confused and agitated.

'Get some rest Aunt Sophia,' Charlie said in soothing tones. Her aunt dreamt of days gone by as Charlie pulled the crocheted blanket over her knees. Now she understood. In memory of the third triplet, she had been christened Charlotte and her father always called her Charlie. Maybe he'd wished for a boy.

* * * * * * * * *

Charlie was relieved to be leaving Boston for St. Mary's at the end of a very long summer spent with Aunt Sophia. Her aunt's dementia was getting worse, and she began to do the strangest things. One day Charlie discovered her planting spoons in the garden.

'When these trees grow and produce their fruit, I'll never have to buy spoons again,' her aunt said, pressing down the soil around the silver handles.

On another occasion, Charlie awoke to the cries of her aunt. She ran downstairs to find Aunt Sophia trying to give her dog cigarettes.

'Aunt Sophia, what are you doing?' Charlie asked horrified.

'I'm giving Dorcas a cigarette,' she retorted as she forced a Marlboro between the poor spaniel's teeth.

'But, Aunt Sophia, she doesn't smoke.' Charlie calmly said.

'What? Well, she always used to!' Aunt Sophia replied with a worried expression. She was rambling again. A week later, at sixty-four years of age, Aunt Sophia was admitted to Yew Tree Lodge Care Home. All alone in her aunt's big house, Charlie counted the weeks until she would leave for St. Mary's.

* * * * * * * * *

As the train pulled into St. Moritz station, a sixteen-year-old Charlie wearily looked out onto the platform. It was a cold October morning, and the platform was lined with suited businessmen eager to earn a day's pay. Charlie struggled to prise her trunk out of the compartment as an old *fraulein* tut-tutted and pushed past, muttering some expletives in German.

'Do you mind?' Charlie shouted after her, not having quite mastered the German language. She turned back to her trunk in a final effort to maneuver it into the corridor. With an anguished tug, it flew out of the compartment, causing Charlie to 'fell' a fellow passenger as he was making his way off the train. With one jerking motion, Charlie had elbowed the middle-aged man in a place where middle-aged men don't wish to be elbowed. He collapsed to the floor gasping for air, his face reddening by the second.

'I... I... I'm so sorry.' Charlie stammered feebly.

'*Scheisse!*' The man's face contorted with obvious agony.

'Here, let me help you.' Charlie started.

'*Nein!*' He replied as he began to stand.

'I am so sorry... here's your briefcase.' Charlie picked up the discarded case and offered it to him. He was in his early forties with a receding hairline and glasses. He glared at her and when he reached out to take the case, she noticed that his hand was deformed. The skin was shiny and wrinkled with red blotches the size of dimes. It looked like a burn, she thought, as he snatched his briefcase from her and limped down the corridor and off the train.

'Welcome to Switzerland.' Charlie muttered as she dragged her trunk off the train with a thud.

Not only did the cold air hit Charlie, but it slapped her around the face. She stood on the platform resembling a refugee returning home. At sixteen, Charlie was developed for her age but in her grey school uniform with straw boater, she was still a child. Her black hair hung down her back and her dark brown eyes opened wide as she surveyed her new territory. Charlie should have started at St. Mary's four weeks earlier, but her Aunt Sophia had taken a turn for the worse. She was immensely fond of her aunt and visited Yew Tree Lodge every day until her aunt's health had stabilized. Charlie pulled the belt of her coat tight and tugged her trunk in search of a taxi.

The taxi ride to St. Mary's seemed to take forever. Charlie sat huddled in the back watching the passing snow-capped countryside, apprehensive of the day ahead. She couldn't help but notice the driver tilt his mirror and cast glances at her with hungry eyes. He must have been nearly sixty and belched every time he took a corner. She stared back in stony silence until he cast his glance back onto the road ahead, shifting in his seat.

The road wound alongside a river and over a bridge and then Charlie could see, looming out of the snow-laden trees, the impressive school with its tower and decorative green roof. They passed through a set of iron gates whose sign proudly read 'St. Mary's - Schule Für Junge Damen'. The taxi crunched to a halt on the gravel by a very grand entrance and Charlie stepped onto the snow-covered ground, staring up the ominous steps. The driver held out his hand through his window and muttered

'*Sechszehn francs*', with no attempt to help Charlie heave her trunk out of the back.

'*Sechszehn francs!*' he repeated, impatiently.

Charlie counted the correct amount and leaned through the window pressing the money into his sweaty hand, causing him to gulp as she stared into his eyes. Slowly she moved back out of the window and beckoned him with her finger, her head disappearing down below his eye level. He slowly leaned out of the window, open-mouthed, to look down. In a split second, Charlie scooped up a handful of snow and forced it into his mouth.

'That should cool you down, you old pervert!' she shouted. The driver spluttered, crunched his gears, and skidded down the driveway. As Charlie laughed out loud, her breath freezing as it hit the cold air, she was suddenly aware of a slow handclap behind her. She turned to see a man standing on the steps.

'Bravo! Bravo!' he applauded sardonically.

The sun shone behind him so brightly Charlie couldn't quite make out his face. As she approached the steps, she caught sight of his hands. They were deformed and very badly scarred.

'You must be Charlotte Black.'

'Er... yes.'

'Your late!'

'I'm sorry... I... mmm... Didn't we meet on the train?'

'Never mind, I am Frank, follow me.' He turned and marched up the steps, leaving Charlie to drag her trunk up the stone stairway and through the giant doors.

The wood-paneled hallway was dark and empty. Her guide was marching up a sweeping staircase lined with pictures of somber-looking men and women. Probably teachers and ex-pupils Charlie thought, and by the look on their faces, they didn't enjoy their time at this *Schule Für Junge Damen*.

As Charlie struggled up the stairs, she heard Frank shout *'Schnell! Schnell!'*

What was this place? Charlie schnelled up the staircase as quickly as possible to a vast hallway stretching left and right. The left corridor loomed into eternity, and to the right Charlie could see the strange man standing by a doorway, looking impatiently at her. She dragged her trunk towards him across the worn carpet. As she reached him, he knocked on the door, opened it, and entered. She followed him into the room.

Although lined with the same dark paneling from the hallway, the room was surprisingly light and airy. There was a large bed behind the door, a magnificent fireplace with two cozy chairs on either side, and a second bed near the window at the far end. To Charlie's left was a large desk with a reading lamp and a bookcase stacked with dozens of tattered books. Next to the desk was a small door. Frank crossed to the window, pulled the latch, and pushed the creaking window open on its tired runners. As

Charlie untied her coat, she heard a girl's voice scream from behind the small wooden door.

'Argghhh…!'

Frank turned his head sharply and cleared his throat nervously. Charlie looked from the door to Frank and then back to the door as the voice let out another scream. 'Argghhh…!' Frank approached and knocked loudly.

'Miss Diakos, are you alright?'

'Fuck!' Came the reply.

Frank shot a glance at Charlie.

'Miss Diakos! Language!'

As Frank knocked furiously, the door burst open. A young girl about Charlie's age stood there clutching a towel to her body, with long curly black hair cascading around her shoulders and a fiery gypsy look in her eyes. Frank took a pace back.

'Miss Diakos, your language is not…'

'There's a spider in my bath!' She exclaimed.

Charlie looked at Frank and giggled.

'Who the hell's this?' Miss Diakos asked the red-faced Frank.

'This is your roommate, Charlotte Black.' Frank replied.

'Oh no, no, no…' she began.

'Miss Black, this is Henrietta Diakos.'

'My father specifically asked for me to have a room to myself.'

'Well, the governess has specifically asked me to show Miss Black to your room.'

Her eight-legged friend suddenly made a dash for it, out of the bathroom, and over Henrietta's foot. She jumped and screamed, flicking her foot out. Her foot caught the open door and sent it crashing into Frank, the large doorknob finding its target accurately.

'*Scheisse!*' screamed Frank as he bent double for the second time that day.

'Miss Diakos!'

Henrietta Diakos glared at Charlie, then at Frank. She turned to the bathroom and dropped her towel. As Frank stared at her rounded backside, Henrietta looked over her shoulder.

'Do one... Frank!' With that, she pulled the bathroom door shut. Frank turned to Charlie looking like he was about to explode.

'I will leave you in the charming company of Miss Diakos. Breakfast is at seven-thirty, do not be late, after which you will receive a full timetable. Goodbye Miss Black.'

Frank marched out of the door and stomped down the corridor, leaving Charlie to survey the room. One bed had clothes strewn over it. That must be the fiery Miss Diakos's, Charlie deduced. She pulled her trunk by the empty bed and opened it. As she crossed to the wardrobe, the bathroom door opened, and Henrietta stood there in a robe with a towel 'turbaned' on her head.

'So, you're sharing with me?'

'Er... yeah.' Charlie replied. Silence.

Henrietta looked Charlie up and down and crossed to her bed.

'Look, I'm sorry about the mix-up over the room...' Charlie started.

Henrietta turned to her.

'Hey, no sweat. I was only ruffling his feathers a bit.'

'Oh.' Charlie didn't know how to take her new friend.

Henrietta approached Charlie with her arm outstretched.

'I'm Henrietta, but my friends call me Henry.'

Charlie shook her hand, 'I'm Charlotte, but my friends call me Charlie.'

'Well Charlie, I see you've met Frank.'

'Yeah, I sort of bumped into him on the train.'

'Oh?'

'Well, accidentally elbowed him in the groin to be precise!'

They both collapsed on the bed in a fit of giggles. Henry looked at Charlie.

'I think we're going to get along just fine!'

Chapter Four

THEN

The Slip

The rain lashed at the French windows as the wind howled around the desolate house. Penelope stared into the glowing fire roaring up the chimney, chasing away the demons of the night. Luke had been away for five long weeks. His mission should have been completed a week ago, but there was no telephone call, no letter, nothing, causing Penelope to fear the worst. She hated his secretive jaunts, shadowing diplomats and ambassadors.

It's not as if they needed the money, she'd inherited more than enough to keep them in their expensive lifestyle. No, he always said he had an obligation, but she knew he loved the sheer excitement of being undercover, but this time she feared the worst.

Suddenly a crack of thunder sent the French windows crashing open, the curtains billowing in like flaying sails on a desperate yacht. The lights went out and Penelope screamed. In the dancing firelight, she crossed to close the windows as the lightning lit up the sky once more. The wet drove in before she finally slipped the latch in place. Candles, she would light some candles and retire to her bedroom. A movement in the corner of the room caught her eye. She whirled around in terror as...

Suddenly she heard hysterical laughter.

'Cut! What the hell's going on?' The director screamed onto the set.

All eyes on the sound stage turned to the corner of the living room set as working lights flashed on. Kitty Wallis's co-star Rick Krane was laying on the floor laughing, a red rose clenched between his teeth.

'You've gone too far, this time Rick!' Kitty fumed.

Rick still laughing took the rose and offered it to her, screaming, 'Happy Valentine's Day!'

'Shove it!' Came the fractious reply.

Rick Krane staggered to his feet. It was obvious to the crew that his old habit had kicked in again. Kitty turned to Philip, the director, who was now striding onto the set.

'I want him off this movie! It's him or me!' Kitty fumed.

'No one is leaving this movie, Kitty!' Philip tried to calm her down, taking her by the elbow. She shrugged him away, turned to Rick Krane, and slapped him across the face, taking him somewhat by surprise. He fell to the ground, his ego wounded more than anything, whilst stifled screams of 'yes!' resounded in the studio.

'Bitch!' he shouted as Kitty turned and marched through the assembling crowd, like Moses parting the Red Sea.

'Brett!' She screamed at her PA. Brett Styles took a breath and turned to Philip with hands down towards the floor in a 'Don't worry I'll calm her' sort of motion.

Philip yelled to the assembled crew, 'Get him off this set and back to his room.'

'Come on Philip...' Rick started to plea.

'Shut up Rick! I'll see you in your dressing room in ten minutes. Lunch break. Everybody back at three.'

Oliver caught the end of this tirade as he tailed Jennifer Castle from her office. A runner had called her on the internal telephone the moment the director yelled 'cut'. She slammed down the receiver and pushed past Oliver. He raced after her, now convinced that he had entered the Twilight Zone.

He arrived at the scene as Kitty Wallis slapped Rick Krane across the face. Kitty Wallis and Rick Krane, wow! They were both huge stars. He'd watched Kitty Wallis in *Passion* three times, and the opening scene in the back of the cab at least thirty-three times. She was the ultimate sex symbol, and here she was in the flesh, her blonde hair bouncing as she stormed off the set, with her pink satin bathrobe clinging to her curves. No one dared move, they all stared at Philip, not knowing what to do.

'Come on!' Philip yelled. 'Get out of here! Screw the lot of you!'

The assembled crew scattered and some of the younger boys stifled a grin. Jennifer and Philip walked toward Oliver deep in conversation and Philip removed his glasses, studying Oliver like an early Barbara Hepworth. He frowned and spoke, as though Oliver wasn't there.

'Quite remarkable.'

Oliver shifted uneasily from foot to foot. Philip suddenly walked away, leaving Jennifer smiling at him.

'Right, your scene is next. Be ready at three on the dot.' She turned to go.

'Just a minute...' Oliver stopped her.

'What now?'

'Well, what do I have to do?'

'Your agent hasn't filled you in?' She bemused.

'Erm... not entirely... no...' Oliver stammered.

'Well... Mr. Wilkins, all will be revealed in time. Oh, a slightly fruitless task, but check in with wardrobe. Philip will fill you in at three.'

Oliver was losing his cool 'Either you tell me what I have to do or... or...' he stammered.

'Now, now, Mr. Wilkins, you seem a bit hot and bothered.' She paused and took a step toward Oliver, 'Have you heard of naked body-doubling?' Oliver stared in disbelief.

'Riiiight,' she continued, 'I have more important matters to attend to, so I will see you at three o'clock prompt.' Jennifer Castle smiled and marched back to her office. The light suddenly dawned. 'Oh... shiiiit' thought Oliver.

* * * * * * * * *

Oliver stared at himself in his dressing room mirror. *What am I doing here?* he thought. He wore a white toweling robe and nothing else. After his confrontation with Jennifer Castle, he'd bumped into Cheryl, the runner slash PA. She was red-haired with a face to match and carrying an array of white lilies in her arms. So many, that she dropped half a dozen or so as she collided with Oliver.

'I'm so sorry, I don't know what's wrong with me today,' she flustered as Oliver bent down to pick up the blooms.

'No problem, it's...' Achoo! He sneezed violently.

'Bless you!' Cheryl looked at him with a concerned look.

'Oh, it's not you, it's the flowers, I have allergies.' Oliver smiled.

'Oh, well that's good... I mean...' Cheryl mumbled.

'It's the day' Oliver explained as he forced the fallen flowers into her human vase.

Cheryl looked vague.

'Well... the date.'

Cheryl's vagueness deepened.

'Friday the thirteenth?' Oliver announced crossing a finger from each hand as though he was Van Helsing.

'Oh, I see.' The light dawned and Cheryl raised her eyes to the heavens. 'Well, thanks for your help, I have to dress the next set by three, it's all go today!'

'Erm... Cheryl, isn't it?'

'Yes, Cheryl Stevens... props and odd jobs. Runner slash...'

Oliver finished her sentence. '...slash PA, I remember.'

'Well, must dash. I'll see more of you later... oh!'

Oliver couldn't help noticing Cheryl's face suddenly flush with embarrassment as she turned and marched away, lilies bobbing around her.

Oliver was ready for his big moment. He'd heard of body doubling before. Many Hollywood A-Listers used doubles in nude shots including shower scenes. But why him? Why Oliver and why today? There was a knock at the door, and a young fresh-faced boy peered into the dressing room.

'Hello, I'm Jeff, a runner, are you ready?' The boy asked, his gaze quickly darting to the floor.

'Yes, I suppose so,' Oliver replied, taking one last look in the mirror.

At twenty-two, Oliver had a well-above-average body. Not too many muscles but very well defined. He worked out when he could and looked after himself, as much as any aspiring actor could. But to stand naked on a sound stage, in front of makeup people, runners, sound technicians, camera operators... The shame of it.

However, there was a plus side, he wouldn't be alone. Kitty Wallis, *the* Kitty Wallis would be his co-star for this 'blink' of a scene. Ok, no one would see his face, no one would know it was him, but he would know, he would remember. 'But what if she also used a body double?' He hadn't thought about that, it hadn't crossed his mind. Maybe that would be better anyway, he wouldn't feel as nervous.

Oliver followed Jeff the runner out of his dressing room. Runner by name, runner by nature. Jeff acted like he was on some game show assault course. After jogging Oliver through a myriad of corridors they finally arrived at the sound stage where the crew was milling about at one end, like a team of worker ants. On set, a shower sat in the corner of a vast black marble bathroom. The cubicle was unusually large, so to shoot the sequence with more ease and one wall was cut away for camera angles. Cheryl was placing the last of her lilies on the marble sink unit. Oliver thought the bathroom resembled a florist's shop in Covent Garden and that maybe Cheryl had overdone it.

She headed for him and gave his arm a gentle squeeze.

'Go for it' she whispered as she scurried past.

'Thanks' Oliver mouthed back to her as she collided with Jeff the runner, sending papers and clipboard flying into the air.

Philip Peters, the epitome of an agitated director, marched up to Oliver.

'You good and ready?'

'I think so,' Oliver replied.

'I don't want this to take the rest of the day. We'll do a full-body take of you entering the shower, then follow up with some close-up shots. When I say 'action' you join her in the shower, back to the camera, you got that?

Oliver nodded.

'Make out you're madly in love with her, it shouldn't be too difficult.'

'No problem.' Oliver snapped, really thinking, *Get me out of here!*

'By the way...' Philip asked.

'What?'

'You're not gay, are you?'

Oliver stared at Philip.

'No,' he smiled, 'are you?'

Philip held his stare and without moving his eyes shouted 'Ok, are we ready to shoot this?'

The ants cleared the set, taking up their positions, and suddenly Oliver sensed a change in the atmosphere. He turned to see Kitty Wallis walking onto the set. No, not walk, glide. She was wearing a pink bathrobe and looked more beautiful than he could ever have imagined. Her blond hair fell over one eye as the makeup girl applied more lipstick to her sumptuous lips. Oliver found himself mouthing Jessica Rabbit and quickly brought himself back to earth. He noted that Brett, her PA, had done a good job of calming her down.

With a toss of her head, she looked over at Oliver. He froze. She stared at him, her gaze slowly dropped down his body and stopped at his feet. Following her eye line, he grimaced as he spotted his footwear. A dressing gown and Chelsea boots were not a winning combination. He clumsily kicked off the boots and muttered 'Damn!' under his breath.

'Standby everyone.' Philip shouted. The water was turned on in the shower. Kitty winked at Oliver, dropped her robe, and stepped into the cubicle.

Looking back over her shoulder she purred, 'Are you joining me?'

'Recording!' Bells sounded everywhere around the stage and silence fell.

'Action!'

Oliver's heart raced as he stood motionless. He was frozen to the spot.

'ACTION!' Philip screamed once more.

Suddenly Oliver started and cast a look from side to side. There were so many people. Through a vase of lilies, he caught Cheryl's eye, and she gave him a secret thumbs up.

'I can do this,' he told himself.

In one movement he opened his robe, dropped it to the ground, and boldly walked up to the shower cubicle. Kitty stood with her back to him. She had the most beautiful body with small, round buttocks facing him. He stepped into the shower, sneezed, slipped on the soap, and fell on his back, legs in the air, for all to see.

Oliver could have died.

THEN

A Sissy Spacek Moment

Charlie and Henry became the very best of friends.

Charlie discovered Henry was of Greek/French descent. The only daughter of self-made millionaire and shipping magnate, Dimitri Diakos, and his erstwhile wife, the famous model, Yvette Paradis, of Afro-French origin. Her dark skin and six-foot, slender body earned her supermodel status. Henry's parents endured a volatile relationship, ending in an acrimonious divorce when Henry was ten years old. In truth, Dimitri couldn't come to terms with his wife's chosen profession. He was a deeply jealous man and constantly accused Yvette of having affairs with stylists, publicists, and fashion photographers. She never had, and in reality, Yvette was in love with Dimitri but couldn't cope with his insane jealousy. One jealous rage too many and she left him for good.

Henry's childhood in Paris had been somewhat sparse of love. Yvette was constantly on some shoot or other, traveling the world, leaving Henry in the hands of Nanny Simone.

With a heart of stone and a wicked mouth, Nanny Simone was a force to be reckoned with. Henry had thought about complaining to her mother, but it never seemed the right moment. On the few occasions she had quality time with her mother, she couldn't bring herself to raise the subject of the nanny from hell. Instead, she learned that she had to take care of number one because no one else was going to. On school holidays she visited her father in Cyprus and cherished her time with him. He may have been running a shipping empire, but he always made time for his little girl.

She adored her parents and they both adored her, but they couldn't live with each other.

At school, Charlie and Henry were attentive but mischievous. Frank Hoffman, their head of year, despised them both and they took every chance to humiliate him. Frank always found an excuse to enter the gym during practice. Eyeing up the girls, their legs wrapped around the ropes, pulling themselves up to the ceiling. He was particularly cruel to some of the 'timid' girls, pushing against them in the hallway and confiscating their newly purchased chocolate. It wasn't that he liked chocolate, it was more the power he felt when they handed it over with shaking hands.

Ms. Kleinhaus was a tall, wispy, thin-lipped woman who took pleasure in others' misfortune. At morning assembly, she stood on a short platform under a sign bearing the school motto, *Nil Sine Labore*. Nothing is gained without hard work or sacrifice. Charlie was determined to make something of her life and would sacrifice anything to be recognized. It wasn't about money; she already had a secret fortune behind a door that was soon to open. No, for Charlie, it was about being a successful, powerful woman.

Charlie awoke early one spring morning as the sun was fighting its way through the curtains. Henry was still sleeping. She kicked off the sheets and scrambled over to the window where, down below, the gardener was mowing the lawns astride the tractor mower. Charlie had noticed him scurrying around the grounds with a wheelbarrow or an armful of shrubs. He worked hard with his head down, not speaking a word. She discovered, through the groundskeeper, that his name was Marcus. Spanish and sexy.

Many times, she'd walk in his path, but he would simply change direction as though he'd found himself going the wrong way. This puzzled Charlie. She was attractive with a blossoming figure and magnificent hair, why did it seem that he didn't even notice her? Marcus was six-foot-tall, in his early twenties, with a strong jawline and a rugged five o'clock shadow. He wore a cap at all times pulled down below his eyes making eye contact difficult. *Maybe he was gay?* she thought absent-mindedly. Well, it was time to find out.

Charlie stepped out into the morning sunshine, camera in hand. She ran down the steps into the gardens following the sound of the lawnmower. Peering around a wall, she watched Marcus as he collected grass cuttings.

'Right, here goes nothing.' she whispered to herself.

Flicking her hair back, she stuck her chest out and stood to fire some shots on her camera, but the lawnmower was standing alone in the center of the lawn, idling away. Marcus's cap was by a large leaf pile but no sign of Marcus. She walked towards the cap and bent down to pick it up when suddenly, an arm shot out of the leaves and grabbed her. Charlie screamed as the leaf pile jumped up into the air and she fell back onto the lawn. Standing in front of her was Marcus, grinning from ear to ear, leaves falling all around him.

'Gotcha!'

Charlie tried to regain her composure. 'You scared me!'

'Yes, that was the general idea!' He reached out and offered his hand to Charlie. He was so damn handsome. She placed her hand in his and he pulled her towards him. She felt herself pressing against his body as he looked steamily into her eyes.

'You a-hole!' Charlie shouted as she threw a clump of leaves at him. 'You've seen the movie *Carrie*, then?'

Marcus smiled 'I don't know any Carrie, but I am hot today. Are you hot?'

'Er... ehm...' Charlie stammered.

Marcus pulled away and ran towards the lake that nestled at the edge of the rambling lawns. He turned and winked before disappearing behind the bushes running along the edge of the water. She turned back to the school building, no one seemed to have stirred, but it was still very early. Intrigued, Charlie walked towards the high hedges. As she approached the lake, a flock of birds swam off the surface and soared over the wood on the other side. She rounded the bushes and there was Marcus, standing beside a pile of clothes, in his boxer shorts.

'What are you...?' Charlie started.

'Sshhhh,' Marcus put his fingers to his lips.

He looked magnificent, everything Charlie had imagined and more. With broad shoulders and a firm chest, his rippling stomach had a line of hair dividing it and moving down his shorts. Marcus put his hands on his hips and slowly, but purposely, pushed his boxer shorts to the ground. He grinned, displaying a stunning row of white teeth, and then dived into the lake. Charlie stared in disbelief as he swam out of sight. He turned and waved. *You're only young once*, Charlie thought. In a matter of seconds, she was tearing off her clothes. She wrapped her camera in her top and dived in after the amorous gardener. The water was freezing but refreshing at the same time. Charlie swam where she couldn't be seen from the school and Marcus swam toward her like an Olympian. He wrapped his arms around her and pressed his wet lips against hers. *God, he tasted good*, thought Charlie. She could feel his excitement brush against her leg as he squeezed his body against hers. After what felt like hours, Marcus pulled away.

'Race you!' he said as he began swimming to the edge of the lake, Charlie following in hot pursuit. He helped her onto the bank and led her into a clearing amongst large rhododendrons, where he pulled her down and caressed her glistening body.

'This place is beautiful.' Charlie picked a crisp white snowdrop from beside her. Marcus looked at her with longing.

'You are a beautiful rose amongst the snowdrops.'

Charlie shuddered as his hot mouth smothered her lips. Slowly she guided him as he enveloped her with his body.

Little did Charlie know that one day soon, Marcus would save her life.

Chapter Six

NOW

A Change of Plan

A seagull cried overhead and disturbed Oliver from his daydreams. The harbor was slowly waking. He checked his mobile – seven thirty-six, still time to enjoy the view. At the far end of the harbor fishermen were returning, ready to hoist their catch ashore. No doubt the lobster would be on dining tables by noon. Oliver wished he could turn the clock back and not have been so naive all those years ago, but a promise was a promise. There was no turning back now.

His mobile beeped.

Drinnng

Oliver pressed the screen to reveal a message from an unknown number.

THIS IS THE LOCATION

A drop-pin appeared on a map.

His thumb hovered over the reply window and he typed his answer.

GOT IT I WILL BE AT THE VENUE AS AGREED AT 12 NOON

He waited

Drinnng

DON'T CHANGE ANYTHING

DO AS AGREED

He typed back

AS I SAID AGREED AND UNDERSTOOD

His mobile beeped again, whoever it was, they were annoying him. But this message was from another sender, this time with a number.

GO TO THE PATISSERIE OPPOSITE THE GEORGE HOTEL 9 AM

LOCATION TO FOLLOW

What was going on? Oliver didn't like this one bit.

A second drop pip appeared showing The George Hotel in Villefranche-Sur-Mer.

He sat upright and hit dial but all he heard were three tones followed by a voice.

'Le Numéro n'est plus en service'

Oliver stared at his mobile, 'No longer in service? Great!'

He had no choice, soon it would be over. But why two locations? He didn't like the sound of this, but to live the rest of his life with Charlie by his side was a risk worth taking. In a few hours, his fate would be sealed. Looking back, would he change anything if he could? Meeting Kitty Wallis all those years ago was a big deal, but maybe he should have known it was all too good to be true. He'd paid for his silence, and then again, if he had lived life differently, he would never have met Charlie. Nothing else mattered.

He slumped back in his chair. Ok, a slight detour...

Chapter Seven

THEN

A Pink Explosion

When Oliver slipped in the shower Kitty hadn't laughed so much in a very long time. She was in her late thirties and at the top of her game. Small movies early on in her career had aroused the interest of some great directors and the movie *Stranger at the Window* catapulted her into the 'big time'. Her on-screen electricity with co-star Rick Krane was the talk of Hollywood. The climax of the film, when her character reveals her secret straight to camera, had everyone gasping. The world adored her and so did directors, mainly because she took notes, exuded sexual chemistry, and worked hard. People like Rick Krane fell by the wayside, they couldn't keep up with her spark and adoration. She'd agreed to do this current movie with Rick as a favor, much to the distress of her assistant Brett Styles. She felt sorry for Rick, he was once a great actor but after getting involved with the new hottest singer on the scene, Vixen, drink and drugs had taken their greedy toll. Vixen was outrageous and Rick couldn't get enough of her.

Kitty helped him on many occasions, but he was a law unto himself, so she offered a final lifeline by letting him co-star with her, mainly because she felt she owed him for her start in the movie industry. Brett tried to convince her it was a huge mistake, but she was adamant and having been her PA for the best part of ten years, Brett Styles knew when to back off. Kitty valued Brett's advice but, on this occasion, she was sticking to her guns. On the plus side, the majority of the shoot was in London. All that shopping! She would spend her free time in Fortnum and Masons, Liberty's, and her favorite restaurants: The Ivy and Joe Allen's.

After Oliver's 'slip up', the shooting went well. So much so, that he was asked to go to Kitty's trailer after the director called a wrap on the shower scene. Oliver walked down the side of the studio as a very hurried Cheryl brushed past him. She half-turned, half ran with a 'Well done you!' making him smile back before making his way outside. He approached the cluster of trailers looking for Kitty's. It was marked with a pink star and as he approached the door Jennifer Castle and Brett Styles hurried out. They looked at Oliver, heaved a great sigh, and stood aside, Brett half leaned back into the trailer.

'Kitty, it's Oliver Wilkins for you.' As he passed, Brett shook his hand.

'Good job today, Oliver.'

'Ehm... thanks.'

Jennifer let Brett go ahead.

'When you've finished here Oliver, come and see me, you know where my office is.'

She smiled and marched back to the studio.

The entire trailer was kitted out in pink.

Literally, everything was pink including the carpet, sofa, curtains, walls, ceiling, the plates, and mugs on the pink side unit under pink towels were hanging on the wall. Kitty was watching a pink television on her pink sofa, looking radiant in a pink tracksuit.

She patted the sofa next to her.

'Oliver, come, sit.' She hit the remote.

'Kitty... firstly I must apologize about this afternoon. I wasn't told what was going on and what, with all those lilies and my allergies....'

'Nonsense, you were wonderful, now, tell me all about yourself.'

'What do you want to know?' Oliver was curious. And why he wanted to say.

'Everything, but first let's have a little drink to celebrate, only one mind, we have a busy day tomorrow.'

Confused, Oliver took a glass of champagne and began.

'Well, my name's Oliver Wilkins...'

'Mmmm, that must change,' Kitty interrupted.

'I'm sorry...?'

'Continue.'

'Well, er...' Oliver talked as Kitty listened. Never once did she interrupt or look the slightest bored, and after five minutes had passed Oliver stopped talking.

'That's about it, my life in a nutshell.'

'Fascinating, but your name, Oliver Wilkins, has no ring to it. It needs to be something more sophisticated, more exotic.'

Oliver looked at Kitty's beautiful face, she was staring into his eyes, lips parted. She leaned forward and he leaned into her with his eyes closed, ready for the kiss.

'There you are!' Kitty exclaimed as she reached down and collected a diamond earring from the floor between them. Oliver swiftly opened his eyes and shot back in his seat.

Kitty looked startled. 'Oliver, were you about to...?'

'What?! oh... no... no! Of course not!'

'Mmmmm... well let's get something straight, we'll not be having any sort of affair. I'm a happily married woman and I intend to keep it that way.'

'Yes, of course!' Oliver stammered.

'Not that I'm not flattered... I am. Now go, you've got a lot of preparation to do.'

'Yes... of course... I'll get off then... erm... preparation?'

'Yes, you have an important screentest in the morning. Now get outta here and go see Jennifer on your way.'

'Screentest? But... I don't...'

'That's it!'

'That's what?' Oliver said, confused.

Kitty looked into her palm at the diamond earring.

'Diamond... Oliver Diamond!'

'Oliver Diamond?'

'Now go!'

Oliver raced out of the trailer, tripping down the step like a clumsy schoolboy. Kitty drew back the curtains watching as he stumbled his way back to the studio. 'Yes... you'll be perfect, Oliver Diamond... just perfect.'

Chapter Eight

NOW

Second Thoughts

Charlie was in the *Groundhog Day* of her nightmare. Two ear-piercing shots, and silence. She stared in disbelief at the body lying before her. Her mouth moved but no sound came out. This time it was different. A man was kneeling over her father's body, holding his hand. She moved towards him as he began searching her father's pockets, then slowly, the man turned his head toward her... Charlie snapped her eyes open and forced the nightmare to stop. Her breathing increased and she was sweating. She could see Oliver through the balcony curtains on his mobile. She reached for her phone, seven-forty, this day had been a long time coming, but she was well prepared. She'd gone over and over every foreseeable outcome and she'd covered every possible scenario. Hadn't she? Was anything missed out, anything overlooked? No, Charlie was meticulous, especially when she had so much to gain but so much to lose. Tomorrow was another day, and it couldn't come fast enough. At least Henry, Charlie's closest friend, would be by her side. Looking back, Charlie and Henry were destined to be friends forever, but her one big risk was losing Oliver altogether...

Chapter Nine

THEN

Carpe Diem

Charlie and Henry lived for the weekends when they would sneak out of St. Mary's and venture into the town of St. Moritz, a mere forty minutes away. On such a Saturday, Henry decided to strike up a friendship with the new grocery delivery boy, Dirk. A pimply nineteen-year-old, eager to please and ready to do anything to get a girl's attention. He gawped at the girls in the quadrangle on his way to the kitchens, his trolley stacked with wooden crates of vegetables, so high he couldn't see over the top. Henry decided to torment him. Leaning on a pillar in the walkway she undid the top button of her blouse, seductively. As he approached with his laden trolley, she dropped her stack of books.

'Oh, now look what you've done!'

Girls turned and giggled as Dirk came to a sudden halt, the top two crates spilling their contents of beetroots over the cobbles. The schoolgirls laughed at his misfortune.

'You need to be more careful.'

'So sorry Miss... please don't tell. I will get such trouble.' His broken English was endearing.

'Yes, well look where you're going next time.'

Dirk scrabbled to recover his load as Henry collected her books from the floor.

'You not say anything, *ja*?' he pleaded in his sweet German accent.

'Well... ok... *ja*, but I need a favor in return,' she replied huskily, her innocent eyes boring into Dirk. She leaned toward him crouching to pick up her last book, her ample cleavage directly in his eye-line. Dirk was so embarrassed, that he matched the color of his beetroot.

'Ok... you want what?' Dirk gulped, averting his eyes.

'I need a ride to St. Moritz. Meet me on the driveway, by the power generator in twenty minutes.'

'But... I cannot... I get big trouble if my boss know, he not nice man.'

'Well, you'll have to make sure he doesn't find out. I won't be telling anyone.'

Henry winked at Dirk, turned, and skipped away to her room, leaving the grocery boy looking after her, half scared, half excited. She was very beautiful. He'd noticed her the previous week during his first drop-off. Maybe, she liked him. Maybe, at last, he could have a girlfriend, and maybe he would finally get to kiss a real, live girl. With a grin and a glint in his eye, he stacked the two boxes back on his trolley and hurried to the kitchens.

Henry burst through the door. 'Charlie! Charlie!' Charlie was sleeping away a late night of chats and a midnight feast with

Marcus. Since their first meeting by the lake, Charlie and Marcus met regularly, he was uncomplicated, unshaven, and so damn kissable.

'Whaaaat? I'm trying to sleep!'

'Oh no, not today.' Henry said, shaking her.

'Why are you so lively in the mornings? And what's so special about today?' Charlie complained, sitting upright.

'Because it's your birthday and we are going to St. Moritz. Now hurry, you have five minutes!'

'My birthday? You know how I feel about my birthday.'

Henry stopped and looked at her friend, 'I know, but Charlie, that has to change. Your father would want you to live your life, come on...'

Charlie caved in, 'St. Moritz? Now?'

'Yes, now! *Carpe diem*!' Henry said excitedly.

'Carpe what?' Charlie screwed up her eyes.

'*Carpe diem*, seize the day! Now hurry and dress.' Henry tugged the bedding off Charlie impatiently and began to dress into her Hermès white jumpsuit with a matching bag and shoes complete with a knee-length white coat.

'Ok, Ok, St. Moritz it is then.'

Charlie leaped out of bed and pulled on subtle black leggings with a tight-fitting black jacket and a bright yellow scarf around her neck. Charlie never had to try hard, she looked fabulous in anything. Chic and understated. Henry stood in the doorway impatiently drumming her fingers on the doorframe.

'Ready birthday girl?'

'As I'll ever be,' replied Charlie, grabbing her camera from her bedside table.

They ran down the drive. It was a beautiful spring day with the promise of a summer around the corner. A good-to-be-alive day, as Charlie called these fresh mornings. They rounded the drive and ran past the ugly electric building to find a nervous Dirk waiting anxiously in his grocery van. He hooted as the girls sprinted for the doors.

'Sssshhhhh,' the girls exclaimed as they climbed into the dusty old van. Ms. Kleinhaus was heading towards them from the main road on her pushbike, looking like a disheveled Myra Gulch on her way to Oz.

'Drive!' Henry shouted as she and Charlie ducked down. The van spluttered into life and Dirk drove past Ms. Kleinhaus who was staring at him, bewildered as to where the van had suddenly appeared from.

The girls squinted through the wing mirror and burst into laughter as Ms. Kleinhaus struggled on her bicycle, looking back after them.

'Oh Dirk, this is my friend Charlie. Charlie, Dirk'

'Pleased to meet you, Dirk.'

Dirk offered his hand.

'Hands on the wheel Dirk, eyes on the road!' Charlie exclaimed,

Formalities over, the girls chatted all the way to St. Moritz. It had been snowing hard and the landscape was covered in crisp white snow. Dirk was happy to have company and the smell of perfume lingering in his dusty vegetable van. The weekend shift wasn't so bad after all.

Chapter Ten

THEN

A Girl's Best Friend

Oliver woke suddenly, the events of the previous day unraveling in his mind. Today he had a screentest, and he was aware of how much this could change his life.

After he met with Kitty Wallis, he had a chat with Jennifer Castle, the executive producer. She'd been vague, but his summary of events was that he had a screentest the next day. He wasn't sure for what, and he wasn't going to push too hard in case she changed her mind. Maybe there was a role still to be cast?

He skipped breakfast, showered, dressed, and checked himself in the mirror. His mother always said, 'Before you leave home every day check yourself in the mirror. See what others see and don't forget to wear your smile.'

His parents were honest, humble people. Born and bred in Sheffield, they'd lived there all their lives.

His father died when he was fourteen years old in an accident at work. He was a plant foreman at a car factory and had been overseeing the installation of some new equipment when the chains snagged and the machinery came crashing down. His father rushed forward to push his new plant supervisor out of harm's way, putting himself into the path of the falling metalwork. His mother, Betty, received a healthy insurance payout and used the majority of the money to send Oliver to drama school. Oliver was devastated when his father died but spent his time making sure his mother was ok and keeping his head down. He took every opportunity to see the latest films showing at his local cineplex. Every genre fascinated him, from Pacino to Hoffman, Depp to Spacey, he soaked up their techniques like a sponge.

Oliver arrived at studio six to find it a hive of activity. The same shy runner greeted him. 'Mr. Wilkins, please follow me.' Oliver followed the young boy down the back corridor. As they were speed-walking, Oliver ran over the script Jennifer had given to him the night before. He was whisked through wardrobe followed by hair and makeup and finally arrived at the studio an hour later.

* * * * * * * * *

The 'set' was the lavish living room where he'd witnessed Kitty Wallis slapping Rick Krane the previous day. Heads turned as he was escorted onto the sound stage and a hush filled the space. Suddenly, he heard the voice of Philip Peters, the director.

'Ok, ok, standby everyone.'

Cheryl was moving candles and clearing the coffee table of coffee mugs and bowls. She caught sight of Oliver and smiled. He winked at her and shrugged a 'what the hell's going on?' look, she pulled a face and shrugged back before scurrying off the set, arms full as usual. Philip Peters approached him with a young girl adorned with a Black Sabbath t-shirt, ripped jeans, Doc Martin boots, and thick black-rimmed glasses. She was clutching the script in her black nail-varnished hands.

'Hi Oliver, this is Zoe,' Philip was much calmer today.

'She's my AD, and she'll take you through what we need. I'll be in the gallery checking things out.'

'Your AD?'

Philip sighed, 'Assistant director?'

'Oh right, yes... mmm... ok.'

Philip looked Oliver in the eyes as if he was trying to work something out in his mind. 'Ok... let's get going on this.' Philip left Zoe to give Oliver the rundown. She stared at Oliver. 'My God, the resemblance is amazing.'

'Resemblance?' Oliver questioned her.

'Yes, you bear an uncanny resemblance to a younger Rick Krane, when he's not drunk that is,' she added, hastily. Oliver hadn't thought about it.

'Well, I was booked as his body double, so...'Oliver stopped as Zoe led him onto the set. She explained what was to happen in the next hour or so. It was a screentest, he knew that. It was a scene with Kitty Wallis where her character, Penelope, pleaded with her husband not to take this last mission. He was a covert spy dealing with Russians, espionage, and atomic warfare.

As Zoe explained what he needed to do his eyes darted around the studio.

'Ok, standby please,' Philip's voice burst through hidden speakers.

Zoe looked at Oliver expectantly, 'You know what you're doing?'

'Yes... I think so... but who will I be acting with?'

'I'll read in, the cameras will be focusing on you, not me.'

'Ok... yes... fine...' Oliver crossed to the drinks bar on set as Zoe stood by the French windows, script in hand.

He heard Philip's voice again, 'Ok, quiet on set.'

Zoe looked back at Oliver, and he gave her a thumbs up.

'Don't forget when I turn to face you from the window, you start talking.'

'Got it.' Oliver swallowed hard, ready to give his all.

'Standby... and... rolling.'

'Rolling!' a voice echoed.

A silence fell across the sound stage. Slowly, Zoe turned to face Oliver and he began his rehearsed dialogue.

'Penelope, I have to do this. You knew what life would be like with me, it's one last mission.' Oliver pleaded.

Zoe looked at Oliver.

'It's always one last mission. Soon it will be your last mission because you won't be coming home alive.'

Oliver moved across the living room.

'I will, I promise I'll be back before you know it. Let's not part this way...'

'You said the same thing last time when you went to Egypt, and the time before that.'

'But this time it's different, we're different…'

'Waaaiiiit!' a voice screamed across the sound stage and Oliver heard footsteps echoing across the studio. All heads turned.

'Cut!' Philip shouted as a bell rang.

Kitty Wallis marched purposefully onto the set looking radiant, with Brett walking briskly behind as Philip came tearing from the gallery.

'Kitty! What are you doing?'

'This is a screentest right?'

'Er, yes.' Philip answered.

'Then let's do it.' She flung off her coat and threw it to one side where it landed squarely in the face of a confused Cheryl.

'But we don't need you at this point of the proceedings,' Philip stopped her.

'But I think you do Philip, so let's not waste any more time. From the top!'

Zoe darted out through the French windows and off the set. Brett smiled at Philip and shrugged his shoulders. Kitty crossed to the living room as Philip threw his hands up, sighed, and returned to the gallery.

Kitty walked up to Oliver. 'Ok Oliver Diamond, we got this. We'll take it from the top. Oh, and say it like you mean it this time.'

* * * * * * * * *

The screentest flew by. Oliver stood on his marks, moved on cue, changed inflections, and was getting such a buzz. All the while Kitty Wallis reassured him, giving his hand or arm a squeeze now and then.

After a particularly tense section of dialogue, Philip stormed on set. *Here goes*, thought Oliver, he knew it was too good to last.

'Oliver,' Philip looked at him intently, 'this is good work, it's looking great on camera.'

Oliver sighed 'Really?'

Kitty knew all she had to do was point Oliver in the right direction and Philip would see the spark she'd felt. Philip couldn't miss it.

'Kitty we need more time on this. I really think...'

Jennifer Castle walked up to Philip and cut him off, whispering in his ear. Suddenly he pulled away and made a decision.

'Ok everyone, break. We resume at two. Kitty, I'll come to see you in twenty minutes; Jennifer, you and I have some calls to make; Oliver, go home.'

'Go home?' Oliver's heart sank. He didn't know why he'd been doing the screentest, he presumed it was for a small role, maybe he wasn't right for it? He was used to rejection, and this had been a rollercoaster ride. As he caught Kitty's eye she winked at him, conspiratorially.

'Hold tight Oliver,' she whispered as she brushed past.

'You were quite something, Kitty's impressed,' Brett said as he tried to catch up with his errant boss. Oliver was struggling to make sense of any of it as Jennifer approached him.

'Oliver, thank you for your time. Go home and rest, I'll be in touch with you direct this evening.'

Now he had no agent, no job, and no money. Great.

* * * * * * * * *

Later that evening, whilst he was making his favorite pasta, Jennifer called him.

'Hello, is that Oliver?'

'Yes, Hi Jennifer,'

'We have some rather good news...'

* * * * * * * * *

Oliver couldn't quite believe what was happening. Before Jennifer had stopped the shoot, she received a call from Rick's PA, Damien. Rick Krane was found completely out of his head in a bar after taking an overdose. He was rushed to a private hospital. The executives and director held an emergency meeting after which Philip and other producers held crisis calls with LA well into the night. His screentest was uploaded, downloaded, and viewed by many moguls and producers.

They unanimously agreed the movie was in good hands with Kitty Wallis at the helm. She was in her prime and her name guaranteed good box office. Many of the producers had been worried that Rick Krane would have an adverse effect on the film's box office, so they welcomed a change of plan. After viewing the screentest they could all see the palpable electricity between Kitty and Oliver. Jennifer called to make an offer to Oliver to play the lead opposite Kitty Wallis in her new film *Stealth*! He was speechless. She gave him his calls for the following morning, told him a courier would drop the script within the hour and a 'car' would collect him at six AM. Before she hung up, she had one caveat. Here it was, there was always a condition.

'What?' Oliver asked cautiously.

'Wilkins, it has to go.'

'Aaaah, Kitty Wallis.' Oliver replied

'Well yes, but Oliver Diamond does have a certain ring to it, don't you think?'

'Whatever you say.' Oliver wouldn't have minded what they wanted to call him. This morning there had been no future and now it was six figures! The production company Golden Hills had made the offer direct which meant his agent, Dan Goldberg, was out of the picture. Literally! Oh, how Oliver would love to see the look on his agent's face when he found out. But first, he had to make a call to Sheffield.

* * * * * * * * *

They hadn't been too far into the shooting schedule for *Stealth,* and the scenes Rick had already filmed were ropey, to say the least. So, with some hard work from the production crew, they were soon back on schedule. Oliver was a natural and slipped into the role of Kitty's 'spy' husband, Luke Starr, like it was written for him. The character was a man's man by day and a woman's man by night, not unlike Oliver. Philip took to Oliver immediately, but then Oliver was a dream after working with Rick Krane.

Rick was dispatched back to California into the arms of his wayward girlfriend Vixen with his tail well and truly between his legs. Initially, he'd tried to fight back at the decision but soon realized he was in no shape to even dress himself in the mornings, let alone work on a movie set.

* * * * * * * * *

Oliver's first few days were a blur. He was whisked through hair and makeup and that's where the transformation began. They chopped his hair and shaped it into an amazing style, a handsome cut but with a flair of the modern-day man. He felt like a hundred hands were on him all day and that his body wasn't his anymore.

Kitty's PA, Brett Styles, turned out to be a great ally, giving Oliver useful tips on how to deal with Kitty Wallis. Not that he needed them, Kitty liked Oliver a lot, but it was always good to have a friend in her PA. Over the ensuing weeks, he would occasionally bump into Cheryl. She was always encouraging and had a smile on her face from ear to ear.

On set, Oliver dedicated his time to listening and learning. He delivered time and time again, take after take. Even managing some of his own stunts, much to the horror of Jennifer, who was already thinking the movie was jinxed.

For one stunt Oliver had to do a simple balcony leap. It involved jumping from one platform to another on the green scene sound stage. Philip needed a full-frontal shot of 'Luke Starr to the rescue'. Oliver loved the satisfaction of doing his stunts. There were plenty of fall mats around the area and in truth, the platforms were only a couple of meters off the ground.

'Ok... rehearsal!' Philip's voice filled the studio, 'Standby... and action!'

Oliver checked his landing mark, pulled back on the rail, and threw himself from his platform. He landed perfectly and rolled on his right shoulder, as taught by his stunt coordinator, Ron, who was watching his every move.

Philip studied the monitor on the ground and gave a thumbs up.

'Perfect. Ron?' Ron nodded his reply.

'Ok, let's go again, another rehearsal. Everyone reset. You ok Oliver?'

'As I'll ever be.' Oliver replied with a smile on his face.

'Ok... standby...' Suddenly bells and alarms rang through the studio, deafening everyone.

'What's going on?' Philip shouted as the crew began to exit through the fire doors.

Brett raced over. 'It's the fire alarm. Thank God Kitty's having a spa day today.' Normally Brett and Kitty were inseparable, but she'd insisted she go to the spa alone whilst Brett caught up on paperwork and emails at the studio. Oliver looked down at Brett and Philip and shook his head. 'Maybe it's a drill?'

Philip sighed 'Yeah well, I wish they'd warn us first! We've little time left to get this scene finished before we have to move on tomorrow.'

Oliver climbed down and walked Philip and Brett out through the fire door, arms around both their shoulders.

'Come on Philip, Brett and I will stand and chat to you whilst watching you killing yourself smoking.' Oliver grinned at Brett.

Twenty minutes later and everyone was back on set, ready to go again. The studio next door had been testing a fire rope. But the rope was old and had given off pungent thick black smoke, and as no one had disabled the smoke alarms, all hell was let loose.

'Let's go for a take Philip, I'm feeling lucky today.' Oliver shouted down.

'Only if you're sure.'

Ron looked concerned. 'It's probably best to have one more run at it.'

Brett nodded in agreement; he didn't want any risks with Kitty's new star.

'Nah it's ok Ron. Let's go for it,' Oliver shouted. 'Mine's a pint.'

Philip laughed, 'Ok Oliver, here we go. Standby... and... rolling.'

'Rolling.' Came the reply.

'Action!'

Oliver checked his landing mark, pulled back on the rail, and jumped, but this time something was off. As he landed the platform shook wildly, sending him off balance. With a feeling of dread, he caught the edge and tumbled like a rag doll down onto the mats below.

'Cut!' bellowed Philip. Medics rushed onto the set as Oliver passed out. Brett didn't like what he saw, Kitty was not going to be happy.

Chapter Eleven

THEN

Caught Red-Handed

St. Moritz oozed luxury. It was peak season, and the snow-draped streets were crowded with tourists and locals alike. Dirk dropped the girls at La Via Serlas, where all the well-traveled models loved to shop.

'I meet you girls later, *ja*? When work finish.' Dirk asked expectantly.

'No, we couldn't trouble you any more than we already have done.' Charlie said, sliding out of the van.

'I not mind.' Dirk quickly interjected.

'No, really Dirk, we're fine,' Henry snapped, 'but thanks, you're an angel.' She winked at him and for the second time that day, Dirk turned beetroot.

'Ok, maybe another day *ja*?'

'*Ja!*' they both chirped.

Dirk turned the wheel and pulled out into the traffic as the girls surveyed the street. The road had been cleared of snow, but the pavements were slushy and dangerous, they had to tread carefully.

'It's so busy today, there must be something going on.'

'There's always something going on in St. Moritz. I can't believe we're holed up in that place, week in week out. I'm going to the perfumery to stock up, you joining me for some fun?'

'Fun?' Charlie was puzzled.

'It's not every day we get to be out here amongst the rich and famous.'

'Well, you may be rich, but famous?'

Henry pulled her sunglasses down to the end of her nose.

'Look here Charlotte Black, if you *act* rich and famous, you *are* rich and famous, get my drift?'

Charlie laughed 'You're incorrigible, I'm going to find a bookstore, I need more reading. Why don't we meet up at The Palace Hotel for afternoon tea at three?'

Henry frowned, 'Afternoon tea? Who are you all of a sudden, the Queen of England?'

Charlie laughed.

'Ok,' Henry continued, 'let's make it a martini cocktail with an afternoon tea chaser.'

'You're on!' Charlie smiled.

'It'll be your special birthday treat on me!'

'Ok, great, see you then. Oh, and Henry...?'

Henry turned back to Charlie, 'What?'

'Be good.'

'Aren't I always?' Henry chirped, as they parted ways.

Charlie turned up the street in search of a good bookstore whilst Henry headed for adventure elsewhere.

* * * * * * * * *

Henry entered the plush store and decided it was time for some fun. The perfumery department comprised lots of little islands, with eager assistants selling their products, wearing over-applied makeup.

That girl's wearing so much makeup you could measure it with a dipstick! Henry thought as she weaved in and out of the perfume archipelago dodging handsome boys spraying their wares.

'Like to test?' said one, as he gaily sprayed into the air. A pair of young twins gawped at him. His black hair was gelled in a sleek, side-parting, and on his lapel, his badge sported the name 'SIMBA'.

'That smells yuck,' the twins said in unison, staring at Simba with frowns.

'You two are simply divine.' Simba spouted in a German-American accent, smiling as he looked desperately for their mother, who was handing over her Amex card to a slavering sales girl.

Henry was transfixed by Simba's skin. *It's like silky chocolate, no 'midnight'*, Henry thought. *I wonder what moisturizer he uses.* Then she had an idea. At the far end of the store, she spotted counters displaying accessories. Hermès bags, Chanel scarves, LV gloves, everything a young girl could want. A few customers were perusing the counters, but no staff in attendance. She noticed a girl standing at a long mirror, leaning in to apply more mascara, and further afield a blonde guy with sunglasses was trying on some cufflinks. *Oooh, Mr. Cufflinks looks handsome.* Henry spotted a delightful Coco Chanel scarf around a hand thrusting itself out of a wooden plinth. The scarf's pattern was made up of small red, green, and blue handbags inside a thick red border. *Gorgeous; not this season, but who cares?* Henry swiftly removed the scarf from the severed limb, deftly tugging the price tag off in one motion. She pocketed the price tag and wrapped the scarf around her neck, looking left and right. The girl at the mirror was now applying red lipstick, contorting her lips in a vulgar fashion, and Mr. Cufflinks was nowhere to be seen. Henry took another scarf from the ample rack and slipped it onto the empty display before marching back into the depths of the store. She slowed down as she approached the main area inside the islands of perfume. Timing was everything. One... two... three... she walked directly into Simba's firing line.

'Like to test?' The assistant sprayed perfume over his prey, like a raccoon in spring.

'Argh!' Henry shrieked causing an unsuspecting Simba to freeze, mid-fake-smile.

'Arrghh!' Henry doubled over gasping for air, her hand over her mouth.

'I'm so sorry,' Simba stuttered, 'is everything ok with Madam?'

'No, everything is not ok *with Madam!'* came the choked reply.

'But it is only perfume?' Simba inspected his bottle, perplexed.

'I have an intense allergy, does that perfume contain Hydroxycitronellal?'

'Hydroxy… what?' Simba was getting nervous and the more nervous he was the camper he became and the higher his voice went. 'It's the latest perfume from Madam Coco!' He exclaimed.

'Yes, but is it lavender-based?' Henry choked back.

Simba scrutinized the label.

'Why yes madam, sensual lavender to capture the spirit of today's strong young woman.' Simba recited the branding as he presented his arms to the cut-out of a young girl astride a horse standing in a field of lavender.

There was quite a crowd forming, with the twins at the forefront staring, open-mouthed, and pointing at Henry as she collapsed, choking, on the ground. 'I'm allergic to laven…' Simba let out a high-pitched scream as Henry passed out, the crowd looking on in horror.

* * * * * * * * *

Charlie was enjoying her freedom. She was wending her way up a particularly steep street of curio shops and small artisan coffee houses when a sign caught her eye. 'BÜCHERWURM'. Perfect. She climbed the worn steps and gently pushed the door causing an old bell to ring, announcing her presence. As Charlie entered the deceptively large shop, her nose was accosted with the musty, glorious smell of books. Dusty books, thousands of them sat floor to ceiling along four narrow rows.

A man, old Deuteronomy himself, peered at her over pince-nez.

'*Guten morgen, fühlen sie sich frei.*' He gestured to the inside of the book emporium. Charlie smiled and made her way to the far end.

Everything was meticulously labeled in German and English. Politics, Autobiographical, Religious, World Affairs, Fiction, Non-Fiction, Crime Novels – her particular favorite – and even Romance. She rounded the end of a long wall of books and found the section she wanted, Photography. It was next to a large wooden chair piled with cushions sporting a very large, sleeping ginger cat.

Selecting a book from the shelf she began leafing through its colorful contents. *Famous Fashion Photographers.* She absent-mindedly sat on the arm of the cat's throne and studied the photographs. She loved the works of Annie Leibovitz and fashion photographer Mario Testino. She was admiring a photograph of Kate Moss lounging in a purple sequined dress when she overheard voices in the adjacent aisle. It was a man and woman in raised whispers, she would have thought nothing of it, but one voice was familiar. She squinted over the top of the row of books to see the back of a girl in conversation. As she moved slightly, she saw the man she was talking to. It was Frank Hoffman, her head of year from St. Mary's. He was clutching an envelope and kept repeating something, she strained to hear what he was saying.

'Das Schloss, A34B.' The woman turned as he roughly grabbed her arm. Charlie lifted her lens and took a photo through the window of books. *Click whirrr.*

Frank shot a glance at the gap in the shelf as Charlie quickly sat down on the ginger Tom. The cat screamed and shot up, vaulting over the bookshelf narrowly missing Frank as it did the feline version of parkour down the length of the shop.

'*Scheisse!*' Frank exclaimed after the cat.

When the girl pulled away, Charlie could see she was in her early 30's, with pale skin, black hair, and very attractive.

'Ingrid! *Das Schloss*, verstehen?' He whispered through gritted teeth. The woman nodded nervously as Frank continued.

'I will see you at White Turf tomorrow, don't be late.' He spat as she stared back at Frank.

'The details are all in here.' He offered an envelope. 'Ingrid, do you understand?'

Ingrid nodded slowly and looked towards the doorway, longing to go outside and away from this horrible man.

'You will be paid handsomely, like last time. And don't forget, you will do *whatever it takes.*'

He whispered into her ear. Charlie saw her physically flinch as he thrust a white shopping bag, tied with black string, into her chest.

'Now go, you need to get to work.'

She clutched the bag and envelope and hurried towards the entrance of the bookshop. Frank looked directly at Charlie through the gap in the books as she ducked down again. Had he seen her? She closed her eyes and heard the bell ring on the door as the woman left the shop followed by the sound of Frank's footsteps walking away from her. What was that all about? What was in the envelope and what was '*Das Schloss*' and 'White Turf'? Charlie was determined to find out.

* * * * * * * * *

Henry opened one eye and surveyed her surroundings. After feigning dizziness, she'd been carried to the manager's office. She was laying on a gold chaise longue opposite a large desk with, what she presumed to be, the manager staring at a computer screen. Simba was taking her pulse with a trembling hand, deep brown eyes, and a concerned expression.

'Ooh, madame! Are you feeling ok?'

'Er, yes... yes, could I have some water?'

'Yes, but small sips.' He passed her a cup and held her head while she took a drink. Behind him, she spotted the Coco Chanel scarf draped over a chair.

'What is your name?' Simba asked.

'Henrietta Diakos... er Henry,' she replied opening her eyes wide. 'What's yours?' She squinted at his badge.

'Simba, like *The Lion King*.' Simba smiled revealing his whiter-than-white teeth.

Henry sat up and smiled, the manager suddenly spoke to Simba without taking his eyes off the screen.

'Ok thank you, Simba, you can leave us now.'

Simba turned swiftly, wanting to be out of there as soon as possible, 'I hope she'll be ok.'

The manager briefly glanced up. 'Yes, I do not doubt that.'

'I have never had someone faint on me before, it is most distressing.' Simba mopped his forehead with a lemon handkerchief. Henry felt a pang of guilt for her 'allergy' and took his hand.

'You have beautiful skin... Simba.'

His eyes lit up as he smiled, 'Yes, I inherited it from my mother in Zimbabwe.'

The manager cleared his throat, 'Simba, I said you can leave us now!'

Simba pouted and Henry squeezed his hand before he smiled, stood up, pocketed his handkerchief, and walked to the door. He threw the manager a haughty look before exiting dramatically. The manager sighed and swung his attention back to Henry.

'How are you feeling now?'

Henry reached for her Hermès bag and removed her face compact.

'Ok, under the circumstances.'

The manager smiled, 'And what circumstances are those, Miss Diakos?'

'Well, your employees shouldn't be spraying everyone that walks past them.' Henry blurted, checking her neck in the mirror of her compact.

'As you can see, I have an acute allergy to lavender. You're lucky I haven't come out in hives.'

'I am sorry to hear this, and what can we do to compensate you?'

Henry studied him over her compact mirror.

'Well, firstly, you can pay for the launder of my suit...'

'Ok...'

'My makeup is ruined... my hair...' Henry had a long list.

The manager was making notes

'Laundry... makeup... hair... anything else?'

Henry sighed 'No, that's about all.'

'What about your scarf Miss Diakos?'

Henry's eyes flicked to the scarf.

'Yes... yes... my scarf also. And then there's the emotional compensation.'

Henry closed her compact, retrieved a handkerchief from her Hermès, and dabbed the corners of her eyes.

'This is *your* scarf?' The Manager looked straight at her.

'Yes... *my* scarf.'

'Well, CCTV says otherwise.' He sat back in his chair with a satisfied look.

Henry stiffened 'CCTV?'

'Yes, we introduced it last month after a spate of thefts in our store. You'd be surprised what people get up to.'

Henry swallowed; this wasn't how it was supposed to go.

'Do you have anything to say Miss Diakos?'

Henry cleared her throat, 'No.'

'Very well, if you wouldn't mind waiting whilst I make a quick call to the local police station.'

'Listen, I'm sure there has been a slight misunderstanding...' Suddenly the door swung open with a bang and Henry, thankful for the distraction, turned to see who the intruder was. Standing in the doorway was 'Mr. Cufflinks', the young blonde guy in sunglasses she'd seen earlier trying on the cufflinks. The manager stood immediately.

'It's ok Gabriel,' said Mr. Cufflinks whilst looking at Henry. 'I'll take over now.'

'But sir, I have everything in hand.'

Mr. Cufflinks smiled, 'You may return to your work, I can handle this.'

Gabriel sighed, stood up, picked up the scarf from the chair, and made for the door. Mr. Cufflinks stood to one side, taking the scarf from his hands.

'I will take this.' Gabriel shot a look at Henry and stormed out of the office. Mr. Cufflinks closed the door and leaned against the front of the desk.

'I do apologize for my head of security; he can be a little overzealous at times.'

Henry regained her composure. 'That's quite alright, we had a little misunderstanding.'

'I am Thomas Hassler, and this is my department store. Well, my mother's, but I run it for her.' He offered his hand.

'Hello, Mr. Hassler.' Henry stood and shook his hand. He was blonde and tall, athletic with a public-schoolboy face. He can only have been in his early forties.

'Now, I believe this is yours.' He wrapped the scarf around Henry's neck and pulled her forward as he fastened it in a loose knot. He was very close to her. Henry studied his face, trying to see what lay behind those sunglasses. He smelt divine.

'Erm... yes, it is. Thank you.' Henry's breathing increased slightly. His dark blue suit was impeccable, with a crisp pale blue shirt finished off with a red and blue striped tie.

'Can I give you a lift anywhere Miss...?'

'Diakos... Henrietta Diakos.' She used her full title. 'Er, no, I'll be fine, thank you.'

'Very well, please take my card, and if I can be of any service, do give me a call.'

He reached into his breast pocket and Henry noticed a pin badge on his lapel. A gold crest sporting a purple turret.

'Here you go.' He passed her a cream card, embossed in gold. It had two words on the front.

Thomas Hassler

In the top right corner, there was the same motif from his pin badge, the purple turret, and on the reverse a solitary telephone number.

'Well, I must go, I'm meeting a friend.' Henry said as she popped the card into the side zipper of her handbag.

'Well, we cannot keep him waiting.' Thomas smiled and opened the door.

Charlie crossed to exit. 'Her,' she corrected him.

He blocked her with his arm across the doorway.

'I have one question.'

Henry looked at him expectantly, 'Yes?'

'Why does a pretty girl like you steal a Coco Chanel Scarf?'

'I don't know what you mean.' She wanted to be out of there, fast.

'Oh... I think you do.'

He looked at her for a few seconds and then removed his arm to let her pass. Henry half-smiled as she hurried out of the room and down the corridor. Thomas watched her, smiling as he closed the door behind her.

She was relieved to be away from Thomas Hassler and soon found a large door with a push-bar and pushed. It seemed to be stuck. She exerted all her might, and it suddenly gave way. She found herself staggering out into the road as a red sports car careered around the corner, just missing her. It was an open-top car, and the driver was laughing wildly.

'Idiot!' Henry screamed after the careless driver. She checked herself and took a breath. *Now to find The Palace Hotel.*

* * * * * * * * *

Charlie left the bookshop and looked left and right. No sign of Frank, or the girl, *hmm... puzzling*. She knew enough German to understand that Frank had instructed the girl about 'Das

Schloss' – The Castle. But what Castle? Secondly, tomorrow he was meeting her at White Turf? *White Turf? What was Frank involved in?* She checked the time, maybe she could meet Henry earlier than planned? She was itching to tell her about Frank. She called Henry's mobile, but it rang with no answer. As she strolled past a souvenir shop something caught her eye in the doorway. In the middle of a stand displaying 'Things to do in St. Moritz' was a pile of leaflets advertising an exhibition called 'Das Schloss'. Charlie snatched one and hurriedly turned the corner into a side street towards the hotel. She didn't see the red sports car as it raced towards her on the slushy road, the horn going full blast. The street was very narrow with high pavements, making it impossible for the car to avoid her, nor could it stop in time. Suddenly two arms wrapped around her, and she was pushed to the pavement out of harm's way from the speeding coupé. Her eyes glazed over as she lay in the arms of her hero. She focused on his face and frowned.

'Marcus?'

Chapter Twelve

THEN

Rose Pharmacy

On the other side of town, Ingrid emerged from a small passage running down the side of an ornate pharmacy. A sign swung in the gentle breeze, '*APOTHEKE ROSEN*'. She clutched the white bag, took a breath, and pushed open the door.

'Ingrid! There you are... twenty-one... twenty-two... twenty-three...' her father peered at her over the counter, 'I've been looking for you. We had a string of customers all morning. I haven't stopped... twenty-four... twenty-five...'

'Sorry Papa, I had to run an errand.' Ingrid replied, anxiously trying to hide her face and puffy eyes betraying the crying she'd done on the way home.

Now in his early 70s, Ingrid's father was American. Having settled in St. Moritz after the war, he'd opened the pharmacy to keep occupied and to use his great knowledge of medicines to the best of his ability. He'd been a doctor and met Teresa, a pretty Swiss nurse, whilst working at the hospital in Zurich. She was the love of his life and as soon as the war was over, they were married at St. Karl Borromaüs Catholic Church in St. Moritz, her hometown. Shortly after Ingrid was born, her mother contracted tuberculosis. She was one of the lucky ones, but never fully recovered. The disease had taken its toll on her lungs, destroying a lot of tissue and her need for assisted breathing left her on oxygen for the rest of her life. '*A small price to pay,*' she would say as she gazed at Ingrid lovingly. She could still get about using her wheelchair, but the oxygen tank was never far behind.

'I'm going upstairs to the washroom papa. You can take a break when I return, I won't be long,' Ingrid shouted over her shoulder as she walked down the shop.

'Ok, ok, take your time.' Ingrid was always dashing about. He looked at the family portrait on the wall opposite and smiled. He was sitting in an armchair with his wife Teresa on one arm and Ingrid on the other. He returned to his task of counting the tablets for his prescription orders 'twenty-six... twenty-seven... twenty-eight...'

Ingrid was full-time at the pharmacy. She'd originally trained in makeup and hairdressing and spent three years working in France for a film company that specialized in the Horror genre. She loved it immensely, but had to return to Switzerland when her mother's health took a turn for the worse. On her return from France, she managed her own hairdressing studio, but it wasn't to be for long. Her mother's illness was worsening, and her father was getting older. She sold the business two years ago and moved back in with her parents so she could keep her eye on both of them.

She pushed through a beaded curtain at the end of the shop where a short hallway led to a metal door with a tiny rectangular window on one side. Her father had installed a small elevator some years ago, at great expense. This meant her mother could gain access to the shop from the living quarters upstairs, where she hated being cooped up day in and day out. There was a rear fire escape onto the back road, but they never used it.

Ingrid opened the metal door and drew back the concertina inner door. She stepped inside and pulled back the grille as the outer door swung shut. The elevator was tiny, with enough room for a wheelchair. She pressed the button marked 1. Nothing happened so she pressed again, nothing. It was an antique. She opened and closed the grille doors again and rattled them, cursing. Through the small outer window, she saw her father look up and hoped he hadn't heard her curse. He shook his head as he lost count of the tablets. One last rattle of the doors and the elevator sprang into action with a whir. She arrived at the first floor, opened the grille doors and outer door, and stepped into the hallway of their very grand apartment.

It was deceptively large with high ceilings boasting cornices and sconces. To her left, a large stained-glass window depicting the Virgin Mary let in a stream of sunlight shooting colored beams onto the parquet floor. The right-hand wall boasted an oak cabinet housing a lifetime of crockery and ornaments. It had a homely feel.

'Ingrid, is that you?' Her mother called from a distant room.

'Yes mother, I won't be a moment.'

'Alright my dear, take your time. I'm only resting.'

She took off her coat and hung it on the stand further down the hall. The coat stand was a deer's head attached to the wall with antlers for hooks. Her father loved it. She looked at the deer's face as she extracted the brown envelope from her coat pocket. The deer's expression seemed to change to a frown, judging her with its eyes.

Ingrid entered the washroom and closed the door, pushing the latch across. She looked into the mirror at her ashen face and swollen eyes. Her mother couldn't see her like this. She scraped back her jet-black hair, tying it in a pony with a band from her wrist, and turned on the tap, splashing water onto her face. She knew what she had to do, she'd done it before and could do it again. Maybe this would be the last time? She emptied the envelope onto the chair and studied its contents. The instructions for 'White Turf' were very precise. She unfolded a second paper labeled A34B, her heart sank.

Yes, she had skills, but surely she could put them to better use? She had to pack everything she needed and then sneak out after dinner, making up an excuse to her parents. Lastly, there were two photographs. She studied the first one, easy, then she took the second photograph and stared at the face intently. Turning it over she read the name written on the reverse, *'Thomas Hassler'*.

Chapter Thirteen

THEN

Hooray for Hollywood

After Oliver's 'fall', the filming schedule was thrown into turmoil. Brett traveled with him to nearby Ashford Hospital, relaying to Kitty what had happened, in a frantic phone call. Luckily the x-ray showed nothing broken but it didn't stop forced bed rest for three days, for observation. It seems that someone had purposefully dismantled the cross-braces, front and back, during the fire-alarm episode. All this occurred on the same day Rick Krane's PA, a shifty guy called Damien, had returned to collect Rick's belongings. Brett sourced the CCTV footage, revealing Damien hiding the braces behind a skip outside. The studio, fearful of more negative publicity, kept the incident under wraps, announcing a freak accident. Oliver knew it was no accident, but at least the feeble attempt at sabotage hadn't been successful and by the end of the week he was fit and well.

The ensuing days turned into weeks and the weeks into months. Not before long, everything was back on track with the end of the shoot looming. One evening, Oliver planned to go for a drink with Brett at the nearby Three Horseshoes. He enjoyed Brett's company and, of course, the occasional beer.

Before he left, Cheryl called into Oliver's dressing room.

'Hey Oliver, Kitty would like you to join her for dinner tonight at Joe Allen's in Covent Garden, nine o'clock sharp.'

'Sorry I've got drinks arranged with Brett,' Oliver put on a sad face.

'Brett said another time. He also said not to worry he won't forget it's your turn to pay.' She smiled.

'No, I'm sure he won't,' Oliver teased.

'I've arranged for your car to drop by your place enroute so you can change.'

Oliver smiled. 'Aren't you the organized one? What if I'd refused?'

'Oh, I know you would never refuse dinner with Kitty. Although I am intrigued at to what she's up to.' Cheryl frowned as she left his room.

'Well, I might let you know tomorrow,' Oliver shouted down the corridor, 'or not!'

* * * * * * * * *

Oliver arrived at Joe Allen's before nine. He walked past the famous gold plaque and down the stairs where the head waiter raised an eyebrow when he mentioned Kitty's name. Oliver bent down and kissed Kitty on the cheek. She was looking radiant in a cobalt blue dress with a sparkling necklace and matching earrings. The table was in a secluded part of the restaurant, so not many people were rubbernecking to see who she was with. Joe Allen's was a regular haunt of the rich and famous, but most guests frequented it for its sumptuous food.

Oliver enjoyed Kitty's company immensely, especially her wicked sense of fun, but tonight she meant business.

'Oliver, it's time we had a serious chat.' She looked at him intently.

'Ok...' He hadn't seen much of Kitty during the filming days. Some nights they would all retreat to The Three Horseshoes, but Kitty would return to her hotel. Oliver welcomed the invitation to be with her, one on one.

'As you know,' Kitty began pouring champagne into to flutes, 'we are rapidly approaching our final day on *Stealth,* and you've been terrific Oliver, truly.'

He wasn't the best at taking praise, especially from someone like Kitty Wallis.

She continued, 'I've been talking to my agent and the studio back in LA, and we're pretty certain that this movie will catapult you into a world far from here. The time has come for you, Oliver Diamond, to brave it in Hollywood.'

Oliver's heart was racing.

'Kitty... I don't know what to say.'

'Well, that may be so, but you did the work, Oliver. I've seen the rushes and you're a bit special.' She passed him his glass and Oliver took a sip and looked her in the eyes.

'Thank you, Kitty, for everything.' Oliver sat back. *Hollywood?*

'Now don't believe for one minute it's gonna be easy, because, easy it is not. You're gonna have to work your balls off and you'll also get some knockbacks on the way. Believe me, I know.'

'I'm ready Kitty.'

'You'd better be. Now, what I'm about to tell you is top secret, you hear?'

'Yes, of course, I won't say a word.' He was intrigued.

'Damn right you won't. I've got a project starting in three months that I want you involved in and it's gonna be big, and I mean B. I. G. BIG. I'm taking on a new role.'

'A new role?' Oliver said taking another sip of champagne.

'You're looking at Kitty Wallis, Executive Producer and Director of Precious Studios, a new company with a new vision.'

'You're going to produce films?'

'Movies! Oh, I won't be hanging up my acting hat, but I've secured a movie franchise that will have *everyone* knocking at my door.'

'I'm thrilled for you Kitty.'

'Well, it took a long time to get here but it's finally happening, and I'm taking you with me for the ride.'

'What do I have to do?' Oliver asked.

'That's all for now, and don't forget, *say nothing*.'

'You can depend on me. I promise your secret's safe.'

Kitty looked at him and smiled.

'Yes, I believe it is. I've always been a good judge of character, and my instincts have never let me down.'

'One day I'll repay you for everything Kitty.'

'That's as maybe. Over the next few months, we'll both be involved in the media circus for *Stealth*, so we'll be seeing a lot more of each other.'

'I've always wanted to travel; I've never even been to Los Angeles.'

'Well, you're gonna love Hollywood, and Hollywood's gonna love you.'

Kitty raised her glass to Oliver.

'To Hollywood!'

They clinked glasses.

'Hollywood,' Oliver replied. Never in his wildest dreams could he have dreamt up this moment.

Chapter Fourteen

THEN

Afternoon Tea Chaser

The Palace Hotel, St. Moritz, stands in a class of its own, with high ceilings, marbled floors, and opulent furnishings. The Grand Hall serves its infamous Afternoon Tea and anyone who is anyone takes part in the ritual. With floor-to-ceiling windows down one side, the elegant room is filled with light and wreaks of sophistication.

In the entrance, a string quartet played Handel to a discerning crowd as Henry managed to secure a table in the corner behind a potted fern. You had to book in advance at The Palace, but she knew how to persuade the Maître D with a flutter of eyelashes and a ten-franc note. Henry perused the vast menu whilst waiting for her friend. There was something about this very English tradition that she loved. The cover of the menu explained – *afternoon tea was created by Anna Russell, Duchess of Bedford, and lifelong friend of Queen Victoria. She believed a mere three meals a day weren't enough, and this new tradition was born to fill the gap until dinner. Mmmm,* Henry thought, *good old Anna Russell,* finger sandwiches and scones were a far cry from the frankfurters and sauerkraut on the menu at St. Mary's.

* * * * * * * * *

Charlie and Marcus arrived outside the hotel as the red sports car screeched to a halt in the drop-off lane. The concierge hurried to open the door as a young guy jumped out and sprinted up the steps to the entrance. He was short and muscly, and he arrogantly tossed his keys over his shoulder for the concierge to catch. Brushing past Charlie for the second time that day, he dashed in front of her through the revolving doors.

'Idiot!' screamed Charlie as she followed him through the ever-turning doors propelling them into the foyer. The reckless driver was nowhere to be seen.

Marcus had probably saved Charlie's life and she would be forever grateful. He'd insisted on escorting her to the hotel where she was meeting Henry, explaining that he'd ventured into St. Moritz to place some bets for the groundskeeper.

Dressed in jeans and a cream roll neck he looked even more handsome away from school. As they approached the Grand Hall the head waiter stepped into their path and pointed at Marcus's legs.

'No jeans.'

Charlie looked at the waiter, 'He's with me.' She pulled Marcus towards her as the waiter stepped into their pathway once again.

'I'm afraid we have a strict dress code madam, no jeans.'

'It's ok Charlie,' Marcus stopped and looked into her eyes.

'No Marcus, it's not ok.' Charlie turned her attention toward the head waiter. 'Today is my birthday and I'm meeting a friend here for afternoon tea. I was nearly run over twenty minutes ago by one of your guests in a red sports car, so I suggest you let me and my friend into your restaurant before I cause a scene you'll regret.'

The waiter sighed and stepped to one side, defeated.

'Happy birthday, Madam.'

Charlie smiled sweetly, 'Thank you.'

Marcus kissed her hand as they entered the Grand Hall.

'Look who I found?' Charlie stood at Henry's table with a grinning Marcus.

'Oh, *happy birthday to you.*' Henry grinned back.

Marcus looked around feeling a little out of place but enjoying the view.

'I've ordered already, don't worry, there'll be plenty for three.' Henry winked at Marcus.

Charlie told Henry about her near accident and how Marcus had been her knight in shining armor.

'Wow, that could've been serious Charlie.'

'I know, I'm a lucky girl!'

A waiter arrived with two Martinis and a raised eyebrow.

'One more of these please,' Henry said to the waiter as she held the Martini expertly. He nodded and backed away, melting into the potted fern.

'So, Henry, what have you been up to?'

Henry relayed her version of events at the department store, ending with her meeting Thomas Hassler.

Charlie frowned 'He sounds a bit creepy if you ask me.'

Henry thought for a second, 'Creepy, but handsome creepy.'

Marcus rolled his eyes as Charlie leaned forward, looking left and right.

'Ok, now I have something very interesting to tell you both.'

As the quartet struck up with 'The Arrival of the Queen of Sheba', waiters appeared from nowhere laden with tiers of sandwiches, scones with cream and jam, and Earl Grey tea. They filled the table with their wares, smiled, and left.

'Come on Charlie, I can't take the suspense.' Henry was intrigued.

Charlie relayed the events in the bookstore as they loaded their plates with the sandwiches. Marcus was particularly enjoying afternoon tea, stuffing a fourth triangle into his mouth.

'Frank Hoffman from school? I always knew he was no good. What's he up to?' Henry puzzled.

'It doesn't make much sense, none of it does,' Charlie countered as she loaded the image on her camera.

Henry looked closely. 'The girl seems genuinely frightened of him in the photo.'

'Yes, you should have seen the way he grabbed her. The key to this is to work out what he meant by Das Schloss and White Turf.'

Henry's attention was spiked. 'Yes, what's White Turf?'

'That's easy,' Marcus said as he took his Martini from a bowing waiter with one hand and grabbed another sandwich with the other.

They both looked at him expectantly. 'Well?'

'Horses,' Marcus said with a nod and a swig of his cocktail.

They were none the wiser.

'Explain.' Charlie was getting impatient.

'Horses. White Turf, it's the name of a horse race held annually here in St. Moritz, and the biggest race takes place on the frozen lake tomorrow.'

'A horse race on a frozen lake?' Henry said in disbelief.

'Yes, it is very famous. The horses, race on the snow and ice, hence "White Turf". That's why St. Moritz is busy this weekend and why I came here today, to place a bet for the groundskeeper.'

'But what about Das Schloss?' Henry puzzled.

'Das Schloss?' Marcus muttered, reaching into his jeans pocket.

'Oh wait!' Charlie exclaimed, searching her coat on the seat between her and Marcus.

'Ta-da!' She placed the leaflet on the table triumphantly. Henry studied it.

'Das Schloss,' she read, 'An exhibition at the Segantini Museum throughout February.'

'An art exhibition?' Charlie thought out loud.

Henry wiped her mouth with her serviette. 'There's only one way to find out, we have to go there, we have to find the Segantini Museum.'

'Ah-ha!' Marcus exclaimed, causing the waitress to jump as she cleared their plates.

'It's not the exhibition.'

'What are you talking about Marcus?' Charlie slowly asked.

Marcus slapped his betting form on the table and pointed. They all leaned in.

'Das Schloss, it's the name of a horse running tomorrow at three o'clock at White Turf!'

Chapter Fifteen

NOW

Oliver Prepares

Oliver reluctantly left the view of the balcony and returned to the bedroom. Charlie was still sleeping as he crossed to the bathroom to take a shower. After his shower, he dressed in a pale blue shirt, chinos, and a brown leather jacket. Pulling on his new season's Balenciagas, he pondered on what his life would hold the next time he saw Charlie. He crept over to her side of the bed and studied her beautiful face. She stirred slightly as he pulled away, holding his breath.

She nestled into the covers and returned to her dream state as he leaned over and kissed her cheek, smelling her scent as he did. Slowly he made his way out of the bedroom and down the spiral staircase.

He crossed to the study and checked his briefcase. The sunglasses were there along with the equipment he needed. Pulling back the far corner of the lining, Oliver revealed a hidden compartment where fixed on a clip was the thumb drive staring at him with a look of innocence. Such a small device with such enormous power. He closed the case and pocketed his smartphone plus an untraceable burner phone before collecting his wallet and keys. He left the penthouse apartment via the private hallway, closing the door as quietly as possible. Oliver was due to meet Charlie with Kitty and her husband, Julian, for dinner in Cannes later that evening. Kitty had become such a strength after Oliver arrived in Hollywood over twenty years ago and had stayed a permanent fixture in his life ever since. He jabbed at the elevator button and cast his mind back to those early days in Tinseltown.

Chapter Sixteen

THEN

Size Isn't Everything

The wrap party for *Stealth* saw the studio transformed into a casino, complete with roulette tables, blackjack, and showgirls. Oliver spent the first two hours dancing the night away with Cheryl, Zoe, and anyone else he could grab. Even Jeff the runner was still jigging about on the dancefloor like a demented zombie long after Oliver left to get another drink. Kitty stayed for a few hours before leaving for the airport.

'Must fly y'all, it's been *your* pleasure,' Kitty announced over the mic, causing everyone to laugh and cheer as she left the building. Brett was staying another couple of days to tie up loose ends before joining her back in LA.

Cheryl stopped Oliver as he made his way to the bar.

'Oliver, I'm so happy that things are taking off for you.'

'Well Cheryl, I couldn't have done it without you.' He reached forward and tucked a stray strand of red hair behind her ear.

'No, of course you couldn't,' she teased back. 'I've got something for you, so you don't forget about me.'

'What?' Oliver looked at her quizzically.

'This!' She produced a small bag tied up with a chord.

'What is it?' He took the bag from her and opened it. It was a keyring of a miniature clapperboard and printed on it was 'Production: Cheryl (Runner slash PA) Stevens'.

Oliver laughed, 'I love it,' he exclaimed, hugging her, 'and I won't forget about you!' She smiled, turned, and gave him a little wave as she crossed to have another whirl around the dance floor. Oliver approached Brett.

'Come on Brett, let's have a last drink together in England.'

'Oliver when you get to LA, I'll show you around. It can be pretty scary the first time, even for a Yank like me!'

'This is still such a blur Brett. One minute I'm scraping along, seemingly going nowhere, and now... this.'

'Well, that's Hollywood for you. More to the point, that's Kitty for you.'

'I'm so grateful to her, it seems there's not enough I can say.'

'Look, Oliver, you do have the talent, there's no doubt about it. She wouldn't do all of this if you didn't, believe me. She's a good girl with a good heart, but she's also a good businesswoman and this makes business sense to her.'

'Well, whatever it is, I still feel like it's all a dream and I'll wake up soon.'

'Don't worry, Hollywood will wake you up quickly enough. Your flight and accommodation are booked, and I'll be at the airport Thursday to collect you.'

'Brett thanks for everything, you're a true friend.'

'Hey, that's what I'm here for,' Brett replied.

'No really, I mean it. If ever I can do anything to repay you I will. And I do mean anything, I'm a man of my word.'

Brett smiled and gave Oliver a sideways look. 'I'll bear that in mind, now let's go and have a drink with a couple of these English "Showgirls"!'

* * * * * * * * *

The following week Oliver dashed up to Sheffield to say his goodbyes to his tearful mum. She said they were happy tears, but Oliver knew differently. She was so proud of him and when he announced he would be returning to England early the following year for the publicity tour of *Stealth* and promised to take her to the première in London, she was beside herself. She, Betty Wilkins, was to attend a film première with her son and Kitty Wallis! She told everyone she came across: the postman, the milkman, and even the Jehovah's Witnesses.

Dan Goldberg, Oliver's ex-agent, had called him on numerous occasions over the past few months and today was no exception. But Oliver ignored the calls and endless e-mails. He'd heard what had happened to Oliver and now wanted a piece of the action but as Dan had said, their contract was 'null and void'. And that was that.

* * * * * * * * *

Business Class to LA was luxury and on arrival, a porter was standing at the gate with his name on a card. 'Oliver Diamond'. He'd always wanted that, to arrive at an airport with someone holding a card bearing your name. It was a far cry from Sheffield. He followed the porter through immigration and out into the LA sunshine where a black DeVille pulled up. Brett stepped out to greet him.

'Hey Oliver, so good to see you!'

'Brett!' They hugged, warmly. 'Wow! I like the car.'

They chatted all the way to his new place, Brett briefed him on plans for the following week and told him a car would collect him Monday morning for his first meeting with Kitty at her offices. The chauffeur placed his suitcases outside the front door as Brett gave him the keys.

'I'm going to leave you to it, Oliver. Enjoy!' With that, he smiled and turned back to the luxurious DeVille.

Oliver's new home was nestled in West Hollywood, near Beverly Hills. Ultra-modern on the inside but looking nothing from the driveway. An ordinary front door sticking out of an ordinary block of concrete, camouflaging any trace of opulence to the discerning passer-by. Once inside, Oliver thought, *Never judge a house by its front door*. Built on a slope over three floors, it boasted 2 bedrooms on the top floor, both ensuites, a living area-cum-dining kitchen on the second floor with terrace, and a small gym, sauna, and utility room on the lower floor. Oliver opened the doors to the terrace from the living room where two sunbeds and an outdoor dining set framed a small dip pool. The size of the house wasn't huge, but it was perfect for Oliver. In the distance, he could see the cluster of tall buildings and the expanse of the city around, The City of Angels. He,

Oliver Diamond, was about to embark on the biggest adventure of his life.

Chapter Seventeen

THEN

Forgiveness of Sins

'Ave Maria' blasted out from the beautiful clock tower of the Church St. Karl Borromäus, nestled by the frozen St. Moritzersee Lake, and drifted down the snow-covered valley. The tower reached for the sky, like the outstretched hand of morality, broadcasting the Schubert classic announcing the start of Mass each Sunday.

Ingrid glanced around the congregation nervously, stifling a yawn. The previous night had been tricky and taken much longer than anticipated. She'd made her excuses to her parents, saying she was meeting friends and wouldn't be home until very late. Although she was thirty-two, they still worried about her and treated her like a teenager.

She left the pharmacy under the cover of darkness and sneaked into the racecourse with ease. The security pass Frank had provided worked without so much as a second look. There weren't many security guys around after dark. She located the stable block, which was deserted apart from a few spluttering horses settling in for the night. The stall was marked, A34B. *Here goes*, she thought as she opened the door and knelt on the straw, laying everything out before her. She looked around and listened – silence, then she began the laborious task.

Today, the church was busier than usual, but they still had their weekly seats near the front. She glanced down at her itching hands and removed a glove. She rubbed her fingers vigorously, then quickly replaced it before her mother noticed the stains. Every Sunday her father insisted they attend Mass as a family. Ingrid knew it was good for her mother to venture outside the apartment, and the wheelchair was fitted with a bracket underneath the seat for the oxygen tank and her mother was quite comfortable. Her chair was nestled at the end of their row, next to Ingrid. Teresa smiled and squeezed Ingrid's gloved hand as she adjusted the rug around her mother's knees.

The organ started up and she rose to sing the first hymn, checking her watch – five minutes past nine. It would be a lengthy Mass, and she didn't have much time to prepare for the afternoon. She had everything planned out, but when did things ever go to plan? As long as she was back at the apartment by midday, she would have the two hours she needed to get ready, but she couldn't afford any last-minute delays. The congregation took their seats, and the priest began his sermon as Ingrid's mind raced over every detail...

'Blessed are you, Lord God of all Creation, for through your goodness we have this bread to offer...'

Had she remembered to pack everything she needed?

'It will become for us our bread of life...'

She had to ensure no one saw her leaving the pharmacy later that afternoon.

'Blessed are you, Lord God of all Creation, for through your goodness we have this wine to offer…'

She had timed the walk from the pharmacy to the racecourse meticulously and she knew every step, every turn.

'It will become for us our spiritual drink. Blessed be God forever…'

The previous night she had raided the special medicines cabinet whilst her father was cooking their meal, he didn't suspect anything.

'Take this all of you and eat of it, for this is my body…'

This would be the last time. She hoped never to see Frank Hoffman and his deformed hands ever again…

'Take this, all of you, and drink from it, for this is the chalice of my blood…'

After today, she would have enough money for her mother's operation, no questions asked.

'…for the forgiveness of sins.'

She squeezed her eyes tight and prayed *her* sins would be forgiven. A choirboy stood and sang as she and her father queued for communion.

'Lamb of God you take away the sins of our world… grant us peace.'

Once they had all partaken the priest approached her mother and offered her the bread and wine. Her mother closed her eyes in prayer as Ingrid shed a tear.

'Let us pray…'

Chapter Eighteen

NOW

D-Day

Charlie closed her eyes, feigning sleep as she heard Oliver
leave the balcony. She didn't want to talk with him this morning,
so she would have to wait until he had left the apartment before
springing into action. At one point Oliver bent down and kissed
her cheek. She so wanted to kiss him back and feel the warmth
of his arms around her, but today she had to be strong with no
distractions. She smelt his scent as he withdrew and listened
carefully as he made his way down the spiral staircase. She
heard him enter the study and after a minute or two, he crossed
to the front door. After it closed softly, she counted to ten before
getting out of bed. She stared out of the window and placed the
elements of the day in order in her head. Firstly, she had to go to
the airport to collect the most important key player in today's
proceedings. The plane was due to land at nine-thirty, so she
needed to get a move on. After Nice airport, she would collect
Henry and then drive into the city. She'd single-handedly staged
everything, name tags, signage, outfits, photographs, all the
accessories they needed. She hadn't missed a thing. A few
months after formulating her plan, he'd finally bitten and now
her life was on the line. Today there was a mountain to climb

and if all went well, she would soon be able to confess all to Oliver and live a life with no more grudges.

It was retribution. It was payback time. It was D-Day.

Chapter Nineteen

THEN

White Turf

Marcus soon discovered every hotel room in St. Moritz was booked. After one last telephone call, he managed to secure a spare room in the hotel's staff quarters where his cousin was working as a commis chef. To not arouse any suspicion, Marcus was returning to St. Mary's later that evening and would return to meet the girls the following morning. He dropped the girls at the staff entrance, where his cousin ushered them into their room. It was sparse with no windows but clean. Not quite the birthday treat Charlie had in mind, but she was with friends.

On the way, the girls had stopped to buy fresh underwear and a change of outfit. They weren't sure what they were doing the following day, but they needed to be prepared.

Frank was involved in something odd, and they were going to see what they could find out. After they'd showered and changed there was a knock at the door.

Marcus was standing there with a bottle of cider and a Chinese takeaway.

'Marcus, you're so sweet!' Charlie exclaimed, grabbing the dinner from him. He was the cutest gardener, but as they were both leaving St. Mary's the following year, she didn't know what their future held. Marcus was only working there whilst his young cousin was settling into the kitchens of St. Moritz and soon he would be returning to Spain. They sat on the floor devouring their beef chow mein and afterward Marcus produced a chocolate muffin complete with candle. After a raucous rendition of 'happy birthday' to a giggling Charlie, Marcus left the girls to get his last bus.

* * * * * * * * *

The following day the girls went in search of breakfast amongst the gathering crowds of St. Moritz. Although still teenagers, once they had applied makeup, they looked like sophisticated young ladies about town.

White Turf was a major event in the yearly calendar and combined exciting horse racing, diverse food, live music, and various exhibitors. It was all staged on the frozen lake with its unique snow-capped mountain backdrop.

The White Turf horse race held a prize fund of half a million Swiss francs. A healthy incentive that attracted trainers and jockeys from all over the world. This was a top-class race meeting complete with champagne on ice, and anyone who is anyone had to be there.

The girls found the excitement palpable in the streets of St. Moritz where the pavements held an endless stream of visitors. They devoured breakfast in a side street café off Via Serlas and made their way past The Palace Hotel towards the racecourse entrance where they'd arranged to meet Marcus. Passing the front entrance of the hotel, the revolving doors sprang into action. Charlie pulled Henry back behind a pillar as the valet drove up in the red sports car with its top down. The young racer appeared from the revolving doors, hand in hand with a beautiful girl dressed head to toe in the latest red Gucci outfit with matching accessories. Red Gucci handbag and shoes, finished off with red Gucci sunglasses and her platinum blonde hair bouncing as she walked. Charlie took a few random snaps with her camera from her vantage point.

Click *whirrrr*.

The doorman touched his hat and opened the car door. She climbed in elegantly, wrapping a scarf around her blonde tresses as he closed the door firmly.

Click *whirrrr*.

The valet held the driver's door open, and the boy racer slipped him a twenty franc note before taking his place behind the wheel.

Click *whirrrr*.

Whilst Charlie watched him driving into the busy traffic, Henry stopped the doorman on his way back up the steps.

'Excuse me, if I'm not mistaken, that was Jennifer Aniston, right?'

'No madam, that is not right,' the doorman replied.

'Well, I could have sworn it was, maybe you didn't see her properly,' Henry quipped knowingly. The doorman sighed.

'Well, it is no secret, he is the famous jockey Piero Ricci from Italy, and his companion is French model Juliette Moreau.'

Henry shot him a puzzled look as he ascended the stairs back to his lookout post. She winked at Charlie.

'He'll be racing today, no doubt.'

'Yes, which explains why he's always in such a hurry,' Charlie quipped as she re-arranged the camera strap around her neck.

'Come on, let's go find Marcus.'

* * * * * * * * *

Ingrid was exhausted. The Mass took much longer than usual so she left early, blaming one of her migraines. Later that day her father was treating her mother to afternoon tea at The Palace Hotel to celebrate their fiftieth wedding anniversary. With Ingrid's help, he'd secretly booked a room for the night, the same room they stayed in on their wedding night. Their love for each other warmed her heart, and her mother had wept when he divulged his romantic plans.

Ingrid was thankful to have the apartment to herself. She unlocked the cabinet in her bedroom and opened the double doors, revealing her masterpieces staring out from the top shelf. They were perfect in every way. She unpacked the bag Frank had given to her the day before and laid everything out on the bed. She then quickly tied her hair up and went to work. She had a lot to do, firstly, nails...

* * * * * * * * *

A few hours later Ingrid looked in the full-length mirror. Sometimes she excelled herself. She studied the photograph taped to the inside door of the cabinet and scrutinized every detail, perfect. After checking the contents of her bag, she took the elevator, cursing the inner doors as she rattled them into place. Leaving through the pharmacy doorway, she ventured out. Everyone was at the frozen lake by now, no doubt. She quickly made her way down the empty street, her red Gucci high heels strumming the cobbled streets with a click-clack.

* * * * * * * *

Marcus stood on a rail looking over the sea of people by the racecourse entrance. 'Charlie! Charlie... over here!' He was wearing grey trousers with a white shirt and grey waistcoat and a cap with an oversized coat with a fur hood. As they joined him, he produced three tickets with a 'Ta-Da!'

'Where did you get those?' Charlie asked with a surprised tone.

'The groundskeeper was hoping to come with his family,' Marcus explained, 'but hasn't been feeling well lately, some bug or other. That is why he asked me to place his bets yesterday. When I saw him this morning he was in a state and told me to take them.'

'Well done, Marcus,' Henry exclaimed. 'He's a keeper Charlie.'

Charlie gave Henry a look as Marcus blushed.

They were soon making their way into the course where the noise was deafening with cheers filling the crisp air. Inside, a huge track wended its way over and around the frozen lake with riderless horses pulling jockeys on skis. Clouds of snow rose from the ground around the stomping horses' hooves like vapor from a jet. The three of them had never seen anything like it.

To their right, a jazz band played on a small stage, and to their left was a row of people standing with eagles on gloved hands. The elegant birds of prey looked around casually, ignorant of their surroundings. Behind the row of eagles was a tent sporting drapes around the doorway. Charlie tugged Henry's coat and they made their way inside.

'Ok,' Charlie said, 'it's time to make a game plan.'

Marcus produced a racing sheet.

'Here are the races on today. The main one is at three o'clock this afternoon and these are the horses racing, including Das Schloss.' Marcus pointed at the listing for Das Schloss with the form, colors, jockey, current odds, and owner details.

Henry and Charlie studied it. Suddenly Henry gasped.

'The racing colors, a gold crest with a purple turret, I've seen that motif before.'

She reached inside her bag and pulled out the card Thomas Hassler had given her in the department store. There in the top corner was the same crest with a purple turret.

'This is one hell of a coincidence,' she exclaimed.

'You're telling me, now listen,' Charlie read from the form, 'Das Schloss's owner is local businessman Thomas Hassler. Henry, look who the jockey is.' She showed her the paper.

'Who?' asked Marcus, looking confused.

The girls read the name in unison, 'Piero Ricci.'

'Our little racing driver from yesterday,' Henry added.

Marcus frowned.

'The guy who nearly took me out with his red sports car, if it hadn't been for you, Marcus.'

'We saw him outside the hotel this morning with his stunning girlfriend,' Henry added.

They studied the photograph of Das Schloss as Marcus read aloud, 'Das Schloss, a five-year-old, dapple grey, gelding. That's strange, look at the form.' Marcus pointed at the figures.

'I don't get it, what does it mean?' Henry frowned.

'It is a very slow horse. Runs eight, wins zero, seconds zero, thirds two,' Marcus read from the sheet. 'Not one win, not even close, and it has long odds at five hundred to one.' Marcus was puzzled.

'Mmmm... the favorite, according to this form sheet, is a seven-year-old black horse called Bullet Train, with even odds.' Charlie frowned.

'Yes, they were even yesterday when I placed a bet for my boss,' Marcus said, looking at the slip in his hand. 'Twenty francs on Bullet Train to win.'

Henry looked around, 'Still no sign of Frank or your mystery girl from the bookstore. We need to split up and meet back here before the three o'clock race.'

'Ok,' said Charlie, 'I'll go and see if I can find anything out at the track. Marcus, you go see if you can spot Frank around the stables, but make sure he doesn't see you.'

'Charlie look!' Henry nudged Charlie, 'There's the jockey's girlfriend, the model, Juliette Moreau.'

They looked sideways as the elegant blonde made her way up a flight of stairs leading out of the far side of the tent. As they watched her red Gucci shoes disappearing, they read the sign over the staircase.

'VIP AREA'

'And that's where I'm going,' Henry announced. 'I'll go and see what she's about and maybe I can find Thomas Hassler lurking up there. He has to be here somewhere.'

'Ok, let's meet back here around two.' Charlie looked at her friends. 'Be careful, both of you, something tells me there is much more to this than meets the eye.'

Chapter Twenty

THEN

In Stitches

Oliver spent the weekend exploring his local area. Coffee shops were in abundance, and he even visited his local cinema showing *Escape from L.A.* He wasn't sure if it was a sign. Post-earthquake and flood, it depicted Los Angeles as an island prison. Being in Los Angeles not knowing a soul, he suddenly felt very alone.

When Monday morning arrived and the car turned up at his house at ten on the dot, Oliver felt more himself and raring to go. Kitty's offices were in a low-rise and, from the outside, very understated. However, Oliver did notice Kitty's love of pink wasn't confined to her trailer in London.

The reception was a sleek, ultra-modern white box of a room, with no obvious doors apart from the entrance where Oliver stood. The central area was occupied by a circular reception with a cubed-shaped LED screen hanging from the ceiling playing MTV. White leather sofas ran against the left wall sporting bright pink cushions and the floor was scattered with pink and white zebra-print rugs. Set into the righthand wall was an enormous fish tank housing dozens of pink angelfish darting in and out of a large pink shipwreck sitting on a bed of pink coral.

On the far wall, Oliver couldn't help but notice the three floor-to-ceiling, black and white posters of Kitty in her most famous films. One on a luxury Yacht – *Still Waters*, one standing by a lighthouse – *Beacon* and one in Red Square looking up to the sky – *Limitless*.

The receptionist smiled with the whitest teeth Oliver had ever seen.

'Hi, how may I assist you today?'

Oliver was thrown for a moment by the brightness of her teeth.

'Er... yes... I have a meeting with Kitty Wallis, Oliver Wilk...' He stopped himself, 'Oliver Diamond.'

'Ah yes, please take a seat, Mr. Diamond, Brett Styles will meet you shortly.' She indicated to the sofa, whilst punching in details on her keyboard. Oliver stared at the LED broadcasting an MTV concert of the latest singing sensation to hit America, Vixen. She was a great singer, known for her wild and over-the-top concerts. As Vixen was belting out a high note whilst swinging from a chandelier over a rapturous crowd, the lighthouse door on the middle poster swung open and Brett Styles appeared as though he was the lighthouse keeper.

'Oliver!' He walked towards Oliver, arm outstretched.

'Brett, good to see you. I'm liking the secret doorway.'

'Yes, Kitty loves her secrets. Follow me, she's waiting for you in the meeting room.'

Kitty greeted Oliver warmly and introduced him to her team. He found her to be a very different Kitty in this environment. Dressed in a fitted white suit, with a pink blouse, she was business-like and very much in charge of everything, a real powerhouse. The main discussion of the meeting was the background of Precious Studios.

It transpired that there were other new faces around the table, so Kitty was killing two birds with one stone. She had everyone running around fetching scripts, lunch, drinks, and presentations. Oliver could also see why Kitty relied on Brett. He often played devil's advocate to some of her more off-the-cuff suggestions. Brett was highly organized but most importantly he treated her as a friend, which meant that Kitty respected his advice and comments.

Later that afternoon Oliver joined Kitty and Brett in her luxurious office where Kitty revealed the franchise that Oliver was to be part of. The movie centered on a seemingly ordinary married couple, Paul Stitch and his wife, Josephine.

'They're living the suburban life, but no children,' Kitty divulged the plot with enthusiasm. 'Unbeknown to his wife, he sees himself as a bit of a vigilante. His clients, who have all been wronged by a corporation or individual, hire him to "get their own back". Whilst she thinks he is an accountant, he's actually targeting the greedy and making sure they get what they deserve. He hires local teams and sets up scams to trap his targets.' Kitty sat back as Brett took the helm.

'The twist is that his wife is also leading a double life. He thinks she's a part-time insurance clerk but she's really an insurance investigator. Part of her job involves undercover work to get to the truth regarding outrageous insurance claims. He keeps his life a secret, for fear of endangering her, and she keeps her life from him because of the dangerous situations she finds herself in. Their secret is safe, until one day their targets are one and the same. It's billed as an Action Comedy. With the emphasis on Action.'

'Oliver,' Kitty leaned on her desk, 'you won't be playing the billed lead role in this movie but, nevertheless, we have a great role for you.'

'Ok.' Oliver nodded slowly.

'And I'll tell you for why...' Kitty continued, 'you did great on *Stealth,* but the movie isn't out yet. We have to see where you lie with the public.'

'I understand and I trust you.' Oliver smiled.

'Yeah, well you'd better!' Kitty spoke direct. 'There's a lot of people with a lot of money riding on this.'

Brett described the role of Mark Rice as the sidekick, and it involved lots of stunts. He was the gadget guy whereas the lead role, Paul Stitch, was 'old school'. A supporting role but still up there on the billing, and his character appeared in all three of the movies in the works. Shooting would run on from movie to movie with gaps for marketing and personal appearances as the movies rolled out. Oliver was thrilled to be part of it and knew that it would secure work for the next two or three years.

'So, Oliver Diamond,' Kitty looked at him over her oversized desk, 'how does all of this sound?'

'Kitty, it sounds amazing. I won't let you down and I can't wait to get started.' Oliver looked at Kitty with newfound admiration. He was also still reeling over the shock of the seven-figure deal.

'I'll have your contract drawn up for the three-movie franchise by next week.' Kitty looked at him squarely. 'It's going to be a tough schedule; I can tell you that.' She turned to her trusted aide. 'Brett?'

Brett took over the proceedings. 'We begin shooting the first movie, working title *In Stitches*, in a month, here in LA. Then a short break for the holidays, and next year out on location in Switzerland. In between locations you will be scheduled for your promotional tour for *Stealth*, and that's when it gets hairy.'

'Sounds good to me,' Oliver enthused.

Kitty leaned forward and smiled. 'Some advice Oliver, keep focused, keep healthy, and keep away from the girls.'

Oliver blushed. Why did she always do that to him?

'Hey Kitty, I'm a good boy,' he complained, with a wry smile.

Brett looked at him squarely. 'They all say that.'

Kitty laughed. 'They sure do, now any questions?'

'Yes, who's playing the husband-and-wife team in the films?'

Kitty looked at him and smiled.

'We call them movies here Oliver, and all will be revealed this weekend at a small party I'm throwing Saturday at my house, Brett will give you the details. It'll be an opportunity for you to see Hollywood at its best.'

'Or worst.' Brett rolled his eyes.

Kitty shot Brett a look and continued. 'Now go, take in the sights, go to the gym, have fun!'

'Sounds like a great plan.' Oliver smiled and followed Brett out of the office.

'If I were you, I'd make the most of it.' Brett winked at Oliver as he opened the door.

'Oh, and Oliver,' Kitty stopped him, 'the party, it's kind of fancy dress,' she grinned, 'Brett'll fill you in.'

Brett rolled his eyes and pulled a face as he ushered Oliver out of the office.

'I saw that, Brett!' Kitty shouted through the closing door.

Chapter Twenty-One

THEN

And the Winner Is...

Everywhere Charlie looked she could see tables of ladies dressed in fur hats and coats sipping champagne and laughing. Beer flowed and there was even a vodka ice bar. *Wow*, thought Charlie, a bar carved from a large block of ice, where girls dressed head to toe in fur served frozen shots to a young it-crowd. Over the noise, Charlie could hear a running announcement of the current race along with cheers and groans from the crowds as people ran from window to window placing bets. A cacophony of sounds, both thrilling and exciting. She snapped photos on her trusty Canon of carriages bearing families with whining children pulled across the ice by weary horses.

Click *whirrrr*.

On the main track, older horses were taking part in a trotting race and receiving lots of encouragement from the jolly crowd.

Click *whirrrr*.

Standing by one of the large stands she saw nothing out of the ordinary. After a good thirty minutes, she decided to chance her luck at the betting area where a row of windows with short queues stretched out under the terrace. As Charlie walked amongst the crowds keeping a low profile, she heard repeatedly from window to window.

'A hundred francs Bullet Train number nine to win.' 'Fifty francs number nine Bullet Train, on the nose.'

Then occasionally she would hear 'Two hundred francs Das Schloss, number five.' 'A hundred francs number five, Das Schloss'

At the far window, marked VIP betting, Charlie spotted the mysterious Juliette Moreau. She lifted her lens and snapped a photo.

Click *whirrrr*.

Charlie made a queue behind her and strained to decipher her rich French accent as she conversed with the cashier.

'I wish to place a trifecta bet on Das Schloss to win, Bullet Train second place...'

'Yes madam, and in third place?' The cashier looked at her expectantly.

She seemed anxious as she studied the race cards before making up her mind.

'Madam?' The cashier waited patiently. 'And in third place...?'

She looked at him. 'The Anniversary.'

'The Anniversary... so that's numbers five, nine, and one, in that order. How much is your bet?'

'Ten thousand francs on fixed odds.' She thrust an envelope through the break in the glass and look nervously around her.

She caught Charlie's eye who feigned a sudden interest in the race card she had collected from a nearby stand.

'One moment madam.' The cashier leaned back and spoke to someone seated at a desk; Charlie presumed he was in charge. He glanced at Juliette and studied her for a moment. Checking the odds on the large board behind him he stood and crossed to the window.

'Is there a problem?' she asked, removing her glasses. He looked at her for a moment and then gave a nod to the cashier, who took the envelope and placed the notes in a counting machine.

'No Madame Moreau, everything is in order,' he said, crossing back to his desk. It was his job to know everybody and although it was illegal for a jockey to place a bet on his own race, it wasn't for his girlfriend. *Now there's loyalty for you*, he thought as he sat down smiling to himself. *Not a chance in hell, oh today was going to be a good day.*

All present and correct, the cashier passed her a printed slip which she examined. Happy with the result, she turned, smiled at Charlie, replaced her sunglasses, and walked away.

'Can I help you, Madam?'

'Er...' Charlie was about to leave. '...yes, I wish to place a bet on Das Schloss, twenty francs to win.'

'Certainly madam,' the cashier smiled.

She'd never placed a bet before, but there was a first time for everything. After the transaction was complete Charlie decided she would drop by the stable block to collect Marcus.

* * * * * * * * *

Marcus made his way past the jazz band as they thrashed out 'The Girl from Ipanema'. He turned by the side of the first building where the smell of straw and manure assaulted his gardener's nostrils like nectar. He found an office, to his left, where a large man was standing with his hands thrust deep in a filing cabinet, cradling a telephone between ear and chin, his back to Marcus. Inside the doorway was a coat hook sporting a lanyard with a pass swinging in the gentle breeze. Marcus deftly reached in, slipped the blue ribbon off the hook, and walked away from the office, placing the ID over his neck. He pulled down his hood and adjusted his flat cap, fitting in like a chameleon in the desert.

A jockey emerged from a stall to his right and began chatting in broken English to a stable boy who was laying down straw near the entrance. A wooden door to his left opened and another boy emerged up a ramp with a wheelbarrow and pitchfork from some sort of cellar where the smell was even stronger. The building had been constructed in the early part of the twentieth century and indeed, was equipped with a cellar for manure. Mainly to protect it from the sunlight, it was both discreet and scientific. Each stall bore a large sign on the door with a code – A12B, A14B. He was scrutinizing the codes when he suddenly noticed someone approaching; it was the girl in red they had all seen entering the VIP area. Marcus ducked back behind a saddle stand and watched her from a distance. Charlie said she was the jockey's girlfriend, so maybe she'd come to wish him luck before his race later that afternoon? Dressed in her finery, she looked out of place in these surroundings, especially her high heels on the stable floor, strewn with straw. He so wished he had a camera phone. She walked by a row of bins at the far end and approached a stall marked A34B.

That was the code Charlie had overheard in the bookshop the day before, A34B. She peered inside and produced a small package from her bag. She crouched down, placed the package inside the stall, stood, and quickly exited the way she'd come in. What was she up to? Marcus walked towards the stall when suddenly a voice called from behind.

'Hey, you!'

Marcus swung around; a jockey was advancing toward him. He needed an escape plan, and quick.

'I need my horse taken out to warm up. It's freezing and my groom is nowhere to be seen.'

'Errmmm...' Marcus stammered.

Suddenly, a young guy shot out of a stall next to Marcus. He'd been sleeping, his hair strewn in hay.

'There you are!' The jockey wasn't pleased.

'Sorry Mr. Hughes, I was taking a rest. He's ready to go.' The boy ran in front of Marcus and opened the stall opposite.

'He'd better be, most horses are out. Take him to the saddling paddock, I want Bullet Train at his peak by three!'

The jockey marched off with the groom on his tail, leading the beautiful black horse out of the stables. As Marcus watched them exit the building, he saw someone else approaching.

There was no mistaking the walk, it was Frank Hoffman. He searched for a hiding place but there was no time, so he threw himself into the stall where the groom had been sleeping and closed the door. It was the adjacent stall to A34B, where Das Schloss was housed. He crouched in the hay, holding his breath as he heard the door open to the next stall. Through a crack in the wood paneling, he could see Das Schloss, the beautiful dapple grey. Frank was standing next to the horse stroking the side of its neck. Then he bent down to pick up the package left by the girl earlier. Marcus squinted through the crack to see what he was doing. After a minute or two, Frank stood up and placed the palm of his hand on the lower part of the neck of the horse, on the left side facing Marcus.

He lifted his palm, took a syringe, and injected the horse with a clear liquid whilst whispering, '*Versicherung.*' Once done, he massaged the neck of the horse, collected the items from the floor, and left the stall.

'*Versicherung*'? Marcus frowned, gently pushing open the door. As Frank was leaving the stable, he hid the white package behind one of the bins before hurrying in the direction of the track. Once out of sight, Marcus crossed to the bins and picked up the white plastic container. It contained a used syringe and an empty bottle with the label – diamorphine. Quickly replacing the container and its contents behind the bin he checked his watch, one-thirty, time to see what Charlie and Henry had been up to.

* * * * * * * * *

Henry grabbed a champagne flute from a passing waiter and made her way up the stairs to the VIP area. Miraculously there was no one checking IDs as she entered the long bar.

To her right, floor-to-ceiling windows gave a spectacular view of the track and crowds below, and the left wall sported a huge mural of horses racing on the snow-covered glacier. A suited waiter approached her from the bar, she had to think on her feet. 'Hey!' Spotting an imaginary friend, she knocked back her champagne and waved like crazy to the far end of the room.

As she passed the waiter, she thrust her empty flute into his hand and said, '*Grazie, calvo cameriere,*' in a loud voice, which roughly translates as Italian for, 'Thank you, bald waiter.' The waiter shot her a look, shook his head, and continued to his post at the top of the stairs.

Crossing to the bar, she helped herself to another glass of champagne and surveyed the room. Exquisitely dressed people of high society were drinking and chatting in every crevice with little focus on the proceedings outside. Henry spotted the Lady in Red sitting alone, obviously here supporting her jockey boyfriend, she looked at Henry and smiled. Henry smiled back and sat down at an empty table nearby, no sign of Thomas Hassler just yet. Suddenly photographers crossed in front of her and shot towards the entrance like a flock of starlings. There, entering the room looking resplendent was Thomas Hassler. Henry swiped the menu from the table, hid her face, and peered over the top. He'd stopped for the press photos but suddenly he looked in her direction.

'Oh no, he's seen me!' She racked her brains trying to think of her next move as he waved in her direction, before approaching. The idea was to shadow him and see what he was up to, not to make contact. Her heart raced as she buried her head further into the menu. She held her breath as his footsteps moved closer and closer on the wooden floor but instead of stopping, he carried on past her table.

'Juliette?' she heard him ask.

'Mr. Hassler, so nice to meet you.'

He bent down and kissed the cheeks of the Lady in Red, Juliette Moreau. *Why would he have been coming to see me?* Henry thought stupidly. As she looked on, Juliette said something, and he smiled. Henry reached for her bag and extracted her trusty compact so she could check her makeup whilst observing Thomas Hassler in the mirror. *I'll have to sit here and keep my eye on him from a safe distance.*

Henry was mid-thought when a waiter approached her with a cocktail that would make any girl blush and placed it on the table in front of her. It was deep pink and sported a large umbrella, slice of pineapple, and a sparkler showering the table with its residue.

'With compliments of the gentleman over there, Madam.'

She turned to see the Lady in Red leaving the table and disappearing through the far door. Thomas Hassler raised his glass towards her, and she returned the gesture with a weak smile. Henry turned back quickly as the sparkler fizzled out in a puff of smoke. Maintaining her composure, she took a sip and decided to sit it out until it was time to meet the others downstairs in the sponsors' tent. A short time later, the Lady in Red returned looking slightly out of breath as she gulped her Veuve Clicquot.

* * * * * * * * *

Charlie walked down the side of the paddock enclosure where horses and jockeys were under careful inspection by officials with clipboards. There was no sign of Marcus. Between the paddock and stables she could see a dapple grey led by a young, pimply groom, but no jockey. The saddle bore the sporting colors of a gold crest and a purple turret. *This must be Das Schloss*, she thought. Suddenly she heard a noise to her right and out of the corner of her eye she saw a shape running from the toilet block. It was too late to dodge, and Charlie was brought down to the ground for the second time that weekend. She sat up as people gawped at her sniggering, she wasn't laughing.

'Look where you're going!' she cried.

Getting up next to her was a red-faced jockey wearing the purple and gold sporting colors.

'So sorry!'

'You?' Charlie exploded.

He frowned and offered his hand as she stood shakily.

'Have we met before? I'm Piero Ricci.' He said, looking over her shoulder at a scowling Das Schloss.

'As a matter of fact... yes we have, you nearly killed me in your sports car yesterday and I also saw you with your girlfriend this morning.'

'I am so sorry; I have to go. Are you sure you're ok?'

'Yes, I'm ok,' Charlie sighed, 'but I shall be going to the VIP area to tell that girlfriend of yours to keep the reins on you.'

'I'm afraid that won't be possible.'

'Oh, why?' Charlie asked.

'Because my girlfriend is back in Paris due to an emergency. I dropped her at the airport this morning and she called me from Charles De Gaulle where she landed an hour ago.'

'But I just saw her...' Charlie began.

'Yes...?' Piero looked confused.

Charlie thought better of it. 'Erm... no... I must be mistaken. You go, your horse is getting impatient.' She pointed at Das Schloss who was stamping the ground and raising his head awkwardly.

'Yes, I have a race to win!' Piero answered as he turned to mount the handsome horse.

∗ ∗ ∗ ∗ ∗ ∗ ∗ ∗ ∗

When Charlie entered the tent, Henry was slumped on the table with a bored expression.

'I hope you've got some news, I haven't much to tell,' Henry said as Charlie sat opposite her. Before Charlie could say anything, Marcus arrived and squeezed between them.

'You'll never guess what I have seen!' he said in a heavy whisper.

'I bet I can trump whatever it is with what I have discovered,' Charlie countered.

Henry looked on. 'All I can reveal is that Thomas Hassler is up in the VIP area with that jockey's girlfriend, Juliette Moreau.'

'Oh really?' Charlie said, bemused. 'Marcus, what do you have to offer?'

'Well...' Marcus relayed everything he had seen in the stables, including Juliette Moreau dropping off the little package and Frank Hoffman administering the mystery injection.

He described the contents of the container, the syringe, and the bottle which had contained diamorphine.

'Diamorphine?' Henry exclaimed.

'Shh! Keep your voice down.' Charlie shot her a glance.

'Diamorphine, it's heroin. Father caught his PA using, it was a scandal in Cyprus.'

Marcus shook his head in disbelief.

'Heroin?' Charlie said in a deep whisper. 'Frank is involved in some crazy stuff! I can only guess what effect that will have on the poor horse.'

'This is heavy.' Marcus was looking worried. 'Frank also said the word "*versicherung*", either of you knows what that means?'

'Yes,' said Henry, 'it means "insurance", but insurance against what?'

'Well, here's the clincher,' Charlie began, 'firstly, there's some crazy betting going on including a large bet placed by the one and only jockey's girlfriend, Juliette Moreau. I saw her with my own eyes, only it wasn't Juliette Moreau.'

Marcus and Henry looked confused.

Henry corrected her, 'But you said you saw Juliette Moreau?'

Charlie produced the shot on her camera she'd taken at the betting windows.

'That, my friends, is not Juliette Moreau. According to her jockey boyfriend, she had an emergency and is now in Paris.'

Henry looked back at the image on the camera viewing window.

'If that's not Juliette Moreau, then who the hell is it?'

* * * * * * * * *

Ingrid checked her face in the bathroom, everything was still in place. Her heart was racing, soon it would be over. She absentmindedly wondered if her mother and father were enjoying their afternoon tea at The Palace Hotel and wished she was with them right now. She took the betting slip from her bag, kissed it, and said a quick prayer. The red stilettos were killing her feet, but it was a small price to pay. It was easy to distract Thomas Hassler, although his reputation went before him, he seemed nice enough. If anyone was to find out what she'd done the night before, she knew she would be arrested. She hoped and prayed that Frank Hoffman would leave her alone once and for all, but if he discovered what she'd done today, she was well aware he would go crazy. She racked her brains, there must be a way. Then it dawned on her that the plan would backfire in Frank's face. She made her mind up, she would switch targets from Thomas Hassler to Frank Hoffman.

* * * * * * * * *

'Come on,' said Henry, 'we must hurry, the main race is about to start.'

They made their way over the snow-covered ground to the outdoor VIP enclosure and snuck under the rope to get a better view of Thomas Hassler. The horses were on the track and raring to go. Charlie spotted Das Schloss, who was behaving strangely, rearing up every so often. Henry pointed to her left at Thomas Hassler and what could only be a doppelganger of Juliette Moreau. But why was this woman pretending to be someone she wasn't? Suddenly Marcus pushed them further into the enclosure.

'Frank Hoffman!' Marcus whispered.

At the front of the stand, Frank Hoffman was looking out to the track. He glanced in Thomas Hassler's direction and then at the betting slips he held in his withered hands, all bearing the name Das Schloss. Suddenly there was a deathly hush followed by a voice squealing over the speakers, '*Und sue sind weg!*'

The crowd erupted as the horses galloped from the start, down the track, snow flying everywhere. How did they not slip and slide? The commentator whipped the crowd into a frenzy as the horses raced past the stands in a blizzard. Das Schloss was in the center of the pack chasing after Bullet Train as they veered around the first bend. At a little over a kilometer, the race was quite something and this was the 'Grand Prix' of White Turf. A horse went down at the first bend as the crowd yelled their 'ooh's and aah's'.

Charlie strained to see Das Schloss making good headway to Bullet Train. It was now a two-horse race as they veered around the final bend towards the finish line. Everyone cheered as the snow flurry raced past and onto the home straight. The crowd roared and the commentator sounded as if he was about to have a heart attack as the powerhouses crossed the finish line.

Chapter Twenty-Two

THEN

First Impressions

Oliver collected his outfit the morning of the party. 'Fancy dress and bright colors', that's what Brett had said. This was Hollywood, and everyone was outrageous in Hollywood, right? He collected a large bunch of pink roses for his hostess and once home he spent the day relaxing. It was so different from his life in England, but different was good he thought, as he picked up the script Brett had couriered over the previous day.

Tonight, Kitty would reveal who was playing Paul and Josephine Stitch, and he was intrigued. Living in a strange town, in another country, was challenging, especially as he didn't know anyone, and maybe tonight he would meet some other people he could call friends. It didn't bother him because the shoot would start next month. He checked the time and made a quick call to his mum in faraway Sheffield. She was sleepy but happy to hear his voice. and with promises to call her the following day Oliver hung up and decided it was time to prepare for his first Hollywood party.

* * * * * * * *

Oliver grabbed the flowers and sneezed as the taxi honked his horn in the driveway. Once out of the front door the driver's reaction made Oliver rapidly regret his choice of costume. Kitty was insistent everyone made an effort and, according to Brett, she adored fancy dress. 'The whackier the better!' Brett had said. He managed to squeeze into the taxi and confirmed the address with the bemused driver.

Oliver looked in amazement at Kitty's mansion at the top of the long drive lined with illuminated palm trees. Cars were dropping guests in a multitude of colors and taxis hooted as valets rushed about parking the private cars. Oliver spotted a girl in a rainbow dress, a boy in a bright orange-sequined suit, and another girl in a dress of multi-colored squares, not unlike a Rubik's cube. He even saw a boy in a bright pink top hat and tails. Everyone seemed very colorful and practical, except Oliver.

He paid the driver and managed to prise himself out of the taxi, by which time everyone else was inside. Oliver took a breath and maneuvered his way up the steps to Kitty's Mansion. On entering the hallway everyone had their backs to him, all focus was on a large sweeping staircase where, halfway down, Kitty's husband Julian Gold was addressing his guests.

'Ladies and gentleman, it's so good to see you all here. As you know my wife loves a party.' The crowd cheered. 'So, let's welcome our hostess, the beautiful and mysterious Miss Scarlet!'

The crowd applauded as Kitty Wallis walked down the stairs wearing the most beautiful scarlet-red, floor-length gown covered in shining crystals. She was Hollywood royalty, and Oliver had never seen anything like it.

'My dear friends, it's so good to see you all looking so...
colorful! This is going to be a party to remember.' More cheers.
'We've got a special guest dropping by later to perform for you,
but in the meantime enjoy yourselves, food will shortly be
served on the terrace.' As the crowd cheered, she scanned the
room and when her eyes fell on Oliver she roared with laughter.
'Before you go to sample chef's delicacies, please welcome my
new friend and protégé, Mr. Oliver Diamond.'

Kitty gestured to Oliver and the crowd slowly turned to face
him. There, standing in the doorway was Oliver holding a bunch
of pink roses and dressed in the biggest, brightest, human-sized
banana you ever did see.

* * * * * * * * *

The party was in full swing. Kitty had found Oliver's outfit
hysterical, as did her husband, Julian Gold. With his arms
poking out from the sides and his face squeezed through a hole
in the front, Oliver was the talk of the party. He made his way
outside to the terrace where tables were laid out like the food
hall of Harrods, with baked hams, roast beef, oysters, lobsters,
you name it. There was a large swimming pool with a stage at
one end with an Indie band smashing their playset. At the near
end stood a large statue of Medusa, complete with her snakey
locks, staring out over the pool where shiny scaffold towers and
lighting trusses straddled water like a gigantic alien spider.
Dotted around the perimeter were statues of naked men and
women, all mid-dive before Medusa had turned them to stone.

Guests smiled and nodded as Oliver passed by on his way to the bar which served pina colada in miniature pineapples. Kitty certainly didn't do anything by halves. A bemused Brett crossed to Oliver with a huge grin.

'Well, what do we have here, old fruit?' He joked in a very British accent.

'Yes... alright Brett, help a poor guy out.'

'No really, I think it's very appealing.' Brett was relentless.

'Very funny,' Oliver smiled. 'The wackier the better you said.'

'Yes, but Oliver, a banana? You took me too literally.'

'Maybe I should go...' Oliver frowned as a table of young guys swung around pointing and sniggering.

'Come with me, I've got a bedroom here with a wardrobe of clothes. Kitty needs me to stay from time to time when she doesn't go into the office.'

'Don't you have a life of your own Brett?' Oliver asked.

'Well, it doesn't feel like it sometimes. But it's all part of the job.'

Oliver left a deflated banana in Brett's room after a quick change into a casual pair of green chinos and a white polo shirt. Brett went in search of Kitty whilst Oliver searched for beer. The enormous kitchen backed onto the end of the terrace and Oliver milling about inside didn't go down well with the chef, who was mid-flambéing. He spotted a spiral staircase winding its way down and thought he would try his luck. Scooting down the staircase he found himself in a short hallway. On his left was a wooden door with a window, leading to a sauna, similar to the one in his apartment. The hallway led to a dimly lit cellar, which resembled a private wine shop. Oliver let out a low whistle as he surveyed row upon row of wines and champagnes. Suddenly he heard movement from the far end and not wanting anyone to think he was snooping he turned back into the hallway, but he was stopped by the sound of a female voice.

'You're drunk...' He heard the girl say.

'Can't a man enjoy himself anymore?' Came the slurred reply.

'You've been at the club all day and now you arrive in this state?' the girl continued. 'She'll freak out if she knows you're here.'

Oliver couldn't see who was speaking but he could hear them clearly in the echoey basement and the man's voice sounded slightly familiar.

'Who cares? I've come to collect what's mine,' the man said aggressively.

'You need to forget about it and move on.' She was getting irritated.

'That's easy for you to say, little miss money.'

She sighed impatiently. 'Get out of here, whilst you can.'

'No, I'll make her pay for what she did to me. There's more on that thing than you think, and I'm gonna make her pay through the nose.' He was very drunk.

'You're pathetic! I don't know why I bother.'

'You bother because I say so.' He was getting nasty and louder.

'Screw you!' she spat back.

'You little bitch!' Oliver heard a slap then the girl began walking, briskly, in his direction.

'Don't think I'm not capable, because I am,' the man shouted after her. Oliver held his breath as the footsteps were getting closer. He quickly opened the sauna door and stepped into the pine-scented room, closing the door quietly. Through the darkened window, he caught sight of a girl with a long red ponytail and a black coat hurrying up the stairs. He strained to see if the man was following her. No sign. He quietly left the sauna and crept up the spiral staircase, his mind racing.

In search of Brett, Oliver lifted a beer from the tray of a passing waiter and moved back outside as Kitty ascended the stage.

'Friends, may I have your attention please?' The crowd fell silent, and guests joined the terrace from inside the house.

'As you all know,' Kitty continued, 'my first movie under Precious Studios starts production next month.' The crowd applauded. 'And it's with great pleasure that I introduce my leading man and co-star...'

So, Kitty was playing Josephine Stitch in the movie, Oliver thought to himself.

'Jason Ross!' Kitty announced with a smile from ear to ear.

Jason Ross entered the stage to rapturous applause from the crowd.

Wow, Oliver thought, *Jason Ross is big news*. A great actor and heartthrob to thousands of girls and probably some boys. He had a reputation with the ladies, but he had recently married his agent of many years. Jason had been acting since his early teens, and his films attracted big box office, he was one of those 'can do anything' actors.

Jason stood with Kitty for photos before Kitty took to the microphone once more. 'I have another surprise for you all.' The speakers played a low chord, resounding around the terrace.

'It's my great pleasure to welcome on stage...' the drone became louder and higher pitched, '...for your entertainment...' Kitty continued the suspense as the drone became even louder and the lights around the stage flickered. Kitty pointed above their heads across the swimming pool as she announced, 'Vixen!'

Then everything happened at once. Pyrotechnics exploded all around, CO_2 burst up into the air as the music surged and Vixen appeared on a zip line, shooting towards the stage upside down, from a high balcony of one of Kitty's upstairs bedrooms. The crowd went wild as she swung her red ponytail around in circles. Oliver gasped; it was Vixen in the basement arguing with the mystery man. She then gave a show of vocal gymnastics that Oliver would never forget.

* * * * * * * * *

Vixen was truly extraordinary, and whether a fan or not, you couldn't help but admire her energy and vocals. After an hour of 'in-your-face' music and performance, the finale saw her swinging on a hooped trapeze hanging from the lighting truss whilst belting out her latest hit song. 'Swimming with Dolphins'.

No one could see Oliver from his vantage point by one of the diving statues, so he took out his mobile to film her swinging above the stage, singing like an enchanting siren. The hundred or so crowd burst into spontaneous applause on her final note as she was lowered into swirling fog. Oliver stopped videoing to applaud and cheer as Kitty sauntered past him.

'Now that's what you call a show!' she exclaimed.

'I've never seen anything like it,' Oliver enthused.

Kitty smiled. 'Welcome to Hollywood.'

'Great music too,' Oliver added.

Kitty smiled, 'Yes, it's a pity she hasn't got great taste in men also.'

Oliver noticed Kitty was wearing a pink gown.

'You've changed outfits. Weren't you Scarlet O'Hara when I arrived?'

Kitty smiled. "And weren't you Bananaman?'

Oliver laughed. 'Where's Julian?'

Kitty spoke out of the side of her mouth, 'My husband isn't a fan of her music. In fact, he wasn't too pleased I booked her for tonight, being the girlfriend of Rick Krane. Blah, blah, blah.' She pulled a face as Oliver smiled.

'Do you always get what you want?' Oliver said through narrowed eyes. Kitty held his gaze. Had he pushed her too far? She suddenly threw her head back and roared.

'Oliver, you crack me up,' she said as she walked back towards the house.

At one AM the party was winding down and guests returned to their homes in the Hollywood Hills with memories of a special night. After the 'show', Oliver and Bret had retreated for drinks in Kitty's home office, but now it was time to make the journey home. Kitty dismissed the staff, informing them, to their relief, that the 'clear-up' would take place the following day. Oliver went in search of his hostess to say goodnight but found the house was empty, it seemed he was the last to leave. Suddenly he heard an ear-piercing scream coming from the terrace outside. He ran across the hall and through the French windows to find Kitty Wallis standing at the side of the swimming pool clutching her mouth. She turned to Oliver and pointed. Oliver followed her gaze and there, floating face-down in the middle of the swimming pool, was the body of a man.

Chapter Twenty-Three

THEN

Chaos

The racecourse fell into silent anticipation as the crowd waited to hear the result. When the announcement came over the speakers loud and clear '*Fotofinish*! *Fotofinish*!', there was an uproar. Thomas Hassler threw his arms around 'Juliette', the excitement too much for him. Ingrid's heart sank as he hugged her, she couldn't take much more of the pressure. Excusing herself she walked back into the stand on shaky feet.

'No one saw that coming,' Henry said, wide-eyed.

'Henry, why don't you follow Juliette?' Charlie said as she caught her leaving Thomas Hassler on his own. 'See what she's up to, and I'll keep close by him, he doesn't know my face.'

'And what should I do?' Marcus asked.

'Keep your eye on Frank Hoffman, he's involved in this up to his scrawny little neck.'

'Ok, will do,' Marcus replied as he scoured the nearby crowd for Frank.

'If any one of us finds anything, call or text,' Henry ordered.

'But I don't have a mobile.' Marcus stopped them.

'Then use semaphore,' Henry answered as she made her way to the building to find Juliette.

'Or smoke signals?' Charlie added as she moved towards Thomas Hassler.

'What is this semaphore?' Marcus asked puzzled. But both girls had gone, he was on his own.

Henry made her way into the building under the stands, it was quite empty. She noticed a sign for ladies' toilets at the far end and ventured inside. The Lady in Red was standing at the sink, dabbing her eyes in the mirror.

'Hey, are you ok?' Henry asked sympathetically.

'Sorry?' Ingrid looked up, adjusting her sunglasses. 'Yes fine, something in my eye, that's all.' She smiled.

Henry looked at her. Something wasn't quite right, but she couldn't put her finger on it.

'Ok, if you're sure...' Henry added.

'Yes... I'm sure,' she smiled again at Henry, 'Thanks for your concern.'

The speakers in the room spluttered into life.

'*Der gewinnerin... Das Schloss!*' She could hear the huge crowd reaction from outside.

Ingrid grabbed her bag to leave. 'Sorry, I must run.' Henry followed her out of the bathroom, determined to find out what was troubling her.

Charlie tailed Thomas Hassler, keeping a safe distance, but he was on his mobile for most of the time. Suddenly there was an electronic whine from the speakers, and everyone held their breaths.

'*Der gewinnerin*... Das Schloss... *Gefolgt von* Bullet Train.... *Mit...*'

The crowd erupted in a mixture of disappointment and shock. She overheard a nearby fellow American...

'Das Schloss hasn't won a race in its life. That horse has had one lucky day!'

Thomas Hassler punched the air and walked towards the paddock enclosure around the far side of the track with Charlie in hot pursuit.

After the girls left Marcus, he sighted Frank loitering at the side of the stage area. The band struck up 'In the Mood', which was quite apt as Frank looked very impatient and certainly not 'in the mood'. He was constantly checking his watch and looking up at a nearby speaker. Suddenly the band stopped playing and as rogue notes fell away the crowd fell silent.

'*Der gewinnerin*... Das Schloss... *Gefolgt von* Bullet Train... *Mit dritter platz...*' The crowd went crazy. Marcus turned back, but Frank was nowhere to be seen. He ran behind the stage and caught him marching towards the stable block. Marcus still had his stolen lanyard, he pulled it over his head, not losing sight of Frank.

Ingrid was aware she didn't have long, but the cashiers wouldn't pay out for another twenty minutes or so. She hadn't heard which horse had come in third place but prayed it was The Anniversary. Either way, she knew what she had to do. She walked past the paddock enclosure, which was surrounded by press taking photographs of the jockeys, trainers, and horse owners. Hurrying to the bins, she extracted the container from the designated place and put it into her bag. She could see Frank pacing at the far end of the stable. Her heart raced as she hurried toward him.

'*Schnell! Schnell!*' He barked at her.

Marcus turned into the stable, and seeing Frank pacing up and down, he quickly ducked down behind a stack of hay bales. He heard footsteps from the far end as the Lady in Red entered the stables.

'*Schnell! Schnell!* Frank screamed at her.

She nervously approached Frank.

'Give me my betting slip Ingrid.' He snapped.

Ingrid? Marcus frowned.

Ingrid put her hand in her side pocket and produced an envelope.

'What is this?' Frank spat at her.

'Your money,' she said evenly.

'You stupid woman, you were supposed to place a bet with it. One thousand francs on Das Schloss.'

She threw the envelope at his feet. Ingrid didn't see it coming, but she felt it. Frank hit her across her face with the back of his hand, causing her to stagger backward.

'Frank stop!' she cried holding her stinging cheek.

'Stop? You pathetic woman, you should have done as you were told,' he shouted, pushing her to the ground. 'You had a simple set of instructions to follow.'

He spat at her as she scrambled inside her bag. Marcus's mind was racing, he couldn't just stand there and watch this man beat her. Suddenly a hand grabbed his shoulder. He turned to see Henry with her fingers on her lips, mobile in hand. Marcus pointed to Frank who was now advancing on Ingrid in a seething rage. They watched helplessly as he bent down and grabbed Ingrid by her Gucci scarf, his right hand lifted high as he was about to strike again.

Marcus couldn't help himself, he stood and shouted. 'Frank, stop!' Henry gasped at Marcus in disbelief as Frank turned his head sharply, not believing what he saw. In a flash, Ingrid produced a syringe from her bag and thrust it into Frank's leg. Frank looked at her with a mixture of hatred and shock.

'Bitch!' he shouted as he slapped her face once more.

Ingrid screamed and kicked him away. Frank regained his composure and knelt over her, raising his hand once more. Henry looked around and picked up a crowbar leaning on the wall. Suddenly, Frank's body twisted, and he fell in a jerky motion landing on the floor with a thud. Henry and Marcus ran over to Ingrid, who was attempting to stand.

'Are you alright?' Henry asked, lifting Ingrid by her arm.

'I'm ok... thank you... but who are you? And what are you doing here?'

Charlie appeared at the far end. 'I got your text, Henry.'

She looked alarmingly at Frank who was now squirming on the floor clutching at his chest. 'What happened to Frank?'

Ingrid shot her a look, 'You know him?'

'No time,' Henry answered.

'Now what?' Marcus looked from Charlie to Henry. 'And he called you Ingrid!'

'Yes, why are you pretending to be Juliette Moreau?' Henry asked.

'It's a long story.' Ingrid looked at the three of them. 'I have no time to explain now, I must go.'

'What have you done to him?' Charlie looked alarmed.

Ingrid bent down by the silent Frank. 'He will be ok, it's my own cocktail of propofol and ketamine. He will be out for a short time.'

'We must hide him,' Marcus suddenly said. 'This place is going to be full of people soon.'

Charlie and Henry looked at Marcus as Ingrid secretly dropped the syringe and empty diamorphine bottle into Frank's pocket.

'Please help me.' Ingrid gave Henry an imploring look.

Charlie wasn't convinced. 'But what are you going to do?'

'You have to trust me.' Ingrid replied as she dusted her jacket off.

The three of them stared at each other and then down to Frank, who wasn't in good shape.

'He looked like he was going to kill you,' Marcus said to Ingrid.

Ingrid stared back at him. 'Believe me, he is not a nice man.'

'Where can we hide him?' Henry looked around.

'I have an idea!' Marcus said as he crossed to a nearby door. 'Let's put him in the cellar.'

'I must go now, there is no time to explain.' Ingrid collected the envelope of money from the ground, turned, and hurried out of the stable.

Marcus opened the cellar door and the girls recoiled, holding their noses.

'What?' Marcus looked at them with a frown. 'Come on, it's good for the roses.'

He grabbed Frank under the arms and dragged him the short distance to the top of the ramp whilst Charlie held the door open. Marcus pushed him inside and Frank rolled down the slope like a rag doll and landed in a pile of manure. He gave a few grunts and groans on the way and then silence. Charlie quickly closed the door as Henry slipped the crowbar in place of the lock.

'That'll hold him for a bit once he wakes.'

'Ok guys,' Charlie looked at them both, 'let's see what this Ingrid's up to. Frank's going to cause a whole heap of trouble once he regains consciousness.'

As they left the stables, the horses were parading around the paddock enclosure. Henry noticed a beaming Thomas Hassler holding up a trophy as the photographers went crazy.

* * * * * * * * *

Ingrid approached the VIP window, composed herself, and produced her betting slip to the cashier. She was early and needed to wait for the verified payout, but on the window were the first three placings.

1st Place Number 5 Das Schloss

2nd Place Number 9 Bullet Train

3rd Place Number 1 The Anniversary

Ingrid took a deep breath as the cashier took his seat and retrieved Ingrid's betting slip.

'Well, you were very lucky today madam,' he said, calculating her winnings. He gave a soft whistle as the manager from earlier approached the window.

'Madam, congratulations are in order. As you placed a trifecta bet and successfully forecast all the first three horses in their correct order, you have accrued quite a sum. This will be paid by bank transfer this evening.' He whispered something to the cashier.

'But I need it to be transferred now,' she answered with a slight panic.

'Now?'

'Yes, now, I am leaving Switzerland tonight. So, unless you wish to receive some extremely bad publicity, you can arrange this, yes?' She held her breath and stood her ground. The other windows were getting extremely busy as the pay-out had opened.

He sighed, 'Very well, madam, if I could please have your bank details?' This was not turning out to be a good day after all.

Ingrid produced a printed slip with her anonymous Swiss bank account which he took and exited through a door marked *'Finanzvorstand'*. Ingrid was living a nightmare and knew the clock was ticking. The cashier interrupted her thoughts with a tap on the glass.

'Excuse me, madam, may I serve the next customer?'

The cashier pointed behind her. She turned and saw a man in a red and yellow bobble hat clutching his betting slip.

Ingrid smiled weakly, 'Of course.'

She was anxious and her face felt very sore. Frank always found his target, and she hoped he was now secure. But who were those young people? She recognized one of the girls from the VIP area and also the bathroom. After what seemed like an age, the manager waved her to the window. He produced a slip of paper and asked for a signature of receipt.

'A total of one million, two hundred and fifty-six thousand francs.'

Ingrid gulped.

'That's after tax.' He smiled a sickly smile.

Ingrid scrawled an illegible signature, and the cashier pushed her copy through the glass.

'Thank you,' she smiled at the manager. 'And thank you for your discretion,' she added.

'Of course, Madame Moreau.'

Ingrid looked at him in the eyes, clutched her bag, and left the window to find a taxi. Her face was stinging, and she needed to get home as quickly as possible. To her dismay, the taxi queue stretched as far as she could see. A car drew up at the front of the queue and a tourist, sporting a red and yellow bobble hat, bent down to speak to the driver through the passenger window. He asked for the railway station which the driver explained was a two-minute walk away, but the man was insistent. As quick as a flash, Ingrid opened the rear passenger door and screamed at the driver. 'Apotheke Rosen, I'll pay double. *Schnell! Schnell!*'

He shrugged at the confused tourist, closed the window, and drove away at speed.

* * * * * * * * *

Charlie, Henry, and Marcus scanned the crowd but there was no sign of Ingrid. The band was playing. The eagles were squawking. It was as if nothing was out of place. Frank was a bad sort and Ingrid seemed genuinely terrified of him, but what exactly was she up to? They stood by the stands, hands in pockets when Charlie suddenly exclaimed.

'I won!'

'What are you talking about?' Henry looked at her, puzzled.

Charlie waved the betting slip from her pocket.

'That's where we'll find Ingrid, she'll be collecting her winnings!'

They arrived at the betting windows as Ingrid was running towards the exit.

'There she is!' Henry pointed.

'But I have to collect my winnings,' complained Charlie.

Henry took her hand. 'That can wait. Marcus, follow her!'

Marcus sprinted down the side of the building towards the exit of the racecourse. By the time the girls arrived there were crowds everywhere. It seemed like half of Switzerland was in St. Moritz. Marcus ran up to them out of breath.

'She just hijacked a taxi,' Marcus panted.

'Did you hear where she was going?' Charlie looked at him expectantly.

'Yes, but it sounded like a shop, not an address. Apotheke Rosen.'

'A pharmacy?'

'Maybe she's hurt?' offered Henry. 'Let's see if we can catch up with her.'

The queue at the taxi stand seemed to go on forever.

'Let's try this one.' Marcus pointed to a car pulling up near them. He reached for the passenger door but was beaten to it by the man wearing the red and yellow bobble hat.

'Oh no,' the man said, pushing Marcus away, 'I'm not losing a second one!'

'We're going to have to walk,' said a reluctant Henry.

'But we have no idea where we are going,' Marcus frowned.

'Well Marcus,' Charlie took his hand, 'We'll have to ask around. Let's hope it's not too far.'

* * * * * * * * *

Ingrid let herself into the shop, turned the lock, and collapsed against the back of the door. She thought through what she had to do. The plan was to make an anonymous call to the racecourse and tell them Frank had injected Das Schloss with diamorphine. She had planted the syringe and bottle in his pocket. It was enough to have him put away for some time and failing that, she had the audio recording of their previous meetings where he stated he was going to inject the horse. She felt a mess and needed to clean up. She crossed behind the counter to the sink and looked in the mirror as she carefully lifted her hairline and pulled off the blonde wig. Then reaching under her chin she pulled at her skin, carefully peeling away the latex mask revealing her face, blotchy and sweaty. She ran the tap and washed her face, removing the glue. Next, the contact lenses. Feeling better already, she kicked off her shoes and removed her earrings. The time had come to go upstairs and make the call.

* * * * * * * * *

They'd decided it was better to split up. Charlie searched behind La Via Serlas, Henry looked around the railway station, and Marcus searched near the clock tower. Marcus tried a few coffee shops whilst Henry asked in the clothes shops, but everyone shrugged and shook their heads, they hadn't heard of Apotheke Rosen. Charlie found her way back to the bookstore she'd visited a day earlier and entered the musty shop causing the old cashier to look up from his book with a frown.

'Back so soon?' The man asked, remembering her from yesterday.

'Good afternoon.' Charlie looked at him. 'I see you like crime.'

'I'm sorry?' He looked at her suspiciously.

'Your book,' Charlie indicated the book in his hands, 'Mary Rinehart's *The Door*.'

'Oh... yes. It is rather gripping. How can I help you, madame?' He was itching to get back to the 'murder in hand'.

'Yes, do you have a map of St. Moritz detailing the shops?'

'Hmmm? As a matter of fact, I do have something somewhere. Was it a particular shop you were after?' He asked as he rummaged under the counter.

'Yes, it's called Apotheke Rosen, a pharmacy?'

'Oh... that's easy.' He replied leaning on the counter, 'I use it all the time for my glaucoma prescriptions.'

'Oh, that's fabulous! I mean... where is the pharmacy?'

'Out of here turn right, then first left, at the end of that road is a junction. You'll find Apotheke Rosen on the far corner tucked away.'

'Thank you, you've been most helpful.'

'Anytime.' He picked up his book and resumed reading in the hope that the next chapter would reveal the identity of the murderer.

Charlie paused in the doorway.

'By the way...'

'Yes?' He looked up, disgruntled.

'The butler did it.' Charlie said as she quickly left the shop.

* * * * * * * * *

As Ingrid made her way to the elevator there was a knock on the pharmacy door. The blinds were down so she couldn't see who was there.

'We're closed today...' she shouted in a feeble voice.

They knocked again, this time a little louder.

'We're closed, please come back tomorrow.'

Nothing, all was quiet. She sighed, pushed through the beaded curtain, and crossed to the elevator opening the outer door. Suddenly there was a crash as the front door window was smashed open and a hand reached for the lock inside.

Ingrid turned and gasped as the door was flung open revealing Frank Hoffman in a seething rage. Ingrid quickly opened the metal grille of the elevator and rushed inside as Frank closed the front door and walked through the shop. She closed the doors and rapidly pushed the button. Nothing. She stabbed again and again. Still nothing. She could see Frank through the outer door window, limping halfway down the shop. Ingrid began to cry.

'No, Frank. Stop!' she screamed.

She looked at the panel and discovered the 'service mode' key was in the slot. She quickly turned it as Frank ripped the beaded curtain down and reached the outer door. The elevator sprang into action. *Wrrrrrr!* Terrified, Ingrid looked at the descending window of the outer door with Frank's contorted face pressed against the glass.

The elevator seemed to take an eternity to reach the apartment. Pulling back the grille, she ran into the hallway in a blind panic. It was approaching twilight, so she switched on the hall light. What was she going to do? Call the police? No, she couldn't yet, he would tell them everything and take her down with him and she couldn't put her parents through that. Think, she must think. If she hid in her bedroom, he would just break down the door and there would be no escape.

She dragged a heavy chair and scotched open the outer elevator door, disarming the machinery. Ingrid then ran into her parent's room and spotted one of her mother's small oxygen tanks by the bed, it was the best she could do. She carried it back into the hallway. Suddenly, the elevator sprang into life. *Wrrrrrr!* Ingrid's heart sank. But how? Service mode! She'd left the service key inside; it didn't matter that the outer door was open. The elevator was descending to collect its caller, Frank was on his way. She sank behind the large dresser in the hallway clutching the oxygen tank with tears streaming down her cheeks. The elevator noise stopped, and she heard the grille open and close on the floor below. Then... *wrrrrrr*. He was on his way up.

Her heart was in her throat. She switched off the light and retreated behind the cabinet, she'd never felt so terrified. She peered around the cabinet as the elevator reached her floor. There standing in the light of the elevator was... the girl from the racecourse! No sign of Frank.

'Hello?' Charlie slowly drew back the grille and cautiously stepped out of the elevator.

'What are you doing here?' Ingrid stood from behind the cabinet clutching the oxygen tank, looking like a madwoman.

'Ingrid... is that you?'

'Yes, but how did you find me?' Ingrid put the cylinder down and rushed to Charlie.

'Marcus heard you getting a taxi and I found the address,' Charlie explained. 'The door was open. It looked like a burglary or something, then I noticed your family portrait on the wall of the shop. You looked different but I presumed it was you... Ingrid?'

'Yes, it's me.' Ingrid was still anxious.

'I'm not sure where the others are. Ingrid, what happened down there, shouldn't we call the police?' Charlie took out her mobile.

'No!' Ingrid shouted. 'Not yet, it's Frank.'

'What about Frank?'

'He's here!'

'But that's not possible, we locked him in the cellar at the stables.'

'Well, he's here. He smashed the front door and chased me down the shop like a mad man. I thought that was him when you came up in the elevator.'

'Ingrid, we have to get out of here, now.' Charlie pulled Ingrid's hand towards the elevator. Suddenly strains of 'Ave Maria' resounded outside, announcing evening Mass. Charlie stepped inside the elevator and Ingrid shot a glance at the Virgin Mary in the stained-glass window. Suddenly there was a crash, and a figure came hurtling through the large window, sending glass flying in all directions. Frank rolled onto the floor, knocking Ingrid to the ground screaming. He'd used the old fire escape at the back of the building. Frank pushed Charlie to the floor of the elevator, and slid the grille in place, wedging a walking stick from the nearby stand into it, firmly holding it shut. 'Ave Maria' was still resounding around the hallway from outside.

'No Frank!' Charlie shouted, shaking the grille door.

'I always knew you'd be trouble!' He spat at her.

Ingrid was a wreck. She crawled up the hallway away from Frank, trying to find the oxygen tank.

'You don't get away this time you bitch!' Frank grabbed her foot as she kicked with all her might. Charlie tried to pull the stick out of the grille, but it was stuck fast. She was helplessly watching Ingrid fight off this monster. Frank grabbed Ingrid and turned her over as she lay on the floor kicking, but she was no match for his strength.

'You had to ruin everything. You're nothing but a cheap whore,' Frank shouted as he pinned her legs down. He stank of manure and was sweating profusely. Ingrid spotted the canister underneath the legs of the oak cabinet. She reached back with her hands as Frank tore at her blouse exposing her bra. Charlie pulled and pulled at the stick through the grille, bruising and cutting her wrists as she did so. Frank straddled Ingrid and as he reached for her arms, she swung the oxygen tank, crashing into his stomach with her full force. As he gasped for air, she struggled free and stood against the oak cabinet.

As Charlie finally dislodged the stick and pulled the grille open, a staggering Frank lunged at Ingrid once more. This time Ingrid had more momentum and sent the tank crashing into his chest, propelling Frank backward across the hallway. His head hit the deer coat-stand with a resounding crack as one of the antlers pierced the base of his skull and broke away. They both screamed as he slid to the floor, smearing blood down the wall.

The strains of 'Ave Maria' reached a climax as the blood pool spread around Frank's head. Charlie took one look at Frank laying on the parquet floor in the growing pool of blood and collapsed.

Chapter Twenty-Four

THEN

Oliver's Dilemma

Oliver stared in disbelief at the body floating in the swimming pool, a cloud of blood growing around the head. Suddenly Brett appeared with Kitty's head of security.

'Kitty, go inside the house,' Brett ordered her whilst scanning the pool area.

'But Brett...' she began.

'Kitty do as I say!' Brett looked around. 'Please,' he added.

Kitty looked from Brett to Oliver and slowly crossed to the house whilst Brett retrieved the pool hooks and net from the side of the pool room.

'Let's get him out,' he said, passing the net to a stunned Oliver.

'Shouldn't we call the police?' He looked at the security guard and then at Brett.

'The police? No, not yet, let's see if he's alive first.' They reached out into the water with pool hooks, indicating Oliver to do the same.

'Oliver...' Brett looked at him.

'Sorry, yes.'

Oliver held onto the nearest diving man statue and reached out with the net towards the floating body. It looked like some macabre 'hook a duck' at the fairground. They dragged the body within reach and heaved it onto the concrete with a rolling motion. Brett groaned when he saw the man's face.

'Isn't that Rick Krane?' Oliver said in disbelief. Brett nodded solemnly.

'Brett, we need to call the police, right away.' Oliver stood.

'Oliver, wait!' Brett stopped him.

'What? He's dead!' Oliver turned to Brett.

'Let me think for a moment,' Brett then searched the pockets of the corpse.

'Think? The police need to know about this, and the sooner the better.' Oliver looked at Brett confused. 'What are you looking for?'

'Just checking to see if he has anything on him. There's no mobile, which in itself is strange.' Brett stood and peered into the depths of the pool.

'Brett,' Oliver sighed, 'we need to do the right thing.'

'But Oliver,' Brett turned and cast a look at the head of security.

'If this gets out, and believe me it will, there'll be police crawling all over this place, to say nothing of helicopters and paparazzi. It will ruin everything. *Stealth* and the new franchise will bomb, and Kitty won't recover.'

Oliver couldn't believe what he was hearing. 'But Brett, the man's dead.'

'Oliver, think about it.' Brett looked into his eyes. 'He has a bad head wound and has been in a fight. This was no accident, and this sort of thing sticks. This is Hollywood.'

Oliver ran his hand through his hair, desperately thinking of what to do. It was Rick Krane he'd heard arguing with Vixen, he was sure of it. The head of security looked at Brett.

'I'll go and bring the car around to the side entrance.'

Brett nodded. 'Ok, John.'

'Now, wait a minute…' Oliver started.

'Oliver, think about what I've said. We can't bring him back. We're not going to dispose of him, just move him to another location.'

Oliver looked at Brett, not believing what he was hearing.

'I'm going to go and help John. Whilst we sort this, I suggest you go inside the house and check on Kitty.' Brett squeezed Oliver's shoulder. 'It will be as if it never happened.'

As he was leaving Brett turned back to Oliver, 'Believe me, Oliver, it's for the best.'

Oliver crossed around the statue and knelt by Rick Krane. He'd never seen a dead body before. He shuddered as he replayed the conversation from the cellar in his head, what had Rick said?

'I've come to collect what's mine. Not after what she did to me. I'll make her pay, you'll see.' What did this mean? Then something caught his eye under the raised heel of a nearby statue. He reached around the leg and retrieved what looked like a skull keyring, with no key.'

'Oliver, what's happening?' Kitty was standing in the doorway.

'Oh my God,' she cried stumbling onto the patio, 'It's Rick Krane!' Oliver quickly pocketed the skull keyring and crossed to her. His instinct was to take her away from the body and calm her down.

'Kitty it's ok, Brett's dealing with it.' He placed his arm around a sobbing Kitty and led her into the living room. He would tell her Brett's plan and he secretly knew she'd be relieved.

He poured Kitty three fingers of malt and sat opposite her in the opulent living room. Kitty's husband hadn't stirred, he'd taken sleeping tablets to ensure a good night's sleep and their bedroom was on the far side of the house.

Oliver repeated Brett's conversation and Kitty listened attentively.

'What a dreadful accident,' Kitty said through bleary eyes.

Oliver was about to enlighten her about the gash on his head but stopped himself, Brett could fill her in on the details.

'Oliver, I must tell you something,' Kitty said when he'd finished.

'What? You can tell me anything.' Oliver shot her a concerned look.

'Yes... well... I feel so guilty.' She looked down, straightening out her dress.

'Guilty? You shouldn't feel guilty Kitty,' Oliver offered.

'Yes, you see, I can't help but feel relieved. Rick was such a volatile man. Oh, years ago he was charming and a great talent, but for a while now he's been off the rails. He'd begun to ruin other people's lives, not just his own. He didn't care anymore, and I'm afraid Vixen hasn't helped. I never knew why she was with him.'

Oliver thought back to the argument in Kitty's basement but decided not to say anything.

'But you were originally filming *Stealth* with him as your co-star. You chose him for the role, yes?' Oliver asked.

Kitty looked away. 'Well let's say it wasn't really by choice and leave it there.' She sighed as Brett entered the room from the patio.

'It's as if nothing ever happened Kitty. John has taken care of everything and don't worry; it will never be traced back here. There's only the four of us who know about this.'

Oliver looked at Kitty and then at Brett. *Yes, but you're forgetting one thing,* he thought, *The four of us know about the body, but it's murder, and someone out there knows the truth.*

166

Chapter Twenty-Five

THEN

Ringing

Charlie opened her eyes and tried to focus. She was staring at a ceiling with ornate cornices, where was she?

'She's coming round.' It was Marcus.

'Charlie, how are you feeling?' Henry reached for her hand.

'Well... a bit weak, where are we?' she croaked, looking at her surroundings.

'Here, drink some water.' Marcus offered her a mug sporting the phrase 'What A Day'.

The recent events filtered through slowly. 'Ingrid! Is she ok?' She looked around the unfamiliar bedroom.

'Yes Charlie, she's ok,' Henry answered, 'She's in the next room with the police.'

'The police? Oh my God, Frank!' Charlie exclaimed.

Marcus spoke very fast. 'We found the pharmacy, saw the break-in, and rushed up to find Frank dead next to a hysterical Ingrid. You were collapsed on the floor.'

'Ingrid told us what happened, and we called the police,' Henry explained.

'She told us not to say anything about Frank and the racecourse,' added Marcus, 'she said to say we were coming here to meet you.'

Henry continued in a heavy whisper, 'She's telling them that he broke in and attacked you both. She's claiming self-defense.'

Henry looked at Charlie with a frown. 'Is that what happened?'

Charlie nodded as her eyes filled with tears.

'It was so awful. He locked me in the elevator and was attacking her.' Marcus took Charlie's hand, 'He was going to kill her, then it all happened so quickly. It was an accident, but he would have killed her, I'm sure of it.'

Henry stroked Charlie's forehead. 'The police want you to make a statement if you feel up to it.'

Charlie nodded.

* * * * * * * * *

The police questioned Charlie and were in no doubt as to what had happened. Self-defense. They left the apartment after taking numerous photographs and removing the body of Frank Hoffman. A team would arrive later that evening to clear the crime scene of blood and mend the broken window. Ingrid knew she had to call her parents, but she didn't want her mother seeing her home until things were looking more normal.

Charlie, Marcus, and Henry were in the sitting room when Ingrid entered.

'I know I owe you all an explanation, but what I'm about to tell you can go no further than this room.' She crossed and sat opposite Charlie, in her father's chair. They saw the real Ingrid

for the first time. She had immense beauty and inner strength.
Charlie looked at her with a soft smile.

'Ok Ingrid, we're all ears.'

Ingrid began her tale of woe. She was desperate to pay for her
mother's operations, and her father's business could never bring
in the sort of money they needed. She'd met Frank Hoffman
online in a chat room for singles three years ago. It was a bit of
fun for Ingrid. She didn't have a boyfriend and her social life was
rather limited. She'd finally arranged to meet him in a bar in St.
Moritz but knew immediately that he wasn't right for her and
decided to call it a night early on in the evening.

'No, stay,' he pleaded, 'just one more drink.'

Feeling a little sorry for him she agreed, but it was the one
more drink she didn't need. He spiked her coke with Rohypnol,
a rape drug. Feeling the effects of the drug, she began to slur her
words and became drowsy. He half-carried her to a hotel room,
raped her, and took photographs of her in different poses. She
woke up the following day naked in a strange hotel not knowing
exactly what had happened. She knew she had been raped, but
the details were rather fuzzy. On arriving home, she showered
and didn't tell a soul, it would have devastated her parents. She
didn't contact Frank but a week later he sent her a naked
photograph to her message account on the dating site. Ingrid felt
so ashamed, she was sprawled on the bed with no clothes on.

'After that, Frank pretty much had me doing his bidding. I'd
told him about my makeup and hair skills over our numerous

chats online before we'd met. He decided I could play many roles and groomed me in all manner of unspeakable tasks.'

Charlie, Marcus, and Henry looked at her in disbelief.

'Ingrid, you poor thing,' Henry said as she sat on the arm of Ingrid's chair.

Charlie was angry. 'The evil man got everything he deserved.'

'He won't be missed at St. Mary's that's for sure.' Marcus added.

Charlie looked at her. 'But what was that all about at the racetrack, Ingrid?'

Ingrid sat forward. 'I had decided that it was to be over, no more doing his bidding. I have another special skill apart from wigs and latex.'

The three of them looked at her expectantly.

Ingrid continued. 'Have you ever heard of ringing?' They frowned and shook their heads slowly.

'I suppose I have grown into a con artist. "Ringing", also known as "horse bleaching", is an old con involving a lot of bleach and the skills of a hairdresser who knows how to dye hair.'

Marcus frowned. 'You lost me.'

Ingrid explained. 'You take two horses, one slow and one fast. You find a slow horse that has run in several races and has a form which isn't great, maybe a second place and a couple of third places, but no winner.'

'Like the form of Das Schloss.' Henry added.

Ingrid looked at her. 'Yes. But only, that wasn't Das Schloss.'

Charlie frowned. 'It wasn't Das Schloss?'

'But people in the horsing world must know what Das Schloss looks like?' Marcus interrupted.

'Exactly,' Ingrid continued, 'and that's where I come in. With a little bleach, ammonia, bandages, and silver nitrate I can turn a bay with a white star on its face into a dappled grey. It was so convincing, even the trainer would swear it was his Das Schloss.'

It was dawning on Marcus. 'So, Frank switched the slow Das Schloss dapple grey horse for a fast racer and you did your dying job to make him look identical!'

'Yes, only me and Frank knew that the slow horse is, in fact, the fast one. The horse goes off at long odds and when he wins, Frank cleans up.'

'Wow!' Henry exclaimed.

'The art of the con,' Ingrid continued, 'is in making the track stewards and the bettors believe the winner was the slow horse having an inexplicably good day.'

Marcus looked at Ingrid, confused, 'If that horse was fast, then why inject the poor animal with diamorphine?'

'Insurance, Frank was making sure the horse "ran like Pegasus". Those were his words,' Ingrid replied thoughtfully.

'Ingrid, it's so dangerous,' Charlie said, not quite believing what she was hearing from this young woman.

'Yes, I know, but it was all for my mother. Only, Frank became too demanding, and this time I decided I was going to be the winner. I didn't bank on Frank turning the way he did.'

'What about Thomas Hassler, the owner of Das Schloss? Did he know?'

Ingrid sighed, 'As far as I know he knew nothing about it. It was my job to keep him distracted during White Turf, so, I became Juliette Moreau. She could walk around without too much suspicion. Thomas had never met her, and I just had to make sure that Piero Ricci didn't see me. Frank wanted me to plant the syringe and diamorphine bottle on Thomas Hassler. Once he had received his payout, Frank would call the authorities and Thomas would be in big trouble, taking all the heat.'

'That's awful, poor Thomas Hassler,' Henry added.

'I know, that was the part I didn't like,' Ingrid confessed. 'So, I decided to plant everything on Frank and... you know the rest.' Ingrid sat back.

'And now Thomas Hassler has the Grand Prix winnings and a racehorse that isn't his, with dyed hair!" Marcus exclaimed.

Charlie was troubled. 'Where's the original Das Schloss?'

'I'm afraid I don't know the answer to that,' Ingrid sighed. 'Frank organized that side of things.'

'No doubt on a butcher's block, somewhere in Switzerland,' Marcus thought out loud.

'Marcus!' Charlie shot him a look.

'Sorry...' Marcus pulled a face.

They sat back, reliving the events of the day. All had turned out ok and their lives would soon be back to normal, apart from Charlie's. Seeing Frank's body lying in a pool of blood had unlocked a memory in her mind. A memory she would sooner forget.

Chapter Twenty-Six

NOW

Sacré Bleu

Oliver headed west on the coastal road. His destination was Nice but first a small detour to Villefranche-Sur-Mer. It was only about twenty kilometers, so he had plenty of time. The sea on his left was glistening under the morning sunshine as the road wound its way past beautiful homes and buildings.

All his life Oliver had tried to do the right thing but sometimes that didn't seem possible. The right thing. What was the right thing, and right for who? The most important part of his life now was Charlie. Most of the crazy stuff had happened before he met Charlie, but he'd never discussed it with her. There was no point, she had enough on her plate, and what she didn't know...

Today, he hoped all would go as planned. But many loose ends seemed to unravel the more he tried to keep them fast. Turning into the quaint streets of Villefranche he found a parking space overlooking the bay. Emerging from his car with a baseball cap and sunglasses in place, he rounded the corner and walked up the steps to the patisserie where he found an outside table tucked to one side overlooking the street. To his right was a large decorative plant pot containing beautiful, vibrant, red geraniums, spilling out towards the street below. *Mum's favorite plants*, he thought absent-mindedly as he picked up a copy of La Monde from an empty chair. The smell of fresh bread assaulted his nostrils as a waiter crossed to his table.

'*Voulez vous un café?*' the waiter asked, pencil poised.

Oliver nodded, '*Oui, Americano et un croissant chaud.*'

He sat back, pretending to read his French newspaper but keeping a firm eye on the hotel entrance opposite, feeling like a stalker. It was a boutique hotel with Juliette balconies running in lines across the façade. The waiter brought him his strong, black coffee and placed the bill in a small rack, with a flourish. A good ten minutes went by before the hotel doors opened and a couple walked out, hand in hand, into the warm sunshine. They looked left and right and then walked in the opposite direction down the hill towards the bay. He checked the time, nine-twenty. *Come on, show yourself*, Oliver thought impatiently. The doors opened again, and an attractive girl emerged mid-conversation on her mobile. She was dressed in a canary yellow suit and wore the largest of sunglasses. Standing with her back towards Oliver, she seemed agitated. Her call must have ended abruptly, he thought, because she stamped her foot before marching swiftly back into the hotel foyer.

A whirring noise distracted him, and he looked up to see a drone pass over the hotel. How strange, what was a drone doing flying around the hotel? Suddenly a flash caught his eye from one of the balconies. He searched to find the source but couldn't see anything. He placed his smartphone on the table, leaned it against the bill rack, and opened the back camera, zooming in with his finger and thumb scanning each balcony. There it was again, that flash. No, not a flash, more like the sun's reflection on a camera lens. Someone was taking photographs of him. Then on a high balcony, he glimpsed a figure. He leaned into the camera to get a better view. Suddenly, on his screen, he saw someone pull the figure back into the hotel room. At the same time, he heard a gunshot and the container of geraniums next to him exploded, sending its crimson petals into the air like spent gunpowder. Oliver grabbed his mobile and ran from the coffee shop towards his car as the waiter shot out of the doors, croissant in hand. He stared at the exploded flowerpot.

'*Sacré bleu!*'

Oliver reached his car catching his breath. *I must get out of here before the police arrive.* He realized it wasn't a camera. It was the sun's reflection on the lens of a rifle. And that was a bullet with his name on it.

Chapter Twenty-Seven

NOW

Hi, Old Friend

Charlie had confirmed everything with Oliver's trusty PA. He had an interview that morning in Nice followed by business in Cannes in the afternoon. Later that evening they were both meeting Kitty and Julian for dinner. After showering, she pulled on a grey tracksuit and packed her clothes for the afternoon meeting. She opened the closet in her walk-in wardrobe and felt behind her rack of Balenciaga and Stella McCartneys. Extracting a large package, she laid it on the floor and carefully released it from its protective wrapping. It was quite remarkable, a new kind of 'art'. She studied its every detail. On the bottom left, nestled in the art, sat the QR code, it looked out of place, but so necessary. She studied the back, checking the security key was in place. It was a masterpiece that would tip the balance of power in her favor. She carefully re-wrapped it and placed it in her portfolio case, hoping that when she returned later that evening her life would be in a different place.

* * * * * * * * *

Charlie took the inland road and reached Nice Côte d'Azur airport in a record twenty-five minutes. She parked in the short stay and marched into the arrivals area. The plane had landed, so she shouldn't have a long wait. Figures passed through the frosted glass partition and Charlie glanced up occasionally thinking she had seen her. Charlie hoped she hadn't lost her nerve and bottled out.

Soon the emerging crowd dwindled and an elderly lady in a wheelchair was wheeled past Charlie to a beaming older gent. He bent down and kissed her, *How sweet*, Charlie thought. She was about to make her way to the information desk when she saw the silhouette of a woman behind the frosted partition. She waited and there from around the glass she finally emerged, wearing a knee-length camel cape, hat, and dark glasses, wheeling a large case behind her. Charlie greeted her with a tight squeeze.

'Ingrid! I thought you'd chickened out.'

'Well, I did think about it,' Ingrid pulled away and smiled at Charlie, 'but I do owe you.' Charlie took Ingrid's suitcase, linked her arm, and pointed her towards the exit.

When they arrived at her car, Charlie removed the portfolio case from the trunk and replaced it with Ingrid's heavy luggage. The portfolio case sat neatly in the trough behind her seat.

Ingrid looked over her shoulder. 'I take it, it is in there?'

'Yes, all safe.'

Ingrid frowned, 'I still don't understand this Bitcoin, how does it work again?'

'It's only a short drive, but I think we have enough time,' Charlie joked, 'and we need to make one stop before we go into Nice and prepare. I hope she's ready for us.'

Ingrid was thoughtful. 'It has been such a long time since I last saw Henry. After all this is over, we need to celebrate.'

'She hasn't changed much,' Charlie said, 'A bit more reckless I suppose.'

'Is that possible?' Ingrid laughed.

Charlie turned on the Promenade des Anglais towards Villefranche-Sur-Mer.

'Back to the Bitcoin. It's like an invisible currency, a digital currency. There's no physical Bitcoin, just a list of transactions. Anyone can have an "address" and you can add or take out Bitcoin like a bank book. It's controlled by a series of computers around the world and is completely anonymous.'

Ingrid frowned, 'Ok, I get that, but how does it have value?'

Charlie smiled, 'Well a good few years ago the US dollar was valued against gold. A bank couldn't print any dollars if it didn't hold that amount of gold in its reserves. Physical gold. In the early 1970s, that system was over, and money held no actual value. Its value now is determined by supply and demand, and people's trust in the economy.'

Ingrid grinned at Charlie, 'How did you get so smart?'

'Well... I read a lot!'

'So,' Ingrid stared out of the window, 'what we are about to do is highly illegal?'

'Yes, stealing someone's Bitcoin is illegal but untraceable. Once a transaction is made, it cannot be reversed and cannot be traced to anyone.'

'It sounds simple, too simple.' Ingrid frowned.

'We have to make the transfer and then convert it back to dollars.' Charlie made it sound easy.

'Surely that will raise suspicion, being such a large amount?' Ingrid asked.

'Yesss... but we find a rich buyer and sell the Bitcoins at a discount that they can't resist. It's not our money to lose so I don't care, but we can't access the Bitcoins unless we get his private key.'

'This private key is the account's code, right?' Ingrid remembered that part.

'You got it.' Charlie smiled. 'That's the tricky part, getting the private key. A lot of people don't keep them on their computers for fear of hackers. That's where you come in, and our little friend back there.'

'Let's hope this works Charlie, for all our sakes.'

The road sign read Villefranche-Sur-Mer. Charlie pulled over and opened the sat nav on the dashboard. 'Now where's Henry's hotel... exactly?' She keyed in the address details.

'The George Hotel... Villefranche-Sur-Mer...'

Chapter Twenty-Eight

THEN

An Interview with a Vampire

After the excitement of White Turf, the girls returned to St. Mary's with Marcus around midnight. They arrived at Monday morning's assembly in time to hear Ms. Kleinhaus announce from her platform that Frank Hoffman had been involved in an incident over the weekend and they wouldn't be seeing him again. There was much gossip amongst the students, but Charlie and Henry kept their mouths well and truly shut.

Ingrid's parents returned home early the following morning, distraught to hear what had happened. Ingrid hadn't told them the full story, of course. They put it down to a break-in and an opportunist, which encouraged Ingrid's father to install CCTV in the shop. Ingrid knew it wasn't needed, but it made her parents feel better. Much to her father's astonishment, she explained she'd been lucky at the races and could pay for her mother's treatment. Teresa was booked in to have her lung reconstruction operation in a month. A procedure doctors carried out mainly on cancer patients, but Ingrid's mother was the perfect candidate.

Soon the events of that Sunday were becoming more of a blur, but seeing Frank's head in the pool of blood on the parquet floor had unlocked a memory, and Charlie's nightmares began again.

She saw the man leaning over her father's body, and there was a reflection of light from a nearby table lamp. The reflection on a large ring on the man's little finger bearing the letters LB. Her father was calling to her, 'Charlie... Charlie...' The man was holding her father's hand... she was helpless. He turned to her. He'd seen her... Then he walked towards her... a white flash, and the next thing she is looking down at the gun in her hand. She needed to be patient and maybe in time, more would be revealed.

The rest of the term flew by with Henry and Charlie spending the odd weekend in St. Moritz, care of their private chauffeur, Dirk. They met Ingrid occasionally, but she was generally busy helping her father in the pharmacy.

* * * * * * * * *

Soon the school year ended and the next was soon to begin. Henry traveled back to Greece to visit her father whilst Charlie stayed at the school. She caught up on her reading and spent most of her days with her trusty camera, taking photographs anywhere and everywhere. She particularly enjoyed having Marcus as her model, along with picnics in the country and swimming in the lake. But it was to be their last summer as Marcus was returning to Barcelona to help his father with the family vineyards. Business was thriving, and his father had secured more land for his Cava production.

Charlie loved Marcus but had always known it wouldn't be forever. They were both young, and their lives would take them in different directions. During the autumn term, her nightmares came and went. However, the ring was a new piece of the puzzle, the letters LB had to be initials, but whose? As soon as the man left her father's body and approached her, there was always a white flash, and she would wake up. Something happened at that moment, and one day she would have the final piece of the puzzle.

During the Christmas holidays, Marcus announced that he would be leaving St. Mary's for Barcelona the following Easter. Although she was also leaving school a term later, she knew her St. Moritz experience would be very different without Marcus.

Finally, the day arrived and as it was Easter break, Charlie rode in the taxi with Marcus and his luggage. Always one for adventure, he was taking the slow route back to Barcelona, traveling by train from St. Moritz to Basel and then on to Dijon in France before reaching his final destination. Henry knew her friend would be sad, so they arranged to meet that night in St. Moritz at her favorite cocktail bar, 'Nosferatu'.

* * * * * * * * * *

The railway station was a smart building with a clock tower and a breathtaking mountainous backdrop. As they both stood on the platform dreading the inevitable, Marcus looked at her with a tear in his eye.

'Charlie Black, I know our lives are very different, but I have loved my time with you.'

'I know, me too, Marcus Garcia,' Charlie replied, swallowing hard. They gazed into each other's watery eyes and an announcement broke their silence. The train was approaching.

'Keep in touch Charlie, and don't forget me,' Marcus said in his heavy Spanish accent.

Charlie brushed a tear away. 'I won't.' She was nineteen and he was her first love.

'Please go now, I don't want a long goodbye.' He gave her a last lingering kiss, picked up his case, and boarded the train.

* * * * * * * * *

Charlie had time to kill before meeting Henry at the bar, so, camera at the ready, she walked the streets of St. Moritz snapping anything that caught her eye. She soon found herself outside the Segantini Museum. A beautiful building with a domed tower by the hillside. A plaque on the outside wall informed her that Giovanni Segantini was an important artist of the late nineteenth century, so she decided to take a look inside. As she rounded the corner of the building, she came face to face with large trucks blocking her way. They were parked down the middle of the small road and people were racing about carrying lighting equipment, microphones, and all sorts of paraphernalia. She took some shots. What was happening? Maybe they were making a tv program? As she approached the side of the building, she stopped a young guy sporting a Mohican hairstyle and a row of earrings down one ear.

'What's happening here?' she asked him inquisitively.

'It's a movie shoot, our last day today... we hope!' He crossed his fingers as he walked away.

'A movie? How exciting!' Charlie exclaimed.

She approached the main door to sneak a peek inside. Suddenly the door flung open, causing Charlie to jump back in surprise. She gave out a short scream as a handsome man walked out followed by a flustered redheaded girl.

'So sorry, did I startle you?' The man stopped and looked at Charlie.

'Er... no, I was looking for...' Charlie faltered, feeling stupid.

'Yes?' He looked at her intently. 'You were looking for...?'

His companion looked agitated.

Charlie flustered 'This!' She held up her camera lens cap and put it back on her camera. 'Yes, I had dropped it.'

'O... K...' He smiled, 'well, I'm glad you found it. But you know you can't take photographs here, it's a closed set.' He added with a grin.

'Right... yes...' Charlie noticed his English accent and thought he looked a little familiar.

The girl was getting more agitated by the second. 'Come on, we have to go to makeup now,' she pleaded with him.

Charlie regained her composure. 'Well, you mustn't keep makeup waiting.' She internally kicked herself as they walked past and turned towards the road. She stopped to take a look back as he did the same, the girl grabbed his arm, pulling him towards a small trailer in the car park.

Nosferatu was an infamous bar in St. Moritz and Henry loved it. It was dark and musty with red drapes. When you arrived the man at the door took your coat and pulled on one of many chords on the walls, dropping a coat hanger from the ceiling. He would then place your coat on the coat hanger and pull the rope, hoisting it back up. The ceiling of the bar was an array of coats, slowly swinging like rows of howling banshees. Henry in a short black lace dress looked like Elvira as she moved through the bar. There was quite a crowd, and at nine-thirty a band was to play from the stage in the corner. A poster on a nearby pillar announced that tonight it was 'The Evil Dead'. *Sounds promising*, Henry thought as she wound her way through the crowded bar of people in fancy dress. Henry spotted a few Draculas, a Frankenstein complete with 'Bride', and two tables of zombies. Who knew the population of St. Moritz was so adventurous? She ordered and pointed to a small banquette in the far corner where a nervous Ingrid was waiting. She beamed when she saw Henry striding towards her.

'Henry! I have never been here before, it's so... different!' Ingrid said as she kissed Henry on both cheeks.

'Ingrid, you look amazing,' Henry enthused, squeezing in next to her. Ingrid had movie-star beauty and didn't have to try hard. Many a vampire was turning their head to catch a glimpse of her black, shiny hair and perfect cheekbones.

'Room for one more?' Charlie's voice cut through their conversation.

'What a great surprise seeing you, Ingrid!' Charlie said sitting next to Henry.

Ingrid smiled, 'Well, I heard you were saying goodbye to Marcus today.'

Henry squeezed Charlie's hand.

'And...' Ingrid continued, 'Henry was quite persuasive!'

They all laughed as a waiter dropped off three cocktails.

'Three Vampire's Kiss!' he announced as he placed the cocktail glasses overflowing with dry ice onto the table in front of them.

'Wooo!' all three girls cheered and picked up their drinks.

'Cheers girls.' Charlie announced. 'Here's to Marcus!'

'And secrets!' Henry whispered, mysteriously.

'And... friendship!' Ingrid added.

They clinked glasses and took a sip of the blood-red mixture, each thankful that St. Moritz had brought the three of them together in a special bond, never to be broken.

Charlie excused herself and went in search of the bathroom. A sign indicated it was behind a curtain through a hallway draped in black rags and cobwebs. She reached a door with a drawing of Elvira, as opposed to the door to her left which had a drawing of Dracula. As she pushed the door, someone was pulling it open from inside and she collapsed onto the bathroom floor with an 'Ouch!'.

'Shorry!' Came a voice from behind her. It was a man with a pair of long bloody fangs protruding from his mouth. He reached out his hand to help her up and she instantly recognized him as the guy she'd seen earlier that day from the film set, outside the museum.

'That's the second time you've done that to me!' Charlie said indignantly, 'And what are you doing in the ladies'?'

'Ehm...the gentsh ish full of zombish shmoking weed?' He explained feebly. He was having difficulty speaking with the fangs in his mouth. 'I wash burshting.'

He looked at Charlie and half-smiled. Charlie hid a grin as he opened the door behind him.

'Well, shee you awound then,' he said awkwardly.

'Not unless I shee you first. You shhcary... vampire, you,' she answered with a grin.

The redhead from earlier appeared in the hallway.

'Oliver there you are!' she said urgently, 'Get a move on, the local news guy is in the backroom for the interview you promised him.'

Oliver looked at Charlie and smiled showing his fangs. The irony wasn't lost on either of them.

He held out his hand.

'I'm Oliver,' he said with a smile.

She shook his hand. 'Hi, I'm Charlie.'

Chapter Twenty-Nine

THEN

Serendipity

After the eventful party at Kitty's, Oliver spent the next day mulling over what had happened. He'd been watching the local news all morning but so far nothing, not a mention of Rick Krane. Brett arrived around midday to check in on him.

'Brett, why is there nothing on tv about Rick Krane?' Oliver asked nervously, as he tried to get to grips with the coffee machine.

'Well, either the body hasn't been discovered or they're keeping it under wraps until the postmortem,' Brett answered calmly from Oliver's white sofa.

'Do you know where he ended up?' Oliver asked, through a heavy whisper. He wasn't sure exactly why he was whispering but it seemed the right thing to do.

'No, but it's best to know as little as possible. You sure you're ok Oliver?' he asked, concerned. Oliver thought about the conversation he'd witnessed between Rick Krane and Vixen during the evening.

'Yes... yes... I'm fine.' He decided not to mention it to Brett right now, everything was complicated enough.

'It's not every day you drag a body from a swimming pool and then agree to cover up what happened,' Oliver said thoughtfully.

'I know, what an awful night.' Brett studied Oliver's face. 'You do understand the effect this would have on Kitty and the movies?'

Oliver took a breath, 'Yes, yes I do, it's ok, I'm not going to say a word.' He gave up on the coffee machine and crossed to the refrigerator. 'Beer?'

Brett stood up. 'No, I'll leave you to it. You've wardrobe calls this week, plus a script reading on Friday.'

Oliver closed the refrigerator door and opened a bottle of Budweiser.

'Can you email all of this?' He took a swig of beer throwing the bottle cap onto the countertop.

'Oliver, I think you are going to need your own PA,' Brett said decisively.

'PA?' Oliver was distracted.

'Yes, your own personal assistant. We are worth our weight in gold,' Brett smiled, indicating himself. 'Things are going to get busy and your daily schedule needs sorting. You'll have enough going on and we can't have you distracted.'

Oliver snapped back to reality.

'It had crossed my mind, but I need someone I can trust, I need a you!' Oliver indicated Brett.

'I'll call an agency if you like?'

'Ok.' Oliver picked up the bottle cap and noticed his keys.

'Can I suggest someone myself?' Oliver asked, not knowing how things worked in Hollywood.

'Yes, I suppose so. Do you have someone in mind?'

'As a matter of fact, I do.' Oliver smiled as he picked up his keys.

'Ok, do you have their contact details?'

'Yes, but there's a small problem,' Oliver looked at Brett, 'She's in England.'

Brett smiled. 'That's ok, I can arrange a permit and fly her over here as soon as. What's her name?' Brett was poised, palm pilot in hand.

Oliver read the small clapperboard keyring to a surprised Brett.

'Cheryl, Cheryl Stevens.'

* * * * * * * * *

The next morning Oliver's television screen was filled with the face of Vixen. She was mid-interview with the running line across the bottom stating 'Rick Krane Missing'. He stared at her face but found her difficult to read. Was she upset? Was she angry? He grabbed the remote and turned up the volume.

'No, I haven't seen Rick for a few days. The last time was Friday...'

Liar, Oliver thought.

'He left my apartment Friday evening to go to some club or other. I think we all know what Rick's like.'

Liar. She had a conversation with him on Saturday evening in Kitty's basement. What was she hiding and why? He'd heard her persuading Rick to leave Kitty's party, but he had refused. 'I've come to collect what is mine... Not after what she did to me... I'll make her pay, you'll see.'

Oliver's mind was racing. What was Rick collecting? Money? Oliver presumed the 'she' was Kitty, but what had Kitty done to him and what did Kitty mean when she'd told Oliver that casting Rick in the film 'wasn't really by choice'? Was Rick blackmailing her? Maybe Vixen had returned to the cellar and they fought? Yes, that seemed to make sense, it must have been an accident. Should he go to the police? No, of course not, that wasn't an option, he couldn't say a word to anyone about the body in Kitty's pool.

He decided to spend some time in his home gym, and after lifting weights and thirty minutes on the treadmill he was sweating like crazy. He put his sweaty clothes into the washing machine, showered, pulled on his favorite sweatpants, and returned to the kitchen to cook a late breakfast of scrambled eggs.

After brunch, he turned on the tv to check the news, and as he channel-hopped, more and more news stations were buzzing with the story of the missing Rick Krane. Some showed photographs of Vixen in concert at Kitty's house on Saturday night which reminded Oliver of his secret filming. He opened his mobile and there she was, swinging from the truss, like a demented ninja.

He zoomed in to get a closer look as she was lowered to the dancers below. Oliver noticed something in the background and paused the video. There in the corner of the shot, he could just make out Rick Krane. So, he was definitely alive during her set. He watched the video a few frames at a time. Rick was talking to John, Kitty's Head of Security, and they seemed to exchange something. He played it over and over but all he could see was Rick Krane take something small and shiny from him. Then Oliver remembered that he had retrieved a keyring from the statue next to Rick's body. A shiny, skull keyring. But where was it now? He'd put it in his trouser pocket when Kitty called him. It had to be in Brett's green chinos mid spin cycle.

He dashed down to the laundry room, pulled out the clothes from the machine, and retrieved the keyring from the damp trousers. It had a button on top of the head and when he pressed it the skull's mouth dropped open revealing a damp USB flash drive. What data was on this storage device? Is this what Rick Krane had been given on the video? And the biggest question, would a sixty-minute wash cycle have ruined it beyond repair? He hurried upstairs, grabbed his laptop and inserted the drive into the USB port, and waited. Nothing happened, it was dead. He removed it, blew into it, and tried again. Nothing. Then he remembered something he had seen on the internet. He found his rice tin in the kitchen and placed the keyring inside, burying it deep in the uncooked rice before replacing it in the cupboard. It worked with mobile phones on YouTube, maybe it would work with this USB?

* * * * * * * * *

Cheryl was ecstatic when Brett called her with the job offer, and a week later she landed at LAX. Oliver spotted her immediately, it was hard not to. She was wearing a white t-shirt with the motif 'Beware the Ginger'. Her red hair bouncing all around her shoulders.

'Come here you.' Oliver exclaimed as he gave her the biggest hug.

'Oliver! I can't believe I'm here in LA. Your PA... in LA!' She laughed.

'Was it a tough decision when you got the call from Brett?' Oliver asked with a serious face.

'Well... I had to think about it for... oooh... ten seconds!' she laughed as they exited the arrivals hall into the warm LA sunshine.

'Ok, I'll take you to your place. We found you somewhere in the downtown area not too far from me. On the way, we'll stop and get some breakfast and I can fill you in on what's happening.'

'Breakfast sounds great, I'm starving.' Cheryl pulled a face.

'Me too!' Oliver pulled her case over the crossing outside. 'And next week I'll take you to the Precious offices.' He said as he loaded the luggage into the trunk of a black four-by-four.

'Don't worry about babysitting me, Oliver. I have a cousin here in LA, he's good fun, and...' she stopped, 'Oh wow, is this your car?'

'Sure is.' Oliver said in his best American accent.

'What... no chauffeur?' Cheryl teased.

'Today madam, I'm your chauffeur.' Oliver bowed opening the passenger door.

'Ok, my good man,' Cheryl joked in her best English accent. 'Show me the sights!'

* * * * * * * * *

Oliver was happy to have Cheryl by his side. She was a fellow Brit, and they shared the same sense of humor. She also proved to be an excellent PA, incredibly organized, and never missed a beat. She knew the industry inside out, having been a runner 'slash' PA for the past eight years. She was twenty-six, dedicated to her work and, more importantly, dedicated to Oliver. He never had to worry about missing a meeting or stunt training session.

Jason Ross, playing the lead role of Paul Stitch, was a name Oliver knew only too well. He was great fun to be around, and they hit it off from the very first reading.

Oliver discovered a comedy streak in his character the scriptwriters hadn't seen. So, the dialogue was changed and scenes altered slightly, giving Oliver's role a tongue-in-cheek English 'buffoon' character, in contrast to the lead roles played by Jason Ross and Kitty Wallis. Oliver watched Jason and Kitty in their scenes, absorbing their skill and timing like a sponge and before he knew it, the first block of shooting was over for a short break for 'The Holidays'.

* * * * * * * * *

Oliver returned to England the day before Christmas Eve to spend ten days with his mum in Sheffield. Schedules had changed and the film was shooting on location in Switzerland in the new year, so he would fly there directly. Cheryl was spending Christmas and New Year with her cousin in LA, so they arranged to meet in Milan where they would travel together by car over the border to St. Moritz.

Oliver's mum counted the days until he arrived home in a flurry of snow that certainly was deep and crisp and even. His mum loved parading him around Sheffield as he caught up with friends and family. Wrapped in a long coat and snow boots, she linked his arm as they walked down the High Street, constantly waving at random passers-by with a knowing look in her eye.

'Who was that Mum?' Oliver asked after the fourth wave.

'Who, Oliver?' She replied smiling inanely at some confused-looking children standing in a shop doorway with their father.

'Those people you waved at, who were they?' Oliver looked over his shoulder at a confused couple walking past a snow-covered churchyard.

'Oh Oliver... enjoy the moment,' she said, grinning and waving at a distressed mother struggling with a pram and two kids tugging at her coat.

Oliver chuckled, 'Enjoy the moment? Ok, Mum... yes... let's enjoy the moment!'

With that, he grabbed her hand and pulled her into the snow-covered churchyard.

'Oliver what are we doing here?' she asked.

'I'll show you!' He pulled her down on the snowy floor.

'Come on Mum, let's enjoy the moment. Let's make snow angels!'

On their backs, they swept the snowy ground with their arms and legs in fits of laughter as shoppers scurried past them with a 'Tut, tut'. After a few minutes, they stopped, out of breath, to find the vicar of the church looming over them, scowling.

'It's alright,' his mother explained to the vicar, 'This is my son, a big Hollywood star. If you like, I'll get you a signed photograph for the church Christmas raffle.'

* * * * * * * * *

Before Oliver left his teary mum, he reminded her he was returning in a few months for the première of *Stealth*. She was counting the days – no, the hours. A red-faced Cheryl was waiting for him in Milan where it had been snowing a great deal and the sky was still full of foreboding. After battling against blizzards, they arrived five hours later in picturesque St. Moritz. Oliver immediately knew why they were filming on location here. It was truly breathtaking, but he only had a short shoot, whereas Jason would be there much longer. Kitty wasn't part of the script in the Swiss section of the story, so she remained in LA shackled to her desk.

The following day, Oliver filmed dialogue with an 'informant' by the lake and on Wednesday, he was to shoot an important scene in the Grand Hall of The Palace Hotel. Cheryl informed him that the hotel was famous for its afternoon teas. For this shoot he had to pass some technology to a waiting Paul Stitch, only to be thwarted by a Russian double agent. His final shoot was scheduled for Saturday in an art gallery in St. Moritz where he was to be seen admiring a famous painting whilst planting a tracking device on The Stitches' 'mark'. It was all part of their con.

The week had gone well, although Oliver hadn't had much opportunity to enjoy St. Moritz, he was grateful for the fresh air and his early morning runs by the lake. Cheryl plagued him to join her for drinks every night, and every night he refused. He wasn't one for drinking whilst he was working but he did promise that after the shoot on Saturday he was 'all hers'.

'So,' Cheryl smiled, 'Saturday you're all mine?'

'Yes Cheryl,' Oliver had given in, 'I will do whatever you want.'

'Oh... whatever I want?' Cheryl teased, 'I may hold you to that.'

Oliver quickly added, 'Within reason!'

On Saturday afternoon they were filming at the museum situated at the far end of town. Traffic was diverted as the roads were narrow and the equipment trucks and dressing rooms had taken over. It was freezing outside so the heating was on full blast inside the museum, causing Oliver to sweat in the dry heat. 'Cut!' the director shouted after a rehearsed run.

'Oliver, go to the makeup van and get sorted, you look like you're melting. And someone turn this damned heating off!' He shouted around the room echoing like the not-so-whispering gallery.

Cheryl grabbed a perspiring Oliver. 'Come on follow me, you look like you could do with some fresh air.' He followed after her into a small hallway where she was grappling with a door, but it was stuck.

'Hurry before I pass out!' Oliver turned into the bigger hallway and pushed open the main doors. As he threw the doors open a young girl on the other side, screamed.

'So sorry, did I startle you?' Oliver stopped and looked at this pretty, young girl.

'Er... no! I was erm, looking for...' she stammered.

'Yes?' He looked at her intently. 'You were looking for...?'

The girl was flustered and so pretty, thought Oliver.

'This!' She held up her camera lens cap and put it back on her camera. 'Yes, I'd dropped it.'

'O... K...' Oliver smiled. 'Well, I'm glad you found it. But you know you can't take photographs here, it's a closed set.' He teased.

'Right... yes...' She went red in the face.

Cheryl poked Oliver in the back. 'We have to go to makeup now.'

The girl looked at him, composing herself.

'Well, you mustn't keep "makeup" waiting,' she said with a hint of sarcasm.

Cheryl pulled Oliver away and whispered, 'Oliver Diamond, you're such a tart!'

He smiled and looking back over his shoulder he caught the girl looking back at him before she turned and hurried away.

* * * * * * * * *

'It's a wrap!'

'Right,' Cheryl was at Oliver's side, 'back to the hotel, change, and then it's party time!'

'Do I have to?' Oliver groaned.

'You promised...'

'I know, I know, I promised I would go anywhere.'

'No, you promised you would do whatever I wanted.' Cheryl reminded him.

Oliver rolled his eyes, 'So where are we going?'

Cheryl reached in her bag. 'It's a secret... but you'll be needing these.'

She pulled out a pair of vampire teeth and plonked them into Oliver's hand.

* * * * * * * * *

Arriving outside Nosferatu, Cheryl stopped Oliver 'What I didn't tell you is... I've promised a short interview.'

'Cheryl!' Oliver interrupted her.

'I know but it's short. Local press, six questions, in and out. We're going to meet in a private room around nine.'

Oliver turned to Cheryl displaying the biggest pair of fangs.

'Ok, come on then, my shweet!'

It was the most extraordinary bar he'd ever seen, complete with vampires, ghouls, and zombies. Cheryl dragged him to the dance floor before he even had time to get a drink.

After the third dance, he crossed to the bar and ordered two 'Bloodbaths'. He was longing for a beer but thought he should join in with the party atmosphere. He jigged his way back to Cheryl across the throbbing dance floor with two glasses of what can only be described as blood with jelly babies floating in it. He found Cheryl sitting with three blood-smeared nurses drinking vodka from a large syringe.

'Get thishh down you,' he ordered, passing her the concoction. 'I'm going to find the thoilet before the band shtarts up.'

'Ok,' Cheryl shouted over the music, 'don't forget we've got the interview soon. It won't take more than ten minutes, but you'll have to remove your fangs beforehand!' Cheryl laughed.

Oliver looked back with his fangs firmly in place. 'My shweeet, how could I forget?' And with a demonic laugh, he turned in search of the men's room.

After pushing his way to the back of the bar he found himself in a short corridor with a door on the left with a drawing of Dracula. He pushed it open to find a crowd of zombies passing around a huge joint. They all turned and looked at him grinning wildly. Feeling like an extra in *Night of the Living Dead* he smiled, flashed his fangs, and backed out into the corridor. He slowly opened the door of the ladies' toilet opposite. It seemed to be empty, so he made his way to the first cubicle.

After washing his hands, he looked into the mirror. No one would believe he'd been shooting a Hollywood movie that same day. He revealed his teeth.

'Ah my lady,' he began, with his eyes staring at his reflection, 'I wisssh to shuck a virgin'sh blood! Can you asshist me in my quesht?'

He moved his head from side to side making sucking noises with his teeth as the second cubicle opened and a worried girl stood there staring at him. She was dressed as Alice in Wonderland, only she wore dark sunglasses and had a trickle of blood from her mouth. He also noticed she was clutching a headless toy rabbit.

Oliver jumped. 'I'm sho shorry, I thought no-one wassh in here.'

The girl smiled and left hurriedly.

Oliver laughed to himself. 'Ooops! Ok, here I come.'

He grabbed the door and pulled it open with a flourish as someone was pushing it from the other side. A girl fell into the bathroom onto the wet floor.

'Oh, I'm sho shorry,' Oliver said, offering her his hand.

It was the attractive girl from the museum, Oliver thought to himself.

'That's the second time you've done that to me!' the girl exploded. 'And what are you doing in the ladies'?'

'Ehm... the gentsh ish full of zombish shmoking weed and...' he sounded like he had a speech impediment, the fangs weren't helping, '...I wash burshting?' he offered as an excuse. He looked at her and half-smiled as he opened the door again and caught her reflection in the mirror grinning to herself.

'Well, shee you awound then,' he said awkwardly.

'Not unless I shee you first, you shhcary vampire, you,' she answered with a grin, causing Oliver to laugh. Cheryl appeared next to him.

'Oliver there you are,' she said urgently, 'get a move on. The local news guy is waiting for the interview we promised him.'

He looked back into the bathroom and smiled showing his fangs.

'I'm Oliver.'

She shook his hand. 'Hi, I'm Charlie.'

'Oliver,' Cheryl was pulling him away as the bathroom door closed, 'let's get the interview over and done with. The Evil Dead is about to start, and we've much more dancing to do!'

'Ok, ok, I'm coming Little Mish Boshy Bootsh.'

Oliver followed her down the corridor to an eager young Swiss reporter who wanted to ask about his experience filming in St. Moritz. During the interview, Oliver was distracted by thoughts of the girl he'd bumped into for the second time that day. At the end of his six questions, the reporter collected his bag and notepad and looked at Oliver.

'Would you say if it had not been for the filming that you would have probably never visited St. Moritz?'

Oliver thought, 'Ermmm... well... no... probably not.'

The reporter nodded, 'Most people discover St. Moritz by accident. I also discovered it that way.'

Oliver looked at him.

'Oh, not by filming,' the reporter quickly added with a chuckle, 'I was sent here by mistake last year from Zurich to cover the local annual horse race held on the lake. Another reporter was supposed to do it, but someone got their wires crossed, anyway the race is called White Turf. It was quite extraordinary; the bookies lost a fortune.'

Cheryl nudged Oliver and mouthed 'Sorry'. Oliver smiled and winked at her.

'That's fascinating er...' Oliver checked the reporter's press badge, '...Hans.'

'Yes, after White Turf I never left the place, fell in love with it.' The reporter had a 'lightbulb' moment. 'Serendipity!' He exclaimed.

Oliver looked at Cheryl and then back at the reporter, 'Serendipity?'

'Yes... a "happy accident"! It was a "happy accident"'. The reporter smiled as he pulled on a pair of hairy gloves.

'Serendipity,' Oliver repeated to himself.

'Thank you for your time, the band is starting soon, so I must go.' With that, the reporter waved his hairy hand, placed a werewolf mask over his face, and promptly left the room.

Cheryl stood. 'How weird! Come on you promised me another dance!' As she opened the door, the band started playing 'The Monster Mash'.

'Ok... ok...' He followed Cheryl, hoping he would see the girl, Charlie, again in the bar. *A 'happy accident' indeed*, he thought but, unbeknown to Oliver, Charlie had already left.

Chapter Thirty

THEN

A Sudden Call

The girls were having the time of their lives at Nosferatu. It was good to see Ingrid letting her hair down and the alcohol and music took Charlie's mind off Marcus. As Henry returned to their table with yet another round of shots, Charlie felt her mobile vibrating in her pocket. She chose to ignore it. She was thinking about the mystery man, Oliver, but guilt quickly consumed her with thoughts of Marcus. She was missing him and wished he was here with her right now. This 'Oliver' was only some glorified movie star who fancied himself with the ladies. Henry soon interrupted her thoughts, 'Ok, let's have a toast to...' Henry looked around for inspiration. The band members were putting on their guitars and a werewolf was taking center stage at the microphone.

'To... werewolves!' Henry was worse for wear already.

They all laughed and raised their shot glasses. 'Werewolves!'

Charlie felt her mobile vibrating again.

'My mobile keeps ringing, I'd better take it outside, it may be Marcus.'

'Marcus Schmarcus!' Henry shouted after her in fits of giggles.

The band struck up 'The Monster Mash' as Charlie answered her mobile on her way out through the doors.

'Hello... hello...?

'Oh... hello!' the caller was taken by surprise. 'Is that a Miss Charlotte Black?' Came the faint voice.

'Yes, this is Charlotte Black, who's calling?' Charlie strained to hear the other end.

'Oh, I'm so glad to have reached you. My name is Nurse Wilding from Yew Tree Lodge Nursing Home in Boston. I'm calling with the sad news that your Aunt Sophia passed away this morning.'

'Oh, no...' Charlie slumped down on a bench at the side of the road and swallowed hard.

'Yes, your name and contact details were on the next of kin list. We thought you'd better know, as soon as possible.'

'Yes, yes thank you,' Charlie was distant. Her aunt had been the only family she'd known, and she'd spent every school holiday with her since she could remember. Nurse Wilding cut into her thoughts...

'She had an aneurysm and peacefully passed away in her sleep. Now, the other name we have is William Black, Miss Sophia's brother, but we don't seem to be able to contact him. The number we have isn't picking up.'

'William Black?' Charlie frowned, remembering her aunt hadn't seen him for quite some time.

'Yes, William, her brother.' The nurse confirmed.

'Nurse Wilding, my aunt hasn't seen William Black in nearly twenty years. I doubt you have a number for him, there must be some mistake.' Charlie frowned as Nurse Wilding continued, 'No mistake, William Black, Miss Sophia's brother, was a regular visitor. He was here only last week.'

'Oh? Mmmm… ok.' Charlie's mind was racing.

'Your aunt left instructions regarding her funeral. We'll be in touch in a few days with details.'

'But can you please tell…' The line went dead.

Why was William Black visiting her aunt after all this time? Aunt Sophia despised him, that's the impression she'd given Charlie. Her uncle William disappeared years ago when Charlie was a very young girl, so why return now?

'The "black sheep" of the family,' her aunt had said. What had he done to make her despise him so much, and what was he up to? He would most likely be at the funeral, maybe then she could discover exactly what was going on.

Chapter Thirty-One

THEN

In the Spotlight

After the interview, Oliver searched the bar for Charlie, but she was nowhere to be seen. Fate had played a different hand and the mystery girl had vanished yet again. The following morning, even though her head was pounding, Cheryl made sure they arrived at the airport in time for their flight back to Los Angeles. Once landed, she dropped Oliver at his place and reminded him of the photo session the following afternoon for pre-publicity for *Stealth*. The media tour was to cut into the filming for *In Stitches*, and he and Kitty would be away for six weeks from February, sharing the premières so they could return to the current shoot as soon as possible.

Oliver was happy to be back in LA. His mobile pinged and he opened a message from Cheryl containing a selfie of their night at the weird bar, Nosferatu. He smiled at the image of him pretending to bite Cheryl's neck and there, in the background, was the girl, Charlie, dancing. He wondered where she was right now. He wished they could have had a proper conversation and spent some time getting to know each other, *but sometimes things are not meant to be,* he said to himself as he switched on the coffee maker and scanned his post. He checked the tv to find the media frenzy seemed to have stopped reporting news on Rick Krane, yet another statistic on the list of 'missing persons'.

Two hours later, a starving Oliver removed some chicken from the freezer and decided to be adventurous and make a curry. When he opened the cupboard in search of the rice he suddenly remembered the flash drive. With the shooting schedule and Christmas, it had completely slipped his mind. He rummaged around in the tin of rice and retrieved the dusty skull. He inserted the USB into his laptop and waited. Nothing. Oliver sighed and he wiggled the USB causing the drive to suddenly spring into action, the eyes of the skull flashing red. Two folders opened in the middle of the screen, one labeled Photos, and the second Brittany.

He opened the first folder which contained three thumbnails. He clicked on the first and a box opened up on the screen.

Enter Password

Damn! Oliver thought. A password, it could be anything. He tried random passwords.

RickKrane Incorrect

rickkrane Incorrect

Stealth Incorrect

It was an impossible task. Then he had an idea.

KittyWallis Incorrect

kittywallis Incorrect

It was no good, he would have to think long and hard. A password was impossible to guess, so he'd probably never open the files. He sighed, closed the password box, and clicked on the second file named Brittany. This time there was no password required. A photograph opened on the screen making Oliver gasp at the image staring back at him.

It was a photograph downloaded from a website he was familiar with called The Spotlight. A site actors use to get jobs through casting agents. The photograph was a headshot bearing the name, 'Oliver Wilkins'.

Chapter Thirty-Two

THEN

The Emerald Necklace

'O God, who gave us birth, you are ever more ready to hear than we are to pray. You know our needs before we ask, and our ignorance in asking…'

The pastor's voice droned around the handful of assembled mourners. Charlie stood alone, head down, staring at her purple patent stilettoes shining in the morning sunlight. Her heels were denting the AstroTurf surrounding her Aunt Sophia's grave. Charlie wasn't one for funerals. She was too young to attend her father's and she hadn't any other family left; 'Uncle William' didn't count.

It was a sharp spring day with a blue sky, and everyone was wearing long coats with hats and gloves. It was so cold she could see her breath, as well as the pastor's. Four representatives from Yew Tree Lodge were in attendance along with an older couple, whom Charlie remembered as her aunt's neighbors in Boston, and a young girl maybe a few years older than Charlie wearing a long black cloak with a hood pulled up, whom Charlie didn't recognize. A sudden gust of wind pushed her hood back revealing shiny red hair and dark glasses, the girl quickly pulled the hood back in place. There was no sign of William Black.

She glanced across the six-foot-deep chasm at a somber Nurse Wilding, the nurse who called her two weeks ago with the news of her aunt's passing. She'd introduced herself to Charlie before the ceremony, saying that she was 'sorry for her loss'. Charlie thought it was a stupid thing to say. Charlie hadn't lost her aunt, she knew exactly where she was, in the coffin being lowered into the ground in front of her.

'Help us to live as those who are prepared to die...' The pastor's voice continued echoing around the cemetery.

Charlie hadn't taken to Nurse Wilding, and she didn't know why. Maybe it was gut instinct, or maybe she reminded her of Ms. Kleinhaus? She looked like a typical nurse, only she was dressed in black with black sensible shoes, whereas Charlie had chosen to wear purple, there was no rule about black. She wasn't a fan of the graveside service, but Aunt Sophia had left strict instructions to Yew Tree Lodge, something called 'Pre-Need Planning'.

The pastor scooped up some earth and threw it into the chasm over the coffin, beckoning everyone to follow suit.

"The Lord bless you and watch over you..."

Charlie removed her glove and took a handful of earth. She cast it over the coffin thinking about the holidays she spent with her blessed aunt and stepped to one side to let the next mourner do the same.

"In the Name of the Father, and of the Son and of the Holy Spirit," everyone chanted, "Amen."

She was staring at the coffin when she noticed the man by her side slip off his glove to collect soil. As he was sprinkling the soil over the coffin Charlie noticed the ring on his pinky finger with the initials LB. She turned and looked at him. It was the man she dreamt about so often, only she had never seen his face before. He held her gaze for a few seconds and then suddenly everything went black.

* * * * * * * * *

Her father was lying in a pool of blood. A man was kneeling over her father's body searching his pockets. She could see his hand with the ring and the initials LB. Her father was in pain. The man was holding her father's hand... Her father turned to her, 'Charlie... Charlie...' The man holding his hand turned sharply and walked towards her... Charlie was trembling... she saw the gun on the floor behind him and started crying as the man moved closer. Then he did the strangest thing. He bent down in front of her, kissed her forehead, and held her. Suddenly he got up and left the room by the far door. She walked slowly towards her father and picked up the gun...

* * * * * * * * *

Charlie opened her eyes. What was that putrid smell? She was laying on the AstroTurf with Nurse Wilding wafting smelling salts under her nose.

'That's it, Charlotte, slowly does it.' Nurse Wilding lifted her head.

Charlie looked around to see her aunt's neighbors standing to one side with a concerned look. To her right Nurse Wilding's coworkers were smoking in a huddle. The young redheaded girl had vanished, as had the man wearing the ring. He was the man in her dreams, it was William Black, her uncle holding her father's hand. He'd murdered her father, but why? With Nurse Wilding's help, she stood and dusted herself down.

'I'm so sorry, I don't know what happened,' Charlie said apologetically.

'Funerals affect us all in different ways,' Nurse Wilding offered in a clipped tone.

She gave Charlie a nod and turned briskly to join her fellow staff returning to Yew Tree Lodge. Charlie decided to spend some time at her father's grave. To her left were her father's parents, Charlie's grandparents, sharing a double plot. She'd never met them, but her aunt told her that they had been in a fatal car crash when her father was ten years old. To her right was her father's headstone with the inscription:

James Black. - 1958 -1985

Loving Husband, Brother, and Devoted Father

Lying next to her father was a smaller gravestone. Charlie crossed to get a closer look at the inscription of her namesake. The third triplet, her father's stillborn brother, and the uncle she never knew she had.

Charles Black - 3rd March 1958

Born Asleep

"Little Charlie"

Rest, Little Angel

Charlie decided to clear her head in the grounds of the cemetery. It was so picturesque with grassy slopes, shaded lanes, and a lake surrounded by mature trees. A plaque caught Charlie's eye, it read…

'The Emerald Necklace' – a chain of parks linked by parkways and waterways

It gained its name by the way it appears to hang from the neck of the Boston Peninsula

* * * * * * * * *

She smiled, now her aunt's ramblings made more sense. Charlie found a bench by the lake and sat in solitude. On the far side of the lake, she saw her uncle William looking straight at her. She stood and walked to the water's edge never taking her eyes off him. He held her gaze for a moment, waved, and then walked away down a path through the trees. Charlie's mind was racing. The police wouldn't listen to the ramblings of a distant memory from an eight-year-old girl, twelve years ago, and she had no proof. But why had he done it, and what did LB stand for? She was determined to find out.

* * * * * * * * *

The next evening Charlie was flying back to St. Moritz, but first there was the matter of her aunt's will. Benefactors aren't normally present at a will reading, but Aunt Sophia had requested her attendance and the family lawyer, a Mr. Thurgood Brown, had been most insistent.

* * * * * * * * *

The following morning Charlie arrived at the lawyer's office in the nick of time. It was in a brownstone building nestled on a pretty avenue lined with large cherry blossom trees. She was uncertain as to whether her uncle William would be there, and she wasn't sure how she would react to seeing him again. She climbed a musty old staircase and entered a door marked Meeting Room A. It was small with two short rows of chairs and behind a table was the lawyer, Thurgood Brown. He glanced up and acknowledge Charlie, who remembered him as the same lawyer who informed her of the trust fund from her father's estate. Nurse Wilkins sat clutching her handbag in greedy anticipation directly in front of the lawyer. For some reason, this bothered Charlie.

'Charlotte, how are you feeling today?' she asked with mock concern.

Charlie smiled, 'Much better thank you, I hadn't eaten yesterday and was light-headed.' Charlie sat on the second row, away from the door by the sash window. Aunt Sophia's neighbors entered and sat on the other end of her row after giving her a small wave. They were a feeble couple who'd always kept themselves to themselves.

As Charlie was looking out of the window at the cherry blossom trees blowing in the morning breeze, the lawyer cleared his throat and began.

'This is the last will and testament of the late Sophia Elizabeth Black. I won't be reading all the details of the will; I will skip to the section pertaining to the distribution of worldly goods.'

He doesn't mess about, Charlie thought to herself.

'To Mr. and Mrs. Fenton…' He stopped and looked at the elderly neighbors, they smiled with watery eyes and held each other's hands as he continued, '…I leave the sum of twenty thousand dollars.'

They gasped and Charlie noticed a tear fall down Mrs. Fenton's wrinkled cheek. 'Ms. Sophia Black adds that "you can now visit your son in Australia, no excuses."' *That was typical of Aunt Sophia*, Charlie thought as they smiled at each other.

'To Yew Tree Lodge…' Nurse Wilding sat up straight in her chair, 'I leave the sum of fifty thousand dollars.'

Charlie looked at Nurse Wilding nodding her head in acceptance with zero reaction. Obviously, Nurse Wilding was already aware of this, Charlie noted.

Mr. Thurgood Brown continued, 'Again another note from Ms. Black, which I will read verbatim, "Please use this money to purchase a new television set for the lounge and goodness' sake do something about the lunchtime menu."'

Nurse Wilding cleared her throat and shifted in her seat as Charlie stifled a giggle.

'Moving on, to my niece Charlotte Black, I leave the sum of two hundred thousand dollars...'

Wow, Charlie thought, *who knew her Aunt had this amount of savings stashed away?*

The lawyer continued '...with the note, "Please keep smiling my dear, your laughter warms my heart."'

Charlie smiled and gazed out of the window; the blossom was whirling down the avenue as the breeze stepped up a gear.

'And finally...' the lawyer glanced back at his papers.

Charlie suddenly noticed her uncle William looking up at her, standing by the cherry tree on the opposite side.

'...to my brother, William Black...'

Charlie turned back to the lawyer, *To my brother?* Charlie thought, *But she hated him.*

'...also known as Liam Black, I leave the house at 12 Sycamore Avenue, Boston...'

Charlie sat up, *Liam Black... LB!* Charlie turned to look outside and stared at her uncle William as he stared back at her.

'...I also leave him...'

He then waved at Charlie from under the cherry blossom, turned, and strode off, down the street.

'...the sum of one million dollars.'

Charlie stared at the lawyer in disbelief. Why would her aunt leave a million dollars to a brother she hated?

'Any monies left over from the sale of stocks and bonds shall be dispersed to a dog sanctuary in Boston, "Paws for Thought".' He smiled and closed his file.

Nurse Wilding stood and left without a backward glance.

Thurgood Brown then announced, 'We have all of your details and will be in touch in due course.' He then promptly left the room.

Charlie stood and looked out of the window left and right, there was no sign of him. She felt a tap on her shoulder.

'Charlotte, I don't know if you remember us?' It was Mrs. Fenton with her husband standing behind her.

'Er yes, of course, you're Aunt Sophia's neighbors.' Charlie looked at them warmly.

'Before your aunt left for Yew Tree Lodge, she visited us and asked if we could take care of Dorcas.'

Charlie frowned, 'Dorcas?'

'Yes, your aunt's spaniel,' Mr. Fenton spoke softly.

'Oh yes, Dorcas, thank you, she was such a sweet dog,' Charlie replied.

'She still is, nine years old and behaves like a puppy,' Mrs. Fenton smiled. 'She also gave me something to give to you... the next time we saw you.'

Charlie frowned. 'What is it?'

Mrs. Fenton reached into her bag and produced a package wrapped in blue tissue tied with a pink ribbon and handed it to Charlie.

Mrs. Fenton continued, 'She said it would give you answers. I'm not sure what that means but... well there you go.'

She squeezed Charlie's hand before they both left the room linking arms.

Charlie sat down to open the package. She tugged the bow and carefully unfolded the tissue. There, laying on her lap, was the framed photograph of Aunt Sophia with her father and uncle William holding the rabbit.

Chapter Thirty-Three

NOW

Gelateria Tony's

Oliver jumped into the driver's seat and sped out of Villefranche-Sur-Mer. The day had hardly begun and someone had taken a shot at him. Why was he someone's target?

His first meeting in Nice was at Gelateria Tony's, an ice cream shop behind the cathedral. He found a parking space tucked away in a corner of the car park and removed the briefcase from the car. No one was there apart from a family climbing out of a Renault Clio opposite. The father was trying to prise a pushchair from the back whilst the mother was carrying a crying toddler, bobbing up and down in a frenzy.

'I told you we should have hired a larger model!' the woman was shouting at her red-faced husband, antagonizing the baby even more, so he flexed his lungs, 'Waaaaah!'

They were American. This wasn't only obvious from their accents but from the stars and stripes pushchair the husband was wrestling with.

'Maybe we should have brought a smaller stroller?' he counterattacked, never a good idea.

'I'm going sightseeing!'

The woman marched off holding the screaming baby as the pram was finally freed from the car. He closed the trunk with a sigh and turned to Oliver giving a half-wave and half-shrug of the shoulders, by way of an apology. Locking the car with a *bleep-bleep*, he ran in the direction of his screaming offspring.

Oliver rounded the corner and discovered the Gelateria. It was a jolly-looking shop front with a blue and yellow candy-striped blind. The facade was painted pale yellow, and the doorway was flanked with pillars on either side, resembling large, striped marshmallows, like two giant flumps. Oliver opened the door with a *ding-a-ling* of the bell. Chairs and tables ran down the left wall and to his right a large glass-fronted counter displayed all manner of mouth-watering ice creams.

'Oui Monsieur? Bienvenue à Tony's!' A well-rounded 'Tony' was beaming at Oliver like a character from Willy Wonka. He wore a blue and white striped apron, complete with a red bow tie, and sported a large curly mustache and greased down hair. He'd sprung from his stool, ready for action.

'Ehm...?' Oliver searched for the first flavor that took his eye.

'One small tub of vanilla please.' *Really? Vanilla? Was that the best you could do?* he thought to himself. It didn't faze Tony. 'Ok Monsieur, one tub of the finest vanilla coming right up!' Oliver sat at the end table facing the doorway. He noted that there was an exit door behind him leading to the back of the shop and outside.

After tasting one spoonful of what was arguably the best vanilla ice cream on the planet, Oliver heard the familiar *ding-a-ling* and looked up to see his stunt double, Kelvin, standing in the doorway.

'Hi Kelvin,' Oliver said holding out his hand. Behind the counter, Tony sprang into action.

'*Oui Monsieur? Bienvenue à Tony's!*'

Kelvin ignored Tony, shook Oliver's hand, and beamed.

'I'm not sure what I have been roped into, but let's hope this does the trick.' He sat at Oliver's table as Tony sat back down on his stool to take another nap.

Oliver retrieved a pouch from his briefcase and handed it to Kelvin.

'Here, take these sunglasses, I don't want anyone to notice you.'

Kelvin took them and put them on. 'Cool.'

'Ok, so you know what to do?' Kelvin nodded as Oliver continued, 'It's very simple, but you haven't got long, the meet is at noon, in thirty-five minutes. Here's the briefcase with everything inside. The USB is hidden, as I showed you online.' He passed the briefcase to Kelvin.

'Oliver, it will be fine.' He winked and stood up. 'I'll let you know when it's done.' He turned and marched out of the door.

Oliver sighed, placed five euros on the table, and pulled out his sunglasses from his pocket. As he was putting them on, he noticed a suspicious-looking man approaching the shop. He was straining to look through the tinted windows from across the street. Oliver couldn't be caught, it would ruin everything, and the man was getting closer, maybe he'd already seen him. He was a couple of meters away when Oliver heard the scream of a baby. The fraught couple had returned and were trying to force their way into the ice cream shop all at the same time, pushchair as well. Oliver took his chance and dashed out of the door behind him. Looking back, he saw the man trying to push past the family jostling with the screaming baby.

Tony jumped up from his stool and shouted at the flustered father.

'*Oui Monsieur? Bienvenue à Tony's!*

Chapter Thirty-Four

NOW

I'm Late, I'm Late, for a Very Important Date

Charlie and Ingrid joined the Boulevard Princess Grace De Monaco running along the coast back into Villefranche. As she rounded a bend, she hit the brakes as the road ahead was packed with coaches. Looking out to sea she spotted a luxury cruise ship sitting anchored a mile out in the Mediterranean.

'Oh no, there's a ship in!' Charlie exclaimed.

Ahead of them, coaches were attempting three-point-turns full of eager passengers ready to spend their euros in Nice. Tender boats were ferrying forty at a time from the colossal cruise ship. Charlie sighed, pulled on the handbrake, and waited for the road to clear.

'We'd better call Henry,' Ingrid said, 'Tell her we are slightly delayed; you know what's she's like.' They both rolled their eyes and laughed.

'Yes ok.' No sooner had Charlie dialed the number on her hands-free, a tetchy Henry answered.

'Hello, at last... where are you?'

'Hi Henry, we're only...' Charlie began.

'Hello? Hello?' Henry was having difficulty hearing them. Then, they heard her scream. 'Arghhhh!' They looked at each other and pulled a face.

'Henry, can you hear me?' Charlie shouted back to her mobile in its cradle.

'Just a moment...' Henry shouted as if she was talking to someone partially deaf, although they could hear her loud and clear.

'How about now?' Charlie asked hopefully.

'Phew! Yes, it's better outside the hotel.'

'We're held up in traffic...' Charlie interjected.

'It's very muffled,' came Henry's reply, 'where the hell are you?'

'We're in a jam near the port, shouldn't be too long now.' Charlie crossed her fingers. The coaches were slowly moving in some form of order, as couples boarded in their pastel windbreakers.

'Ok hurry, I'm a bag of nerves as it is!' Henry shouted before the line went dead.

The car behind sounded its horn, long and hard indicating the road ahead was clear. She slipped the car in gear and drove past the queue of cruise passengers who were waving and smiling inanely at them.

As they approached the hotel, the road was cordoned off by three police cars, a crowd was gathering.

'Oh no, now what?' Charlie was flustered.

'There's police everywhere Charlie, we won't get through.'

'I hope this has nothing to do with Henry.' Charlie checked her rear-view mirror at the traffic building up behind her.

'Charlie,' Ingrid turned to her, 'what if we went on ahead in the hope that Henry can find a taxi? We need time to prepare, and you have to be at the bank no later than 2 PM.'

'But I need Henry with me...' Suddenly Charlie was interrupted by a knock on her window from a sweating Henry, looking somewhat disheveled in a canary yellow Chanel suit and enormous sunglasses. Charlie pushed the door unlock button and Henry lugged her case onto the back seat and climbed in.

'Be careful of the picture!' Charlie warned her.

'Never mind the effing picture, turn around and drive!' said a flustered Henry.

'Hi, Henry.' Ingrid smiled at her friend.

'Ingrid, so sorry, it's been one of those mornings' Henry offered an apology as Charlie maneuvered the car through a five-point-turn.

'What's happening at your hotel?' Charlie asked.

'I was all ready and waiting for you – by the way, you're twenty minutes late – when there was a commotion outside. It didn't help that Vixen's staying in the penthouse.'

'Vixen? Why is she staying there?' Charlie puzzled.

'Any... way...' Henry continued, 'there was a gunman apparently.'

'Someone was trying to kill Vixen?' Charlie was confused.

'No... that's just it. They fired a shot *from* the hotel to a pâtisserie opposite, then all hell broke loose.'

'I wonder what that was about?' said a worried Ingrid. 'St. Moritz is so tame.'

'That's not quite how I remember St. Moritz,' Charlie joked.

Henry slapped the dashboard, 'Anyway… back to me… I wasn't staying to find out what was going on, so I snuck out through the gardens at the back of the dining room and went 'off-road' with my suitcase.'

The girls caught up with Ingrid's news from St. Moritz and reminisced about the first time they had met and that fateful day at the races. They arrived at the Hotel Prince Albert as the clock in the foyer chimed noon. Charlie gestured outside and whispered to them as they waited for their key cards.

'The bank is only a two-minute walk down Boulevard Victor Hugo.'

The girls arrived at their suite and Ingrid gave a soft whistle as she opened the double doors, revealing floor-to-ceiling windows looking out onto the Alsace Lorraine Gardens. The room was filled with Louis XIV furniture and the duck egg blue carpet was like a calm sea lapping up to ivory walls boasting sconces and gold cherub light fittings. It was, indeed, a room fit for a king, or even three queens. The porter arrived with their luggage and opened the double doors leading to an even more elegant bedroom. In the center was an oversized canopy bed sporting an enormous peacock-feathered headboard. Charlie gave the porter a handsome tip, fifty euros. He couldn't hide his reaction and almost tripped over a turtle-shaped pouf as he backed out of the suite with his head bowed. Henry jumped onto the bed, face down, and groaned as it enveloped her.

'Oh, I wish we could enjoy this place first,' she whined.

'Come on, we must change, Ingrid has work to do!' Charlie shot her a look.

'First things first Charlie, where's the mini-bar?' Henry jumped up and began opening and closing doors in the elegant furniture.

'Help me clear this dressing table, it has the best light,' Ingrid said, dragging her heavy case.

'Ok, Henry why don't you change first? Ingrid can make a start with me.'

Ingrid took three photographs from her bag and taped them next to each other on the large dressing table mirror.

'Aha!' Henry said, triumphantly turning to Charlie with a handful of miniature whiskeys.

'Henry, seriously!' Charlie exclaimed as Henry pouted her lips like the petulant schoolgirl she used to be.

'Let's go over the details one last time.' Charlie sat on the bed with Henry and Ingrid. 'Henry, you and I must be at the bank by two, I confirmed the appointment with them yesterday. He's due at two-thirty and then we have thirty minutes to convince him.'

'But how do you know he'll show?' Henry was unsure about that part of the plan.

Charlie smiled. 'Oh, I'm sure he'll show, he won't be able to resist the temptation. Once I'm in place you'll look out for him and bring him to me, I have your lapel badge.'

'Have you got the security code for the door in the bank?'

'It should be coming through at any time, don't worry.' She turned to Ingrid.

'He should leave his office at around two o'clock, so you'll have approximately one hour. That should be enough time, yes?'

'I don't see why not,' Ingrid replied, 'after last month's test run the groundwork is done.'

'Ok,' Charlie continued, 'we'll meet back here no later than three-thirty.'

Ingrid looked over at the luggage. 'Can I take a look at the "Cryptoart"?'

'Yes, it is something else.' Charlie retrieved her portfolio case and extracted the frame.

Sitting on the end of the bed they all gazed at the framed art, depicting a large white rabbit, like the one in Alice in Wonderland, with a blue sky and white clouds. Only he was standing on a stack of gold ingots looking out of the frame wearing a blue military uniform and a pair of flying goggles. He was surrounded by stacks of US dollar bills and hundred-dollar bills were falling like confetti from the clouds. He even had one rolled in his mouth and was smoking it like some giant Cuban cigar. The picture was bordered with an art-deco look of gold and blue, intertwined lines.

'How crass!' Henry screwed up her face.

Ingrid stared at the picture. 'It may be crass, but it's an extraordinary copy. It's amazing Charlie.'

Ingrid took the frame and turned it over, revealing the security key sitting behind its plastic, protective strip.

'So, the key is here intact, yes?' Ingrid pointed at the strip.

'Yep,' Charlie nodded, 'a series of sixty-four letters and numbers that hold the key to a fortune.'

'What about the Rothschilds' *representative*?' Henry asked Charlie.

'Don't worry, that's all arranged. Just think, this time next week this will be over, and we'll be sipping cocktails at the red-carpet party in Cannes. You're both invited, by the way.'

At that moment there was a knock at the door.

'Who can that be?' Henry said in a heavy whisper.

'They can't come in Charlie!' Ingrid looked over at the photographs stuck on the dressing table mirror. The knock came again followed by a voice, 'Room service.'

Henry was agitated, 'But we haven't ordered anything.' She looked at Charlie, 'Have we?'

Charlie crossed into the living area to open the door.

'Don't worry girls, it'll be the champagne.'

Ingrid and Henry looked at each other, 'Champagne?'

'Now you're talking!' Henry's face lit up.

Ingrid and Henry looked through the double doors from the bedroom as Charlie returned followed by a waiter pushing a trolley with glasses and a bottle of Veuve Clicquot nestling in an ice bucket. Charlie turned to the waiter.

'Thank you, here is fine.'

Ingrid and Henry were stunned as the waiter stood beaming at them both. They couldn't believe their eyes.

'Marcus!' They both said simultaneously. Standing with the trolley, looking as handsome as ever, was Marcus wearing a dark suit and a grin. He gave them both the biggest hugs.

'But I don't understand, what are you doing here?' Henry looked from Marcus to Charlie.

'You didn't think you were going to pull this off without a little help from me, did you?' he said with a smile.

'Marcus, it's so good to see you.' Ingrid smiled at him, remembering his help at White Turf. 'But Charlie, what about Oliver? Does he know you are in touch with an old flame?' Ingrid poked Charlie.

'Hey, Ingrid, less of the *old*,' Marcus joked.

Henry looked Marcus up and down, 'A very handsome old flame, I might add. I've never seen you looking so good.'

'Ok ladies,' Charlie addressed them, 'Marcus knows I'm very happily married, and Oliver knows all about my past, well, most of it. Please meet our Rothschilds representative, Santiago Rodriguez.'

Marcus gave a half bow.

'Charlie has briefed me, so I know what to do.' Marcus became serious, with his heavy Spanish accent. Charlie crossed to the trolley and poured the champagne.

'Come on girls,' she looked at Marcus, '...and boy, it's time to prepare.'

'Ok Charlie,' Henry stood and announced, 'let's go get your money back.'

They 'clinked' glasses and took a sip.

Charlie heaved a sigh. 'Ingrid, let the transformations begin.'

Chapter Thirty-Five

THEN

Byte Size

Oliver hadn't been able to sleep. He spent all night wondering why the USB he'd found at Kitty's party contained a photograph of him. He needed to open the other password-protected files; they must hold the key to all of this. He made a coffee and as he was taking his first sip his door buzzed, it was Cheryl.

'Hi,' she bounced in, her red hair shining in the morning sun, 'I know it's early, but I thought we could go over some details for the photoshoot over breakfast.' She held up a brown paper bag brimming over with all sorts of breakfast goodies.

She looked at Oliver. 'Wow.'

'What?' he looked back at her through squinted eyes.

'You look like I felt yesterday... awful.'

'Yeah, couldn't sleep,' Oliver mumbled, glancing at his laptop.

'Go and take a shower whilst I do breakfast.'

'Cheryl... I only need some coffee... I'll be...'

'Go!' Cheryl interrupted.

Oliver caved in and as he made his way upstairs, he shouted into the air.

'I like my bacon crispy.'

'Shower!' Cheryl ordered as she unpacked the groceries and got to work on her favorite meal of the day.

* * * * * * * * * *

'Cheryl, one day you'll make the perfect wife for somebody,' Oliver said as he finished the last slice of fried bread.

'Mmmmm,' she replied, 'there's no man who'll live up to Mum's expectations I'm afraid, and in the meantime, we've got work to do.'

Oliver grabbed his laptop.

'There's something I need to share with you.'

Cheryl looked at him suspiciously. 'Oh no, you're not going to declare your undying love for me, are you?'

Oliver turned sharply. 'What? No!'

'Oh, that's ok then, because I'm on a promise tonight with the delivery boy, hence all the bacon.'

Oliver laughed and then sighed. 'Cheryl this is serious.'

'Ok... now you're spooking me out.'

'Come sit,' Oliver tapped the stool next to him, 'I need to show you.'

He relayed the entire story about Kitty's party a few months earlier. Rick Krane, the argument with Vixen and the USB. She sat and listened to his every word and when he had finished, she was dumbfounded. Oliver looked at her expectantly.

'Well?'

Cheryl shook her head, 'I can't believe you've known all of this and haven't told me until today.'

'Well, to be honest, I didn't want to involve you but I'm at a bit of a dead-end.'

'Rick Krane was *murdered,* Oliver.' Cheryl's mind was now on overdrive.

'I know, but Brett convinced me that it would ruin Kitty, and now it's all too late. His body still hasn't been found, and here's where it gets even weirder.' He opened the USB.

'It gets *weirder*?' Cheryl said sarcastically.

'On this USB there's a photo... of me.'

Cheryl couldn't believe what she was hearing. Oliver opened the image and showed her.

'Oh my God, it's your Spotlight photo, now that is weird,' Cheryl confirmed his thoughts.

Oliver continued, 'There are three more image files, but they're password protected. I've tried all the usual passwords, rickkrane, kittywallis, nothing works.'

'Ok, you have to think laterally about these things.'

Oliver frowned, 'What do you mean?'

'Well, what would Rick Krane use? A password that's easy to remember and something important to him.' They both fell silent.

'I know!' Cheryl exclaimed making Oliver jump in his stool. '*Try Stranger in the Window,* their first film together.'

'Ok...' Oliver typed in strangerinthewindow.

'Nope...' Oliver sighed, '....and I've tried upper and lower case.'

'It must be something catchy, more personal.' Cheryl racked her brains.

'Wait! That's it... try Brutus.'

'Brutus?' Oliver began typing it into the box.

'Yes, he used to have a dog called Brutus that he took everywhere with him. A Jack Russell, I think.' Cheryl replied, knowledgeably.

The password box disappeared with a 'ping'.

'That's it, Cheryl, you've cracked it!' Oliver exclaimed.

Cheryl heaved an exaggerated sigh, 'I'm not just a pretty face you know. So, what is it?'

Oliver looked confused and turned the screen towards Cheryl. The file opened to reveal a picture of a waterfall cascading into a lagoon surrounded by trees and flowers.

'Well, that's hardly worth the password.' Cheryl sighed, 'Try the other two image files.' Oliver opened the second image. It was a landscape of mountains and clouds and the third was a forest in the early morning mist.

'What's so important about these Cheryl? It doesn't make sense.' Oliver was confused even more.

'They'll have to wait, we've got a photo shoot to get to,' Cheryl sprung off the stool. 'And I need some time to absorb all of this so we can figure out what to do,' Cheryl added as she snapped the dishwasher shut to begin its daily cycle.

* * * * * * * * *

Over the next few weeks, Oliver spent hours staring at the images on his laptop and eventually gave up trying to fathom what they meant. He and Cheryl departed LA, with Kitty and

Brett, to take on the promotional tour of his first movie, *Stealth*. It was a huge hit and soon Oliver Diamond was on the lips of every production house in Hollywood. He parted ways with Kitty for some legs of the tour, but he always had Cheryl by his side. From time to time, they discussed the mystery of the USB but drew no conclusions. After touring America, Singapore, Manilla, and Bangkok, they were reunited with Kitty and Brett in Europe.

The UK première took place at The Odeon, in London's Leicester Square. Oliver bought his mother a black sequined dress from Yves Saint Laurent on Rodeo Drive, which Cheryl helped him choose. She looked a million dollars walking down the red carpet on his arm. She held onto him so tightly and didn't want to let go. After the screening, they were driven to meet the others for a meal, and en route, she told Oliver she had a new boyfriend by the name of Alan Marshall. She'd known him since junior school, and they'd met up again at the Tuesday Bridge Club. He was a widower whose wife had died from breast cancer five years before. Oliver was pleased for his dear mum, and he couldn't help noticing her eyes had their sparkle back for the first time in forever. The supper was at The Ivy, on West Street in Covent Garden. They sat at a large round table with Kitty Wallis, her husband Julian, Brett Styles, Cheryl, and some of the media team. Oliver's mother was a huge hit, regaling them with stories from Oliver's childhood that made him blush like a schoolboy. After the main course, Kitty stood to make a toast.

'Ok everyone, I propose a toast to my wonderful co-star... no, actually, to his mother.' She looked at Betty and raised her glass.

'Betty Wilkins, you're a star and you raised a star. To Betty Wilkins!'

'Betty Wilkins!' They all raised their glasses as Betty looked around the table beaming. Oliver pulled her towards him and kissed her cheek.

'Now then Oliver,' his mum whispered, 'next time I want to be sitting between you and your girlfriend.'

Oliver looked at his dear Mum and smiled. 'You and me both! There never seems the time with the shooting schedules and...'

'What about you and Cheryl?' His mum threw Cheryl a not-too-subtle smile.

'Mum... she's a dear friend, like the sister I never had.' Oliver turned to Cheryl and mouthed *'help'*.

'Well, *dear friend or not,* you couldn't do much better than a girl like that.'

'Mum...' Oliver started.

'Sorry dear, we'll chat later,' his mother stood, 'I have to pay a visit to the little girl's room, I think I just saw Shirley Bassey going in there.'

* * * * * * * * *

After a tearful goodbye, Oliver departed London to complete the tour of Europe and return to the filming of *In Stitches,* which finally wrapped the following February. After the success of *Stealth,* Kitty and Precious Studios were rubbing their hands.

Oliver had signed a three-movie deal for the *Stitches* franchise, and although his role wasn't the lead, it proved to be a strong, story-led, character. The second movie in the franchise, *A Stitch in Time*, was due to begin shooting in July and, in between, he had photo calls and the media tour of *In Stitches* to fill his time. But thoughts of the USB were never far from his mind.

* * * * * * * * *

One rainy April day, Cheryl messaged to say she'd e-mailed the new script for *A Stitch in Time, so* Oliver opened his laptop to take a look. On the wall by the countertop was a row of key hooks and there staring at him like a head swinging in a noose was the skull keyring, daring him to have another go.

He sighed, lifted it from the hook, and plugged it in. The photographs still held their mystery, no matter how many times he zoomed in and out, scrutinizing every pixel. He shut them down and was about to close the directory when something struck him. His curser was resting on the first photograph, of the waterfall, and at the bottom of the directory it read '1 item selected 4.41MB'. Oliver was no IT wizard, but he knew that photos were usually around a couple of hundred kilobytes, not four megabytes, that was a pretty large file. But it was only an ordinary photograph. He held his curser over the next photo, 4.52MB, and the third, 2.80MB. This wasn't right, photos didn't contain this much computer information. Oliver had had a breakthrough, but what to do about it? It was time to bring in an expert. So, he called Cheryl.

Cheryl frowned at the screen.

'You're right, these aren't just photographs, they contain something else.'

'Yes, but what?' Oliver was frustrated.

Cheryl checked the laptop, 'Look at the time.'

Oliver frowned, 'What? What does that tell you?'

'It tells me it's wine o'clock! Make yourself useful and pour some.' Cheryl enjoyed ordering him about.

'Ok, wine coming up.'

Cheryl typed away as Oliver poured two glasses and waited in anticipation.

Cheryl struck a key. 'Got it!'

'Got it? Got what?' Oliver sat next to her.

'Ok, so I downloaded some software which opens hidden files within files.' She was staring at the screen impatiently, as a blue line was filling up an empty chamber.

'And...?' Oliver looked at her.

The chamber was now full.

'Eh, voila!' Cheryl exclaimed. 'Each photograph contains two files. The first one is the photograph of the waterfall but embedded in that photograph is another file that you can't see.'

'Cheryl, how do you know how to do all of this?'

'I was head of the computer club at school, and besides, I'm a PA, you pay me to know all of this stuff.'

Oliver looked at the screen. 'But what is it?'

'It's a sound file, a recording of some sort.' Cheryl frowned as she double-clicked on the audio icon. They both listened intently as the file opened.

It was Brett's voice.

'*But you know it's illegal Kitty.*' Cheryl stared at Oliver and mouthed '*It's Brett*'.

'*Yes, but I had to raise the money somehow,*' this was Kitty. '*And it's not hurting anyone.*'

'*Well not physically, no, but I'm uneasy about it, Kitty. Is there no other way? No other investors?*'

'*Look, Brett, we have to drive up the stock prices a little more and then we sell high and make the shortfall we need.*'

'*Are you talking weeks or days?*' Brett seemed anxious.

'*Only a few days, then it's all over and Precious Studios can get off the ground.*'

Cheryl pulled a face; she couldn't believe what she was hearing.

'*I'll be glad when it's at an end.*' Oliver could tell Brett was pacing. '*Won't the authorities be suspicious?*'

'*Apparently not, nothing can be traced back to me. The media hype for the shares came from unknown sources, so the trail of breadcrumbs leads nowhere. We're in the clear Brett.*'

Then the recording ended.

'Wow!' Oliver sat back and reached for his wine.

'Double wow.' Cheryl did the same. 'So,' she continued, 'Kitty is involved in some illegal transactions. I've heard of this sort of thing before.'

'Have you? What does it mean?' Oliver looked at Cheryl with a frown.

'You own majority shares in a company and drive up the price of the shares with misleading information in the media. Information that makes people buy shares and when the value is high, because of the sudden interest, you sell your majority for a healthy profit, then the shares plummet. It's called Pump and Dump.'

'That sounds *really* dodgy.' Oliver wasn't sure what to think.

'Yes, but she got away with it.'

'Until now maybe, but I have this recording. What do I do with it?' Oliver's mind was struggling to get to grips with everything.

'Oliver, don't forget there are two more files.'

'Oh Christ, what will they hold?' Oliver frowned.

'There's only one way to find out, and whilst I'm extracting the other two files, we need more wine.' She held up her empty glass and got to work on the two remaining image files.

The second audio was again, Kitty and Brett.

'I want that man off my film. He's useless and now he's becoming a nuisance.' Kitty was angry.

'Well, I could say I told you...' Brett was interrupted.

'Brett, I don't want to hear I told you so! Do something about him. He's done all of this to himself. God, how I've tried with him, he's had more chances than I care to remember.'

'What if he sues us? It could cost a fortune,' Brett reasoned with Kitty.

'I don't care what it takes, do it!' Kitty raised her voice

Then another voice was heard in the background, but it was muffled.

Kitty raised her voice, *'Julian, is that you?'*

Then louder, 'Julian darling?'

Julian's voice could be heard in the distance.

'Kitty! I've come back for my hat, this sun's not good on a bald coot like me.'

'He can't have heard anything Kitty.' Brett was whispering again.

Then the file ended.

Cheryl sighed. 'Well, they certainly didn't like Rick Krane.'

'Yes, but that wasn't news, everyone knew that,' Oliver puzzled.

'Yes, but Rick Krane's dead, remember.'

The audio suddenly took on a different meaning.

Oliver stared at Cheryl, 'You don't think that Kitty...?'

Cheryl pulled a face in a 'maybe she did think' kind of way.

'Let's hear the third recording.' Oliver looked back at the screen and Cheryl clicked play.

Kitty's was the first voice they heard. *'Hmmmm, Oliver Wilkins...'*

Oliver looked at Cheryl with wide eyes as she pointed back at him.

'He fits the bill, Kitty.' She was, again, talking with Brett.

Kitty answered him, *'Doesn't he just? Let's get him in and see what he's about, we might have got lucky with this one.'*

'Ok, I'll get Jennifer on it first thing tomorrow, but not a whiff of this to Rick, he'll sue your ass off.' Brett was being his usual efficient self.

'After all his drinking and drugs, he won't be able to afford to sue anyone,' Kitty snapped... and the recording ended.

Chery looked at Oliver. 'So, they planned to replace Rick from the beginning.'

'Yes... and people are always saying I have a resemblance to him.' Oliver sighed. 'These files are damning, especially the first one about the stocks, they could ruin Kitty.'

'Yes, they could, and we don't know what their involvement was with Rick Krane's death.'

'He was blackmailing her with this. Do you think I should speak with Kitty about it? Or Brett?' Oliver looked to Cheryl for answers.

'No, not yet. I think we should wait and think things through first.'

Oliver put his head in his hands, 'They only booked me to get rid of Rick Krane.'

'Hey, buck up!' Cheryl jibed, 'At least you proved your worth. They wouldn't have used you for the *Stitches* films otherwise, and you're a huge hit with the public, something they could never have foreseen, so get over yourself. And you, Oliver Diamond, can pour me another glass of wine whilst we figure out what this all means and what we're going to do about it.'

Cheryl was a great personal assistant.

Chapter Thirty-Six

THEN

All Will Be Revealed

Charlie returned to her hotel after the lawyer's meeting. She wasn't flying until that evening, so she relaxed in the large ornate bathtub, going over the events of the past two days in her head. The funeral yesterday was weird, with William showing up and then seeing him lurk outside the lawyer's office that morning. Also, who was the young girl at the funeral with the sunglasses and where did she vanish to? The will reading wasn't without its moments either, but why had Aunt Sophia left so much to William? She'd always said she despised him and whenever she spoke of him, she got so worked up.

* * * * * * * * *

After Charlie dressed, she sat down at the desk to study the photograph. Her father and uncle looked so sweet and innocent, grinning out of their space helmets. She rubbed the misty glass with her sleeve to get a better look, but it was still blurry. She lifted the back off the frame and the photograph slipped onto the desk along with a folded piece of paper. When she looked closely, her father wearing the 'J' jumper was smiling sweetly whereas William, in the 'W' jumper, seemed to be sneering whilst strangling the albino rabbit in his hand. Yes, James was definitely grinning, but William had an evil smile. The dead rabbit's pink eyes staring ahead sent a chill down her spine. No wonder Aunt Sophia had a strange look on her face. She'd called William the black sheep and it looked like he was a very odd child indeed. Charlie turned the photograph over and discovered her aunt's handwriting...

'Me and my little babies... July 1969'

It was at the same time man had landed on the moon. *So that's why they were wearing those homemade helmets,* Charlie thought to herself. She opened the folded document. It was baby Charlie's death certificate.

Name: Charles Black

Sex: Boy

Date of Birth: 3rd March 1958

Cause of Death: Placental Abruption

Father's Name: this box had a line through it.

Mother's name: Sophia Black

Charlie frowned as read again, 'Mother's Name – Sophia Black? *My* little babies?' Then it hit her, 'Of course!' She wasn't her aunt at all, she was her grandmother. Sophia was James and William's mother, that's what she wanted Charlie to find out. Her aunt's... no... her grandmother's ramblings about James and William now made perfect sense. The triplets were *her* babies and that's why she'd been so upset about the third triplet, '*Little Charlie*', dying during childbirth.

Charlie read the last box on the death certificate.

Distinguishing Marks: Albino

Albino? Poor Sophia and poor little Charlie. She looked at the photograph one more time, then it struck her. William was playing a cruel joke. This eleven-year-old boy was holding a dead albino rabbit in place of his dead brother. Charlie shuddered, that was some sick child. She gathered her belongings and left her room to check out. She asked the concierge to collect her suitcase and organize a taxi in thirty minutes. Crossing the foyer, she ordered a coffee and sat reviewing old shots on her camera.

The photograph in her bag was never far from her thoughts. She retrieved it and as she was studying the macabre group intently, she didn't notice the man at the next table looking at her. Her coffee arrived and she looked up to see William Black sitting there, smiling.

'You!' Charlie didn't know what to do, he'd taken her by surprise.

'Please don't be alarmed, I wanted to see you before you left.'

'How did you know...? Have you been following me?' Charlie wasn't happy.

'Yes, I'm sorry to admit it, I needed to explain...' He began to say.

Charlie looked across at the receptionist who was staring at her computer screen.

'Explain what? How you killed my father and now have inherited a million dollars from your sister, who isn't your sister but your mother?' Charlie spat out her words, her eyes darting around the empty foyer. Thankfully they were tucked in a corner and not many people were around at that time of the day.

'Charlie...' he sighed.

'What?' She'd caught him off-guard. 'Sophia made sure I knew the truth, she left me Charles' death certificate with this'. She threw the photo on the table in front of William.

'You know that much, yes Sophia was our mother, but we didn't discover the truth ourselves until we were in our mid-teens. The truth that we're bastard children.'

Charlie stared at William, 'Look at yourself in this photograph, holding a dead albino rabbit in place of your brother Charlie. You were some sick child.'

William looked at the photograph and then at Charlie. He opened his mouth to say something and then sat back with a sigh. Charlie looked at him intently.

'The nurse from the home said you visited Sophia.'

William looked down. 'Yes, to say goodbye.'

Charlie stared at him, her eyes searching his face.

'I saw you that night, the night my father was killed.' A tear ran down her face. 'I've had nightmares all my life, with parts missing but now they're complete. It was you I saw over his body.'

'Yes Charlie, it was me...' William started to say.

'Don't call me Charlie, you don't have that right.' Charlie was getting upset, her heart racing.

'I promise you, it's not as it seems,' he tried to calm her.

'Then exactly how is it *Uncle* William, or Liam, or whoever you are?'

'Yes, I was there the night my brother died, but I didn't kill him, I swear.' He looked at Charlie directly as she searched his eyes. Charlie was confused, he looked as if he was telling the truth.

'Then who did kill him?' A tear ran down Charlie's face.

William moved closer to Charlie. 'We were in business together, me and… James. We'd bought a large warehouse ripe for conversion. One of our business partners raised the money, only we found him out to be dishonest. We discovered he'd been portraying himself as an investment banker and swindled hundreds of people out of their life savings.'

'But why did he kill my father?' Charlie wiped a tear away.

'James threatened him, he said he was going to go to the police and that would have ruined him. It transpired he had mafia connections and was not the sort of person you threaten. I'd come to warn James but arrived too late.'

'But you disappeared, why?' Charlie was trying to piece everything together.

William looked at Charlie and sighed. 'It's complicated. He'd got what he wanted. It was too late for James, but not for me; I couldn't bring James back.'

'So, you ran?' Charlie looked at him in disbelief.

'He was my *brother*, my *brother*! I loved him and I think about him every day.' He looked at her in earnest.

Charlie stared at her uncle, 'What's his name? This crooked partner, who killed my father.'

William sighed, resigned to his fate. 'His name is Thomas Hassler. He was arrested trying to leave the neighborhood and sent to prison.'

Charlie was stunned for a few seconds. No, it couldn't be the same man, could it? The blood drained from her face.

'Are you ok?' William leaned into her.

'Er, yes... yes I'm fine.' She didn't know what to do. Could Thomas Hassler from the department store and the racecourse have been the man responsible for her father's death? She needed to think. Charlie composed herself.

'How long had you known him, this Thomas Hassler?'

William sat back in his seat. 'James first met him in St. Moritz at a business conference before you were born.'

'St. Moritz?'

'Yes,' James continued, 'in fact, it was the same conference where he met your mother. He kept in touch with Thomas, and they would meet up occasionally in New York.'

Charlie stopped him. 'My father met my mother in St. Moritz?' This was news to her.

'Yes, she was on holiday with her family and they both instantly "clicked". A year later they were married in New York, and you came along shortly after.'

Charlie looked at William, 'I've met Thomas Hassler.'

William's face changed, 'What? Are you sure?'

'Yes, I'm certain. But you said he was arrested.'

'He was sentenced to life imprisonment for the shooting but was released after only nine years. He always pleaded self-defense, saying there was a fight. There was no fight, but evidence became shaky, to say the least, and after a retrial, he was out.'

Charlie told William about the events at *White Turf*. She couldn't believe she'd been in the presence of her father's killer. Had Thomas Hassler known about the fixed horserace all along? Ingrid said he didn't have anything to do with it, or so she'd thought. *He* was Ingrid's original target, unless Frank had gone rogue and decided to work alone, framing Thomas Hassler?

'I must go.' Charlie stood, her mind racing.

William stopped her, holding her arm. 'Are you ok?' She turned to him, he looked genuinely concerned.

'Yes, I'm fine, I have to get to the airport.'

He handed her a card. 'Please take this and call me when things have settled down. I mean it... Charlie.'

Charlie looked at him and then at the card. She put it in her pocket and turned back to him, 'By the way, who was the girl at the funeral yesterday?'

'Girl? I didn't notice, to be honest, I was too preoccupied.'

Charlie caught the concierge waving at her, 'One more thing before I go...'

William looked at her, 'What?'

She fixed her eyes on him. 'In my dream... my nightmare,' she corrected herself, 'you left my father's body and hugged me...'

'Yes...'

'Why?'

At that moment the concierge bounded up to her hopping from foot to foot.

'Madam, your taxi is waiting for you.'

She didn't wait for his reply. 'I have to go, goodbye William.'

She turned and left him staring after her, wondering if he'd said too much. Charlie had already crossed paths with Thomas Hassler and that wasn't good. That wasn't good because William Black knew that Thomas Hassler was a very, very dangerous man.

Chapter Thirty-Seven

THEN

Puuuurfect

Oliver's mother called to say she'd received a telephone call from a Jonathan 'somebody-or-other'.

'He said he worked with you at The National Theatre in… hang on, I wrote it down. Tight as a… Drones Knickers or something. He saw your film, *Stealth* and thought it was great. Do you remember him, Oliver?'

Oliver pulled a face, 'Er… *Titus Andronicus*, yes Mum, I remember Jonathan.'

'Well, next time you're back in England, he wants to meet you, for old times' sake. He said he was a close friend.'

'Ok Mum, thanks for the message.' Oliver had no intention of meeting up with Jonathan.

'I've got to go now love,' she began speaking quickly, 'Alan's picking me up in five and I've still got my hair-rollers in. We're going for a rubber tonight.'

'A rubber?' Oliver hoped he didn't know what she was talking about.

'It's a Bridge term darling, speak soon, oh and find yourself a decent girlfriend.'

Oliver laughed as he put the phone down, then he frowned. Jonathan told his mum they were 'close friends'. Close friends? There weren't too many of those in Hollywood, he only really had Cheryl. Since they heard the voice files, he'd kept his distance from Kitty and Brett. The second film, *A Stitch in Time,* had begun production, and Oliver was loving his role yet again. The majority of his screen time was with Mr. Stitch himself, Jason Ross. They would be shooting in LA until the new year, after which the shoot moved to Europe for a couple of months.

Oliver and Cheryl discussed the secret recordings between Kitty and Brett on many occasions. What were they supposed to do? Cheryl told him he should have left the keyring where it was, by the pool. This only antagonized Oliver, he wasn't one for hindsight.

As he was leaving for the studio one morning, his post arrived. He flicked through it, and all was pretty standard apart from a black envelope with gold writing. It was a hand-written invitation, but who sends invitations in the post anymore? Oliver opened the black velvet card and two small silver bracelets fell out with tags bearing a barcode. It was an invitation from Vixen to a 'sci-fi' themed party at her Malibu mansion this coming Saturday. *How interesting*, Oliver thought, *that would be one hell of a party*. He tossed the invite on the countertop along with the bracelets and left for a long day of gadgets and stunts.

* * * * * * * * *

After a grueling day on set, Brett visited Oliver's dressing room.

'Hey, Oliver.'

Oliver looked up from his script, 'Hi Brett, come in, how are you?'

Brett sat on the sofa by Oliver. 'I'm great, everything's great. Your dailies look awesome by the way.'

'I'm loving it.' Oliver had known Brett long enough to know he was after something.

'Oliver?' *Here it comes.*

Oliver looked up expectantly 'Yes?'

'Is everything ok?'

'Yes of course, what makes you say that?'

'Well... you've seemed a little distant recently. I noticed it a few weeks ago, and now Kitty's mentioned something to me.'

Oliver smiled, 'I'm fine Brett, it's probably the schedule, there's so much to do and think about. I've not meant to be distant; I promise,' Oliver lied.

Brett studied Oliver's face. 'Kitty's having a small dinner party a week on Saturday, she'd love you to come.'

Normally, Brett would have gone to Cheryl but now he was cornering him directly.

'Erm, next Saturday...?' Oliver started.

Brett leaned forward from the sofa and put his hand on Oliver's knee.

'Kitty wants you to be there.' He looked at Oliver and smiled.

Oliver caved in, 'Yes of course.'

'Great!' Brett stood and turned to leave.

Oliver called after him. 'Don't forget, no...'

'...peanuts.' Brett chimed, 'Your allergy... I remember.' He stopped at the door. 'Bring someone if you wish.'

Brett left the dressing room, leaving Oliver feeling guilty. They'd both changed his life beyond recognition and had been there for him when he moved from England. Maybe the dinner party would re-establish their friendship? But that was next weekend, this weekend he was taking Cheryl to a party she wouldn't forget for a very, very long time.

* * * * * * * * * *

Cheryl was beside herself when Oliver broke the news that she was to be his 'plus one' at Vixen's *party of the decade.* She agonized over what to wear.

'Sci-fi... mmm?' She sat on his sofa cradling a gin and tonic, whilst browsing magazines for inspiration.

'After turning up at Kitty's party as a banana a few years ago, and feeling a *right banana*, I'll be looking at something more subtle.' Oliver announced.

'Boring!!!!' Cheryl admonished him whilst staring at a photo of a much younger Jane Fonda as Barbarella.

Oliver peered over the back of the sofa.

'Look again Cheryl, I'm not going to Vixen's party with you dressed in a see-through Perspex corset'.

'I've got it!' Cheryl exclaimed turning her magazine to face him.

'A Smurf? They're not sci-fi.' He said, straight-faced.

'It's the Blue Man Group!' Cheryl threw a cushion at him.

He caught it. 'Again, not sci-fi!'

'What are you going as?' Cheryl pleaded.

'I'm going in a black suit and tie as *MIB – Men in Black* – and I don't care what you say, little Miss Bossyboots. While you choose your outfit I'm going to listen to some Kylie Minogue.' Oliver sat back and put on his black headphones.

Cheryl looked at him and exclaimed, 'That's it! I know exactly who I'm going as!'

* * * * * * * * *

Vixen's Malibu mansion was perched on a cliff overlooking the Pacific Ocean. Music could be heard drifting – no, thundering – down the coast for miles. Vixen liked it loud, and no one complained, after all, she was Vixen and could do exactly what she wanted. The house was an illuminated modern mansion at the end of a hidden driveway. The car dropped Oliver and Cheryl on the white gravel, and they crunched their way to the security gates. It was like a hi-tech airport with guards in black face masks scanning everyone and checking bags. Every guest had to pass through an x-ray before gaining entry. Oliver and Cheryl had their bracelets scanned by a faceless guard and then walked through the x-ray machine. Oliver, dressed in his *Men in Black* attire, was good to go, but as Cheryl walked through the x-ray an alarm sounded followed by blue flashing lights, causing everyone to stop and look at her.

'What?' Cheryl blushed.

Oliver sighed, raised his eyes to heaven, and looked back at Cheryl with a questioning expression, whilst a guard without a mask escorted her to a table at one side.

'Princess Leia!' the guard smiled at her... 'Do you have a mobile telephone on your person?'

Cheryl was wearing a large cream sheet, tied at the waist with a silver belt. Her look was completed by a huge brown wig, with the trademark side-cinnamon-buns framing her head, like old-fashioned headphones.

'A mobile telephone?' She repeated innocently, looking at him as if he was speaking an alien language. Oliver joined her side.

'Cheryl...' He frowned at her like a disgruntled parent, '...I told you, *no* mobiles.' She looked at him and sighed.

'Mobile?' She laughed as though it was the most ridiculous suggestion. 'As if I would bring a mobile...' She was persistent.

The guard nodded at Oliver and looked back at Princess Leia, with a smile.

'I have a photo... from the scanner... of a mobile phone.' The guard looked her in the eyes and as she stood her ground he continued, 'And I know *exactly* where it is.' He didn't break his smile.

She sighed and then did a 'not very princess-like', move. Hoisting her dress up she retrieved the mobile from her pants.

'Ok, ok, it was for emergencies.' She slammed her mobile on the table and snatched a key from the guard.

'You may collect it on your exit Princess. Have a nice night and I hope you find your Luke Skywalker.'

Cheryl turned to a bemused Oliver and mimed 'Sorry'.

'Come on Cheryl, let's go party. I think I spotted Elton John and David Furnish dressed as Batman and Robin.'

* * * * * * * * *

The entrance to the mansion was lined with CO_2 machines blasting up into the air, with a loud 'whooshing' noise. As Oliver led Cheryl up the steps, the CO_2 shot up causing Cheryl to scream and grab the nearest guest to steady herself. She thanked him and he smiled as he leaned into her.

'No problem, it's not the first time I've done that.' The guest, wearing a Ghostbusters jumpsuit, chuckled as he went ahead through the entrance.

'Who was that?' Cheryl asked. 'He looked familiar.'

Oliver roared with laughter again, 'That was Mark Hamill.'

She frowned at him quizzically.

'Luke Skywalker... Mark Hamill?' Oliver grinned.

Cheryl's eyes widened. 'Let's find the bar, I need a drink!'

The hallway was an amazing sight, with all manner of space suits and superheroes chatting, drinking, and generally drifting around. Huge planets were suspended from the ceiling at varying heights, all slowly turning and changing places like some demented galaxy, far, far away.

Cheryl downed her Galactic Cocktail and turned to Oliver. 'Come on let's dance!'

Outside, the music was frenetic, and the pool was covered with a black dance floor. '*Wise move*' Oliver thought absently. Girls in white body paint, holding spherical lights, were suspended from the trees. Hanging on silver silks, they moved with the music, swaying like some bizarre tree lanterns. At one side stood a large rocket reaching for the starry sky, and perched inside the airlock was a group dressed in spacesuits playing the latest hits.

Cheryl's jaw dropped open as she recognized the singer emerging through the smoke from within the rocket.

'Oh my god, it's Cher!' Cheryl exclaimed, transfixed as the crowd cheered to Cher's 'Believe'.

Five songs into the set, Oliver shouted over the music.

'I'm going to look for the toilets.'

Cheryl nodded. 'Ok, you know where to find me. Whilst Cher's here, Cheryl's here!'

Oliver moved back inside as a 'Chewbacca' dragged Cheryl off for a frantic dance. There were so many famous faces that he didn't know where to look. What he didn't realize was that he too was now a famous face. When he was looking at the likes of Leonardo or Demi or Brad, *they* were looking at Oliver Diamond. He eventually found a bathroom on the first landing off a silver staircase and entered as Matt Damon was leaving.

'Hey! Hi, Oliver Diamond!' Matt Damon was beaming at him. 'Loved *Stealth,* by the way, see you around!'

Oliver was speechless and couldn't wait to tell Cheryl he'd been in the bathroom directly after the very *Talented Mr. Ripley*.

Making his way downstairs he grabbed a beer from a roller-skating 'space-waiter' and leaned on a marble pillar watching a girl twisting and winding herself on a silver silk. Suddenly a voice whispered in his ear.

'I hear Men in Black save the universe, how about saving a damsel in distress?'

He turned, the red hair and amazing blue eyes gave her away, it was Vixen dressed like Catwoman in a black leather zip-up jumpsuit, with thigh-length purple boots. The zip was virtually all the way down, exposing her navel, and she wore an eye mask and a pair of ears, her red hair falling around her shoulders.

Oliver smiled. 'I think you're more than capable of taking care of yourself.'

She purred at him, 'Follow me, I can show you where the real party is.' She then turned and walked upstairs without a backward glance. Oliver couldn't help himself, he took a swig of his beer, deposited the bottle with the roller-skating waiter, and took the stairs two at a time.

Chapter Thirty-Eight

Seize the Day

Charlie returned to St. Moritz to finish her last term. She couldn't wait to tell Henry all about the meeting with her uncle William and what he'd told her about Thomas Hassler's involvement in her father's death.

'I knew there was something bad about that man,' Henry said as Charlie divulged the details.

'Yes, but what are the chances that years later, I come across the man who killed my father?'

'What do you mean?' Henry frowned.

Charlie sighed, 'Well, it seems one hell of a coincidence, that's all.'

They called Ingrid for more information on Thomas Hassler, but she didn't know any more than they did. He must have been involved in the horse scam, but she only ever received instructions from Frank Hoffman. However, she always suspected Frank was working for someone else.

Charlie and Henry visited St. Moritz in search of more information on Thomas Hassler. They decided to visit their favorite coffee shop behind La Via Serlas before dropping into the department store in search of him.

'Charlie, find a table whilst I order the coffees. We'll be in and out in no time.'

Charlie looked around, it was rather full apart from some spare chairs at a table in the window where a young guy was cradling a hot chocolate. He was closing his eyes and didn't see Charlie approach.

'Ahem.' He didn't flinch as Charlie stared at him. 'Erm, excuse me, do you mind...?' She indicated the spare chairs. He opened his eyes startled and pulled the cord of his earphones in a downward motion causing the buds to spring out of his ears, one landing in his hot chocolate.

'I'm so sorry *mademoiselle*, I was a million kilometers away.' He spotted the floating earbud. 'Shit!'

'So, it's ok if I sit here?'

'Yes, of course!' He scooped the earbud from his drink and wrapped it in a tissue.

Charlie sat and noticed that he was dressed in a suit and was wearing a badge from the department store. His skin was smooth as glass and the color of midnight.

'Please, do get back to your music video, or whatever you were watching.'

The boy looked puzzled, 'Music video? Er *non*, I was watching a demonstration on how to locate a tracking device if someone were to plant one on you.'

Charlie looked puzzled, 'Er, oh, I see... as you do...', she read his badge, '...Simba.'

'I am studying criminal law, but I am more to the technology side of things.'

'Is that Simba like the...'

Simba rolled his eyes, '...*The Lion King*, yes.'

'...and you work at the department store around the corner?'

'Yes, to help me through university, well, more like pocket money. Next year I move back to live with my father in Los Angeles.'

'I see...'

Simba looked up and exclaimed, 'Miss Henry!'

Charlie turned to Henry who was approaching with two rather full Skinny Lattes.

Henry had the expression of, 'I know the face but...'

Charlie jumped in, 'Henry, Simba was telling me that he works at the department store.'

The penny dropped, 'Oh, yes, of course! Simba, how are you?'

'How are you Miss Henry, have you had any more fainting episodes?'

Henry and Charlie exchanged glances, 'Er, no Simba, I'm perfectly fine now.'

Charlie was bemused, 'How exactly do you two know each other?'

Henry sat and squeezed Simba's arm, 'This is my friend from... Zimbabwe? Simba, this is Charlie.'

Charlie frowned, 'Zimbabwe?'

'My mother...'

'How are things at the store?' Henry butted in.

Simba smiled showing a set of beautiful teeth, 'Oh you know, really boring actually.'

Charlie looked at Henry, 'Er, Simba, have you seen your boss, Mr. Hassler, recently?'

'Mr. Thomas? Er no, not since he went back to America.'

Charlie felt deflated, 'He's back in America?'

'Yes, he was only here for a short time.' Simba looked around the shop and then fell into a deep whisper, 'Rumour has it that he is not in his mother's best books.'

Henry moved closer, 'Really?'

Simba continued, 'Yes, he's a bit of a bad boy. He was always ok with me, but staff heard his mother shouting at him in his office many times and then he disappeared.'

'What was the argument about?' Charlie was curious.

'The only thing worth remembering was her saying you'll send me to an early grave. Staff say he returned to America, permanently.'

'Simba, can you do me a favor?' Henry turned on the charm, opening her eyes wide.

'Yes Miss Henry, but you can stop it with the flirting. I bat for the other side, so to speak.'

Charlie chuckled, 'Henry, you're gaydar is way off.'

'What do you want Miss Henry?'

'Here are our numbers,' Henry scribbled on a paper napkin, 'if you hear anything more about Thomas Hassler can you give one of us a call?'

'But of course,' Simba reached into his jacket pocket and produced a smart business card, 'and if you ever need any IT work doing, then please call me.'

Henry frowned, 'IT?'

Charlie studied his card. SIMBARASHE SIBANDA I.T. Wizard.

'Information Technology, Henry.'

'Yes, basically, I can provide a good service in spyware or other useful gadgets.'

Henry looked at Simba, 'Really?'

'My main customers are wives spying on their husbands, but I can even hack a hacker. Don't be fooled by my expert perfume-spraying technique.' With that, he smiled, produced a small sample bottle, sprayed the air between them, and left the table with a flourish.

Charlie and Henry sat back and laughed.

'He is one hell of a character Henry.'

'Isn't he just, but how did you know he was...?

'Henry, open your eyes. I'll keep his details though, you never know.'

'Come on, drink your latte, we've got shopping to do.'

* * * * * * * * *

Any further digging resulted in a blank regarding Thomas Hassler's earlier life, and it seemed his mother was hiding a few secrets of her own. Charlie wrote Marcus a long letter about her discoveries. After his return to Spain, phone calls became more infrequent. They both knew their relationship was over but would remain firm friends.

As the term was drawing to an end, Simba contacted Charlie with some news. He heard gossip from the shop floor that Thomas Hassler had been arrested in New York for an attempted horserace scam at Belmont Park.

'Simba, thank you. I owe you one!'

'No problem, Miss Charlie. I never liked him anyway. Don't forget, if you want anything hacked, I'm your guy.'

'Mmm, I will remember that, Simba.' Charlie's mind had drifted. Justice at last, and she had to admit that the news of him behind bars did instill a little relief.

* * * * * * * * * *

After St. Mary's, Henry arranged to visit her father, Dimitri, on his luxury yacht in the South of France. A few days later Charlie would join her for a week's holiday before deciding what to do with her inheritance and the rest of her life. She'd reached her twentieth birthday in February, and the funds were due from her father's estate. Henry's father had recently made a fortune in a new scheme and whilst on his yacht, Charlie wanted to find out more about his investment.

Charlie decided to drive to St. Tropez. It would take about seven or eight hours and she was looking forward to the open road and solitude. As she drove her rented BMW sports past Lake Como her mind turned to William Black. She still couldn't think of him as 'Uncle William', after all, she didn't know of his existence until a few years ago. She hadn't contacted him since their meeting in Boston and felt bad about it, she didn't know why, but she did. Maybe one day she'd be in the right frame of mind to make the call, but not today. She also secretly hoped that one day she would come face to face with Thomas Hassler again.

* * * * * * * * *

Charlie arrived in St. Tropez early evening and parked off the harbor making her way on foot to Henry's father's yacht. Everywhere was busy with people strolling in the warmth of the evening and artists lined the edge of the harbor sketching eager faces in the amber light of a nearby lamppost. A band played the last notes of a song to enthusiastic applause from the gathered crowd. The lead singer, sporting a cream fedora hat, leaned into the microphone, 'Any requests?' A family strolled by. The mother was holding hands with a teenage boy and girl and the father, sporting their younger son on his shoulders, shouted 'Mac the Knife!' to an agreeable crowd. Charlie looked at them with a tinge of envy, *one day*, she thought to herself. As the band launched into the song Henry emerged from the crowd.

'Oh, I'm so glad you're here,' she hugged her friend tightly, 'I've missed you so much!'

Charlie looked at her and laughed, 'But I only saw you two days ago.'

'I know! That's forever when you've spent a day with my father.' Henry linked her arm and walked her to where her father's yacht was moored.

Henry called it a yacht; Charlie called it a galleon. It resembled something from the ultimate pirate movie, constructed from brightly polished wood with brass fittings. Charlie noticed the name painted on the stern in gold.

'Carpe Diem,' Charlie pointed, 'I remember you saying that to me on my birthday. The day we went to St. Moritz and met Ingrid for the first time.'

Henry frowned, 'Did I?'

'Yes, you said it means "seize the day".'

Henry shrugged, 'Maybe, come on, there's lots to show you.'

A short 'gangplank' led them onboard where Charlie was greeted by a butler dressed in tailcoats and bow tie. He nodded and took her car keys, saying that he would arrange for her luggage to be brought aboard immediately.

'Henry this is incredible.' Charlie wasn't often lost for words.

The deck was dark wood and the brass fittings around the ship were highly polished. The mast stood proud and strong, with its cream sails neatly stowed away on its cross beams.

'Come on, I'll show you to your cabin and then we can change for dinner.' Henry grabbed Charlie's hand, dragging her towards the living quarters.

* * * * * * * * *

An hour later they arrived on deck ready for dinner. A large wooden table was laid with the finest gold cutlery, white plates, and dishes. The centerpiece was a large gold candelabra with arms stretching out in all directions. Henry oozed sophistication wearing a figure-hugging white dress with a scooped neckline and low back. Her raven hair fell around her shoulders, shining in the moonlight. She completed the look with large-hooped earrings and lashings of lip-gloss. Her big, brown eyes sparkled mischievously as she showed Charlie the view from the deck.

Charlie wore red, high-waisted trousers and a white sleeveless shirt with her hair curled and just the right amount of make-up. At twenty years of age, these two girls were ready to take on the world. Charlie snapped photos of Henry, who was giving her over-the-top poses as she giggled and pouted her lips. They stopped and looked out into the harbor at the many beautiful yachts moored for the night.

As Charlie was thinking about how much she would like to own a yacht, her thoughts were interrupted by a booming voice.

'My gorgeous daughter!' Charlie turned to see Henry's father, Dimitri Diakos, with a beautiful woman on his arm. Charlie knew exactly who she was, the resemblance was quite remarkable, it was Henry's mother.

'*Maman*?' Henry shrieked, running to her mother, throwing her arms around her like a clumsy infant.

'What are you doing here?' Henry couldn't believe her eyes, 'And how did you sneak on board without me knowing?'

Her mother kissed her cheeks and smiled. 'I know how much you like surprises.'

Her father looked down on her, 'Where are your manners, Henry? Please do the introductions.'

Henry introduced Charlie and took her father by the arm leading him to the table.

'Papa, you invited Maman for a holiday! What's going on? Tell all!'

Charlie smiled at Henry's mother. Yvette Paradis was a very famous French fashion model. She was immensely popular, and the most beautiful woman Charlie had ever seen, she took her breath away.

'So, you're a keen photographer?' Yvette indicated to Charlie's camera.

'Er, yes, I take lots of photographs. It's always been my thing.'

Yvette looked back at Henry and her ex-husband, Dimitri.

'She's always been a daddy's girl, and you can assure Henry for the record, we're not back together again.'

Charlie smiled as Yvette linked her arm. 'I happened to be in town for a Vogue shoot and Dimitri told me Henry was visiting with her friend from school. I couldn't resist, but I had no idea her friend was so beautiful.'

Charlie blushed, not knowing what to say. Yvette Paradis said *she* was beautiful. Yvette smiled at her. 'Come on let's eat, I'm starving.'

Dinner was a grand affair and the champagne flowed. After a dessert called 'floating island' which involved meringue, cream, cream, and more cream, Dimitri looked at Charlie.

'So, Henry tells me you are moving to Los Angeles.'

'Yes, that's the plan.'

'I do business there from time to time, it's a tough city. What will you do there?'

'Well, the one thing I love is taking photographs. I was thinking of setting up my own studio.'

'I've tried to convince her to be a lady of leisure,' Henry joked as she prodded Charlie, 'but she won't hear of it.'

Dimitri looked at his daughter sternly, 'Maybe you should listen to Charlie, there's nothing wrong with working for a living.'

Henry frowned, 'It's not like she needs the money, she has a ton of it coming to her any day.'

'Henry!' Charlie shook her head and laughed. 'It's true, I don't have to work but I need to. I want to do something I enjoy, and I want to be a successful woman.'

'Here, here!' Yvette banged the table a little too loudly and held her glass up for a refill.

Henry glared at her mother for being overzealous with her friend. 'I'll be settling soon and getting myself a job, just watch this space.'

Yvette smiled and turned towards Henry, 'And what industry will my princess be working in?'

Henry thought quickly, 'Something to do with music... erm... maybe a music producer.' Yvette rolled her eyes and took another drink from her bottomless wineglass as Dimitri frowned at his daughter.

'Mmmm, I'll believe it when I see it.' Dimitri leaned toward Charlie, 'After dinner, I'll take you to my office and show you the portfolio I invested in, it's quite remarkable.'

'Yes, Henry did mention something,' Charlie looked at Dimitri, 'That would be wonderful. I want to put the money somewhere safe and earn some interest before deciding what to do with it.'

'You're a very wise girl and I hope some of your wisdom will rub off on Henry.'

Henry screwed her face up. 'Don't worry about me Papa, I'll be successful, you wait and see.'

Yvette raised her glass, 'To successful women!'

She looked across the table at Charlie. 'I tell you what Charlie, tomorrow I have a free morning, why don't you test that camera of yours on a new model?'

Charlie was confused, 'New model?'

'Yes... moi!'

Eight courses and dinner was finally over. Yvette took to her bed a little worse for wear whilst Dimitri led Charlie to his study leaving Henry on deck finishing off the champagne, alone.

Dimitri talked Charlie through his investment portfolio and explained that in a space of sixty days he had received a whopping fifty percent return on his second investment. Charlie thought it sounded too good to be true and he admitted he'd felt the same, which is why his initial investment had been relatively small. When he gained a return of four hundred and three thousand dollars on a one-million-dollar investment over a mere forty-five days, he knew he couldn't lose. He plowed in much more the second time around to get a fifty percent return over sixty days.

The company, Hase International, had an office address in Nice. Charlie wanted to meet face to face, and so decided when she'd finished her time with Henry, she would pay them a visit.

'I'll set up a meeting with the CEO, a Mr. Beau Boucher.' Dimitri said as she left his office.

The following morning, Charlie was up early, leaving Henry sound asleep. Yvette had promised to be her model, and although she'd made the promise after her sixth glass of champagne, she was a woman of her word. Their location was the gorgeous yacht and with a backdrop of the Mediterranean, it couldn't be better. Charlie was in her element and Yvette looked stunning in her gold bikini. She was in her late thirties with the body of a twenty-year-old. After several shots around the deck, Yvette was sweating.

'Yvette, you're sweating,' Charlie frowned, 'have you had enough? I've plenty of shots.'

'No, we're not finished quite yet. Let's spice things up a bit.'

Yvette turned and climbed towards the center mast. Charlie had no idea what to expect but went with it. Yvette took a wooden bucket of water and emptied it over her head with a squeal of delight. Pulling her hair back off her face, she leaned back on the mast and tilted her face up towards the sun.

'Ok, shoot away.'

Charlie clicked from every angle.

Click *whirrrr*.

Click *whirrrr*.

Click *whirrrr*.

The shots were terrific, and Yvette looked a million dollars.

'Now we're done!' Yvette said climbing back down to the deck and into the doorway. Charlie followed, feeling elated, she'd never had such fun with her camera.

'I will sign a release for those photos, but I must vet what you use, that's all I ask.'

Charlie couldn't believe what had just happened. The photographs held more than monetary value and she well was aware that the world's top photographers would give their right arm to have taken them.

* * * * * * * * *

Yvette stayed for two more days and whilst Charlie found her to be great company she now knew where Henry's mischievous nature came from. Dimitri was a great host and Charlie and Henry spent most of their time together enjoying a week of shopping, drinking, and sunbathing. It was now time to do the 'grown-up' things, Charlie had to organize her life.

The following month, Henry's father was visiting LA on business. Henry would travel with him before moving back to her mother's apartment in Paris, so they arranged to meet up. But first Charlie would travel to Nice for her meeting with Beau Boucher, CEO of Hase International. *What a name, 'Beau Boucher'?* Charlie thought as she drove on the coastal road away from St. Tropez. She'd received confirmation of the inheritance deposited into her bank account and would feel much happier once it had been invested. She had plans for her new business but in the interim her lawyer, Thurgood Brown, reminded her that her father had been very shrewd. He believed money should make money. 'Earning not yearning,' he would say. This was a guaranteed high return on a short-term investment, and she knew her father would be proud of her. The inheritance from Sophia was set aside, two hundred thousand dollars for her photography studio space in Los Angeles. After her meeting at Hase International, she would drive to the airport hotel, return her hire car, and catch the early morning flight to LA, where a new chapter would begin.

The offices of Hase International were located in a building on the corner of Avenue Des Fleurs in the center of Nice. The building was built at the end of the nineteenth century, in the La Belle Epoque style, and Hase International took up residence on the upper two floors. The receptionist was dressed in an outfit from a Christian Dior runway show of the 1950s and completed her 'look' with horn-rimmed glasses.

Charlie read a framed quote on the wall opposite.

'Curiouser and Curiouser.'

Charlie removed her camera from her bag and crossed to get a better look. She took a shot of the quote. Click *whirrrr*. The receptionist looked up, cleared her throat, and smiled; Charlie smiled back.

'I like that. It's from *Alice in Wonderland*, isn't it?'

The receptionist looked at her with a cold stare and said, 'Lewis Carroll,' as she reached into her desk drawer. A door opened at the far end of the reception and a young, handsome guy strode out, arm outstretched.

'Miss Black, so sorry to have kept you, I'm Beau Boucher, please come into my office.'

Beau Boucher transpired to be a very amiable, thirty-something guy. Charlie shook his hand, smiled at the receptionist, who was now flicking through the latest edition of *Cosmopolitan*, and followed him. His office was very grand with a huge mahogany desk at one end and two sofas on either side of a low marble table, opposite. The walls were lined with sports photographs, which Charlie noted to be superb action shots: The Monaco Grand Prix, The French Winter Olympics, a Mediterranean Regatta, and even White Turf, in St. Moritz.

When Charlie mentioned Henry's father, Dimitri Diakos, Beau Boucher opened the champagne. The figures Beau gave her were very impressive and promised an incredible return in a relatively short space of time, as Dimitri had told her. Charlie was in no rush to use the money and decided to invest for a three-month period. Dimitri had reaped a good return, so Charlie should do even better with a longer investment. After Beau explained the contracts, Charlie took a breath. It was only for a few months, after that time she would be settled in LA and could then invest her money in property.

'Ok, where do I sign?' Charlie was eager to seal the deal.

After she put pen to paper Beau explained to Charlie what to expect over the following months. As he was talking, she noticed a photograph behind his chair of a girl in her late teens with ginger hair and freckles. She was holding up a large trophy that was so big it covered half of her face. The trophy read 'Paralympic Games – Atlanta'. Charlie thought she looked familiar.

'Is that your daughter?' Charlie blurted out.

Beau looked up, 'Sorry?' He followed her eye line and settled on the photograph.

'Er... no... that's my business partner's daughter... Siobhan. She's a champion swimmer, deaf and ninety percent blind.'

'What an accomplishment.' Charlie smiled.

Beau looked at Charlie, 'Yes, it's amazing what you can do with determination.'

Charlie shook Beau by the hand and after an 'Au revoir' to the receptionist, she made her way out into the Nice sunshine. She called into the bank to arrange the bank transfer, as promised, it was all very straightforward. However, she wasn't aware that after she left, Beau Boucher received a call from the Federal Correctional Institution in New York.

'Well? How did it go?'

'It was as you said Mr. Hassler,' Beau was beaming as he studied Charlie's signature, 'she was a pushover.'

'Good, good.' Thomas Hassler was smiling on the other end of the telephone from the prison corridor. 'Ok, Beau, it's time to move offices.'

Chapter Thirty-Nine

THEN

An Unexpected Guest

Vixen was as wild as they came. However, behind all the façade she was vulnerable and lacking in confidence, albeit a little out of control at times. Oliver awoke in her bed the following morning with an almighty hangover. They'd drunk countless bottles of champagne between them, before spending two hours in her dip-pool of a jacuzzi. He'd no idea what had happened to Cheryl, but she was a big girl and could look after herself. He showered in the luxurious bathroom, dressed quickly, and made his way downstairs in search of a ride home.

He was met with hordes of staff in black and white outfits, scurrying about like pieces in a manic chess game. Everyone was tidying and cleaning, removing all traces of the party. With no sign of Vixen, he ducked through the front doorway as two boys were struggling with an enormous red planet. The universe had finally imploded. A boy, standing on the gravel drive, shouted back to Oliver.

'Hey... can you bring out Mercury?' Oliver frowned as he continued, '...then we can get them all loaded in the lorry.'

Still dressed in his *Men in Black* attire, he blended in with the rest of the staff. He laughed looking down at his suit, causing his head to pound even more. The boy recognized Oliver and apologized profusely.

'Mr. D-D-Diamond...' he stammered, 'I'm so sorry sir, I didn't see it was you.'

'Hey it's ok, do you know where I can find a ride?'

'Yes sure, I'm Carl, one of Vixen's drivers, I can take you anywhere you wish.'

'That would be wonderful... thank you.' Oliver was grateful, all he wanted was to go home and sleep for a week.

During the ride home Oliver was awoken by the sound of a ringing telephone, Carl answered.

'Hi, Carl speaking.'

Vixen's voice filled the limousine. 'Carl, I believe you have some precious cargo.'

'Er... yes ma'am.' Carl smiled as he looked through his rear mirror.

'Don't call me ma'am, it makes me sound a hundred!'

'Sorry, ma'am... I mean, Miss Vixen.' Carl was getting hot under the collar.

'Oliver, I know you can hear me.' Vixen's voice bounced around the car.

'Yes Vixen, I can hear you, as can Carl your driver,' Oliver quickly added.

Vixen laughed. 'Well, my party turned out to be quite something else.'

Carl caught Oliver closing his eyes in his mirror.

'I hope you're not the type who gets what he wants, then never calls a girl again.'

Oliver cringed, 'No Vixen, I'm polite and very English.' Then he smiled, 'And I hope you're not the type who teases a vulnerable guy when he's many miles from home.'

Vixen roared, 'That's what I like about you English guys, you don't take yourself seriously.'

'But the question is...' Oliver said as Carl waited for his reply in anticipation, 'do you take anything seriously?'

There was a pause on the line and then Vixen chuckled.

'I can't help it if my default state is happy,' she countered. 'So, aren't you going to ask me to the movies or something?'

Carl locked eyes with Oliver.

'What? Popcorn in a lover's double seat at the back?' Oliver shouted into the air.

'I could book the entire movie theatre, and I was thinking more of a hotdog.'

Carl choked, making Oliver laugh.

'I tell you what Vixen, Kitty's having a dinner party this coming Saturday, why don't you come along?'

'What? As your date?' Vixen teased.

Carl looked into his mirror and grinned, he liked Oliver.

'Yes ok, as my date,' Oliver conceded.

'Fabulous!' The line went dead.

* * * * * * * * *

Kitty was expecting ten people for her 'soirée', as she liked to call it. To say she and Brett were surprised when Oliver showed up with Vixen on his arm would be an understatement. Julian, Kitty's husband, wasn't a fan. Not of her music at any rate, but that evening they saw a different side to the on-stage performer. Dressed in a long black dress cut down to her navel, she looked very chic. She was the perfect dinner guest, Oliver thought, as he observed her chatting to Brett.

They were in Kitty's living room enjoying pre-dinner drinks. To Oliver's left was Brett's plus-one, some wannabe actress from Texas called Lilly-May. Sitting on a low sofa across from Oliver and Vixen were a timid husband and wife from Idaho, who Julian had known since childhood, Dorothy and Vern, now retired and on vacation in LA. Dorothy couldn't take her eyes off Vixen and to her dismay, neither could her husband. Oliver noticed her poking Vern in the ribs when his drooling became too obvious. Vixen was leaning over the arm of the sofa chatting to Brett, her dress falling away revealing her long slender legs, causing Vern's eyes to nearly pop out of his head.

'Vern!' Dorothy chided him, 'Focus!'

'So, what advice do you have for a struggling actress Mr. Diamond?' Lilly-May on his left was leaning into him, showing her ample cleavage in the process, her accent thick and deep-south.

Lose the Southern drawl for a start, Oliver wanted to say.

'I mean, what should a Texan girl do to make it in Hollywood?' Her eyes were wide, but not that innocent.

'Well, you're not doing too bad, you're at Kitty Wallis's dinner party after all.'

She looked at him, not getting it, 'Yes, but what can I do to get a role in her next movie?' She pulled a face and looked expectantly at Oliver. At that moment the doors opened, and a maid ushered in the last of the guests.

Kitty stood, 'Ah, there you are! I'd almost given up on you.'

A handsome man entered with a younger, beautiful girl.

'Now let me introduce you. Everyone, this is one of our investors, Dimitri Diakos, and his beautiful daughter Henry Diakos.'

* * * * * * * * *

After dinner Vixen was gossiping with Henry and at the dinner table, Dimitri was mid-story with Kitty and Julian. Meanwhile, Dorothy was chastising a timid Vern in the corner for gawping at Vixen for most of the meal. Lilly-May was applying more lip-gloss, and Brett took his opportunity and invited Oliver to join him for a liqueur in Kitty's office. The food and drinks had flowed, and Oliver felt like his old self with Brett, and Kitty for that matter.

'So, how does Kitty know this Dimitri Diakos?' Oliver asked as Brett poured him a generous glass of Disaronno.

'They were introduced by a friend of a friend of a friend, you know how it is.'

'He seems like one of the good guys, and his daughter is quite something else.' Oliver hadn't been able to resist Henry's infectious personality.

'Now Oliver, we don't involve ourselves with the investors, it's not good for business,' Brett admonished him.

'What? No, wouldn't dream of it, Brett,' Oliver laughed.

'Anyhow, you and Vixen, what's going on there?' Brett asked sipping his liqueur.

'Nothing really, she's nice, but I think there's too much baggage for me to be honest.'

'Well, yes,' Brett frowned, 'but I have to say, she's well-behaved with you. Better than when she was with Rick Krane.' Brett stopped and looked at Oliver.

'Mmmm.' Oliver frowned.

'Oliver, I know we don't talk about... you know... the incident, but there's something I need to confess.'

Oliver leaned in, 'What?'

Brett took a deep breath, 'Rick was blackmailing Kitty. It was all quite nasty and, although I've no idea how he ended up the way he did, I can't help saying that I, well Kitty, was so relieved.'

'I understand.' Oliver looked at Brett stony-faced, wondering how much he would tell him.

'Yes, but what you don't understand is that Rick had physical evidence about something Kitty had been involved in. It's nothing too bad, don't worry.'

'Brett, why are you telling me this?' Oliver didn't know where this was going.

'This "evidence" has disappeared with Rick. We checked his body; it wasn't on him. As you were there that evening, did you see anything out of the ordinary?' Brett looked deep into Oliver's eyes.

Oliver held his gaze, thinking back to the skull keyring, 'No, no Brett. I didn't see anything.'

Brett suddenly smiled and sat back.

'Ok, let's hope this all passes, for all our sakes.'

Oliver smiled. 'Let's get back to the others, by now Lilly-May's probably doing a cheerleading routine on the dinner table!'

* * * * * * * * *

Oliver said his goodbyes and Dimitri passed him his card promising to show him the sights of the South of France if he was ever in Europe. Dorothy and Vern left hurriedly, in a taxi. Dorothy making Vern sit in the front with the driver because she wasn't talking to him. Meanwhile, Brett was trying to talk Lilly-Mae down from sliding down the banister rail of Kitty's sweeping staircase.

Kitty and Julian hugged Oliver with Kitty holding him a little longer than usual.

'Oliver,' Kitty said to him as she pulled herself away, 'you're doing ok kiddo.' Oliver smiled as she winked and walked back into the house linking arms with her husband.

'Ok Oliver Diamond, let's go party!' Vixen was back. The demure girl at dinner had finally been sent home. Oliver smiled and looked at this wonderful woman as they crossed the driveway where an eager Carl was standing with the limo door open.

'Do you know,' Oliver said, 'I'm going to go back and get some sleep. Script to learn and all that.'

Vixen pulled a face. 'Well, I'm going to hit "Secrets" and dance the night away.'

'I'll take a rain check, ok?' Oliver squeezed her hand.

Vixen looked at him, 'You can say it,' she sighed, 'I'm a big girl now.'

Oliver kissed her on the cheek. 'Sorry Vixen, it's just...' he started.

Vixen put two fingers against his lips and smiled, squeezing his hand.

'I will settle down at some point you know, Oliver.'

He looked at her, 'I know, meanwhile, I think I need a little more "single" time.'

Vixen nodded. 'And meanwhile, I need to party! You know where to find me, Oliver Diamond.' With that, she climbed into her Limo as Carl shrugged and waved to Oliver.

Oliver called over to Kitty's driver to take him home and on the way, he mulled over the conversation with Brett. He knew one thing, he had to hide the USB keyring somewhere safe. It was his insurance policy. He'd been involved in a murder cover-up, and the evidence against Kitty could never get into the wrong hands. He didn't need any more distractions; he'd throw himself into the movie. After all, it was the millennium fast approaching, which meant a whole load of new beginnings.

Chapter Forty

THEN

The Daily Grind

Charlie had been in Los Angeles for a month living in a temporary studio apartment in the Downtown area of Hollywood with one room for eating, sleeping, and cooking, plus one bathroom. It was small, but she called it home. She was hunting for a photography studio and didn't want a long lease on an apartment until she knew exactly where she was settling down. One Saturday she decided to take a stroll in her local neighborhood, itching to find a decent coffee shop. Henry was arriving in LA with her father, Dimitri, the following week, and she was looking forward to catching up with her friend. Turning a corner, she discovered a promising coffee shop standing alone amongst the office blocks, 'The Daily Grind'. When she entered, the smell of coffee filled her lungs. It's the nicest smell in the world, Charlie thought to herself as a young Hispanic guy greeted her with the warmest smile.

'*Señorita, hola* and welcome! What would you like?' He was handsome with dark curly hair, ripped jeans, and a red t-shirt bearing the slogan 'I Can't See Dead People.' Charlie perused the extensive chalkboard menu. 'Ooh, I don't know, surprise me!'

He turned away and then quickly turned back shouting, 'Boo!' making Charlie scream and jump, along with a few of the other customers. The boy laughed as another guy appeared from behind the counter.

'José! Stop frightening the customers.' He was blonde with cute dimples and dressed similarly to José, only his t-shirt read 'I survived Lake Placid'.

The other customers returned to their coffees and books.

'I do apologize for José, he's from Colombia. I'm George, please take a seat and I'll bring you one of our finest coffees.' George smiled at Charlie, who smiled back.

'Ok... and I'll take one of your half-fat blueberry muffins.'

José looked at George pointedly, 'Very little here is half-fat.'

George rolled his eyes, 'Don't mind him, he's very temperamental.'

Charlie chuckled and looked around the coffee shop. It was an eclectic mix with pop memorabilia hanging from the ceiling and on the walls. There was all manner of chairs and sofas, scattered with cushions. Charlie found an empty sofa sharing a table with a wing-back chair where a young red-headed girl was curled up with a book.

'Is it ok if I sit here?' No reply. 'Excuse me, do you mind if I sit here?' Charlie asked again.

The girl looked up, 'Yes, of course! Sorry I was miles away, engrossed in my book.' She revealed the cover – *Bridget Jones: The Edge of Reason.*

'Mmmm good choice.' Charlie sat on the sofa smiling at the girl's English accent.

'I'm trying to get some tips from Bridget.'

'Yes, I could do with a few of those myself.' Charlie smiled. 'I'm Charlie by the way.'

'Hi Charlie, I'm Cheryl. You seem familiar, have we met before?'

Charlie frowned, 'I don't think so, but I know what you mean.' Suddenly Cheryl's mobile danced on the table.

'Sorry...' Cheryl picked up the mobile and answered.

'No please, go ahead.' Charlie grabbed a magazine and began to browse but couldn't help overhearing Cheryl's conversation.

'No, I'm not telling you what I'm going to the party as. You'll have to wait and see.' Pause. 'Yes, I'll collect your suit, everything's in hand.' Cheryl looked at Charlie and raised her eyes to heaven. Charlie smiled as José brought her coffee and muffin.

'Ta da!' Announced José as he put the enormous frothy coffee cup on the table beside a muffin oozing with blueberries.

'Yes, I know, no mobile phones.' Cheryl continued. She then whispered heavily into the mobile, 'I'm in a coffee shop, I can't sound too excited!'

José raised his eyebrows and pulled a face at Charlie indicating Cheryl, as he backed away. Cheryl ended her call and Charlie pointed at her book.

'Well, it doesn't sound like you need Bridget's advice.'

Cheryl laughed, 'What? Oh, that, no, that's my boss, he's very demanding.'

'What do you do?' Charlie asked, genuinely interested.

'I work in the film industry. Surprise, surprise in LA, right? How about you?'

'I'm setting up a photography business but finding the right space is proving difficult.'

Cheryl thought for a moment, 'I saw a place go up for lease opposite my apartment block only yesterday. It's an old warehouse and it would make a perfect photography studio.'

'That sounds cool!' Can you give me the address?' Charlie was thinking fast.

'I can do better than that,' Cheryl picked up her book, 'let me finish this chapter, whilst you taste the best coffee in LA, and I'll take you there.'

Charlie smiled, 'It's a deal, only if you share my muffin.'

* * * * * * * * * *

Charlie loved the warehouse instantly. The lease was signed, the deposit paid, and the keys were in Charlie's hands by the following week. The large warehouse was divided into separate loft-style apartments. Charlie's was on the second floor with a great view of Downtown LA. A large metal door slid to one side to reveal the huge space. With floor-to-ceiling windows down the entire length, daylight flooded in, giving it a bright and airy feeling. Charlie decided to add false walls to create a living area at one end, a separate bedroom, and a large lounge area cum kitchen. Blackout curtains at the opposite end would help control light for photoshoots, plus a roller system on the far wall for large backdrops. She was so excited about showing Henry her plans. Henry had arrived in LA with her father earlier that morning and she was escorting him to some fancy dinner party in Beverly Hills that night with 'boring movie people' as Henry had put it.

'Papa said you can come too.' Henry called her within minutes of landing, wanting her friend by her side.

'No... it's ok. I've got a lot of planning to do for my new place.' Charlie wasn't one for imposing herself.

'Oh, ok, suit yourself.' Henry didn't like not getting her way.

Charlie smiled to herself; she knew Henry inside out.

'Look, I'll meet you tomorrow for coffee and show you the loft, how does that sound?'

'Ok, and I'll tell you all about the dinner party you missed out on.' Charlie hung up and began sketching her ideas.

The following morning Charlie met Henry in The Daily Grind.

'You missed out on a great dinner party last night Charlie.' Henry gushed as she winked at José behind the counter.

'You know me, I don't like to intrude. Anyway, I was drawing up plans for my new place, so I was pretty busy.'

'But Vixen was there,' Henry enthused.

'Really? Oh wow, maybe I should have gone.' Charlie kicked herself.

'She was with some movie actor and a bunch of people I didn't know. Papa was in his element.'

José arrived with their coffees and two blueberry muffins. He wore a bright pink t-shirt with the slogan 'Not In A Month Of Sundays'.

'One muffin for you,' then he placed one in front of Henry, 'and a nice big one for you *Señorita.*' He winked at Henry and licked his lips before skipping back behind the counter.

Henry leaned in, 'Charlie, I think I'm in with the barista!'

Charlie laughed, 'I don't think so Henry.' She nodded towards José, who was blowing George a kiss across the coffee shop. George's t-shirt of the day stated, 'I Can't Even Think Straight'.

* * * * * * * * *

The following week was consumed with renovations for the loft. There wasn't a tremendous amount to do as the brick walls and floor were already glazed. The false walls were up in a day and plastered the day after, with curtain rails fitted and curtains up by the Friday.

Charlie spent most of the week with Henry shopping for furniture, bedding, and rugs. She also ordered some photography equipment to be delivered over the next few days, and by Saturday all was complete. Charlie and Henry sat on a very large cream sofa surveying the spacious apartment, a glass of wine in their hands.

'I've got to hand it to you, Charlie, it's amazing.'

Charlie chinked her glass against Henry's. 'I need some clients now!'

Suddenly a buzzer sounded.

Henry looked at Charlie, 'Who can that be?'

'Well at least the entry system works, let's find out.'

She crossed to a pillar where a small monitor lit up and there on the screen was Cheryl, shaking a bottle of wine with a huge grin on her face.

* * * * * * * * *

The following week Henry traveled to Paris to stay with her mother, promising Charlie she would return next month. Charlie needed to kickstart her business if she was to survive in Hollywood. Her investment was due to mature soon, but for Charlie, it wasn't about money, it was about being fulfilled. Nothing excited her more than the thought of having her photographs in magazines and on billboards. Then she remembered the photoshoot with Yvette Paradis on board the yacht. They were the perfect way to make a name for herself and generate some business. She decided to choose her favorite shots and tout them around some publications, once she had Yvette's blessing, of course.

Charlie picked out a dozen photographs and forwarded them to Yvette for approval.

She instantly replied, saying that she loved them and gave her a contact at *Cosmopolitan* magazine. Within a week not only had she struck a deal with *Cosmopolitan*, but they told her she had the front cover of their next month's issue! They even fixed a six-figure sum for the photographs. Charlie was ecstatic and called Henry immediately. On hearing the news, she screamed down the telephone and Yvette shouted 'Congratulations!' in the background.

Charlie was finally making herself known. She hadn't seen much of Cheryl after that first night. She was constantly busy and kept unsociable hours with her needy boss, but Charlie decided to call her anyway.

'Hey, that's great. *Cosmo*, wow!'

'I can't believe it, Cheryl, talk about lucky! I've opened the wine; do you want to come over later?'

'I wish I could, but I've got schedules to sort. Sometimes I think the studio is of the mind that I have no life.'

'You know why, don't you?' Charlie said smiling to herself.

'Yes, because, it's true, I have no life!' Cheryl sighed. 'Anyway, Charlie I need a huge favor. Can I book you for a photoshoot tomorrow? The company we use has had a flood in their studio and we must get some promo shots for this film as soon as. It's a very tight deadline.'

'I'd be delighted!'

'Phew! Charlie, you're a lifesaver and your place is perfect. I'll bring him myself and go through the shots we need to come away with. It's for my boss, Oliver.'

'Oh, I finally get to meet your big bad boss!' Charlie laughed.

'Well actually, you've already met him,' Cheryl said mysteriously.

'What? When?' Charlie frowned.

'All will be revealed tomorrow around ten,' and with that Cheryl hung up. Charlie soon forgot about Cheryl's cryptic message and began to set up the equipment for the following day. Her mobile rang, it was her lawyer in Boston, Mr. Thurgood Brown.

'Hi Charlie here, I mean Charlotte.'

'Ms. Black, Thurgood Brown here, I'm afraid I have some rather bad news.'

'What?' Charlie's heart sank. Maybe something had happened to William?

'You asked me to keep hold of your papers regarding your recent investment with a...' he paused, '...Hase International.'

'Yes... is everything ok?' Her heart was pounding in her chest.

'It seems everything is far from ok.'

'The initial investment period should be over any day.' She racked her brains trying to figure out today's date.

'The news is very bleak, Hase International is no more.'

'What are you saying?'

Charlie's mind was racing as she digested the information from her lawyer. The company had gone into liquidation and dissolved overnight.

'But my best friend's father, Dimitri Diakos, received a healthy payout from a similar investment.' Charlie was desperate.

'I've done some research on your behalf, Ms. Black, and it seems you have fallen foul of a scam.' Thurgood wasn't enjoying the conversation.

'B-but it was low risk and M-Mr. Diakos had no problems,' Charlie stammered, 'He told me he received a large return and I trust him implicitly.' She'd had a gut feeling it was too good to be true, and knew when you felt that way, it usually was. Why hadn't she listened to her gut?

'Ms. Black, this is something known as a Ponzi Scheme,' her lawyer went on to explain, 'a company has initial investors and pays them a good return using money received from new investors. They never really invest your money; they use it to pay investors further down the line.'

Charlie was stunned.

'Everything seems completely legitimate. I've no doubt Mr. Diakos did receive a high yield, but it was someone else's money. The strange thing is, it seems to have stopped with you.'

Charlie frowned, 'What do you mean?'

'Well, you were the end of the line. If you ask me, it feels personal.'

'But the CEO Beau B-Boucher, the offices, everything, seemed so... so...' Charlie sank to the floor of her apartment thinking wildly.

'Beau Boucher is recorded as the CEO,' Thurgood explained, 'but I feel there is someone else behind this.'

Charlie ended the call, her heart beating out of her chest. She knew the answer, but she contacted Simba for confirmation.

'Simba, it's Charlie.'

'Miss Charlie, I was thinking of you, I am back in LA, for good. How about...'

'Simba, I need you to do something urgently,' she interrupted him.

'But of course. Are you alright?'

'Yes, I'm ok. I need details on a company called Hase International. I'll text you all the details I have.'

Charlie texted Simba and waited, staring at her mobile. She picked it up on the first ring.

'Miss Charlie, you won't believe this.'

'Go on, Simba...'

'The CEO is a Beau Boucher, but I dug up someone else higher up. It's Thomas Hassler.'

Charlie closed her eyes and ended the call. Thomas Hassler, that name again. He'd murdered her father and now he'd stolen her inheritance, from prison. What did he have against her? She was determined to find out, and one day she would exact her revenge.

* * * * * * * * *

Charlie finally fell asleep around five and awoke again at nine, the sun streaming in through the window. Her heart sank as the conversation with her lawyer replayed over and over in her head. The photoshoot was the last thing she wanted to do that day, but she couldn't let Cheryl down. She showered and made herself look half decent. With puffed-up eyes and hair that wouldn't do anything it was told, she felt a mess. As she pulled on a white jumpsuit, her door monitor buzzed.

'Hi, it's only me.'

'Hey Cheryl,' Charlie tried to be chirpy.

'I know we're a little early, I'm sending him up with the coffees whilst I nip back to The Daily Grind because someone left the muffins on the counter.'

'Ok sure, I didn't sleep much so... Cheryl? Cheryl?'

She'd disappeared from the monitor. Charlie pressed the unlock button and slid the bolt open on her door. As she checked the camera and lighting setup there was a knock at her door.

'It's open!' she shouted, checking the flash was working. The door was still rattling. Charlie turned towards her large metal door and called out, 'Slide it across!'

The rattling and banging continued. She sighed, crossed to the entrance, pulled the handle, and slid the huge door across to the left. As it slid open Oliver fell into her apartment, coffee cups hurled in all directions. Hot coffee going everywhere, but mostly over Charlie's jumpsuit.

Charlie screamed, 'Aargh!'

Oliver looked up at her. "So sorry! I was pushing instead of sli...' He stopped.

'You?'

Charlie was open-mouthed. 'You? You're Cheryl's boss?'

Charlie scowled at Oliver who collapsed on the floor in fits of laughter. Cheryl came running in behind him and took in the scene before her.

'Oh, I see you've been re-acquainted then?'

Chapter Forty-One

NOW

Saved by the Bell

Kelvin left Gelateria Tony's with the briefcase and as he walked around the corner, he noticed a family fast approaching him. The mother was half running with a pram carrying a screaming child, whilst the father was doing his best to keep up.

'You're the one who promised him an ice cream,' the woman was shouting over her shoulder as the child reached a hundred decibels. The husband was frantically searching Google maps, on his mobile.

'There's an ice cream shop around this corner, let's hope to God it's open.'

At that moment the cathedral bells began to chime. Kelvin looked up, eleven-thirty, he had thirty minutes.

Kelvin entered the cathedral through the main doors where an old woman was dragging a mop bucket on wheels across the hallway and a gaggle of nuns was whispering inside the entrance. As the woman dragged the bucket further one of the nuns looked up and 'shushed' her. She gave the nun a not-too-Christian look and picked up the bucket, sloshing water over the stone floor. She opened a nearby door and a young blonde schoolboy wearing round gold glasses ran out and bumped straight into Kelvin.

'Woah!' Kelvin said as the kid ran into the cathedral.

The gaggle turned and scowled as Kelvin followed the schoolboy. He pushed his glasses up to his forehead and took in the sight inside the vast cathedral with its row upon row of highly polished pews. Moving toward the pulpit he noticed a small school party of boys, around eight or nine years of age, complete with a guide who was well into her seventies. The small blonde boy was standing amongst them.

'In London you have St. Paul's Cathedral, here in Nice we have Cathédrale Sainte-Marie et Sainte-Réparate. Now if you would all cast your eyes heavenward...'

The boys slowly looked up to the incredible ceiling, mouths open as the guide fed them more information.

'Do try to keep your mouths closed, we do get the odd pigeon in here.'

The boys closed their mouths swiftly.

'You will notice the ornate ceiling. The style is baroque, very popular in the early seventeenth century...'

Kelvin spotted choir pews running vertically facing the pulpit. He crossed to the last pew.

'The magnificent high altar is surmounted by the most beautiful painting of Glory of Saint Reparata. The virgin martyr to whom the cathedral is dedicated...'

Hymnbooks and bibles were stacked across the top of the pews and there was a pillar in the middle, the ideal position.

'Now let's move on towards the high altar...'

The guide's voice drifted away, the boys following her every move. Kelvin crouched on the floor and removed the tiny camera and hidden USB from the briefcase. Pocketing the USB, he placed the camera carefully between the stack of bibles and pointed it towards the pulpit.

As he checked the image a young blonde boy's frowning face filled the screen. Kelvin lifted his head from the camera and gestured for the boy to move to one side, but the boy stood his ground, folding his arms. Kelvin checked the time, eleven forty-five, he didn't have long. He looked towards the high altar and noticed the party returning with their guide leading them like the pied piper of Hamlin.

'Now we shall visit one of the ten chapels in here, called "Our Lady of Sorrows".'

He glared at his eight-year-old obstruction and held out five euros, which the boy took, re-joining his group with a grin. Kelvin sighed and went back to his camera. The side of the pulpit was in view with the long stone corridor to the left, leading to another chapel. He pressed 'send image' and crossed to the pulpit, placing the USB on the floor.

Returning to his car, he called Oliver.

'Hi, everything's set.'

'I was beginning to think there was a problem,' Oliver said, relieved.

'Well, I did have an eight-year-old problem, but I bribed him away. Do you have the signal?'

Oliver checked a second mobile phone cradled on the dashboard.

'Yes, the feed's coming through now.' Oliver was looking at the image the camera was sending and at the same time recording it.

'It also has sound, but you shouldn't need that. It's amazing what spyware can do nowadays. I'll hit the road, let me know if you need anything else.'

'Will do, and thanks, Kelvin, I owe you one.' Oliver scrutinized the video feed.

'Yes,' said Kelvin, 'and you also owe me five euros.'

Oliver closed his mobile and checked the time, noon. Today he was to be finally rid of the USB, but not before he knew who he was up against and who killed Rick Krane over twenty years ago. Suddenly on the screen, a young blonde-haired boy approached the camera, staring straight at Oliver, frowning.

'No, no,' Oliver whispered into his mobile, 'go away, little boy.'

The boy was getting nearer, curiously looking forward, tilting his head side to side like an inquisitive puppy. As he screwed his face up Oliver could hear him whispering, 'Who are you?'

'He's going to ruin everything!' Oliver felt helpless and hit his steering wheel in frustration, knocking the mobile onto the floor of his car, as the bells chimed the half-hour.

'Damn it!'

After scrambling on the floor, he eventually retrieved the mobile. The screen showed the pulpit and corridor but no boy. Surely the USB had been collected by now. He stopped recording and hit rewind back to when the boy was approaching the camera, whispering.

Suddenly the cathedral bells chimed and the boy looked to his right and shot back down the corridor. A few seconds later Oliver could see a figure crossing slowly to the pulpit but at that angle, he couldn't see his face. The man crouched down out of sight, then stood and left the pulpit, pocketing the USB. This time he did get a good look at his face. Oliver couldn't believe his eyes. He rewound the recording, pressed pause, and zoomed in on the face of Brett Styles.

Chapter Forty-Two

NOW

Do the Hustle

Charlie and Henry stood in front of the full-length mirror inspecting Ingrid's extraordinary handywork. Charlie wore a light blue skirt and jacket with a crème blouse, a blonde shoulder-length wig, in a smart bob, and blue contact lenses. Four-inch, cream stilettos completed the outfit. The most remarkable feature was the prosthetics, making her face take on a completely different shape. The more she looked, the more she didn't recognize herself.

'Mmmm, business-like but sexy with it, I like it,' Charlie said, crossing to the sink to spray perfume on her wrists.

Henry scowled into the mirror. 'Whereas I look like a fifty-year-old virgin!'

She was dressed in dark jacket and trousers, a white frilly blouse, and flat, black shoes. Her auburn wig scraped back in a low bun did her no favors, and neither did the dark-rimmed glasses. She too was wearing prosthetics on her chin and nose. Even close-up you couldn't see any joins. Their transformations were remarkable, but nothing as remarkable as Ingrid's. When Ingrid entered the bathroom the girls stared, wide-eyed.

'Oh. My. God.' Henry was speechless.

'Who are you? And what have you done with Ingrid?' Charlie said jokingly.

'Is it ok?' Ingrid looked at them both.

'Ingrid, you look amazing,' Charlie enthused. 'I think I've seen her somewhere before, but I can't put my finger on where.'

'The freckles aren't too much, no?' Ingrid looked in the mirror.

'You're perfect Ingrid,' Henry said, checking her lack of makeup in her reflection.

'Knock, knock!' It was Marcus.

'We're coming out now Marcus,' Charlie shouted as she looked in the long mirror. 'Ok, girls, let's do this.'

'Wow!' Marcus gave Charlie a wolf whistle. 'I would never recognize you.' Marcus' hair was gelled in a side parting, and he was wearing a navy-blue suit, pale blue shirt, and a red tie, sporting an authentic Rothchild's pin badge.

Charlie crossed to him.

'You're not looking too shabby yourself, Rothschilds would be proud.'

Henry looked at him. 'Your prosthetic nose suits you, Marcus.'

'Well, it feels weird.' Marcus said, crossing his eyes to take a look.

Charlie took a breath and faced them.

'Ok, are we ready for this?' They all nodded.

'We're ready, Charlie Diamond,' Ingrid used her full title.

'Hey!' Henry exclaimed. 'We're like… Charlie's Angels!'

'Well, I am not going to be Bosley!' Marcus laughed.

Charlie cleared her throat, 'Let's get back to the matter in hand, shall we?'

Henry, Marcus, and Ingrid stood like a bunch of naughty school children.

'Ingrid, do you have the portfolio case?' Charlie asked.

'Yes, it is here.' Ingrid gave a half-smile.

'Marcus, you have your case with the props?'

'Yes boss,' Marcus grinned, 'and I've checked the contents five times.'

'Henry, you've got your name badge?'

'Yes, but what about the code?'

'The code! He should have sent it by now,' Charlie's mobile *tringed,* displaying a message.

Henry frowned, 'That's spooooky!'

Charlie looked at her mobile, 'Good old Simba!'

'Simba?' It was Marcus's turn.

Henry smiled, 'He's a friend of ours from St. Moritz.'

Marcus laughed, 'Simba? From St. Moritz?'

'It's a long story. We've always kept in touch. 7-1-4-3, Henry.'

Marcus looked puzzled, 'But how did he…?'

'He's a hacker Marcus,' Charlie explained matter-of-factly.

Marcus turned to Ingrid, 'Who are these people?'

Henry repeated, '7-1-4-3, Ok, let's go.'

Henry led Marcus out of the hotel room whilst Charlie stopped Ingrid in the doorway.

'Ingrid, we'll meet you back here at three-thirty.' She took her hand, 'Thank you, dear friend, for doing this.'

Ingrid smiled, 'Let's hope you're saying that in a couple of hours.'

* * * * * * * * *

Oliver felt sick, he found it difficult to believe Brett was the blackmailer. What was he thinking of? He must have known for some time that Oliver had the USB evidence, and he was one of Oliver's best friends, for over twenty years. But was he capable of murder? Now Oliver knew who he was up against, he decided to face Brett and deliver the real USB in person. He'd planted the fake one in the cathedral to smoke out his blackmailer. But why would Brett send letters threatening to ruin his name and destroy his life, including his marriage?

Firstly, he would collect the original USB from his bank safety deposit. The only ace up his sleeve was that Brett wasn't aware Oliver knew it was him. He parked down a side street and made his way to the Première Financière Bank. It was an 'old-fashioned' establishment that had been in business for a hundred and fifty years, running on a 'the customer is paramount' principle. A floor manager would greet all customers, sporting a purple frock coat with matching trousers, a white shirt, a purple tie, and the biggest smile.

Once you were through the large mahogany and brass revolving doors, he would point you in the direction of Bureau de Change, Securities, or wherever you needed to go on that particular day.

Oliver approached the doors to be greeted by the ever-smiling Monsieur Lagarde.

'*Bonjour* Monsieur Diamond.'

'*Bonjour*, I need to retrieve an item from my safety deposit box.'

'Certainly sir.' Monsieur Lagarde clicked at a young girl who came running over. 'Louise, please take care of Monsieur Diamond, he requests his safety deposit box.'

'Of course, Monsieur Diamond please wait here for a moment, I will arrange a private room.'

Oliver walked into the busy banking hall and waited by a pillar.

* * * * * * * * *

The bank was a short walk from their hotel, and as they approached the doors Henry held back, allowing Charlie and Marcus to go ahead.

'I'll text the code as soon as I have it.' Charlie said to Henry, who nodded and waited out of sight, by a low hedge.

Charlie and Marcus walked through the revolving doors to be welcomed by the floor manager, beaming at them.

'*Bonjour* and welcome to The Première Financière Bank... ah, Mademoiselle Mars, it is good to see you again.'

'*Bonjour*, Monsieur Lagarde.'

'What can we do for you today?'

'I need to access my safety deposit box. I've booked room 'G' for one hour.'

'Very well mademoiselle, please wait one moment I will have someone take you there, *toute de suite*.'

He indicated an empty chaise down three steps in the banking hall, smiled, and nodded at Marcus. 'Monsieur.' Marcus noticed that he'd spotted his lapel-pin badge.

Charlie and Marcus walked down to the chaise and sat, surveying the hall. The bank tellers were behind low glass, and the long counter was carved from beautiful shining mahogany with brass foot stands. Charlie had chosen the date very carefully, the banking hall being rather busy was no accident. It was the end of the month, payday, and everyone was visiting the bank to complete their finances. Marcus whispered to Charlie whilst fixing his eyes on the tellers in front of him.

'How come he recognized you, Ms. Mars?'

'When Ingrid flew in last month for her research, we had a little test run. I took out the safety deposit box and made sure Monsieur Lagarde didn't forget my face.'

'Well, I don't know what you said to him, but he knew you as soon as he set eyes on you.' Marcus smiled.

'To a man like that, a little flattery from a blonde girl and he never forgets.'

'How is he going to be distracted when Henry makes her entrance with "you-know-who"?'

'Don't worry, I've also got that covered.' Charlie winked at Marcus.

'You think of everything.' There was a pause. 'Are you nervous?' Marcus whispered in her ear.

'Yes of course, but I have my eye on the finish line. It will all be worth it.'

Marcus was looking around as he spoke to her. 'And you are confident that he will do everything you say?'

'Nothing's guaranteed,' Charlie whispered back, 'don't forget, he's ruthless.'

'Mademoiselle Mars?' Charlie looked up to see a young girl in a dark trouser suit standing in front of her. Charlie and Marcus stood.

'Yes, *bonjour*...' Charlie smiled at the young girl and read her name badge, '...Louise.'

'Please wait one moment. I have to take another customer to a private room and then I will return for you.' Louise indicated behind her and left them, crossing the foyer. Charlie followed her gaze and quickly turned back to Marcus.

'It's Oliver!' she whispered heavily.

Marcus froze, 'What?'

'It's Oliver, he's coming!' Charlie was desperate. 'What are we going to do?'

Louise was walking in their direction with Oliver close behind her.

Marcus looked at Charlie, 'Act natural, you look nothing like you. You've got prosthetics and a blonde wig remember? I have only met him on a few occasions, so I don't think he'll remember me.' He said in a sing-song voice, smiling inanely at Charlie. They both turned away as Louise marched Oliver past them and up the large staircase to the next floor.

'He's gone,' Marcus sighed.

'That was close! What's he doing here?' Charlie screwed her face up as Marcus took her hands, 'And breathe… Charlie, breathe.'

Charlie looked at him sharply, 'If you say "breathe" one more time, I'll slap you.'

They both sat, their minds racing.

'She's coming back.' Marcus collected himself.

'So sorry about that, Mademoiselle Mars. Please follow me, I'll take you to your room and bring you your safety deposit box.'

Charlie and Marcus followed the bank clerk up the large staircase. Charlie walked ahead of a sweating Marcus and did her best to make small talk with Louise. The staircase opened onto a small landing area with doors to the left and right. Louise approached the right-hand door.

'What a great view of the banking hall from up here,' Charlie said as Louise was studying the keypad.

'What? Oh yes, it's *magnifique*.' She turned back to the door.

Charlie continued, 'And such a busy day for you.'

Louise began to punch in the numbers as she spoke to Charlie over her shoulder. 'Yes, end of the month and a bank holiday on Monday.'

Charlie checked the code, 7143, good old Simba. There was a buzz and click as the door opened inwards. Louise escorted them down a dimly lit hallway with a deep carpet and photographs of Paris through the ages. Charlie sent a message to Henry on her mobile as Marcus's eyes darted around in search of Oliver.

They finally reached a door at the end of the hallway with a brass plate announcing 'Room G'. The room had a rich purple carpet, wood-paneled, and wall lights with purple shades. At the far end was a desk and leather, wingback chair set in front of a large Georgian window framed by bookshelves. Heavy net curtains dressed the window with large purple drapes swagged at either side.

'Please take a seat, I will return with your deposit box in a moment.'

She smiled, leaving the room through a second door by the desk.

'Charlie, it's already two-fifteen, I hope he's not early.' Marcus was feeling apprehensive, to say the least.

'I'm aware of that Marcus, we'll have to set up in record time. I'm more concerned about Oliver ruining everything, what's he doing here?'

They sat, anxiously waiting for Louise's return.

* * * * * * * * *

When Ingrid left Charlie, Henry, and Marcus, she walked in the opposite direction.

Stopping by Alsace Lorraine Garden she put on her dark glasses and extracted a collapsible white walking stick from her case and continued up Boulevard Gambetta. Twenty minutes later she stood outside the offices of Thomas Hassler. Ingrid tapped her way up the steps to the main door and took a breath before looking vaguely in the direction of the camera and pressing the buzzer. After a few seconds, she heard the tell-tale buzz and click as the large wooden door opened into a hallway leading to a staircase in front of her. To her left, a large vase of blue hydrangeas took pride of place on a cream and gold half table. Ingrid glanced at herself in the ornate mirror before managing the stairs one step at a time. On reaching the first floor she entered the reception where the receptionist smiled and spoke very loudly. '*Bonjour* Siobhan, Mr. Hassler is out at an appointment, he should be back a little after three.'

Ingrid smiled back and 'signed' to the receptionist, who stared at her with an uncertain look on her face. Ingrid tapped her stick through the reception and pushed open the door to Thomas Hassler's office.

'Oh, very well, you wait in his office,' the receptionist leaned over her desk, still over-speaking as Ingrid closed the door of his office behind her.

She turned the lock without a sound, removed her glasses, and crossed behind the oversized desk to where the artwork had pride of place. Opening her case, she extracted her tools and got to work.

* * * * * * * * *

Henry looked up and down the street but there was no sign. In the distance, a group of men in suits was walking in her direction. They must be the law students as Charlie had predicted, but still no sign of 'him'. She received a message on her mobile, 'Oliver's here!'

Oliver's at the Bank? What did Charlie mean? Henry's stomach turned over. *Seven, one, four, three. Seven, one, four, three,* Henry repeated the code in her head. With the law students fast approaching Henry checked her watch, two-fifteen. Then, out of nowhere, a car pulled up and Henry marched through the crowd of students with her hand outstretched.

'*Bonjour*, Monsieur Hassler?'

'Yes, hello Miss...?' He held her hand and squinted at her name badge, '...Patricia.'

'Please follow me.' Henry said in her best French accent.

She escorted him through the entrance where the crowd of students was milling around a befuddled Monsieur Lagarde. They all had appointments for two-thirty to open bank accounts so they could have their student loans paid in for the new term. That's what Charlie had overheard their bursar asking a bank clerk the previous month. Henry smiled and raised her eyebrows at Thomas Hassler as they crossed into the banking hall.

'Please follow me, Monsieur Hassler.'

They walked up the stairs, Henry not daring to look behind her. She secretly checked her watch, two thirty-three, and reached for the keypad.

Seven, one, four, three. The red light turned green, and the door opened with a loud click.

Henry smiled and led Thomas Hassler down the long hallway towards room G.

* * * * * * * * *

Marcus was pacing, 'Charlie it's two-twenty-four, they could be here at any minute and we're not ready!'

Suddenly the door by the desk sprung open.

'So sorry to have kept you.' Louise approached the desk carrying a large metal box with handles. She placed it on the table and produced a key unlocking one of the two locks.

'Ok, I'll leave you to it. You have your key, yes?'

Charlie nodded.

'I apologize again for the delay; the gentleman next door is taking a little longer than anticipated.' Henry and Marcus stared at the adjoining wall. 'However, I'm afraid this room is booked again at three, so you must be finished by then.'

Charlie sighed and smiled, 'That will be fine, thank you, Louise.'

'I will return a little before three to return your box to the vault.' She turned and exited through the same door.

Marcus pointed at the adjoining wall and mouthed 'Oliver!' Charlie frowned.

'Come on Marcus, we need to focus on the job at hand.'

He sprang into action, opened his bag, and produced a brass plate with sticky-sided tape. He opened the door leading to the hallway and pressed it over the existing plate. It now read:

MME. RUBY MARS

INVESTMENT PRESIDENT

Charlie lifted the safety deposit box and hid it under the desk whilst Marcus placed framed photographs on the bookshelves behind the desk. They showed a beaming Charlie as Ruby Mars, shaking hands with various businessmen and women, all set against differing backdrops. 'International Finance Corporation Awards', 'Finance with flair Awards'. They looked impressive.

'Marcus, are you nearly done? It's two-thirty.'

Marcus was sweating as he checked the room.

'There's just the portfolio literature for the desk.'

Marcus retrieved paperwork from his case.

There was a knock at the door, they looked at each other.

'Here goes.' Marcus nervously sat down, and Charlie sitting behind the desk took a deep breath, *'Entrer.'*

The door opened to reveal Henry standing with the one and only, Thomas Hassler. Charlie swallowed as Henry announced, 'Your two-thirty appointment Madame Mars.'

'Thank you, Patricia; please do come in Mr. Hassler.'

Henry stepped to one side as Thomas Hassler marched up to Charlie in his usual dark shades. Her heart rate increased as she shook his hand vigorously. It was the hand of her father's killer, but she had to remain in control. Henry crossed to pour some water and caught Marcus looking like a rabbit caught in headlights, she glared at him.

'Please take a seat, Mr. Hassler.' Charlie indicated.

Thomas Hassler sat forward on his seat.

'So, Madame Mars, please tell me more about these highly lucrative investments.'

'Yes, here at Première Financière Bank, I have access to some very elite portfolios. As you can imagine these aren't available to everybody Mr. Hassler, only privileged investors. When I first had contact with your company, I was informed that you may be interested in making a sound investment. Am I right?'

Thomas Hassler smiled, 'Madame Mars, I'm always interested in something that isn't available to everyone else.' Charlie held his gaze for a split second.

'Let me introduce you to Mr. Santiago Rodriguez from Rothschilds in Spain.'

'*Hola* Señor Hassler, it is very good to see you.' Marcus beamed and held out his hand. Henry heaved an inward sigh of relief as she distributed the glasses of water, Marcus had stepped up to the plate.

He continued, 'Now, Miss Mars, if you don't mind, I would like to take Mr. Hassler through some of these portfolios.'

Charlie smiled and sat back as Marcus talked this evil man through the fake investments. She wanted to scream about what he'd done to her family, but she had to keep her cool.

As Marcus concluded, Charlie looked at Thomas Hassler expectantly.

'Well Mr. Hassler, with an investment of say fifteen million US dollars, to begin with, we can ensure a fine return with the bank's current investments.'

Thomas Hassler looked at Marcus and then back to Charlie.

'Madame Mars, it sounds like an excellent investment, and I feel privileged that the Première Financière Bank deems me to be a, how did you put it? "A privileged investor".'

Charlie smiled, 'Then let's sort out the paperwork and we can start getting you some high returns immediately.'

Thomas Hassler smiled and stood up, Marcus and Charlie followed suit. He first looked at Henry and Marcus to his left. He checked out the photographs on the bookshelf and finally settled his eyes on Charlie.

He smiled, 'There is one tiny problem.'

Charlie didn't blink, 'And what is that Mr. Hassler?'

'I don't do business with amateurs.'

Charlie, Marcus, and Henry stared at him in disbelief. Marcus perspired heavily.

'I'm sorry Mr. Hassler, I don't quite follow you.' Charlie said flatly.

He tilted his head and smiled, 'Nice to see you... Miss Black, maybe next time you won't have your pathetic friends with you.'

Charlie closed her eyes; he'd known all along. Thomas Hassler turned and chuckled as he marched out of the room, slamming the door behind him.

Chapter Forty-Three

THEN

The Man with the Teardrop Tattoo

Oliver's photoshoot with Charlie was going extremely well. Cheryl sat back and watched as Charlie snapped shot after shot after shot. Cheryl had never seen him so relaxed, and it was obvious there was a spark between the two of them. When Oliver went to change his outfit for the third time Cheryl joined Charlie in the kitchen area.

'I've never seen him so relaxed on a shoot. He's usually trying to end early.'

'I have to admit, I'm enjoying it myself.' Charlie smiled at Cheryl as she poured some apple juice,

'Are you ok though?' asked Cheryl. 'You look tired.'

'Yeah... sorry... I had some bad news last night.'

'Really? What happened?' Cheryl was concerned for her new friend and Charlie felt the need to share her news with someone.

'When I was very young my father died, and I recently received my inheritance.'

'Oh Charlie, I had no idea.'

'It was a long time ago; I was only seven.' Charlie stared out of the window revisiting the image that tormented her.

'Nevertheless, it can't have been easy,' Cheryl sympathized. 'So, what happened last night?'

'My inheritance was a large sum of money and I invested it, only last night I discovered that I was part of a scam. I've lost the lot.' Charlie began to cry.

'Charlie I'm so sorry. Have you been to the police?'

'I don't know what to do. My lawyer's dealing with it, but he said not to hold out much hope. I can't believe I was so stupid.'

'There are some pretty awful people about.' Cheryl frowned and looked at Charlie sideways, 'When you say a lot...?'

Charlie closed her eyes, 'Millions.'

'Oh, my goodness Charlie, I don't know what to say.'

'There's more to it, but I won't bore you, I'm still trying to get my head around the fact my father's money has gone for good.'

Oliver's voice shot down the apartment

'Is there only me working today?'

Cheryl rolled her eyes, 'See, he wants you back where he can see you. I'm a good listener if ever you need to talk...'

'Thanks, Cheryl, I'll be fine.' Charlie wiped her face.

'Come on,' Cheryl squeezed her hand.

Charlie smiled and walked back to the studio.

'Right Oliver Diamond, let's see what you've got.'

* * * * * * * * *

As Cheryl packed Oliver's outfits in the bedroom Oliver approached Charlie.

'So, are you going to give me your number, or shall we wait another couple of years before we bump into each other again?'

Charlie smiled, 'I tell you what, you give me *your* number and I'll be in touch.'

Oliver smiled, 'Oooh... I love it when a girl plays hard to get.'

'Mmmm, I bet you do.'

Charlie passed him a notebook and pen from the counter. Oliver jotted down his contact details and as she went to take it, he pulled it out of her reach. They held each other's gaze for a few seconds before Charlie laughed and snatched the notebook, breaking the silence.

'Did I hear happiness in here?' Cheryl, faking a mock American accent, came bounding out of the bedroom. Oliver and Charlie looked at her quizzically.

'It's a quote... Miss Hannigan?... *Annie*?' Cheryl rolled her eyes, 'Oh never mind, come on Oliver, you've got a script to look at.'

'Thanks for a great shoot, Charlie.' He winked at her and attempted to push the door open.

'It's "*slide*"!' Cheryl shrieked. 'Oh, you're so un-cool,' she said, sliding the door open and pushing him out into the hallway.

Charlie looked at the note he had given her. He'd written his mobile number with his name underneath and inside the O of Oliver, he'd placed a small 'x'.

* * * * * * * * *

After the *Cosmo* piece was published, Charlie proved to be very popular. From fashion shoots to private 'at home' shoots with the glitterati, her diary was filling fast into the new millennium. Over the next few weeks, Cheryl pleaded with Charlie to call Oliver as he was *driving her insane.* Thomas Hassler spending her father's money was all-consuming to Charlie and she needed a diversion which came in the form of an interesting booking.

A local company contracted her to photograph a secret event. Charlie had to sign a 'Non-Disclosure Agreement', meaning she had to promise to keep everything under wraps. It was called 'The Cage of Hades'. After the success of the movie *Fight Club*, a local company was launching regular cage fights.

Promising to be 'high on energy' and 'high on volume', their marketing team agreed on her exclusivity. Charlie was curious and thought it would be fun to take Oliver on a 'working' date with maybe a drink or two.

The event was held on the Monday before Christmas, a few days before Charlie was to visit Henry in Paris.

Oliver was relieved when Charlie called him.

'You remember when I was at your studio, and I said I loved it when a girl plays hard to get?'

'Yeeeees.' Charlie smiled.

'You didn't have to take it literally!'

Charlie laughed. 'I'm calling you, aren't I?'

'Ok I forgive you, but cage fighting? Seriously?'

Charlie laughed again. 'Come on, it'll be fun, and we can grab a drink after.'

Oliver was sold, 'Ok, deal, I'll pick you up at eight.'

His filming had overrun, and Oliver dashed home to change before swinging by for Charlie. It was their first date, and he didn't want to mess up. He dressed in black with a black baseball cap, to keep some anonymity. On the way, he nearly took a wrong turn but managed to switch lanes, cutting up a black Jeep. The Jeep sat on his horn at the red light and Oliver waved, by way of an apology, he didn't want road rage on tonight of all nights. As he waited at the lights the Jeep drew up next to him and Oliver gave his best 'I'm sorry' face. The window slid down and the driver, who was bald with a rough lived-in face, scowled, revealing a rack of gold teeth. Oliver couldn't help but notice that the man had a tattoo in the shape of a teardrop under his left eye. When the lights changed, the Jeep sped away with a screeching of tires. Oliver finally arrived to find Charlie outside her apartment. She wore a dark blue jumpsuit, and her hair was tied back.

'I thought you'd stood me up.' She joked as she jumped in his car.

'Finished late at the studios, now where's this place?'

'I forgive you, and yes I'll be your Sat Nav, now drive.'

The address led them to an old building further downtown. The bouncers checked Charlie's invite and radioed inside. After a minute a young Asian guy came bounding through the door.

'Miss Charlie, hi! My name is Cong Jing. Cong from Hong Kong.' He laughed, 'Please, come with me.'

They followed him through two large metal doors and down a flight of stone steps. Music drifted up from the depths below, getting louder and louder. Cong Jing turned and smiled as he waited by a pair of large doors.

'Welcome to Hades!' He announced, pushing the doors open into a vast room with music blaring out all around them.

The 'spectators' ranged from punks and rockers to businessmen and women. At the very center was a large hexagonal cage with a lighting rig suspended over it. Charlie watched two young guys fighting inside the cage as lights pulsed in every direction in time with the heavy music. They were kicking and punching. Charlie noticed they weren't wearing boxing gloves, just fingerless leather gloves, this was going to hurt.

'You really know how to show a guy a good time,' Oliver shouted into Charlie's ear as they made their way through the raucous crowd.

'I've never seen anything like it!' exclaimed Charlie.

Cong Jing gestured for them to follow him towards the cage. They eventually reached a VIP area with no seating; this event was standing room only. He produced a security tag for Charlie and Oliver and placed them around their necks.

'You can go anywhere you like, but not inside the cage.' Cong Jing laughed raucously.

'I'll leave you to it, Miss Charlie.' He stopped and bowed his head.

Charlie nodded as she slowly walked around the cage. 'Ok, thanks, Cong Jing.'

'Don't worry, I will ensure your boyfriend, Mr. Diamond, is ok whilst you take your photos.' Cong winked at her. 'He very cute.'

Charlie cast Oliver a quick look. 'Yes, I agree with you Cong Jing, he is cute... and thanks.'

'They don't call me Cong for nothing.' He smiled, showing his perfect white teeth. 'Cong, it Chinese name. It mean "smart".' He added with a wink.

There was a grating buzzer noise as the lights snapped to bright white, all pointing into the center of the cage. One of the boys stood with his arms up to thunderous applause.

'Ok, Miss Charlie. We are about to begin the first proper fight.'

'The first *proper* fight? What was that then?' As she pointed, the cage door opened at the far end and the losing boy, his face streaming with blood, was carried off by two boys in grey outfits with yellow crosses on the front.

Cong Jing laughed, 'That was only the warm-up.' He backed away. 'See you later and enjoy!'

Suddenly there was a loud siren and the lights began to sweep all around the room as smoke cascaded down from the ceiling with a deafening hiss.

Charlie crossed back to Oliver.

'Have you ever seen anything like this?' Charlie was feeling fright and flight simultaneously.

'Never! This is a first date I won't forget in a hurry!' Oliver laughed.

'Ladies and gentlemen!' a booming voice interrupted them over the music which was pumping like a giant mechanical heart.

'Please welcome your Hades cage models, Mary-Lou and Lilly-May!'

The crowd went wild as two girls entered the cage and paraded around the inside, in opposite directions. Oliver instantly recognized Lilly-May as Brett's plus one from Kitty's dinner party.

She was strutting around the hexagonal ring like a prize pony. A tiny black sports bra squeezed her ample breasts together and she wore the minutest pair of black shorts which left nothing to the imagination. She was chewing gum and holding a large sign over her head, which read *'Round 1 – It's Gonna Be A Bloodbath!'*. Smiling inanely at the crowd she spotted Oliver and jumped up and down waving like a demented cheerleader. Charlie looked at Oliver who was grimacing.

'It looks like you've been spotted by an old girlfriend,' Charlie teased as she took photos of the two girls.

'I assure you she was never a girlfriend of mine.'

Lilly-May stopped by Charlie for a photo and then continued strutting her stuff.

'Put your hands together for our first fighter of the evening – Hades' very own, Cage Rage!'

The crowd roared as a young guy ran into the cage dressed in a pair of black shorts and nothing else apart from his gloves. His face bore a large black lightning streak and revealed an incomplete set of teeth as he screamed at the crowd. Charlie darted around the perimeter, snapping away.

'Opposing Cage Rage please welcome – The Dark Angel!'

Again, the crowd roared as the music pumped, and even more smoke filled the arena. The Dark Angel was anything but dark. He was a young guy with silver-grey hair and silver-grey shorts, and he had two enormous grey angel wings strapped to his back. His chest was covered in silver glitter and when he smiled, he showed a pair of huge dimples in his babyface cheeks.

A ten-second countdown began, and the lights swirled around the arena like a giant clockface whilst bodyguards marched around the circle in time to the music. As they passed by, one guard stopped in front of Oliver and smiled, showing his gold teeth. Oliver instantly recognized the teardrop tattoo, below his left eye. Suddenly a loud buzzer sounded and the guard moved away. The Dark Angel shrugged off his wings and the fighting began.

Oliver watched as Charlie darted around the cage, taking photo after photo of the two boys knocking the hell out of each other. Kicking, slapping, punching, it was brutal. A buzzer signified the end of the round as the boys parted and Lilly-May strutted back on with her co-star Mary-Lou. This time their signs read 'Round 2 – There's Gonna Be Tears!'

* * * * * * * * * *

After the third fight, Charlie had enough material and they left Hades for a round or two of tequila shots chased down with some old-fashioned beers.

'Well, Charlie Black,' Oliver grinned, 'finally, we get to spend some time together.'

'Yes, but short-lived, I'm going to Paris next Friday to spend Christmas and New Year with a friend.'

Oliver smiled, 'Oh really? Well, it just so happens that I'm also traveling to Paris next week.'

'You're kidding me?' Charlie said with a cheeky grin.

'Seriously I am, I'll be in Paris on the twenty-eighth and twenty-ninth, after a day in Monte Carlo. We've got a break in shooting and I'm looking at buying a property down there.'

'Why Monte Carlo?'

'My producer Kitty Wallis has a place nearby and she was telling me of a great investment near the harbor.'

'Maybe we can meet in Paris then?'

Oliver smiled at her, 'They do say it's the most romantic city in the world.'

'This time you get to choose the date.'

'Ok, and I promise, no blood sports,' Oliver teased her.

Charlie was warming to Oliver with every minute that passed.

'You can meet my friend. You'll love her.'

Oliver rolled his eyes, 'I'm glad you said *her*!'

Charlie pulled a face as Oliver smiled.

'What?' she questioned him.

Oliver looked at Charlie and sighed, 'Why do you feel so inevitable to me?'

Charlie pondered on his words as she ordered another round of drinks.

They called it a night around one in the morning and Charlie insisted on getting a taxi home. She didn't want any of that kissing goodnight on the doorstep. When the taxi pulled up, she kissed him tenderly on the cheek. 'See you in Paris, handsome.'

Oliver couldn't help but notice his heart skipped a beat as he waved goodbye. What he didn't notice was the stranger in the doorway watching his every move. The stranger with a teardrop tattoo.

* * * * * * * * *

The night at Hades was a huge success in more ways than one. Charlie's photos were published in many industry magazines. A photo showing The Dark Angel knocking out Cage Rage, with sweat hanging in mid-air around their heads made the front cover of the Christmas edition of *Cage Fury*, a monthly magazine.

Oliver wrapped for the year on the movie and spent Christmas Day with Cheryl at Kitty and Julian's house. It was an open house for Kitty's friends and the management team from Precious Studios. Brett was holding fort with Bruce Willis and Demi Moore who were listening to Matt Damon and Ben Affleck regaling stories from their 'drama geek' days. At one point,

Cheryl, after her sixth glass of champagne, could be seen laying across Kitty's grand piano, draping a feather boa around Elton John as he duetted with her singing 'Don't Go Breaking My Heart'. Oliver was looking forward to teasing her relentlessly about that over the next few years. He called his mum at eight, which was late afternoon for Betty. She was spending the day with Alan and sounded like she'd had one too many gins. Betty and Alan had planned a summer wedding and Oliver promised he would do his best to be there. All in all, Oliver had a good Christmas, but he couldn't stop thinking about meeting Charlie in Paris.

* * * * * * * * *

Charlie and Henry spent Christmas with Yvette, Henry's beautiful mother. Paris was divine, the food was divine, and Yvette's apartment had an amazing view of the Eifel Tower from the balcony. Henry was appalled to hear what had happened to Charlie's inheritance.

'And to think that Thomas Hassler is behind it. I feel like marching up to him and... and...' Henry was seething.

'Henry, there's nothing I can do, by the law he's blameless. One day I'll get my revenge, but in the meantime open another bottle of champagne.'

'So, what's all this about a new love interest?'

Charlie widened her eyes, 'Did I tell you about the guy I bumped into a couple of times in St. Moritz?'

'Oh, only a hundred times,' Henry teased, 'he's in movies, right?'

'Yes, and I met him again, quite by accident. He's called Oliver Diamond, he was in that movie last year, *Stealth*.'

'I remember, and... I've already met him.' Henry looked at Charlie.

'You've met him? What do you mean?'

'Oliver Diamond was at the dinner party I went to with Papa. Remember, the one you were too busy to come to. Papa's an investor in the studios he works for.'

Charlie smiled. 'What a small world.'

'He was with Vixen.'

Charlie frowned, 'Oh, was he? Well, he's taking me out on Tuesday. He'll drop by here first to say hi and then we're going on a date. "Somewhere special", he said.'

'That sounds very mysterious. Maman's off to Milan for a week, so we'll have the apartment all to ourselves. I've got a date on Tuesday, also.'

Charlie sat up, 'Who with?'

'Oh, some gorgeous designer Maman set me up with.'

Charlie smiled at Henry, 'Well, aren't we the lucky ones?'

Henry laughed, 'Yes, but I'm agonizing over what to wear, "old" slutty or "new" slutty?'

* * * * * * * * *

Henry smiled at her date, a handsome Italian clothes designer called Giovanni, and leaned into Charlie.

'Maman did good!'

'Henry, you're incorrigible…' Charlie laughed.

Oliver remembered Henry from Kitty's dinner party, mainly because she'd hit it off with Vixen, not many girls did that by all accounts.

'So, Oliver,' Henry said as she passed him a glass of bubbly, 'what's this mysterious date you're taking my friend on then?'

Oliver grinned, 'She'll have to wait and *see*. Oh… there's a clue there already.'

Charlie frowned at Henry and then at Oliver.

'First of all, you tell me to wear a dark outfit and now you're being all mysterious.'

Oliver checked his watch. 'Ok, it's time we were going Charlie, I promise you a meal you won't forget.'

And how right he was.

* * * * * * * * *

Charlie stood outside the restaurant, reading the sign over the door.

'*Les Tables Noire*? What *is* this place, Oliver?'

'It's a different style of eating that I thought would be fun.' He laughed, half wishing he had booked a restaurant on the banks of the Seine.

Charlie frowned, 'The black tables? I don't understand.'

Suddenly the doors opened, and the maître d' beckoned them inside, clapping his hands twice. 'Attention! Attention!'

'Oliver Diamond, what have you done?' Charlie whispered out of the corner of her mouth as they made their way inside the entrance. The waiter opened another door and half-pushed them into a pitch-black room.

'Oliver, what's happening?' Charlie began to get a fit of the giggles.

'It's a new dining experience,' Oliver giggled back, 'It's called dining in the dark.'

'Dining in the...? Ow!' Charlie shouted as her leg struck a table. An arm grabbed her and guided her to a seat nearby.

Oliver sat opposite Charlie and whispered across to her, 'Are you ok?'

'Apart from a bruised leg, yes.'

'I didn't think it through, did I?' Oliver whispered.

'Er no,' Charlie was crying with laughter, 'I hope that's your leg I'm stroking with my foot.'

Oliver grinned, 'It's all quite exciting.'

'So, what happens now? How do we read the menu?' Charlie said as a waiter cleared her throat by her side making her jump.

'Monsieur et Madame, I will explain a few things.'

'Ok.' Charlie was having trouble stifling another fit of giggles.

'Your food is a blind menu, which means you don't know what it is. Please let me know if you have any allergies. Madame?'

'Allergies? Er no...apart from dates who don't want to see your face when they're eating.'

'Touché,' Oliver laughed.

'Monsieur, any allergies?'

'Er... yes... I have a peanut allergy. Nothing can go near a peanut.'

By now Charlie was nearly under the table in hysterics. 'It's serious Charlie.' This made her laugh even more. 'The cooking utensils cannot be shared... and no cooking in peanut oil.'

'Very well, leave it to Chef. Just to let you know, most of our waiters are blind or partially sighted. I will be serving you this evening; I am blind, and my name is Rosalyn.'

Charlie sat upright 'Thank you, Rosalyn,' she then whispered heavily to Oliver. 'Why would you come to a place like this when you have a serious allergy?'

Oliver reached across the table. 'Give me your hand.' After clanging her cutlery and nearly knocking her wine glass over Charlie eventually found Oliver's clammy hand.

'It's ok, I have an EpiPen on me at all times,' Oliver whispered.

'A what?'

'If I go into shock, you stab me in the leg with it.'

Charlie lifted her head and roared, she'd no idea if there were other people around her and she didn't care. She felt the room go quiet and stifled her laughter.

'Oliver Diamond, you are something else.'

After the initial shock of complete darkness, and it was totally black, they were soon accustomed to eating 'blind'. The food tasted so much better. They never stopped talking and couldn't wait to go outside and see each other's faces again.

'So how was the apartment in Monte Carlo you viewed?'

'Terrific, I'm seriously thinking about buying it. I would show you some photos but...'

Charlie laughed, 'Er... yeah... maybe later.'

'I propose a toast.' Oliver lifted his wine glass.

'Ok,' Charlie lifted her glass, 'a toast to what?'

'The new millennium and a new beginning for...' Oliver stopped.

'For...? For what Oliver?' Charlie giggled.

'For... for...? Oliver began choking.

'Oliver, stop messing around, you were being all romantic,' Charlie chided him.

'I'm choking... my EpiPen... quick... Charlie... help me...'

Oliver collapsed on the floor, pulling the tablecloth, and its contents, crashing all around him.

'Lights! Please someone switch the lights on!' Charlie shouted frantically.

After a few moments, bright ceiling spotlights snapped on. Charlie was blinded but she could make out Oliver on the floor gasping for air, lying wrapped in a tablecloth with cutlery and up-turned plates of food, around him. He reached into his pocket for his EpiPen. It looked like a large plastic tube, pointed at one end with a button on the other end. Charlie snatched it from him, noticing his face swelling up at a disturbing rate.

'Here goes!' She stabbed his leg pushing the button at the top.

'Someone please call an ambulance! Hurry!'

Rosalyn knelt next to Charlie.

'I have already called one. It will be here soon. We are very near the hospital.'

Charlie hated seeing Oliver in such a state. The other diners looked on in horror, shielding their eyes from the glare of the bright lights. Charlie heard a distant siren and collected her bag from the back of her chair. There, lying in the middle of their empty table was a business card. She picked it up and looked around the room at the concerned guests. A man crossing to the exit smiled, catching the reflection of the strong lights on his gold teeth. The card was blank apart from a goldcrest with a purple turret. Immediately, she knew the calling card belonged to Thomas Hassler.

Chapter Forty-Four

NOW

A Problem Solved

Oliver retrieved the USB from his safety deposit and sat contemplating his next move. He'd sent a message to the number Brett had messaged him from disclosing that the USB at the Cathedral was fake. He waited to see what his response would be. Who would have believed Brett Styles was capable of blackmail and possibly murder? He turned over the USB in his hands as the young bank clerk, Louise, re-entered.

'Have you finished Mr. Diamond?'

'Yes, all done, thank you.'

Suddenly there was a loud bang from the next room.

Oliver turned his head sharply and Louise frowned, 'I must apologize, There's a young couple next door. I think someone has left in a hurry and slammed the door, maybe I should check if they are ok.'

Louise opened the side door and disappeared into the corridor. She knocked on the door and gently pushed it open.

'Nearly finished,' Charlie called out, as she nervously looked at Louise's head poking through the partially opened door.

'Is everything ok?' Louise looked into the room and settled on Marcus, who was sitting, white-faced, in the chair.

'Yes, everything's fine. We need another five minutes, ok?' Charlie smiled, having regained her composure.

Louise looked from one to the other. 'Yes, of course, I'll return in five minutes.'

She closed the door and Marcus and Charlie both let out a sigh of relief as Henry unwrapped herself from the large curtains behind the desk.

'That was close.' Charlie took a breath, 'We need to finish up quickly.'

'What about Thomas Hassler, Charlie?' Henry looked at her friend.

Marcus reached for a glass of water. 'He rumbled us from the start.'

Charlie looked first at Marcus and then at Henry.

'Yes... I wanted to strangle him but... it couldn't have gone any better.' Henry and Marcus both frowned as Charlie smiled, 'We've got him, hook, line, and sinker. It's game on!'

* * * * * * * * *

'It's game on!' Oliver threw the skull USB into the air and caught it as Louise returned from the next room.

'Can I place your deposit box back in the vault now Mr. Diamond?'

'Yes, thank you.'

Oliver exited the room and marched back down the corridor with purpose. Henry opened their door and spotted Oliver.

'Oliver's in the corridor, he's leaving now.'

Charlie looked up. 'What's he doing here, today of all days?'

'I've no idea, but let's go meet Ingrid,' Henry said, removing her lapel badge as she slowly opened the door again. 'Marcus are you ok? You're sweating like crazy.'

Marcus looked up, 'Er, yeah Henry, I'm fine. I'm just *so* hot in all of this getup.'

'Ok, I'll meet you both in the street.'

Charlie checked the room, 'Everything's perfect.'

Louise knocked and re-entered to remove the safety deposit box.

'We must go now, thanks for your help.' Charlie shouted over her shoulder, as she and Marcus left. On the way out, Marcus lifted the nameplate from the door and slipped it into his case.

* * * * * * * * *

Oliver returned to his car. He'd lived through the nightmare of that night for over twenty years and it was now time to face the music and put an end to Brett's blackmailing. But how did Brett know he had the USB in the first place? On leaving the bank he received an irate reply to his text telling him to make his way to the Precious viewing rooms in the basement of The Portman Building in Cannes. It was a small viewing cinema leased by Precious Studios for the Festival. He was to wait in the auditorium at four o'clock until contact was made.

Cannes was only a short drive down the coast and it was buzzing with the festival. Movie buffs and industry professionals had flown in from all over the world. News reporters loitered on street corners vying to grab interviews with the rich and famous.

Oliver valet parked nearby and pulled his cap down as he entered The Portman Building.

The art deco cinema was small, holding hundred and fifty people, and had no screenings until that evening. Oliver let himself in through the back entrance into the dimly lit auditorium and sat in the fifth row, waiting impatiently. Suddenly, the curtains in front of the screen slowly opened and the lights dimmed. He looked around. There was no one in the auditorium but he could see a figure in the control room. After being shot at earlier that morning he was feeling very uneasy.

'Hey, I know who you are,' Oliver shouted into the air, 'Come down, let's talk about this.' Silence.

Then a film began playing on the screen. Oliver turned to see Kitty's swimming pool with Rick Krane's body floating on the surface. Then he watched his younger self staring at the body. Brett and John, the bodyguard, joined him and between them, they retrieve the body.

Then John moves out of the shot leaving Brett and Oliver. There's no sound, only black and white images of that night twenty-four years ago. Brett searches the body and looks into the pool. Then he leaves Oliver alone, staring at the body. Oliver is then seen picking something from under the nearby statue and pocketing it as Kitty appears at the door of the house. Oliver swallows hard. *Why now, after all these years?* Oliver leaves the pool and joins Kitty, taking her arm he enters the house. The film ends and Oliver stares at the blank screen.

He then hears someone walk slowly from the back of the auditorium and sit in the seat behind him.

'Ok, Brett, it's over,' Oliver said over his shoulder, 'I know it was you who killed Rick and I know it's you who's been blackmailing me these past few months.'

Then Oliver heard a voice from the seat behind him.

'But, Oliver Diamond... I'm not Brett Styles.'

* * * * * * * * * *

Charlie and Marcus walked down the staircase into the bank foyer as quickly as they could. As they approached the revolving doors Charlie heard a voice.

'Mademoiselle Mars!'

She stopped in her tracks, turned slowly, and smiled, 'Monsieur Lagarde!'

The floor manager looked strangely at Marcus.

'Are you alright Monsieur?'

Charlie looked at Marcus and stared in horror at his crooked nose. He'd been sweating so much, that the glue holding the prosthetic had finally given in. She scowled at him, staring at his nose as it slowly slid down to one side. Marcus was cross-eyed trying to see what she was looking at. Monsieur Lagarde, now open-mouthed, slowly pointed at Marcus's nose. Charlie had to think fast.

'You see, Monsieur Lagarde, I was checking an insurance policy from my safety deposit box. My boyfriend has recently had plastic surgery... and...' Charlie was now heavily whispering,

'...and as you can see... it hasn't gone *that well.*' She mouthed the last two words. Marcus took a handkerchief from his pocket and held it to his nose with a horrified looked in his eyes as Charlie continued,

'We need to go right away to the hospital.'

'Yes of course Mademoiselle Mars... immediately!' Monsieur Lagarde stepped to one side. 'I do hope your boyfriend recovers.'

'Yes, so do I.' Charlie now had tears in her eyes as she held a hand to her mouth. As she passed by Monsieur Lagarde she whispered in his ear.

'You should have seen him *before* the operation.'

* * * * * * * * *

Oliver turned in his seat. There, smiling back at him, was Julian Gold, Kitty's husband.

'Julian? I... I don't understand.'

'Don't you? Well, it will all make complete sense soon, come sit by me.'

Oliver climbed over the seat and sat with one seat between himself and Julian.

'What you have in your possession could ruin Kitty, and I simply can't let that happen.'

'But why now, after all this time?' Oliver was confused.

'Because I didn't know the whereabouts of the evidence until a few months ago. John, our head of security, is a very keen gambler and recently he's been down on his luck. Twenty-four years ago, we were in the middle of installing CCTV and as far as we were aware, it wasn't functioning during that party. Recently we discovered that it was. John had been testing a hidden camera and had footage that, quite frankly, incriminated all of us. Well, you, Brett, John, and Kitty at the very least.'

'So how did you come across the footage?' Oliver asked.

'A few months ago, John found himself in trouble with a casino and came running to me. He was blackmailing me with the video evidence, even though it incriminated himself, stupid man. Said he'd been keeping it for a rainy day and now it was torrential.'

'So, you paid for the CCTV footage which revealed me retrieving the USB.'

'That's about it. I take it you know what's on the USB?' Julian looked at Oliver

Oliver waited a beat, 'Yes, I've heard the recordings.'

'So, you know why I need it.' Julian held out his hand, 'Hand it over, Oliver.'

'But what about Rick Krane? What happened that night?'

Suddenly it hit Oliver and he turned to Julian.

'You killed him, you murdered Rick Krane!'

Julian sighed, 'No, not me.'

Oliver's eyes fixed on Julian's, 'Then who?'

Julian looked at Oliver with watery eyes. 'Ok, I'll tell you what happened. The party was in full swing. Vixen had begun her set and I was on my way down to the cellar to find a brandy I'd been keeping for special occasions...'

Julian wasn't Vixen's greatest fan, he figured he would turn in during her crazy concert and have a secret brandy in bed. When he entered the cellar, he heard voices and some kind of struggle. Behind the wine racks, Rick Krane was laying on top of someone. Then Julian realized it was Kitty. She was struggling, trying to push a drunken Rick away, Julian saw red.

'Rick! Get off of my wife!' he screamed, as he tugged at Rick's shirt. Rick turned and, seeing Julian, launched into a demented rage. He grabbed Julian by the throat, pushing him hard against the wine racks. Kitty managed to get herself off the ground.

'Rick, leave him alone, haven't you done enough?' She screamed.

Rick pushed Julian's head against the rack and choked him harder. Kitty was desperate, her hands found a bottle of brandy and she brought it down hard on Rick Krane's skull. He immediately let go of Julian, who fell to the ground choking. Rick collapsed with blood running down his head in two lines.

'Julian, are you alright?' Kitty rushed to her husband's side.

'Yes, I'm ok, I'll get security to sort this out. Once the party's over we'll deal with him.' Then Julian continued, 'What were you thinking of? Being down here with him, alone?'

'Vixen told me he wanted to talk. I should have told you, I know, but I thought he'd be drunk and I could send him on his way. But he was trying to blackmail me. He said he'd

'acquired' voice recordings and evidence of me pumping up the share values illegally. He also had a recording of me asking Brett to get him off the movie. He said it was all on a USB and enough to see me in jail.'

'How the hell did he get this stuff and where is it now?'

'I'm not sure, but I told him I wouldn't be blackmailed. Then he spouted off about how we used to be close and he started to try and kiss me.' Kitty was shaking.

'We need to check his pockets.' Julian bent over his body and searched him.

'Nothing... maybe he hasn't got it with him.'

'I feel a mess, Julian. I need to go and change; I can't be absent for too long.' Kitty wanted to be out of there.

'Yes, you go back to the party, and we'll sort Rick Krane out later. It looks like a mild concussion; he'll sober up in a couple of hours or so.'

'Julian, thank God you arrived when you did.'

'Yes, yes, now go and don't worry.'

Kitty left to change, and Julian tied Rick to a pillar with some rope hanging from a nearby hook.

Later, as the last guests were leaving, Kitty went outside to find John, their head of security. She wanted to know what he was going to do with Rick Krane, but John was nowhere to be seen. As Kitty crossed by the swimming pool Rick emerged from the kitchen door, staggering towards her, holding his head.

'You bitch! Thought you'd tie me up and leave me for dead, did you?'

'Rick, you don't know what you're saying. You attacked Julian!'

'I have everything on here!' Rick spat as he held up a skull USB. 'This will ruin you, Kitty Wallis!'

He was getting nearer Kitty as she edged by the side of the pool, backing up to one of the statues. 'Rick, calm down, let's go inside and talk about this.'

Rick looked at her with hatred in his eyes. 'It's too late for that. If you don't do as I say, this will go out to the press, and you'll be all washed up.'

Kitty looked around desperately, she was trapped against a statue as Rick moved toward her. 'Don't do this Rick. Look at yourself, you're a mess, a drunken mess.'

At that moment Rick lunged for Kitty. She moved to her left as he twisted and banged his head on the outstretched arms of the diving statue. He let out a noise as he fell into the water. Kitty stared into the water, but Rick wasn't moving. Suddenly he floated to the surface of the pool and Kitty screamed.

'The next thing she remembers was you running out of the French windows towards her.' Julian looked at Oliver, 'The rest you know.'

Oliver sighed, 'But how did Rick Krane get hold of these voice recordings in the first place?'

'Again, it was all down to my head of security. John's gambling habit was way out of control. He confessed to wiring our home office in the hope to get some *juicy* material. It was all insurance for him, and he was in the perfect position to do anything without getting found out. At the time of the party, he owed fifty thousand bucks to some loan shark and sold the USB to Rick Krane. He knew Rick would be hungry for anything against Kitty and would pay any price.

After the party, he kept the CCTV footage you saw on the screen, and some twenty-odd years later he decides to sell it back to me.'

'That's some story. But at the cathedral, it was Brett who took the fake USB.'

'He was only helping me out, I'm not as young as I used to be.'

Brett entered the auditorium from the back.

'Oliver, you're doing the right thing,' Brett said as he crossed to stand behind Julian.

Oliver nodded slowly, 'Brett, I certainly hope so.' Oliver frowned and then a sudden thought struck him.

'But, why the hell did someone take a pot shot at me this morning?'

Brett frowned, 'What are you talking about Oliver?'

'This morning in Villefranche, someone was using me as target practice.'

Julian and Brett were stunned. Julian leaned forward to Oliver,

'I have no idea what that was about. We'd never do anything to hurt you Oliver, you know that.'

Oliver nodded, 'But, there's a file on here with a photograph of me, from a casting company…'

Brett smiled, 'Yes, Kitty came across you in London. You reminded her so much of Rick years earlier.'

Julian added, 'It was a practical choice Oliver, you must understand that?'

Oliver sighed as Julian continued, 'Oliver, it all turned out better than we could ever have imagined. Kitty's very fond of you, as we both are… and proud.'

Oliver took the USB from his pocket and stared at the skull for one last time. 'Here,' he dropped it in Julian's palm. 'I can't say I am sorry to get rid of that thing.'

'I promise you this Oliver, the footage at the pool will be destroyed today.'

Oliver was relieved, after all these years he'd finally given up the USB. He also knew that the day wasn't over yet. Whoever had taken that shot at him could be back for more and maybe they wouldn't rest until he was dead. Suddenly his mobile vibrated and an unidentified message came through.

Important. Meet me at Café Bleu on Quai Saint-Pierre, in the harbor at 5 pm

Meet who? Oliver didn't like cryptic messages. He looked at Brett and Julian.

'I have to go; I'll see you at the restaurant later.'

* * * * * * * * *

Charlie and Marcus caught up with Henry and as they rounded the corner, Charlie bent double in fits of laughter.

Henry stopped, 'What? What's so funny?'

Charlie couldn't speak, she pointed at Marcus who was still holding his handkerchief over his nose. He lifted it to show Henry.

'Oh Marcus, that looks nasty.' Henry laughed, 'Come on, we'd better get you back to the hotel without anyone noticing.'

They made it to their room a little after three-thirty to find Ingrid sitting on the bed waiting for them. Charlie took a step towards her.

'Well? How did it go?'

Ingrid looked at all three of them. 'It was... perfect!'

Marcus and Henry said 'Yes!' simultaneously and punched the air.

'Let's see it then, Ingrid.'

Ingrid opened the zip portfolio and produced the picture. Charlie's heart skipped a beat as she scrutinized it.

'And you replaced this with the fake one easily?'

Ingrid sighed, 'Well, I wouldn't say it was easy, but yes, he'll never know until he tries to use the private key on the back.'

Marcus frowned. 'Now, explain to me exactly how this came about.'

Charlie looked at Ingrid and Henry, 'Well, it all *came about* by accident. As you know, I help out on a charity for the Paralympic Games. In one of their lead articles was a photograph of a Paralympic swimmer, Siobhan Hassler, standing with her father, *Thomas Hassler*. I'd seen her photograph before in the office of Hase International when I invested my money here in Nice. I couldn't believe I was looking at the man who murdered my father and also cheated me out of ten million dollars. There he was looking all smug. I showed Henry, who remarked on the picture on the wall behind Thomas Hassler. She recognized it as Cryptoart.' Henry gave a little curtsey as she was pouring out the champagne.

Marcus frowned, 'Crypto-what?'

It was Henry's turn, 'Cryptoart Marcus. When people hold bitcoins, they need a "private key", like a long PIN, to access their coin. In these days of computer hacks and viruses, people are less likely to keep a record of their private key stored on a laptop or personal computer.'

Charlie interjected, 'Yes, and if you lose your private key, you lose all your money, it's irreplaceable.'

Henry looked at Charlie as she handed out the champagne, 'Yes... so back to me... the trend nowadays is to store your private key in plain sight. That's where Cryptoart comes into play. People commission bizarre art pieces and the key is located behind a security sticker on the back of the picture. Papa has three hanging at his home in Cyprus.'

'Look,' Charlie took the *art* from Ingrid, 'here's the key.' She showed them a sticker with a pull-off strip on the back of the frame. Charlie continued, 'Also, on the bottom left of the front of the picture you will notice a QR code.' Marcus frowned again. 'It's like a barcode at the supermarket Marcus. Whenever you want to buy more bitcoin to add to your account, you scan this QR code with your mobile app and top up as much as you like.'

Ingrid looked at him, 'Fascinating, eh Marcus?'

'Yes, it's like a whole world I know nothing about!' Marcus laughed, as he pulled the rest of his nose away from his face.

'So, not only did Henry recognize the style as Cryptoart, but she also knew someone who designed such artwork.' Henry sat back on the bed drinking her champagne, looking pleased with herself.

Marcus nodded, 'So, you used the photograph you had to make a copy of the artwork and Ingrid switched the artwork this morning.'

Charlie nodded, 'Yes, but the private key behind the art sitting in Thomas Hassler's office right now is a string of useless numbers and letters.'

Ingrid looked at Charlie, 'But first I had to set up my alias. I disguised myself as Siobhan, his daughter. She was the only person who would have access to his office and not raise any suspicion.'

Charlie nodded, 'Yes, that was the tricky part.'

Ingrid continued, 'Charlie discovered that Siobhan now lives in St. Moritz with her grandmother, so I was able to study her quite easily. A month ago, I carried out a test run. Charlie tracked down his offices and discovered that Thomas Hassler was away for a few days at a conference. I visited his office as Siobhan, his assistant didn't take any notice. Siobhan is partially sighted and deaf, so it was easy. This set up today's visit, she'd seen me once already, twice was normal.'

Marcus had a thought, 'But why the elaborate scam this morning at the bank? Why not wait for him to be away and carry out the switch?'

Henry looked at Charlie who answered Marcus, 'I had three reasons. Firstly, if something went wrong switching the art, we may have gained his signature at the bank and scammed money from him anyway. Secondly. I needed to catch him off-guard. As I suspected, he knew we were trying to scam him, and now thinks we failed. He won't think twice about his precious Cryptoart.'

Marcus looked at Charlie, 'And thirdly?'

Charlie looked out of the window. 'Thirdly, I had to see him face to face. The man responsible for so many bad times in my life and so much hatred in me.'

Henry looked at Charlie, 'Now what do we do with this?' She looked at the picture of the White Rabbit surrounded by money.

Charlie turned and lifted her glass, 'You leave that to me. I'm going to drink this champagne and then empty his bitcoin wallet dry.' She lifted her glass, 'To Thomas Hassler.'

They all joined in, 'Thomas Hassler!'

Chapter Forty-Five

THEN

Doctor's Orders

Charlie and Oliver sat on the balcony of Henry's mother's apartment and looked on in awe, as the Eiffel Tower showered the sky with a pyrotechnic feast for the eyes.

Charlie chinked glasses with Oliver, 'Happy New Year, handsome.'

'Happy New Millennium, beautiful one.'

Charlie looked into Oliver's eyes, 'It's not quite the way I pictured celebrating the millennium.'

Oliver smiled, 'Me neither, but I wouldn't have it any other way.'

Charlie sighed as she snuggled up close to Oliver under a fleece blanket.

'A few days ago, you were in hospital fighting for your life.'

'Yes, well I'd rather not think about that, thank you.'

It had been a close-run thing, but thanks to the EpiPen pumping Oliver with a quick dose of chemicals and the proximity of the hospital, he'd been discharged the following day. He wasn't telling Kitty, or his mother for that matter, about his brush with death. The hospital was private and promised not to disclose anything. *In Stitches* was due for release in the spring and nothing could overshadow that. Charlie had been amazing, insisting he stay with her at Henry's so she could take care of him day and night. He slept in her bed whilst she slept on the sofa a mere three meters away. Henry's new relationship was at the early honeymoon stage, and she was spending every waking and sleeping moment with Giovanni.

Oliver was feeling back to normal and well-rested. As the fireworks continued, he picked up Charlie and carried her into her bedroom. Fireworks lit the room in different colors with a loud fizz, bang, bang as he laid her on the king-size bed.

'I don't think the patient should be doing this,' Charlie teased him.

Oliver looked down at his beautiful Charlie, 'Doctor's orders, I'm afraid.'

* * * * * * * * *

Charlie didn't mention Thomas Hassler's business card, for the time being; she didn't want Oliver thinking he was involved with some crazy woman. But she knew that Thomas Hassler had something to do with Oliver's collapse. She shuddered at the thought of anyone involved with that evil man being beside her in the darkness of the restaurant.

Oliver was due back in LA on the second and Charlie a few days later. He was embarking on a short marketing tour for the first film of the franchise, *In Stitches*, and then on location in Italy for *A Stitch in Time*. Kitty and Jason Ross were shifting their part of the shoot to Greece before returning to LA for some final scenes with Oliver in April.

Oliver and Charlie promised to keep in regular contact with each other and meet whenever they could over the next few months. It wasn't easy, but between them, they spoke three or four times a week. Charlie had a full diary and wasn't always available when Oliver was and vice versa. But with Cheryl's help, Oliver managed to sneak away for twenty minutes here and there.

Since scoring a few front covers, Charlie was in high demand, but she was distracted by thoughts of Thomas Hassler. So much so, that she decided to call William Black, her estranged uncle. He'd given her his business card in Boston, and she'd thought many times about contacting him but had resisted temptation until now.

'Hello?'

She paused, 'Hello… William?'

'Yes, this is William, who's this?'

Charlie sighed, 'It's me…'

'Charlotte…? Charlie? I thought you'd never call, are you ok?'

Charlie hesitated, she was wishing she hadn't made the call, what should she say?

'Charlie…?' He repeated. The thought of William stirred her memories again.

'Yes… sorry… I don't know why I've called,' Charlie began to backtrack.

William spoke before she could cut him off. 'Listen, whatever you think, whatever has happened, I'm here for you.'

A tear fell down Charlie's cheek.

'That's good to hear. There are some things I haven't told you...'

Charlie revealed everything to William. When she told him about Thomas Hassler embezzling her investment, he didn't sound surprised.

'I was aware Charlie, may I call you Charlie?'

She hesitated, 'Yes... ok.'

'The lawyer, Thurgood Brown, let it slip. I wanted to call you but decided to wait for you to contact me. I'm so angry that he took your inheritance, was there any other contact?'

Charlie swallowed hard, 'Yes, in Paris recently.' Charlie told William about the night at the restaurant and the card she found on the table. He was disturbed.

'What? That's gruesome, let me see if there's anything I can do about Thomas Hassler.'

'I don't expect you to do anything, it's good to get it off my chest and talk about it.' Charlie wondered what her life would have been like if her uncle had been around when she was growing up.

'Thomas Hassler is very dangerous. He's locked up for fraud, but look what he can do from a prison cell,' William said sternly.

Charlie had to ask the question, 'But why has he got it in for me? He already murdered my father.'

William spoke slowly, 'I'm not sure yet, but I will get to the bottom of this. He'll be in contact with some pretty nasty pieces of work on the inside. Be careful Charlie, I'll be in touch,' then he hung up.

It was strange how Charlie felt a little lighter after speaking with William. It was also strange that after that phone call she heard nothing else from Thomas Hassler. Nothing else, that is, until the night of the fire.

Chapter Forty-Six

THEN

A Spontaneous Gesture

When *In Stitches* was released, it hit the ground running. It was an overnight box office success.

'Just what people need!' 'You'll be "in Stitches"!' 'Oliver Diamond, breakout success!' 'First *Stealth* and now *In Stitches*… what's next for this Brit in LA?'

The reviews were tremendous, and Kitty was over the moon. The follow-up movie, *A Stitch in Time*, wrapped at the end of June. Oliver had a couple of months before the final film in the franchise, *All Stitched Up*, began pre-production and was looking forward to spending some time with Charlie. He was thrilled to make the call to his mother to tell her that he'd be attending her wedding. Betty screamed down the phone when he broke the news. She'd missed her boy, but she was more excited that he was bringing a girlfriend with him to the UK.

'Oliver's girlfriend will be joining him for the wedding.' She told her hairdresser the week before the ceremony. 'She's a very famous photographer, she shoots all the stars,' Betty announced to the salon. Tracy nodded in the mirror as she was applying the peroxide. Betty's little black poodle, Marky Mark, sat curled up by her chair as she gloated; Betty loved nothing more than a good gossip at the hairdressers.

She smiled at Tracy.

'Yes, she knows all the stars. The likes of Streisand, De Niro, Hanks, Roberts, the Beckhams. No doubt she'll be putting some of the photographs from my wedding into *Hello* magazine.'

Betty reached down and stroked her poodle.

'We'd like that, wouldn't we Marky Mark? Yes...'

As Betty sat upright again Tracy accidentally dropped some peroxide which landed squarely on Marky Mark's black back. Tracy looked down in horror, but Betty was none the wiser.

'Do you get *Hello* magazine, Tracy?' Betty said as she leafed through an old edition of *Woman's Weekly* from the stand by her chair.

Tracy frowned, staring at the peroxide on the sleeping poodle.

'Er... no I don't get *Hello* magazine, is it like *Inside Soap*?'

Betty ignored her, engrossed in an article about Fifty Natural Ways to Stay Young. Tracy carefully slipped off her left trainer and gently stroked Marky Mark's back with her socked foot in a vain attempt to wipe the peroxide off him. This only made matters worse. Tracy hurriedly finished her hair, disappearing for an early lunch as Betty paid the cashier.

'Well, I must go and check the seating plan for the wedding.' She turned to give Tracy her tip. 'Here you go Tracy, a little... Oh...?' Tracy was nowhere to be seen, so Betty turned to leave the salon.

'Come on Marky Maaaaark!' Betty screamed out as she stared horrified at her pride and joy. Marky Mark, who this morning looked like a cute black poodle, now looked like an ugly old skunk.

* * * * * * * * *

Charlie was thrilled Oliver had asked her to accompany him to England to attend his mum's wedding. On arrival, Betty instantly fell in love with Charlie, she knew a good match for her boy, and she was looking right at her. Oliver could see that Alan adored his mum, they looked so happy. The ceremony took place on a private estate with a select gathering of fifty-five guests. The paparazzi were out in force as soon as they heard Oliver Diamond would be attending. Oliver paid for Betty and Alan's honeymoon, a luxurious ten days in a villa on stilts in the Maldives, one of Betty's dreams.

'It's in the Arabian Sea of the Indian Ocean, you know,' She told everyone on her wedding day.

'Another one off my bucket chart!'

'List,' Oliver corrected her.

'Yes, that's right,' she said as Alan whisked her off around the dancefloor to the strains of The Black-Eyed Peas.

Oliver and Charlie rounded off their visit to England with a night at The Dorchester on London's Park Lane. 'A night of five-star luxury for a five-star girl,' he told her when they were in the limousine driving down the M1 motorway.

Oliver looked out of the window at the English countryside speeding by. His thoughts were on his future, a future he knew he couldn't spend without Charlie.

* * * * * * * * *

Back in LA, they divided their time between Oliver's apartment in the hills and Charlie's loft apartment downtown. Oliver bought the property he'd viewed in Monte Carlo and decided to buy his own place in LA. His bank balance was healthy, and now was the time to buy. He temporarily moved in with Charlie. A big step, but the next natural stage of their lives together.

Cheryl loved living across the street from Oliver, it made everything so much easier having her boss at hand.

One evening Oliver couldn't contain himself anymore.

'Charlie…?'

'Yes, handsome?' She was distracted, reading the latest Danielle Steel.

'I need to ask you something…'

She turned a page, 'What's that…?'

Oliver cleared his throat and Charlie looked up from her book. He was on bended knee about to open a ring box in his hands.

'No!' Charlie screamed.

Oliver snapped the box shut and looked around. 'What? What's the matter?'

'It's all wrong.' Charlie was frowning.

'All wrong? What's all wrong?' Oliver had no clue what she was talking about.

'This…' she gestured to his ring box. 'It's all wrong! I have it in my head. In my head it's perfect, and this is… all wrong!'

Oliver swallowed and looked from side to side uneasily. 'O… K… then how do we make it "all right"?'

Charlie jumped up. 'First, I need to change. You need to change. You're wearing grey sweats for goodness' sake!'

'Right, I'll change.' They both ran into the bedroom.

'Anything else?' Oliver asked, pulling on a pair of chinos.

'Yes… champagne… we don't have any… and… and… candles.' Charlie pulled on a white cotton dress. She looked beautiful.

'Ok… champagne and candles.' Oliver was now standing anxiously in his cream chinos and a black t-shirt.

Charlie pulled him towards her, 'You look so handsome.' They kissed.

'I'll go to the bar around the corner and pick up the champagne whilst you sort out the candles.' She grabbed her bag and ran back to Oliver, kissing him again.

'This is going to be absolutely perfect.'

As Charlie raced out of the apartment, Oliver opened the ring box. Sitting there, on its silk cushion was the most beautiful solitaire diamond on a platinum band.

'A diamond for my Charlie Diamond,' he muttered. Suddenly he sprang into life and rushed around, collecting any candles he could find.

* * * * * * * * * *

On her way back to the apartment Charlie called Cheryl. It was five in the morning in Paris, Henry would be sleeping.

'Hi Charlie, I didn't expect to hear from you until after the weekend.'

'He's about to do it, Cheryl!' Charlie couldn't contain herself.

'What? He's about to do wh... oh my God!'

Charlie laughed, 'I know, I can't believe it. I've dashed out to buy a bottle of bubbly, not a word though Cheryl.'

'Your secret's safe with me.' Charlie heard Cheryl's door buzzer in the background.

'Oh, have you got an assignation tonight?' Charlie teased.

'No, I wish! It's my cousin Brian borrowing some DVDs. He's trying to impress some actress with his knowledge of Martin Scorsese.'

'Ok, you go. I had to call you... I couldn't wait, we'll talk tomorrow, and don't forget, act surprised when he tells you!'

Cheryl laughed as Charlie ended the call and turned the corner. Speeding towards her was a fire engine, lights on and siren blaring out. Charlie looked up, horrified, as glass shattered over the street, followed by a fireball of flames leaping out of her apartment.

Charlie ran towards her doorway, screaming.

'No! No! Oliver!'

* * * * * * * * *

Charlie stared at the flames. The firemen moved her out of harm's way, but she didn't care, the love of her life, Oliver Diamond, was up there. She screamed to the fireman and told him her boyfriend was trapped on the second floor engulfed in a ball of fire. How had this happened? She stood in a crowd of bystanders, helplessly watching the firemen trying their best to abate the raging flames. The police stopped traffic and a crowd was building near the burning building, all apart from one man walking in the opposite direction. Red lights flashed across his face as another fire engine raced past. It was the face of the man with the teardrop tattoo.

Suddenly Charlie heard a voice calling her.

'Charlie! Charlie!' She turned, and there, pushing through the crowd, was Oliver with Cheryl close behind him.

'Oliver!' Charlie cried as she ran towards him. His big arms wrapped around her as she sobbed onto his shoulder.

'I thought you...' She cried squeezing him as tight as she could.

'I know, I know, I'm ok. We're both ok.'

Charlie looked into his eyes. 'What the hell happened?'

Cheryl joined Charlie and put her arms around her.

'Well after you left,' Oliver explained, 'I found some candles but couldn't find a lighter anywhere. I knew Cheryl would have one, so I quickly ran across to borrow one.'

'Yes, when you called me, it was Oliver at the door, not my cousin,' Cheryl added.

'As soon as Cheryl answered the door, we heard the sirens and came out to see what was going on. Thank God we found you here.'

'Let's go back to mine,' Cheryl suggested.

'I want to stay around a bit,' Charlie said.

Oliver looked at Charlie, 'In that case let's sit in The Daily Grind and have a coffee, we can nip back whenever you want.' She nodded feebly and looked back at the flaming apartment. Then it hit her.

'To think, we could have been in there Oliver.'

Oliver slowly nodded and put his arms around Charlie and Cheryl.

* * * * * * * * * *

After the fire, they stayed in a temporary unit until they found a new home. Oliver worried about Charlie; something didn't add up. He was convinced that he'd seen a familiar face when he found Charlie outside the burning apartment. As he was moving through the crowd, a man had pushed past him. He recognized the teardrop tattoo instantly and had watched enough prison documentaries to know what that signified. A teardrop tattoo in prison culture stated that a man was dangerous; it signified he had committed murder.

Charlie canceled her studio shoots and bought a new set of camera equipment, at least that way she could keep her on-location bookings. The insurance assessor declared the fire as 'suspicious', with no evidence of arson.

However, he did suspect the presence of accelerants. There were some localized burn patterns to the floor, which was a sign of overheating in that area, suggesting something was thrown in to cause the fire, but it was inconclusive. The door was found to be locked and no sign of forced entry.

The insurance would payout eventually, and Charlie decided it was time to look elsewhere for a new studio. She retrieved everything she could, which wasn't much. The fire had raged quickly, and the damage was severe. She took a last look around and felt sad as she remembered how excited she was when she first viewed it with Cheryl. She slid the door back across the entrance for a final time and walked down to the foyer to open her mailbox for any last post. It contained a credit card bill, electricity bill, flyers for pizza, and a hand-written cream envelope. Charlie frowned and opened the envelope. Inside was the purple turret calling card of none other than Thomas Hassler. Charlie's heart raced; would this ever end? She sat on the stairs and thought hard. What good was it going to the police? The card proved nothing, there was no evidence.

She would speak to two people about this. Firstly, Oliver. The time had come to tell him everything, after all, his life had been at risk, twice. Secondly, she had to make another call to the only man who may be able to stop this, William Black.

* * * * * * * * *

William Black was devastated and angry when he heard the news from Charlie. Thomas Hassler had gone too far.

'Charlie, he's crazy, he feels he's won. He's taken your money and now he's threatening Oliver.' It was time for William to do some digging of his own. He smiled to himself, 'Every dog has its day.'

Thomas Hassler had caused Charlie enough pain and grief, but he wasn't going to hurt her anymore, of that William was determined.

* * * * * * * * *

When Charlie told Oliver about Thomas Hassler, his first thought was to inform the police, but Charlie made him promise not to do that. It would rake up the past and there was no concrete proof of anything. Nothing linked him directly to the fire, or any of the bizarre events, for that matter. When she called William Black, he assured her Thomas Hassler would go away and stop targeting her and Oliver. He told her in such a way that she believed him and only then did she begin to sleep at night.

Oliver's real estate agent found them the perfect house in Hollywood Hills. It was three triple-story houses, linked together with glass walkways. Ultra-modern with an infinity pool on ground level and sweeping gardens complete with a tennis court. There was the obligatory gym, sauna, and a cinema room on the lower level. Every room had floor-to-ceiling windows opening up to breathtaking views, and the décor was grey and white with cream soft furnishings. Complete with electric curtains, hidden lighting, and under-floor heating, it exuded luxury. There was also, a separate annex with its own entrance. This had two bedrooms, a living area with a kitchen, a small gym, and a rooftop terrace. It was perfect for when Oliver's mum and Alan wanted to visit. With that and the penthouse in Monte Carlo, his bank account was empty. He had to arrange a small mortgage for the purchase, but he was Oliver Diamond and in high demand. Many studios were vying to win him over, but he was always transparent with Kitty about their lucrative offers. Next year, after the final movie, *All Stitched Up,* she promised him the lead role in her next blockbuster. The much-anticipated adaptation of the bestselling book *Poison*, a dark thriller with twists and turns.

Oliver occasionally thought back to the night of Kitty's party. The conversation in the cellar between Vixen and Rick Krane, Rick's body in the pool, and the mysterious skull USB. But now his mind was on Charlie. His proposal had been interrupted the night of the fire and it was time to make amends.

Chapter Forty-Seven

NOW

The Man Who Sold His Soul

Oliver sat outside Café Bleu looking out onto the harbor, it was five minutes past five. After his orange juice, he heard a voice in his ear.

'Teetotal are we now, darling?'

It was Vixen, she was wearing blue sweats, sunglasses, and a red baseball cap. She sat down in the chair opposite.

'Vixen…' he whispered. The café wasn't too busy, but the last thing he wanted was to draw attention. 'I'm not having a good day, what's all this about?'

She pulled down her glasses revealing her big blue eyes, flashing mischievously. 'No, I know your day's not good, it never is when you're being shot at.'

Oliver stared at her. 'How do you know about that?'

She continued, 'I was staying at The George Hotel last night.'

'So, it was you who sent me the text to meet you across from that hotel?'

'No, of course not!' Vixen snapped. 'What text?'

'The text said to go to the patisserie opposite The George Hotel and wait, then you shot at me!'

'Why would I shoot at you?'

'Well, someone did. Someone who knows me.'

'Look, I came here to warn you to be careful. Yes, I was at the hotel this morning and before leaving my security detail was carrying out one last sweep. I get all sorts of death threats, daily! The drone spotted a gunman setting up on the balcony one floor below mine.'

Oliver looked at her in disbelief, 'You have drones?'

Vixen sighed, 'Yes, I have drones. My security burst in and wrestled him to the ground. He managed to escape but we did find this on the floor of the room he was in.'

Vixen produced a small photograph from her pocket, a photograph of Oliver.

'Christ...' Oliver felt sick.

'Go carefully Oliver,' Vixen warned him, 'You've got your première next week, right?'

Oliver sighed, 'Yes, you're singing at the post-screen party remember?'

She drank from Oliver's orange juice. 'What's the movie called again? Oh, yes, cute title, *The Man Who Sold His Soul*.' She stood and held his chin.

'Let's hope you don't end up selling yours.'

Oliver gave her a half-smile and stared at the photograph. Vixen produced a small zip bag and placed it on the table in front of Oliver. He looked up, 'What's this?'

'Open it somewhere secluded, I worry about you.'

Oliver slowly unzipped the bag; it contained a revolver and ammunition.

'Jesus, Vixen! What are you playing at?'

'I'm serious! You may need it.'

She turned to leave.

'One more thing, my security described your shooter as bald with gold teeth and a teardrop tattoo.'

* * * * * * * * * *

Charlie raced back to Monte Carlo as fast as the traffic allowed. With the film festival in full throttle, everywhere was unusually busy. She'd said her goodbyes to Ingrid, Henry, and Marcus. They were all looking forward to meeting again the following week at Oliver's première.

When she was five minutes from the apartment, she facetimed Cheryl from the car.

'Cheryl, hi!'

'Hey Charlie, how's everything going?'

Cheryl was bobbing around her hotel room. Charlie could tell she was dashing about, as usual.

Charlie smiled, 'Today's good, a very good day.'

'Glad to hear it, we're getting ready to leave. We're still meeting at the restaurant, right?'

'Yup, La Vue restaurant on top of Hotel Du Palais. We have the entire place to ourselves.' Charlie squinted into the sunshine and dropped her visor.

'How have they been today?'

Cheryl laughed, 'I want to say "as good as gold" but I'd be lying. My mobile was dropped into the hotel fish tank at lunch and it's not been the same since.'

The image flashed and went black and then Cheryl came back hitting the screen. Charlie laughed as the lights ahead turned red. She pulled up the hand-break. 'Put them both on.'

Cheryl moved to one side to reveal the most gorgeous twins you ever saw. Nine years old with dark brown hair and faces of angels. They were sitting on a sofa, staring out of Charlie's screen with enormous grins.

'Now then you two, you must behave for Auntie Cheryl.'

They nodded slowly, eyes full of mischief.

'Blue... Raven, you're not supposed to drop mobiles into fish tanks!'

They shook their heads, 'Sorry Mommy.' They both chimed. Blue's hair was gelled down on his head in a side parting and Raven's shoulder-length hair was in loose curls. They both had the stunning looks of their parents.

The screen flashed black once more and then Cheryl came back into the shot.

'Hey, it was a great sleepover, I love having them.'

Charlie smiled at Cheryl, 'I'll get you a new mobile tomorrow, I promise.'

'Don't worry about it.' Cheryl said as she tickled the twins, who squealed with delight.

A car hooted behind Charlie as the lights ahead turned green.

'Listen, I've got to go.'

'Ok, see you at the restaurant.' Cheryl's camera shook as she ended the call mid-giggle from the twins.

Charlie smiled and felt guilty that she hadn't thought about her twins all day. But it had been one hell of a day. Once back at the apartment she would store the Cryptoart, shower and change, then drive back to Cannes to meet everyone. She hadn't heard from Oliver, but that wasn't unusual. He was always wrapped up in one thing or another. After the day she'd had, she longed to hug him and her babies.

* * * * * * * * *

Oliver was at a loss for what to do, he was due to meet Charlie and the others at the restaurant in a couple of hours. Cheryl was bringing the twins with her. As soon as they had discovered Cheryl was staying at The Hard Rock Hotel, they had begged for a sleepover. He opened a message on his mobile from Brett.

It's out on social media that we're all at Hotel Du Palais, so we've changed the venue. Now Palm room of Hotel Belmont. Please tell Charlie.

Oliver sighed; it was a good thing. He'd been a target this morning and he didn't want to put Charlie or his children in any danger. No one would know about the venue change, he called Charlie.

'Hey, you.'

'Oliver, I've missed you today.' Charlie stood in her apartment and looked out into the harbor.

'You missed me?' Oliver smiled, 'It's good to know after twenty years I still have the same effect on you.'

Charlie grinned, 'I'm on my way back to Cannes soon.'

'I'm in Cannes now, I'm gonna stay here. I'll buy a change of clothes.'

'Oliver, you need to shower. You've been out all day.'

'I'll sort something, but there's been a change of plan, we're now dining at the Hotel Belmont, Brett messaged.'

'Gotcha, I'll call Cheryl on the way and tell her. That's a shame though, we were having the Hotel Du Palais's special kebabs tonight.'

'Kebab, lamb shank, it's all the same. And Charlie... drive carefully.'

'Of course.'

'And Charlie...'

Charlie sighed, 'What?'

'I love you.'

Charlie's heart skipped a beat, 'I love you too, handsome.'

* * * * * * * * *

Charlie was soon on the road heading back to Cannes. She called Cheryl once more but her mobile rang and rang with no answer. Facetime gave out the 'not connecting' tone, so she called her mobile again until it went to voicemail.

'Cheryl, hi! Hope you get this in time. There's been a change of venue, the meal is now at a private room at the Hotel Belmont, see you there.'

This is what happens when a mobile is dropped into a fish tank! Charlie thought to herself. She slowed down as the traffic ahead ground to a halt and cursed herself for taking the coastal road, it was a big night for the film festival. Charlie considered her options and decided to take the inland road at Nice, Google agreed. She would arrive at The Belmont in around fifty minutes, twenty minutes late was quite a result for Charlie.

* * * * * * * * * *

Françoise, the Head Waiter at the private rooftop restaurant of the Hotel Du Palais, slammed the phone down. '*Merde!*'

He'd been informed by the hotel manager that the private room, complete with an outside balcony, would not be in use that evening. He was so looking forward to meeting Oliver Diamond in person, let alone Kitty Wallis. A last-minute cancellation! He regretted switching rotas from the swimming pool bar-b-que to the rooftop VIP meal, but he knew it was all his fault. He'd leaked the details of the private party on his Instagram page, he couldn't help but show off to his friends. He'd deleted the post quickly and hoped he wouldn't be in too much trouble.

Françoise sighed as looked around the room. The large round table was set out so beautifully with a floor-length, powder-blue tablecloth, crystal glasses, silver cutlery, and white dinner service with ivy running around the edges. Next to every other place setting, gigantic kebab stands reached up in anticipation of their skewered delights. Well, they would remain empty this evening. Inside the doorway was a display holding a large poster depicting a flame with the face of a man with devil horns. It read...

The Man Who Sold His Soul - Starring Oliver Diamond

Palme D'Or Nominee

The hotel would invoice the studio for their work but that was irrelevant to Françoise, he wanted his selfie with Oliver Diamond. He ordered the staff to take up positions elsewhere in the hotel and decided to try his luck with the suckling pig at the swimming pool party.

* * * * * * * * *

Cheryl arrived five minutes late. The traffic had been a nightmare but she, as always, had booked her Uber driver early. The twins were eager to see their parents and tell them about the waterslides at Cheryl's hotel. The elevator doors pinged, and Cheryl stepped out into the short hallway. Through doors to her left, she spotted a poster for *The Man Who Sold His Soul* and frowned. *This must be the right place*, she thought as she entered the empty room. The lights were on, and everything was laid out. I must have got the time mixed up!

Blue frowned. 'Auntie Cheryl, where is everyone?'

Raven giggled to Blue, 'I think Auntie Cheryl got the time wrong.'

'No, Auntie Cheryl didn't get the time wrong,' Cheryl said, trying to open her mobile for the umpteenth time that evening. 'Everyone else got the time wrong.'

Raven shrugged her shoulders.

'What do we do now?' Blue asked, throwing a baseball into the air and catching it.

'Blue! I told you to leave that at my place, why have you brought it here?' Cheryl wasn't happy.

'It's my lucky ball. It goes everywhere with me.'

'Yes, but to dinner?'

'It's signed by Jim Thome!' Blue said indignantly as he showed Cheryl the baseball.

'Yes, you told me a hundred times. You showed me his photo, Jim Thome, a major league player.'

'He holds the record for the most walk-offs in history.'

'What's a "walk-off", Mr. know-everything-about-baseball?'

'Everyone knows what a walk-off is,' Blue replied mischievously.

Raven looked at Cheryl and raised her eyes to heaven. 'Boys!'

'Yes, Raven, boys!'

Raven ran through the room and outside onto the terrace.

Blue grinned at Cheryl. 'You liked Jim Thome, you said so.'

'Yes, well he is quite handsome,' Cheryl laughed.

'Blue! Come and look,' Raven shouted from outside.

'Be careful kids.' Cheryl ran after Blue as he joined his sister, pocketing the ball en route. Music was drifting up from the streets below. The terrace was on the 12th floor and the view over Cannes was stunning.

'Keep away from the edge you two,' Cheryl warned them.

Blue and Raven decided to gaze through the telescope fixed at the side of the terrace.

'Me first! Raven took hold of the telescope and climbed onto the metal walkway, standing on her tiptoes, gazing through the lens around the city.

Armchairs were scattered outside, and Cheryl decided she would sit and wait there. She was too far away to hear the lift *ping* in the hallway. And she was too preoccupied with the twins to notice the man with a teardrop tattoo standing in the doorway looking at Blue and Raven as they tried to pull the telescope from each other.

Chapter Forty-Eight

THEN

Emerald Bay

As the low sun glistened on the crystal-clear emerald sea, Oliver looked out onto the Straits of Malacca. *No wonder they call it Emerald Bay*, he thought absently. Brett came to his side. 'How are you holding up?'

Oliver looked at Brett and exhaled deeply, 'Apart from the heat, I'm good. I hate to ask, but you do have the rings, don't you Brett?'

Brett's face filled with horror and then he smiled. 'Of course I do. Apparently, she's on her way.'

There were a handful of guests, exactly as they wanted it to be. Oliver looked over his right shoulder and smiled at his mum as she was wiping away a tear. Behind Betty and Alan sat Kitty and Julian, looking resplendent in matching cream linen suits. Kitty beamed at Oliver as she squeezed Julian's hand. Next to them was Philip Peters, the director of the movie *All Stitched Up*, which had finally wrapped. Over his left shoulder Oliver smiled at Henry's boyfriend, Giovanni, who was wearing a loud, Indian-style Kaftan, and on either side of Giovanni sat Cheryl and Ingrid. Cheryl looked radiant in a cream, flowing dress and fanned herself desperately with a battery fan she'd purchased at the airport in Kuala Lumpur. She caught Oliver's eye and gave him a thumbs-up as Giovanni passed her a tissue to wipe away a stray tear. Ingrid was elegant as ever, in a lemon chiffon dress with matching fascinator and sandals. In another life, she could have been a supermodel. Seated behind them were Henry's parents, the stunning Yvette Paradis and Dimitri Diakos. Charlie was surprised they could make it but when Yvette learned of the location, she wasn't going to miss it for the world. Charlie asked Henry if they were back together, but Henry denied it saying it was her mother's way of 'making him realize what he was missing'. Next was Charlie's Uncle William. Although he'd never been part of her life, he was her only living relative and Charlie had decided she wanted him there. He would hold a low profile at the ceremony, and he seemed genuinely pleased when Charlie had invited him. When Oliver met him, he couldn't help but think about what a mild-mannered man he was. Intelligent and very easy to talk to. Oliver liked him.

Pangkor Laut Resort was halfway around the world off the west coast of Malaysia. It had melted Charlie's heart when she saw the photos in a wedding magazine. Billed as 'One Island, One Resort', it lived up to expectations. Frequent visitor Pavarotti even had a suite named after him when he declared it to be paradise. And if it was good enough for the likes of Michael Schumacher or Joan Collins, then it would do for Charlie Black.

Following tradition, Oliver and Charlie hadn't spent the previous night together. They slept alone in their separate Sea Villas and in the morning, they had been escorted to their individual, private spa by the resort staff. After hours of spa treatments befitting a warrior and his princess (or a prince and his warrior!), they were ready to pledge their lives to one another. Oliver's thoughts were interrupted by the acoustic band sitting nearby. As the soft music played, he slowly turned. Standing at the end of the shell-lined aisle, amongst the palm trees, was the love of his life, Charlie Black, looking nothing like he could have imagined. Thin diamanté straps were holding a white lace dress with a 'V' shape at the front and back. She was the ultimate glamour bride, her black hair pinned up with tiny strands falling, here and there. Her hair was dotted with miniature white orchids, making her look like a fairy-tale princess. Charlie chose to walk down the aisle with Henry at her side. Her trusty friend, with whom she'd been through thick and thin. Henry looked every bit as stunning in a pale lavender bridesmaid dress complete with orchid-strewn hair.

As they made their way towards Oliver, the select gathering gasped as their eyes fell on the bride for the first time. One or two guests were shedding more tears than expected as Charlie walked slowly between a line of seashells to join her handsome groom. At one point Cheryl let out a loud snort which made everyone laugh and suddenly all nerves were displaced as Oliver and Charlie faced each other hand in hand. The pastor recited the service under the silk wedding arbor where they stood not taking their eyes off each other as the sun slowly sank into the glistening sea.

Chapter Forty-Nine

THEN

The World Is Your Oyster

Life settled down, as much as the life of any Hollywood couple could. A movie star and a famous photographer, a perfect fit.

Shortly after their honeymoon, the world was devastated as the events of 9/11 took every headline. Hollywood was in mourning, as was the entire globe.

Movies centering on terrorist threats or plots ground to a halt and many premières were postponed or canceled.

But Hollywood soon became a fountain of hope and the American spirit survived, as always, in the face of adversity. Everyone reflected on that day. The world was brought to its knees but would soon be dusting itself down and getting up again.

* * * * * * * * *

Oliver and Charlie's house in the Hollywood Hills was perfect and Charlie had discovered a new photography studio in Beverly Hills, nearby. She resisted the temptation to give up her photography and live life as a Hollywood housewife, she was still Miss Independent. The franchise movies from Precious Studios were all huge box office successes. The third film, *All Stitched Up*, was 2002's highest-grossing movie. The industry nicknamed Kitty the producer with the Midas touch, as she had the knack of turning any script or screenplay into gold. She surrounded herself with the best of the best. She hadn't gotten where she was without having a ruthless streak, but she always sought fairness and justice. If you didn't play ball then you were out, it was that simple.

The first movie after the Stitches franchise was *Poison*. It was a great script and she'd received many offers from agents and managers pushing their clients for the lead role. Some tipped this role to be 'Oscar worthy' well before the first frame was shot. Kitty had promised Oliver the role and she was aware that he was more than capable, and the public loved him, not only in the US, but worldwide. He had a homely, honest way with him. When you first met Oliver, you felt you'd known him all your life and he never forgot where he'd come from.

Kitty's instincts were spot on, but then she knew that. *Poison* made a big impact at the box office and in its first weekend, it became the movie with the third-highest box office takings in history. Then it happened. What every actor wants. Oliver Diamond, the boy from Sheffield, was nominated for an Oscar for best actor. Betty and Alan flew in for the ceremony.

'I wouldn't have missed it for the world!' red-gowned Betty proclaimed to the Fox News reporter on the red carpet. Alan hovered in the background as Betty was commandeering the interview with her arm firmly in Oliver's.

Oliver wore a white tuxedo and looked as handsome as ever. Charlie and Henry looked dazzling in their red-carpet gowns, Charlie in a glittering gold Versace and Henry in a cream Jean-Paul Gaultier.

They were followed down the carpet by Henry's supermodel mother, Yvette Paradis with her toyboy lover and singing sensation, August Moon. Yvette's Elie Saab dress was the most revealing of the night, with its white lace and strategic embroidery that left nothing to the imagination. August wore an ultra-white tuxedo with no shirt, just a white bow tie. A singing sensation at twenty-six, he didn't care what the press thought of him. Henry glanced back at her mother and knew her father would be furious when he saw her on the front page of the tabloids the following day. Maybe Yvette was trying to make her ex-husband jealous?

It was Charlie's proudest moment when Oliver's name was called out by Ewan McGregor as the winner of the Oscar for best actor. Oliver hugged Charlie and then his hysterical mother before making his way to the podium. In his speech, he thanked his mother Betty, who had sacrificed so much to send him to drama school. He also paid tribute to Kitty Wallis, without whose help and friendship he wouldn't be standing there. And last, but not least, to his own private Oscar, Charlie Diamond, his absolute inspiration and the love of his life.

After *Poison*, Oliver was in even higher demand as A-listers fell over themselves to work with him. He had a great reputation on set and his career was skyrocketing. Charlie was always supportive, as he was of her career.

She too was fending off a heavy workload and seemed to be forever living in the troposphere as she jetted to one part of the world or another on location shoots for every front cover imaginable. Over the years she forced thoughts of Thomas Hassler out of her head. She would speak with William sporadically; he was always happy to hear about her success and even happier to hear Thomas Hassler was leaving her alone.

* * * * * * * * * *

As the years went by, Charlie and Oliver organized their work life so they could spend maximum time with each other. Summers in Monte Carlo meant Oliver could spend time on his latest hobby, yachting.

It was there he discovered the second love of his life, *Serendipity*, a forty-meter-long luxury yacht. He also added a house in Mayfair, London, to his property portfolio, which his mother used more than they did. When Oliver was on location, Charlie would spend time with Henry whenever she could. Henry was still looking for Mr. Right but seemed to only find Mr. Wrong or Mr. Not-Quite-Right. Giovanni was long gone after she caught him skinny dipping with the pool boy one time too often.

In the summer of 2009, Charlie was thrilled during a shoot in Barcelona to catch up with Marcus. He was finally married to a lovely Spanish girl, Angelina, whom he'd met in Madrid at a wine export conference. The family business was booming and so was Angelina, as they were expecting a baby that Christmas. Charlie couldn't help but feel a pang of jealousy. The one thing missing from her life with Oliver was children. Charlie was desperate to have a child but although they tried and tried, it seemed it wasn't meant to be. They visited the top doctors, but no one could find anything wrong with either of them. Charlie was fast approaching her thirty-second birthday, and although by today's standards she was still young, she yearned to be a young mother with young children.

Charlie told Oliver about meeting Marcus in Barcelona and their history together, much to Henry's dismay. But Oliver was cool about past boyfriends, even if Marcus was her 'first love'.

Oliver and Charlie were spending Thanksgiving at Kitty's open house. Oliver's mother was visiting with Alan, and Betty was having the time of her life. Although she didn't celebrate Thanksgiving, a turkey was a turkey in Betty's mind. They arrived at Kitty and Julian's a little before noon and Betty couldn't resist taking photos wherever she went. She had 'The Facebook', as she called it, and thought it was an excellent way to show her friends in Sheffield her glamourous life.

Oliver gazed out of the living room window at his mum and smiled. She was taking a selfie of her and Alan by the Medusa statue at the end of the swimming pool, encouraging Alan to pull a face like Medusa. Charlie linked her arm in Oliver's as he looked out onto the terrace.

'You're so lucky to have your mum in your life.'

Oliver sighed, 'I know, and I count my blessings every day.'

Betty was dying for a swim, even though the temperature was in the sixties, but she would have to wait until she was back at Oliver's. There would be a photo upload, of course. 'Look at me, swimming in November!' She was dressed in a bright pink Vera Wang with a yellow hibiscus flower print. Oliver had taken her to Vera Wang's shop on Rodeo Drive and told her to pick whatever she liked. He chuckled as she draped herself over one of the statues whilst bossing Alan where to stand to take the best shot.

Oliver leaned down and kissed Charlie, and as he opened his eyes he looked out into the pool and saw Rick Krane's body floating, lifeless, on the surface.

'What's the matter?' Charlie frowned. 'You looked like someone walked over your grave.'

Oliver shuddered, 'I'm thinking back to the early days when I first came to Kitty and Julian's. Something happened the first night...'

'There you are!' Kitty glided into the room looking ultra-glamorous in a red velvet dress complete with a red bow in her blonde hair, 'I do hope I'm interrupting,' she said with a grin. 'We're having an early dinner before the others join for cocktails, so we'd better get seated.'

The Thanksgiving table looked resplendent. Complete with miniature gold pumpkins on long garlands stretching down the table, wending their way between the lit candlesticks. Oliver sat with Charlie opposite Betty and Alan and Kitty sat at one end with Julian at the other. Either side of Kitty was Brett and his current girlfriend, a painfully thin model who went by the name of 'Sparrow'. She announced she was 'a vegan' numerous times and the chef had prepared a nut roast especially for her. Oliver kept his distance. Either side of Julian were his old friends Dorothy and Vern from Idaho. Oliver remembered them from the dinner party some years back, he smiled at Vern starring at Sparrow's cleavage. Dorothy was nudging Betty, pointing at Sparrow as she chased some vegan sushi around her plate with chopsticks. Charlie squeezed Oliver's hand, happy to spend Thanksgiving with him.

Julian stood to propose a toast whilst the waitress delivered a huge dish of fresh oysters.

'Ladies and gentlemen, no, dear friends, my darling Kitty and I welcome you to our home.' Kitty smiled across the table. 'We wish you all a wonderful Thanksgiving. Let us be thankful for the food we have on our table and the drink in our glasses.' Everyone laughed, 'Most of all, let us be thankful for friends and family.'

Everyone raised their glasses and chimed, 'Friends and family!'

As Charlie was about to take a sip, the waitress placed a silver bowl of oysters in front of her. She stared into the oysters, put her glass down, and ran from the table, holding her hand to her mouth.

Oliver stood, 'Charlie, are you alright? Sorry, everybody, I'll check she's ok.'

Kitty looked at Betty and winked.

'She's ok, she's more than ok.' They both smiled.

Chapter Fifty

NOW

The Perfect Walk-Off

'Auntie Cheryl, Blue's looking at a lady undressing in the building opposite.'

'No, I'm not!'

'Yes, you are!' Raven snatched the telescope back from Blue.

Cheryl stifled a giggle, 'Oh, come on Blue!'

'But it's my turn!' Blue shouted.

Cheryl sighed, 'Blue, you have to share.'

Blue stormed past Cheryl in a sulk, baseball in hand.

'Oh,' Cheryl laughed, 'is that what a "walk-off" is?'

Blue looked at her, 'No, a walk-off is the hit that ends the game.'

He ran into the room and hid under the table.

I'll hide from them, that'll annoy Auntie Cheryl, He thought smugly.

Cheryl crossed to Raven, 'Well, I think I'll go and try to find out where the others are Raven.'

'Yeah, they should be here now, right?'

'There must be a phone behind the bar. I'll call reception and see if they can shed some light on what's happening.'

'Ok, Auntie Cheryl, I'll stay here.' Raven pointed into the room and whispered, 'Blue's hiding under the table, he thinks we don't know where he is.'

Cheryl rolled her eyes, 'Boys will be boys.'

She crossed to the telephone on the wall behind the bar. As she picked up the receiver a hand grabbed the telephone and ripped it from the wall.

'Hey! What the hell...?'

She turned and saw a man standing there with a gun. She looked at the doors leading to the elevator, but they were closed and presumably locked.

Cheryl was shaking, 'Who are you? What do you want?'

He looked at her and then at the terrace where Raven was still looking through the telescope. Raven couldn't hear from where she was, the music from below drowned any sound out. Cheryl looked around for something, anything to defend herself with but there was nothing.

'Leave us, go now and we'll forget anything happened.'

He stared at her not saying a word. She looked at his ugly face with the teardrop tattoo. Suddenly, he grabbed Cheryl's arm and twisted it behind her back, pointing the gun at her head. Cheryl screamed in terror and Raven looked up, she heard the scream but she couldn't see anything. He dragged Cheryl across the room as she struggled to break free, but he had her firmly in his grasp. Cheryl turned to Raven as she stood in the terrace doorway, crying.

'It's ok Raven, don't be frightened.'

Cheryl had no idea what to do. With one arm free, she was flailing around but was powerless. Raven cried out again as Cheryl pushed her attacker into the table with all her might. He released his grip and Cheryl grabbed a nearby kebab skewer and swiped at him blindly.

He dropped the gun and grunted as she slashed his face, opening a fresh wound. Angered, he pushed Cheryl to the ground. She kicked him between the legs, winding him momentarily. Suddenly, there was a knock on the hallway doors and they began to shake violently as voices were calling from outside. He regained control and drew his fist back to hit her with all his might. Suddenly a baseball hit him square on the back of the head. Cheryl saw the astonished look in his eyes as he fell forward on top of her. Scrambling her way from under him, she ran to Raven who was being cuddled by Blue.

'Blue, you saved me!'

'That's a walk-off,' Blue announced as he held Raven tightly.

Cheryl looked them over, 'Are you both ok?' They both nodded their heads slowly, but Raven was sobbing and Blue was shaking.

The doors were locked fast so Cheryl took them outside hoping there was another way off the terrace, but there was no other escape route. She turned to leave, and there he was, standing in the terrace doorway, blocking their exit. He rubbed the back of his head, pointing the gun at them. He was angry and Cheryl knew he would stop at nothing to hurt them.

'Please no,' Cheryl pleaded, 'leave us alone, just go.'

She was desperate. She pushed the twins behind her, knowing she would fight him to the end. She picked up a chair to defend them like a lion tamer at the circus, but he snatched it from her hands, tossing it to one side. She pulled the twins across the terrace towards the telescope and shielded them. He gave her a golden smile, knowing full well there was no escape. Cheryl knew the only way out was for her to run at him and try to push him over the edge. He slowly advanced towards the cowering group, blood pouring down his face.

Blue and Raven closed their eyes tightly as Cheryl took a deep breath. Suddenly a shot rang out and a bullet struck their attacker in the side of the head. His lifeless body collapsed on the floor as Charlie ran onto the terrace holding a small revolver in her hand.

'Mommy!' The twins rushed to her as she knelt to cuddle them. She was followed by an ashen-faced Françoise.

He surveyed the scene, 'Oh *merde*!'

Cheryl looked at him.

'More like murder.' Françoise gave a weak smile and frantically called the manager on his mobile.

'Cheryl are you ok?'

Charlie held out her hand as she slumped into a nearby chair. Cheryl looked at Charlie and sobbed, 'I thought he was going to kill all of us, he went crazy. I'm sure he was trying to get to the twins, but why and who is he?' Cheryl looked into the empty room. 'And where the hell is everybody?'

'The venue changed, last minute, I couldn't reach your mobile and as I was late anyway, I came to get you. I heard something going on through the locked doors and found the waiter to open up.' Cheryl stood and took the twins' hands.

'I'll take them inside, nine-year-olds shouldn't see such things,' she gestured to the body.

As Cheryl moved the sobbing twins into the room, Charlie stared at the body of the man she had shot. Yes, this time it had been her who'd fired the gun. He was sprawled on the terrace in a pool of blood, his head turned to one side. Charlie was about to leave when she noticed something on his neck, under his right ear. It was a tattoo of a purple turret. She knew then that Thomas Hassler was out for revenge.

Chapter Fifty-One

THEN

Everything Has Changed

'…Happy birthday to you.' As the singing finished the twins leaned forward to blow out the eight candles on their cakes. Blue's cake looked like a flattened baseball, with red stitching, whilst Raven's resembled a large microphone laid on its side. They squealed with delight as the candles kept re-lighting themselves and everyone clapped and cheered. In the garden, a large bouncy castle shone brightly in the California sunshine next to a stage, complete with a mirror ball and LED screen for the karaoke. Charlie slid her arm around Oliver's waist as they watched their twins running towards the bouncy castle with friends from school.

'Come on, let's join the others for an adult drink.'

Oliver pulled Charlie to the terrace where Henry was holding court with stories of her misspent youth.

'Hey Marcus, have another beer,' Oliver offered him a bottle; Marcus looked at Angelina before taking it.

She laughed, 'I don't know why you're looking at me! You're going to have it anyway, and I'm driving.'

Marcus smiled and grabbed the beer, clinking bottles with Oliver.

'Ok, one quick one.' He turned to Charlie, 'We're so pleased to have seen you and met Oliver and the twins on our trip out here.'

'Me too, Marcus; we go back a looong way.'

Angelina called out towards the bouncy castle.

'José, Maria, we have to go soon, say your goodbyes.'

Oliver looked at Marcus, 'Don't be strangers, ok?'

Marcus smiled. 'We've got a big day at Universal tomorrow, so we need to get these two in bed.'

José and Maria ran to Angelina, out of breath. José was seven and Maria six. They were dark-haired, olive-skinned, and had impeccable manners.

Angelina looked at them both standing there smiling. 'What do you say?'

'*Adiós y gracias.*' They chimed together.

Charlie kissed them, 'It's so good to meet you two. Next time we'll go to Universal together.'

They said their goodbyes and Charlie walked them out to their hire car.

'Bye Charlie,' Angelina kissed her on both cheeks, 'Come on you two.' She fastened the children in the back of the car as Marcus waited to say goodbye. Charlie hugged him.

'Marcus, thank you for agreeing to help me in Cannes with Thomas Hassler, Ingrid's gonna be there too.'

'You only have to say the word.' The car horn hooted, 'Must go, but give me notice though, Angelina likes to keep tabs on me.' Marcus grinned as he opened the car door and shouted to Angelina.

'My dear, have no fear, *tu Marcus es aquí.*'

As Angelina pulled out, another car pulled into the driveway. Charlie peered inside to see who was arriving so late. Emerging from the car was William Black.

'Charlie! Apologies for turning up unannounced.'

'William?' Charlie was surprised, 'Oh my God. No, it's fine, really.'

He'd never been to their house and Charlie was puzzled as to what he was doing there. They'd kept in touch from time to time, but she hadn't seen him for over fifteen years. He'd aged but still looked handsome.

'It's the twin's birthday, we've had a few people over.'

'I won't stay long. I had some business in town which finished earlier than expected and I fly back later today.'

Oliver joined Charlie. He'd only met William Black briefly at their wedding. Charlie had shown him the photograph she had of him with her father and their mother, Sophia. He thought the dead rabbit was gruesome and that William was indeed a strange and mysterious man.

'Oliver, you remember William Black, my uncle.'

Oliver held out his hand. 'William, good to see you again.'

'Good to see you too, Oliver, I'm not staying,' he looked over their shoulders at the twins running towards Charlie.

'Mom, can we do karaoke soon? Pleeeeease,' Raven grabbed Charlie's hand as Blue stared at William.

'Hello.' Blue held out his hand and William smiled and shook it.

'This is Blue and this little one is Raven.' Charlie ruffled Raven's hair.

Raven turned to him and waved an uneasy, 'Hi,' then she turned back to Charlie. 'Come on Mom!'

Oliver took them both by the hand and winked at Charlie.

'Come on you two, let's get things started,' they squealed with delight as Oliver chased them towards the tiny stage.

'They're lovely kids,' William smiled awkwardly.

'Yes,' Charlie sighed, 'they sure are. Now, what's this about?'

William looked at her. 'I've heard that Thomas Hassler is out of prison.'

Charlie's heart sank, 'I thought as much. I received something in the post last week, his calling card with the turret, I've told no one.'

William frowned, 'Be careful Charlie, he's been quiet all these years and now he's getting restless.'

'But why? Hasn't he done enough?'

'Well, let's face it, you and Oliver aren't exactly low profile. I suspect now he's out of prison, he can't stand seeing your success. You must be alert.'

The driver hooted, William waved and turned back to Charlie, 'And don't do anything to antagonize him, he's very dangerous.'

William kissed her and turned back to the car. Her mind was racing as the car pulled away. Thomas Hassler, it was finally time to put her plan into action.

A plan that would avenge her father's death and retrieve her inheritance.

* * * * * * * * *

As William drove away from Charlie he reflected on the past. His life had been very troubled and not the way he imagined it should have turned out. But he'd had no choice, he never had a choice. As he was wondering if he could have done things any differently, his mobile rang.

'Hello.'

The voice at the other end came through loud and clear.

'I have the information you requested regarding Thomas Hassler...'

* * * * * * * * *

As Blue belted out the Taylor Swift song 'Everything Has Changed', Oliver leaned toward Charlie.

'Don't you find it strange that your uncle turns up out of the blue?'

Charlie looked at him, 'Yes, I do, but he's always been a mystery.'

'He stays for five minutes and then leaves?'

'Well, he was never in my life. I get the odd telephone call but nothing else.' Charlie was deep in thought. She knew her family life was far from normal but now she had her own family, and that's all that mattered. As if on cue, Oliver reached over and kissed her. She smiled after him as he went into the kitchen, to grab a diet coke. The tv was on in the background playing Fox News.

He opened his can and his stomach sank as he heard a news flash.

'A body was discovered under a garden patio on an estate in Beverley Hills two days ago. Forensics announced today that it is believed to be the body of movie star Rick Krane, who went missing over twenty years ago.'

Chapter Fifty-Two

NOW

Time to Make a Plan

Cheryl and the twins slept in the back of the car as Oliver and Charlie sat in silence on the journey back to Monte Carlo. Cheryl had refused to go to the hospital and after Charlie gave her initial statement to the police they were allowed to go home. They weren't sure if it would reach the papers. The hotel didn't want bad publicity and Oliver would rather keep everything quiet, at least until they could figure out what was going on.

Cheryl was staying the night in their apartment, and they would see how she was in the morning. Kitty, Julian, and Brett were shocked when they heard the news and pledged their support.

As soon as they had put the twins to bed and settled Cheryl into their spare room, Oliver and Charlie sat on the balcony replaying the events of that day.

A tear slid down Charlie's face as she held Oliver's hand. She turned to him.

'I have a confession to make.'

She told him the entire story of what she had done that day, with the help of Henry, Ingrid, and Marcus. He sat bewildered as she relayed meeting Thomas Hassler in the bank and their scam of switching his Cryptoart.

'I can't believe you didn't tell me any of this, and I was in the bank today!'

'I know! What were you doing there?'

'Oh, it's a story for another time. So, Thomas Hassler knew all along that it was you?'

Charlie nodded, 'I've lived with this man and his effect on my life for too long. He murdered my father and drove my mother to suicide.'

Oliver put his arms around her, 'And look what he's still capable of, look what happened tonight.'

Charlie cried as Oliver held her. He decided not to mention the bullet he'd escaped from earlier that morning.

After all, the man with the teardrop tattoo was now lying on a slab in the police morgue. Nor would he mention the USB, that could wait.

'Charlie, we're in this together. We have to put an end to this for the twins' sakes.'

Charlie wiped her eyes and sat up. 'I've already put into operation selling his Bitcoin. It has a value of approximately eighteen million dollars. I'll take back what's mine and donate the rest to charity. After what happened tonight, he must already know it's missing.'

'Yes, and when he doesn't hear from his hitman, he will put two and two together.'

She looked at Oliver, 'I've antagonized him by taking my money back and it's time to call it even. We need to confront him, but first, we need to draw him out of his hiding place.'

'And how do you propose we do that?'

Charlie was formulating a plan which needed the help of Henry and her old hacking friend Simba. Charlie sat back in her chair, 'I have an idea.'

* * * * * * * * *

Oliver was restless and couldn't sleep. He got out of bed, leaving Charlie sleeping heavily with the help of a temazepam. Oliver hated keeping secrets from her, but they were both guilty of not giving full disclosure.

When the first blackmail letter for the USB had arrived some months earlier it was for his attention in a hand-delivered envelope. I know what you did. Your involvement will ruin you. I want the USB. Message this number. He hadn't discussed it with Charlie because he didn't want to involve her in his past. Little did he know that it was Julian Gold behind the blackmail letters.

After he'd heard the news about Rick's body being discovered there was a very high-profile investigation. But the police had nothing, no evidence, no murder weapon, and nothing linking Rick Krane to Kitty's house that evening. Only a handful of people knew that he'd been there that night and none of them, including Vixen, were about to rock the boat.

Then Oliver's mind went to Thomas Hassler. What is he capable of and why was he intent on ruining Charlie's life?

The murder of her father, the attack on Oliver, the fire, embezzling Charlie's money, and now their precious twins.

The man was relentless. Charlie did have a plan to call a truce, but Oliver didn't trust Thomas Hassler, so he decided to call on some insurance. As Charlie slept, he gently slid her mobile off the side table and scrolled through her contacts until he found the number he wanted.

The telephone number for William Black.

Chapter Fifty-Three

NOW

It's in the Cannes

The venue for the world première of *The Man Who Sold His Soul* was The Grand Auditorium. Searchlights swept the sky as cars pulled up with their precious cargo. It was the highly anticipated movie of the festival, and the theatre was filling up rapidly as the crowd waited in anticipation. The red-carpet arrival was televised and broadcast as 'the place to be'. Oliver stepped out of his limousine wearing a red tuxedo with black trim. The crowd cheered as he waved, waiting for Charlie to join him. She stepped out of the car to a rapid succession of flashing cameras. An eager crowd gasped at her outfit. Neon signs around the city suddenly burst to life with the live feed of Charlie standing on the red carpet in the garish design. Her dress was short and sleeveless with a print, that no one had seen before. It depicted a large, grotesque white rabbit, wearing flying goggles, surrounded by falling money. The dress they were photographing and filming bore a design identical to Thomas Hassler's Cryptoart. Charlie spotted the LED signs around her – Simba had worked his magic. He'd hacked into the broadcast feed and projected Charlie's image all over the city. She was sending out her message loud and clear. A message that Thomas

Hassler could not, and would not, ignore. Oliver crossed to Charlie's side.

'Are you sure about this?'

Charlie smiled at the row of photographers, 'Absolutely certain. I've no doubt he will be watching from somewhere. Let's see what rock he crawls out from underneath.'

They made their way into the VIP room where Charlie was excited to be reunited with Marcus, Henry, and Ingrid.

'Charlie!' Henry ran over and hugged her friend tightly. 'The dress turned out well! I might order one myself.'

'Thanks for your help, Henry,' Charlie held Henry's hand firmly. 'Ingrid!'

Ingrid crossed the room with Marcus by her side and kissed Charlie on both cheeks, 'You look fabulous.' Then Ingrid screwed her face up, 'Even though the dress is a little creepy.'

Marcus couldn't contain himself. 'I've never been to a première before, it is so exciting!'

Charlie laughed, 'The twins want to see José and Maria again, soon.'

'Yes, we'll arrange something for the summer. Are Raven and Blue here tonight?'

'No, I feel a little guilty, but we took them for a sleepover at their friends.'

The truth was Charlie wanted them safely out of harm's way. They'd complained at first but with the promise of their first smartphones, they soon conceded. She scanned the room, no sign of Thomas Hassler, but give it time.

Vixen approached Oliver from the bar.

'I'm looking forward to your movie, Oliver.'

Oliver smiled, 'Why thank you Vixen.'

'Maybe next time we can shoot a movie together?' she purred.

'Seriously?' Oliver smirked as she nodded. 'Well, you'd better get your people to talk to my people then.'

'Oh... I will,' Vixen pouted, 'see you at the afterparty...'

Cheryl grabbed his arm and pulled him away.

'She's trouble, Oliver.'

'Nothing I can't handle,' Oliver smiled as they made their way back to Charlie.

'I can't seem to shake this one off,' Oliver joked, gesturing to Cheryl who slapped his arm.

'Don't forget we've got the "influencers" conference immediately after the party in one of the VIP rooms, we'll only be about an hour.'

'Cheryl, what would I do without you?' Oliver smiled.

Kitty and Brett approached him.

'Where's Julian, Kitty?' Oliver looked around the room.

'Oh, he's not feeling too good. Sends his apologies but I'm in good hands with this one.'

Brett smiled. 'Oliver, you're gonna wow them once more.'

Oliver took a breath, 'Let's hope so, Brett.'

Brett caught the eye of Henry's father, Dimitri Diakos.

'Kitty, let's go and chat to Dimitri, we still need investors for the next movie.'

Oliver raised his eyes to heaven, 'It's non-stop Kitty.'

'Oh, you have no idea how much creeping I have to endure!'

Whilst Brett and Kitty were schmoozing Dimitri, a buzzer sounded requesting everyone's presence in the auditorium. Oliver entered nervously; he was aware that all eyes were on him.

The Man Who Sold His Soul was packed with stunts, chases, intrigue, and plot twists that had everyone gasping. Oliver was outstanding in the role and Charlie squeezed his arm so tight he thought she'd stop the blood flow. After the final frame played on the huge screen the auditorium sprang to its feet with thunderous applause, all eyes were on Oliver. Kitty requested no speeches or theatricals at the movie theatre, she was saving that for the post-party. Oliver was relieved, although at the top of his game, he was still humble and intensely shy. He and Charlie left the auditorium through a private exit and made their way to the after-party at a nearby nightclub, aptly named The Seven Deadly Sins.

* * * * * * * * *

The club was way over the top. The entrance doorway sat inside the huge mouth of Beelzebub himself, complete with horns. Machines shot yellow flames into the night, whilst his eyes flashed red and purple.

The press lapped it up. Inside was a sunken dance floor with a wrap-around balcony and stairs at either end that joined the two. Stairways off the balcony led to various private karaoke rooms. In keeping with the movie, they were themed like the seven sins – Greed, Envy, Pride, Lust, and so on. Some rooms were open to everyone, but others were for private use only and each was decorated with a myriad of props. Cheryl checked out 'Gluttony' with its Henry the Eighth-style banquet table, for the press call. It was aptly named for the hungry influencers. 'Lust' was decked out in the style of Cleopatra, complete with Anubis statues and a gold sarcophagus. The 'Greed' room had a pirate theme with treasure spewing out of a large sunken chest surrounded by wooden seats and palms.

Security was ramped up but still no sign of Thomas Hassler; maybe he was planning his next move. Charlie stayed alert but as the party continued, she began to relax more and more. The evening was a huge success, and everyone was buzzing about the movie. Charlie and Oliver left the dance floor as Ingrid was putting Marcus through his paces to the latest hit song by Vixen, who was throwing herself around the stage like a she-devil. Charlie checked her mobile, Raven had messaged saying that Blue was teasing her and could she go on her own for the next sleepover. This was followed by a message from Blue saying that Raven was acting like a princess, and he hoped that Mommy and Daddy were having a good time.

Cheryl shouted over to them, 'Oliver, the party's winding down soon, time to have the influencers' press conference. It's in the Gluttony room upstairs.'

'But I'm having fun, Cheryl!'

Cheryl looked at him like a displeased schoolteacher.

'Ok, ok... I'm coming,' Oliver teased her as he kissed Charlie. 'I'll be back before you know it.'

'The champagne's still flowing, I'll see you later handsome.' Charlie kissed his cheek.

He waved and pushed through the crowds with Cheryl pulling at his arm. Kitty said her goodbyes with the promise of seeing Charlie and Oliver the following week. Marcus and Ingrid shared a taxi back to their hotel. Henry, a little worse for wear, was regaling Charlie with stories of her failed relationships.

'But that's not the point, I said to him, if I wish to spend time on my own then I shall! Even my father is luckier than me with relationships, I saw him leaving earlier with Vixen.'

'Oh no Henry, you can't call Vixen Step-Maman!' Charlie teased as her mobile beeped with a message from Oliver.

Meet me in the Lust room upstairs... x

Charlie laughed, 'Henry, hold that thought, I'm going to meet Oliver upstairs in the Lust room of all places.'

'You, see,' Henry pointed at Charlie, trying to focus but not succeeding, 'You and Oliver have it right.'

Charlie smiled as Henry slumped back in her chair. She walked towards the short staircase with a sign that read, Gluttony, Lust, and Avarice this way. Ascending the stairs, she pushed open the outer door of the Lust room at the end of a short corridor. She slowly opened the inner door. Soft music played and gold lights danced on the ceiling.

'Hey, Oliver, I'm here.' Charlie said, her eyes darting around the room.

Anubis statues, half man half dog, towered over her, framing a gold sarcophagus in the center. On the far wall was a large stained-glass window with backlight, depicting Tutankhamun. She felt uneasy and swallowed hard.

'Oliver, stop messing around, it's been a long day.' Silence. She looked at her mobile and pressed dial on Oliver's text message. Suddenly she heard his mobile ringing in the room, but it was very faint.

'Oliver, I know you're in here. I can hear your phone ringing as I'm calling you.'

She walked in the direction of the ringing, it seemed to be coming from inside the sarcophagus. Slowly she reached out to open the Egyptian coffin.

* * * * * * * * *

'We're locked in!' Cheryl looked at Oliver as she pulled at the door of the room.

'Cheryl, my mobile phone's gone!'

Cheryl turned to Oliver, her face white, 'What? How?'

'It must have been on the way here, as we pushed through the crowds.'

'Mine's got no signal! I hate this new phone!'

Oliver was white, 'Cheryl, I've got a bad feeling about this.'

Oliver was pacing around the room, frantically trying to find anything that could help them. The press conference had finished after forty minutes but a lingering influencer had kept Oliver and Cheryl back at the end, eager for a scoop. Oliver politely smiled as Cheryl informed him that the interviews were over. The security guard led him from the room, and they followed a minute later but the door was locked. They hammered on the door, but the room was completely sound-proofed.

'I have to get to Charlie! This is the work of Thomas Hassler.' Oliver was desperate. 'Cheryl, there must be another way out!'

Where was Charlie? And what was happening?

* * * * * * * * *

Charlie pulled open the door of the sarcophagus and the ringing volume increased. Laying on the floor was Oliver's mobile, she picked it up, not liking this one bit. She slowly turned around and standing in front of her, pointing a gun, was Thomas Hassler.

He smiled, 'We meet again Charlotte Black.'

Her breathing increased, 'It's Charlotte Diamond.'

'Oh, you will always be a Black to me.'

'What do you want?' Charlie shot a look at the exit.

Thomas Hassler walked over to the door and turned the lock fast. He smiled.

'What do I want? Let's see now.'

Charlie walked to her left, towards one of the Anubis statues.

'Let's start with you returning my Bitcoin, shall we?'

Charlie looked at him coldly, 'You stole that money from me. That was my father's inheritance.'

He laughed, 'I owe you nothing!'

'Why are you doing this? Why did you hate my father so much?'

'Your father was going to expose me. He was ruining all my hard work.'

'But you were cheating people out of their life savings!'

Thomas snorted, 'Life savings? These people had more money than sense, I was relieving them of a fraction of their wealth. Anyway, it's not the only thing James Black took from me.'

'What are you talking about?' Charlie was trying to keep him talking, surely someone would come to find her soon.

'He took Elizabeth from me, your mother.'

Charlie couldn't believe what she was hearing. 'What?'

'I met her in St. Moritz. I loved her and she loved me!' His voice was getting louder, 'Then James came along and stole her. I was in love with her! She didn't want to know me after that.'

'So now you're ruining my life because of my father?'

'You don't understand. Your father took everything from me, and I mean everything. Elizabeth should have been my wife! You should have been my child.'

Thomas was standing by a gold pillar at the end of the room. His usual dark shades shone in the beam of the gold lights around him.

'It's time to finish this. I won't let you harm Oliver or my children. You can have your Bitcoin, but it has to be over.'

Thomas lifted his head and laughed. 'Oh, that's not how this ends. I have a different ending in mind.'

'What do you mean?'

'Have you not worked it out yet?'

He walked around the room, looking at her with contempt. Thomas stood in front of the stained-glass window and raised his gun toward Charlie. 'Yes, Charlotte Black. This ends now.'

She froze, tears cascading down her cheeks. Where was Oliver? She thought about him and her twins as she closed her eyes.

Suddenly a hidden door in the sidewall swung open, knocking Thomas Hassler to the ground. Charlie scrambled towards one of the statues. She looked back and standing there, with a gun, was William Black. He'd found the staff passage to the private room.

Thomas wrestled him to the ground, knocking his gun away. During the struggle, William ripped Thomas's glasses from his eyes as Thomas turned his gun on William.

Charlie screamed out, 'No, don't shoot him. We can sort this.'

'Sort this? We can sort this?' Thomas turned to Charlie in a fit of anger.

She looked at his eyes, they were red with steel blue pupils, and the skin around them was puckered and pink.

'It's time she knew the truth don't you think William?' Thomas spat. 'You'll both be dead soon anyway.'

Charlie could see William's gun, laying by the statue about two meters away.

She stared back at Thomas.

'Truth? What do you mean?'

Thomas Hassler laughed, 'What do I mean? Well, after all, we're all family.'

William sighed, 'Charlie, Thomas Hassler is my brother and your other uncle.' Charlie couldn't believe what she was hearing. 'He's Sophia's third triplet, Charles Black.'

Charlie stared in disbelief.

'But Sophia said the third triplet died during childbirth, this is impossible.'

Thomas's breathing increased and his eyes flashed from side to side.

'Curiouser and curiouser!'

Charlie remembered reading that quote in Thomas Hassler's office.

'Alice in Wonderland,' she mumbled.

'Yes, and I'm the white rabbit.' Thomas snarled.

William nodded, 'Sophia was told the third triplet, Charles, had died, she knew no different.'

Thomas screamed at Charlie, 'An albino baby. The doctors saw me as deformed, a worthless life! Lucky me.'

William tried to calm Thomas, 'It wasn't like that. Sophia couldn't cope at the best of times. Our mother wasn't a well woman, that's why we were brought up by our grandparents.'

Thomas turned to William, 'Yes, but I was sent to Switzerland, a newborn, discarded like a rabid animal. I endured operation after operation like some tortured lab rat!'

Charlie looked at William, 'You knew all of this?' Then at Thomas, 'and you murdered my father... your own brother...?' She was trying to make sense of everything.

William looked at her, 'I only discovered the truth recently. He was adopted by a good family in St. Moritz and became successful. He discovered his parentage by accident.'

'Yes, mother was careless with her papers. Can you imagine what I went through?' Thomas was screaming hysterically. 'It was no accident when I met your father at the conference. He had no idea I was his brother. Our joint venture was going well until he began to mess things up, threatening me with the police. My life had been ruined once and I wasn't going to stand by and let it happen again.'

He stared out into the stained-glass window, reflecting on the past. Charlie saw her moment and lunged for the gun on the floor, but she wasn't quick enough. Thomas Hassler was fast. He grabbed Charlie roughly as William dived across the room trying to get the better of him. But Thomas had her by the throat, pointing his gun at her head.

She cried out, 'William! Help me!'

'Stop this now!' William shouted at him. 'Let her go, you won't get away with this.'

Charlie struggled, but he held her firmly in his grip.

'You were the daughter I wanted. The perfect Charlie.'

'But you have a daughter, Siobhan,' Charlie tried to bring him back to reality.

Thomas sneered, 'Siobhan? She nearly ruined everything. She couldn't resist attending dear mother's funeral.'

Charlie thought back, she was the girl at Sophia's graveside, it made sense now. She was saying goodbye to her grandmother.

Thomas pressed the gun against Charlie's temple, 'Anyway, she's a half-blind mute, defective, like me!'

'Defective? She's not defective, she's your daughter!' William shouted.

Thomas turned blindly and squeezed the trigger. William screamed in pain, as he fell back against the wall.

'Don't do this!'

Charlie stared in disbelief as William lay on the floor, blood oozing from his chest.

He was squeezing the life out of her. As Charlie struggled, she knew her life would end soon. Thomas pushed her away against the sarcophagus. She stood there helpless as he laughed and pointed the gun at her.

'Goodbye my little niece, Charlotte Black.'

A single shot rang through the air.

Epilogue

Charlie shielded her eyes as she looked down the gangplank towards the harbor. There, walking towards *Serendipity*, was Henry and Ingrid. Marcus and Angelina were close behind holding hands with their children, José and Maria. She waved frantically and they all cheered. It had been a month since that awful night but, at last, Thomas Hassler was out of her life for good.

She'd heard the shot ring out and watched as Thomas Hassler fell forward onto the ground. Dead.

In the hidden doorway there stood Oliver, revolver in hand. But that was then and this is now. Today is going to be a good day.

'Charlie, loving the yacht!'

Kitty walked up behind her with Brett and squeezed her arm. Charlie smiled at Kitty, 'I've not had a chance to say, but I'm so sorry about Julian, Kitty.'

Kitty took a breath and looked out into the sea.

'I'll leave you two to it,' Brett said as he walked down the deck.

'He was the love of my life, and we had a great inning together.' A tear slid down Kitty's cheek. 'As you know it wasn't a shock, we'd known for some time, but it still gets to you, you know.'

'I can only imagine.'

Kitty took a quick breath, 'Anyway, today's not a day for being morose, let's drink to happy times ahead!'

Oliver slid down the steps from the upper deck like a seasoned seaman.

'What are we drinking to?' He smiled.

'Well, I would drink to something if I had a glass in my hand,' Cheryl laughed as she bounded down the deck sporting the biggest sun hat you've ever seen.

'Well, let me do something about that Cheryl!' Oliver kissed Charlie on the cheek and linked Kitty and Cheryl's arms.

'Come on girls, let's go and check out the champagne.'

Henry and Co stepped onto the yacht from the gangplank.

'Charlie, how are you?' Henry hugged her friend tightly.

'I'm better for seeing you lot.'

José and Maria ran to her, 'Hi Tía Charlie!'

'Blue, Raven, come and see who's here!' she called down the deck.

Marcus hugged her, 'Are you ok now things have calmed down a bit?'

Charlie looked at him and Angelina and sighed, 'Yes, I'm doing ok.'

'Yeeaayyy!' Blue and Raven came running to José and Maria.

'Come and see our bedroom,' Blue said as Raven tugged at Maria's hand.

'Raven, be gentle, and Blue it's not a bedroom, it's a cabin,' Charlie teased.

Ingrid hugged Charlie as the children ran down the deck, through the door leading below.

'Charlie, I was so worried about you.' Ingrid pulled away and held Charlie's face in her hands.

'All is good, and the sooner we can put all of that behind us, the better,' Charlie said as she spotted a lone figure on the jetty, walking towards the yacht.

'You all go and get a drink; we should be casting off soon and then we shall eat.'

Charlie stood back as they all walked towards the bow of the huge yacht. She looked back at the limping figure getting nearer and nearer and eventually walking up the gangplank.

'William, I'm so glad you could make it.' Charlie smiled, as she helped her uncle onto the deck. He was using a walking stick, but only to assist him, soon he wouldn't need it.

'I wouldn't have missed it for the world, Charlie.'

'Come on, let's go get you a drink.'

'Charlie,' he stopped her, 'before we do, is there somewhere we can talk in private?' William looked deep into her dark eyes. 'Just the two of us?'

Charlie couldn't help noticing that his eyes were glistening in the sunshine.

'Of course, let's go up top if you can manage it.'

'I'm not an invalid yet.' William smiled as he walked up the stairs, one at a time.

Oliver rounded the deck and stopped when he saw Charlie going up the stairs after William. He decided to leave them to have some private time and turned back to the others. 'Right, let's get some music on! Anyone up for a bit of Kylie?"

Charlie and William sat under a white canopy. The air was fresh, and they were secluded from the rest of the yacht.

As strains of Kylie's 'The Locomotion' drifted from the bow, William sat next to Charlie and looked deep into her eyes.

Charlie frowned, 'William, are you ok?'

'Yes... yes... I'm ok.' He took a breath, 'There's something I have to tell you. I think the only way is to show you something.'

Charlie had no idea what he was meaning. The events of the past few months had been heart-wrenching enough.

She knew that when he'd come crashing through that door in the club, he'd saved her life, as Oliver had a few moments later. William had taken a shot from Thomas Hassler and thankfully it wasn't too serious, he was lucky, and in recovery. He reached into his pocket as a tear fell down his cheek.

'William,' Charlie held his trembling hand, 'are you sure you're ok?'

He withdrew his wallet from his jacket and slid out two photographs from inside and passed one to Charlie. She stared at it, then at William, and then back at the photograph. It was a copy of Sophia's photograph showing William and James with Sophia and the gruesome William holding the dead albino rabbit.

'Why are you showing me this? I already have this photo.'

'Yes. In Boston you said I was a sick child, holding the dead rabbit.'

'Well... yes... it was a strange thing to do, even for an eleven-year-old.' Charlie didn't know where this was going.

'That wasn't me. The boy in the jumper with a W isn't me, Charlie.'

Charlie frowned, 'What? You mean you swapped jumpers?'

'No. Take a look at this.'

He passed Charlie a second photograph. She was looking at a werewolf family at Coney Island. A cut out with three, smiling heads poking through the holes. A lone tear trickled down her cheek as she remembered the perfect day. Her seventh birthday. The last birthday with her mother and father.

'You see Charlie...' tears streamed down his face as Charlie stared at him for what seemed like an eternity, her eyes also filling up with tears.

'...I am your father; I am James Black.'

Charlie was silent, speechless. Words wouldn't come.

He continued, 'I've watched over you all of these years. I've not been able to tell you for fear of not only my life, but more importantly, yours. I knew Thomas Hassler would stop at nothing. He was obsessed. He wanted me dead all those years ago but, unwittingly, he killed the wrong brother. William and I were identical. He wasn't interested in William, only in me, James, so I took William's identity. I knew it was the only way I could protect you.'

'But all these years I believed my father was dead. I thought you were dead.' Charlie was in shock.

'If he knew he'd killed the wrong brother, he would have killed me also, and then I couldn't protect you. Don't you see? It was the only way I could be sure of you living.' Tears streamed down James's face as he held Charlie's hands.

'Your mother, Elizabeth, knew. She was the only one who did. She kept my secret for your sake, but she was fragile and before she died, I promised her I would protect you forever.'

Charlie looked at him for what seemed an eternity, processing everything. Then she wrapped her arms around him and, for the first time in thirty-five years, she hugged her father and wept.

* * * * * * * * * *

Serendipity sailed out of Monte Carlo harbor and plowed its way into the beautiful Mediterranean Sea. They would stay close to the shore and sail down the coast past Nice and Cannes towards St. Tropez.

* * * * * * * * * *

Charlie and James rejoined the party on the main deck as Blue and Raven, and José and Maria were dancing around Cheryl's hat. Three glasses of champagne later, Cheryl hadn't a care in the world. Charlie passed James a glass of champagne and looked at all of her friends. Marcus and Angelina were dancing, staring into each other's eyes, Kitty, Brett, and Oliver were laughing together, Ingrid was attempting to jive with Henry whilst Cheryl was standing on the front seat, arms out, facing the sea, doing her best Kate Winslet impression.

Charlie turned the music down.

'Everyone, can I have your attention?'

They all turned to face Charlie. She walked up to James and put her arm in his.

'Oliver and all of my dearest friends, I have an announcement to make. I would like you all to meet... my father, James Black.'

They all stood dumbfounded as silence filled the air. Then Oliver walked up to James and shook his hand firmly. 'Pleased to meet you, James.'

Charlie whispered to Oliver, 'I'll explain everything later,' as everyone burst into applause.

The End

BIOGRAPHY – CHRIS COLBY

Chris has spent all his life in the Entertainment Industry, mostly as a Theatre Director. Originally from Blackpool, United Kingdom, he now lives in Thailand with his soul mate and life-long partner, David.

His most recent work has been as a Creative Director in television on Asia's Got Talent and also The Masked Singer, Australia. He feels very fortunate to be well-travelled and has worked with some truly amazing people.

In theatre, as an actor and subsequently a director, Chris worked with the likes of Edward Woodward, Su Pollard, Anita Harris, Anita Dobson, Sue Hodge, Anne Charleston, Shirley-Anne Field, Ruth Madoc, Norman Wisdom, Lynne McGranger, Linda Lusardi, Vicki Michelle, Gorden Kaye, Lynda Baron, Michele Dotrice, Sinitta, Mart Wynter, Jade Goody, Ken Morley, and many more.

He uses his wealth of experiences in his writing and hopes that all his readers enjoy getting to know his colorful characters.

Serendipity is the first of three novels detailing the lives of Oliver and Charlie Diamond. Book two will be out early next year.